STORM UPON THE DAWN

IMMORTALITY SHATTERED BOOK FOUR

Christian Warren Freed

This is a work of fiction. Names, characters, businesses, places, events, locales, and incidents are either the products of the author's imagination or used in a fictitious manner. Any resemblance to actual persons, living or dead, or actual events is purely coincidental.

Excerpt from *Hammers in the Wind* 2020 Christian Warren Freed
Cover design by BRoseDesignz
Cover copyright 2021 by Warfighter Books
Author Photograph by Anicie Freed
Map by Jamie Noble

Warfighter Books
Holly Springs, North Carolina 27540
https://www.christianwfreed.com

Second Edition: August 2021

Library of Congress Cataloging-in-Publication Data
Name: Freed, Christian Warren, 1973- author.
Title: Storm Upon the Dawn/ Christian Warren Freed
Description: Second Edition | Holly Springs, NC: Warfighter Books, 2021. Identifiers: LCCN 2021900274 | ISBN 9781957326306 (hardcover) | ISBN 9781735700014 (trade paperback) Subjects: Epic fantasy | Military fantasy | Paranormal

Printed in the United States of America

10 9 8 7 6 5 4 3 2 1

ACCLAIM FOR CHRISTIAN WARREN FREED

HAMMERS IN THE WIND: BOOK I OF THE NORTHERN CRUSADE

“I love this book. This book hooked my attention on the first page and it was hard to put down. There is darkness in this book, you know something is going to happen so you keep reading to find out what. The author writes it so good, it’s like you are there experiencing what the characters are. And I love it.”

“I purchased this book to read to see if it would be suitable for my daughter to read. She is advanced in reading, but some books for kids older than her can be a little to much content wise. I think this one will work out great for her and she would enjoy it as much as I did. I'm glad I came across this book and can't wait to read the rest of the series.”

WHERE HAVE ALL THE ELVES GONE?

“This story is fresh and a little tongue-in-cheek, a nice fantasy change of pace with twists here and there that make you have to keep on turning the pages.”

“Christian Warren Freed is a very gifted, well-spoken author and his story took me in from page 1. His descriptions of situations, momentary happenings and his vivid characters of the world within the story made my fantasy run wild. As a reader, I felt like being part of the carefully woven net of this book.”

THE DRAGON HUNTERS

"Excellently written. The author is able to really capture the stress, fear, and panic of life and death situations such as combat. Greatly looking forward to the next installment in the series!"

"Mr. Freed weaves the parts of this tale together smoothly, keeping the story moving at a good pace. He uses his own military background to paint powerful battle images and then he moves on. With only a little background, he makes the reader care about the members of the band - to worry about them and want them to do the 'right thing'. He adds depth to the characters through their actions and his dialogue is very realistic."

ARMIES OF THE SILVER MAGE

"Armies of the Silver Mage was a great read...any fan of Lord of the Rings or Game of Thrones will love this book. I'm looking forward to next book."

"The book is almost an homage to the great classics like Sword of Shannara and the Lord of the Rings. The author has cleverly used his past military and combat experience to make the battle scenes more realistic."

Other Books by Christian Warren Freed

The Northern Crusade

Hammers in the Wind

Tides of Blood and Steel

A Whisper After Midnight

Empire of Bones

The Madness of Gods and Kings

Even Gods Must Fall

The Histories of Malweir

Armies of the Silver Mage

The Dragon Hunters

Beyond the Edge of Dawn

Forgotten Gods

Dreams of Winter

The Madman on the Rocks

Anguish Once Possessed

Through Darkness Besieged

Under Tattered Banners*

Where Have All the Elves Gone?

The Lazarus Men

Coward's Truth: A Novel of the Heart Eternal*

Tomorrow's Demise: The Extinction Campaign

Tomorrow's Demise: Salvation

A Long Way From Home: Memories and Observations From Iraq and Afghanistan+

Immortality Shattered

Law of the Heretic

The Bitter War of Always

Land of Wicked Shadows
Storm Upon the Dawn

War Priests of Andrak Saga
The Children of Never

SO, You Want to Write a Book? +
SO, You Wrote a Book. Now What? +

Forthcoming + Nonfiction

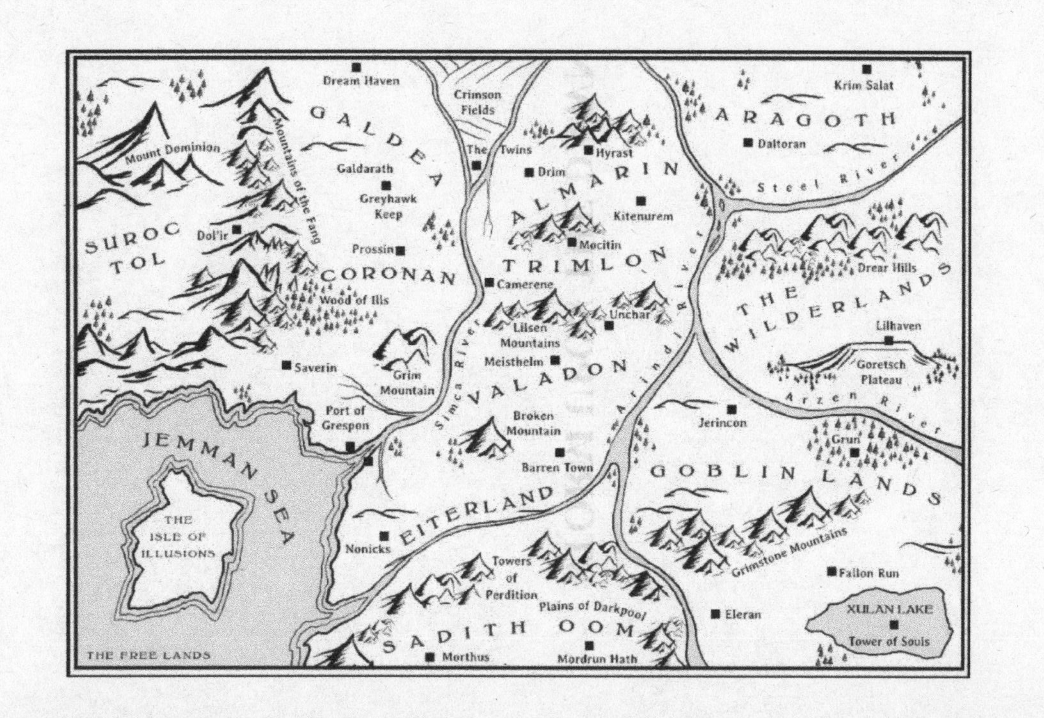
Dream Haven
Crimson Fields
Krim Salat
ARAGOTH
GALDEA
Mount Dominion
Mountains of the Fang
The Twins
Hyrast
Daltoran
Galdarath
Drim
ALMARIN
Steel River
Greyhawk Keep
Kitenurem
SUROC TOL
Dol'ir
Mocitin
Prossin
TRIMLON
CORONAN
Camerene
Drear Hills
THE WILDERLANDS
Wood of Ils
Unchar
Lilsen Mountains
Lilhaven
Meisthelm
Goretsch Plateau
Saverin
Grim Mountain
VALADON
Simca River
Arindi River
Port of Grespon
Broken Mountain
Jerincon
Arzen River
Grun
JEMMAN SEA
Barren Town
GOBLIN LANDS
EITERLAND
THE ISLE OF ILLUSIONS
Nonicks
Grimstone Mountains
Towers of Perdition
Fallon Run
Plains of Darkpool
Eleran
XULAN LAKE
Tower of Souls
SADITH OOM
Morthus
Mordrun Hath
THE FREE LANDS

STORM UPON THE DAWN

PROLOGUE

She watched her younger sister picking wildflowers with mild interest. The colors did nothing for her, nor did watching Essie. In fact, she'd come to view their relationship most unfavorably the older they got. Essie was only six years old and already a thorn in Arlie's side. Her parents practically forced her to watch over Essie, even when Arlie had other plans.

She'd lost friends because of it and missed out on important events that no parent would understand. How could they? It had been so long since they were eleven. Every child knew that parents were simply out of touch with the true goings on in the village. Arlie fumed when her mother sent her after Essie, today of all days! Arlie and her friends were supposed to meet by the old town square fountain to discuss the technicalities of the upcoming summer dance.

Only she couldn't go now and was going to miss everything! All because of her stupid sister. Arlie wished things were the way they used to be, before Essie came along. Life had been perfect then. A happy family with no conflicts. Essie changed it all. Arlie found herself grinding her teeth. Her jaw was sore and she swore tiny bits of tooth were floating in her saliva. Arlie frowned. Yet another calamity to heap upon her sister.

"Arlie! Look!"

She glanced up, despite knowing better. Essie stood in the middle of a bed of lavender flowers. Several were clenched tightly in her small hand. The smile stretching across her face radiated joy. Arlie snorted. They were just flowers.

"Mama will be pleased!" Essie beamed.

Of course, she will. You've become her favorite, robbing me! Arlie's eyes narrowed dangerously thin. Her fist clenched as fresh rage sparked. She wondered what her friends were talking about. "They're just flowers, Essie. No one cares."

Despite being scolded, Essie maintained her smile. "Mama said you need to be nicer to me! I heard her tell it."

Arlie rose, placing both fists on her hips. "Why should I? You ain't done nothing but ruin my life, Essie! They loved me most before you came along."

Essie threw the flowers down. Tears threatened to spill. "How can you say that? We're sisters! We're supposed to be best friends."

"I liked my life better before you were born! Mama and Da only talk about you now. They forget all about me," Arlie raged, feeling relief at finally being able to express herself. She didn't care if she hurt Essie's feelings. Hers had been getting abused for years. "Sometimes I wish you had never been born."

Essie broke down and cried harder than a newborn babe. Between sobs she managed, "That's not fair, Arlie. I love you."

The admission fell on deaf ears. Arlie was no longer listening. She closed her eyes as years of pent up anger flushed through her. She felt it suddenly, unbidden and … powerful. Her entire body began to vibrate. Softly at first. A gentle caress from her inner core. The intensity quickened until she felt as if she were being torn in two. Arlie threw her head back and screamed.

Essie dropped to her knees, hands over her ears, as she watched in horror as her sister began to fade. A kaleidoscope of colors rippled over Arlie's flesh, pushing through her organs before bleeding off through her fingertips. The ground trembled, tearing in places. Steam issued from the gaps. Bushes and grass wilted, dying in the span of a breath. Arlie fell.

She writhed on the ground. Her body contorted into impossible shapes as it was being remade from the inside out. And then the remarkable happened. The pain faded, ever so slowly. Replacing it was an overwhelming feeling of euphoria. Arlie relished the previously unknown sensations taking control. She wanted more.

Arlie's screams turned to unchecked glee. She'd never felt so alive. Never dreamed such was possible. A tiny hand stretched forth. Bolts of electricity danced between the fingers. Arlie had once heard rumors of a magic user in the Port of Grespon, but chose to ignore it as foolish gossip. Everyone knew magic was rare in the Free Lands, if it even still existed at all.

"This is …" she gasped, as the hem of her dress caught fire.

She vaguely heard Essie scream. The poor fool! If she only had an idea of what was truly occurring. But Arlie didn't care. It was her anger at her sister that was responsible for sparking this dramatic change. A change she knew she'd never be able to undo or return from. Nor did she wish to.

Every feeling and emotion became amplified as the raw magic consumed her. She looked upon Essie and felt contempt. The root of all her problems and she now had the strength to act upon it. Righting what had previously seemed impossible. Flames sprang up around her collar, singeing the little hairs on the back of her neck.

Essie reached out, her fingers barely scraping against Arlie's forearm. "Arlie, no!"

Arlie watched in muted awe as her sister burst into white hot flames, collapsing in a pile of ash a heartbeat later. It would be many years before Arlie realized the full extent of her actions, but by then, her plans had already formed. The world would kneel before her. Ironically, she knew none of it would have been possible if not for her sister.

ONE

A Wounded Land

Scenes of devastation unfolded as Galdea's army marched south through the kingdom of Valadon. The men, already war weary from months of fighting, took in each new village with growing despair. Charred and partially eaten human remains lay undignified in open fields or stuffed into tight alleys. The darklings were compassionless. A travesty to the civilized world. Their plague, having been unleashed from their eternal prison of Suroc Tol, seemed limitless to many of the Galdeans.

Yet despite the intensity of conflict, most of the rank and file remained in good spirits. They saw their coming into Valadon as salvation. Words of hope were whispered among each other when the senior leadership was bedded down for the night, for no self-respecting soldier would risk fate turning on him so close to what he perceived to be the end of the war. It was a game long played by armies throughout history.

Lord Aron Kryte of the Hierarchy's elite Golden Warriors rode at the head of the Galdean columns. His once soft eyes were now hardened, sharp, as he continually scanned the way ahead. Though Valadon was his home, he was forced to view it as enemy territory. The armies of the Black Imelin had swept down from the north on a murderous spree with the capital city of Meisthelm as their inevitable target. Already scouts had returned with reports of the city being besieged.

"You look so glum," Karin Ilth said from his right side. Her roan was slightly smaller than his war stallion, giving the impression of shortness. "We are not engaged with the enemy yet."

He kept looking forward, unsure how to convey his feelings without offending his love. She'd become dear to him, especially since Jod Theron pulled him from the banks of the Simca River, half dead and frozen. Aron knew the notion of falling in love in the middle of a war was foolish. How many times had they brushed against death's cloak? But the heart was not to be denied. He fell more in love with Karin with each passing day. He wondered if the potential cost was worth the journey.

Lips cracked and dry, Aron offered a tight smile. "The enemy controls this kingdom, insofar as we know. It would be foolish to let our guards down."

She frowned. "You know what I am talking about, Aron."

Sadly, he did. His last attempt to use the Staff of Life, the horrid weapon created by wizards long ago, nearly cost him his life, while destroying thousands of darklings in the span of a single heartbeat. He lived but felt as if he were missing a piece of himself. The sensation was unlike any other he'd ever felt and he had yet to wrap his mind around the concept. One fact was certain, however, he was loath to use the Staff again unless absolutely necessary.

"I do and I have no wish to discuss it," he replied. *Not here, or now*.

Dissatisfied with the answer but willing to give him space, Karin made a show of huffing. "Very well, Lord Kryte. Keep your secrets. There are other ways to get a man to talk."

She wasn't sure if he blushed or it was the effect of the cold wind striking his exposed cheeks. She laughed.

"What?" Aron asked.

Karin shook her head, long dark hair swishing over her cloak. "Nothing. Nothing at all."

He let her have it, already knowing better than to provoke her ire. "Valadon lies in the heart of the Free Lands. Though not the largest kingdom, it is the core of all we hold dear. I fear for those in the hamlets and villages ahead of us. Imelin has already shown us the levels of depravity he is willing to sink to. The longer we delay, the more lives are put at risk."

"Not even you can control destiny," she said, her voice oddly smooth. "All we can do is the best with what we have. Do not be in such a hurry to confront tomorrow, Aron."

"Meaning I should enjoy today," he finished.

Her nod was barely noticeable.

He sighed. A great breath exhaling as he relented. "Perhaps you are right. The winter doesn't seem as bad this far south."

She struggled to contain her laugh. "Weather? That is your big change of subject? My dear Aron, I was thinking more along the lines of sharing a tent tonight."

His sheepish look was all it took for her to lose control. Laughter spread over the head of the Galdean column, garnering several odd stares. Only Amean Repage, Aron's mentor and longtime friend, remained passive. The old veteran understood the value in a strong relationship. More so, he was pleased for Aron. The lad deserved love and so much more. Amean's thoughts drifted away from the rigors of campaign and what might await in the coming days and centered on his daughter and grandchildren. They were the reason he continued to fight, not for the Hierarchy or any other. Especially not for the man at his side.

Ute Hai, the Rover turned traitor, cast a sidelong glance. His natural mistrust of the Hierarchy and those among its ranks, continued to rankle him, but it was useless sentiment. He could never return to Denes Dron and the Rovers, or Aragoth, again. Betrayal was a wicked tool used by lesser men. His disagreements with pitching in with Imelin and the darklings caused an impossible rift with his people and left him on the outside. The ride south through the Unchar Pass invoked unpleasant memories of the day he'd ridden north to find a new life. He never imagined that life would be spent among his once mortal enemies.

The army wormed south with unprecedented authority, despite being so far from home. Field Marshal Dlorn rode at the very head of the snake. His iron resolve was determined to see the matter of the darkling army ended for good. Had he any inkling of what was happening in his home kingdom, he would have turned the army around.

Dlorn was a proud, tired man. He'd once dreamed of retiring to a quiet village far from the bustle of court life in Galdarath, but the return of evil prevented those dreams. He lamented that his life had become one of war, with little room for anything else. A man should have more to look forward to in the waning days of his life.

Still, he was committed to finishing the task at hand. Twenty thousand healthy Galdean warriors looked to him as an example. His bones ached. Body bruised and battered more than from any other campaign. Dlorn needed a long rest, but what he needed and what was required were vastly different. A leader of men, Dlorn intended on ending the siege of Meisthelm and forcing the Black's armies into a fatal confrontation.

They'd come so far already, and through hardships worse than any in recent generations. The battle of the Crimson Fields left his army ravaged, but in fighting spirits. Pursuit down through Trimlon and into the Unchar Pass further drained his strength, but the men persevered. Campaign made men hard. The weak and unwilling fell first or were washed away under a tide of violence. What remained was the iron core of Galdean strength. They reclaimed the fallen Hierarchy garrison at Unchar and with more than a little help from Lord Kryte, destroyed what Dlorn assumed was the entire host of the darkling army in the north.

The men needed a rest as much as he, and he promised they'd get it, but only after Meisthelm was relieved. All other concerns were secondary. Horses screened the main columns of infantry. Heavy boots clumped down on the muddy road, weary and ready to arrive at their destination. Sergeants barked cadence. Officers provided words of encouragement to those soldiers looking as if they were about to fall out of formation. The leagues passed by and the army continued to grind.

Jod Theron, former Hierarchy diplomat turned hermit, drank lightly from his mug of watered down ale. He'd worked his way into Dlorn's inner circle, and an odder group he'd never encountered. From the silent lord from across the sea, to the fallen elf prince, to the troop of Golden Warriors, the combined army of Galdea offered broad representation from across the Free Lands. He watched and listened, speaking only when asked direct questions. After all, how was a man to learn if he always ran his mouth?

It was Prince Warrien of Almarin who had his attention. The young lord of the far northern kingdom was inexperienced and brash but held potential. The Free Lands would be in desperate need of strong leadership in the aftermath of this war, regardless of the outcome. Jod wondered if the youth's love for Princess Elsyn of Galdea would interfere with what had to be done.

"I had been of mind to return to my kingdom but the battle at Unchar Pass has given me pause," Warrien admitted to the small group.

Dlorn rubbed the stubble on his chin. He was frustrated with being shackled with not only one, but two heirs to kingdoms. Yet what could he do? Bind Elsyn and have her forcibly removed from *her* army? That would be the equivalent of career suicide. Not a bad option, the more he thought about it.

"We are about to run into a formidable storm and you've only a handful of soldiers to guard you," Dlorn countered, careful not to provide insult.

Elysn's eyes narrowed but she held her tongue. She was beyond tired of hearing how much of a hazard the way ahead was. She'd lost more than any other and wasn't about to be denied seeing the man responsible for her father's murder brought to heel. Whether Dlorn wished it or not.

Warrien sipped his now lukewarm tea. "I understand but there is compulsion driving me on. I cannot explain why, but I feel it is in my kingdom's best interest to see the end of the war firsthand."

"What think you, Master Theron?" Dlorn asked unexpectedly.

Jod nearly choked, as he was caught off guard. "Eh? Me? Why should I think anything? I'm no royal."

"No, but you hold more opinion and I daresay, sway than any other I have met in a long time," Dlorn countered. He knew Jod bore a great secret. One the old man was unwilling to divulge.

Making a show of being unprepared, Jod set his mug down and rubbed his hands. "Well, I would say the young prince has valid points. His presence in what might well be the final battle of the war, provided we are triumphant, will ensure continued support from the Hierarchy in the coming years. On the other hand, he is endangering the future of his line by continuing with the army. Should we lose…."

He let the thought drop. Speaking the inevitable served no purpose. What would be, would be. Jod settled back on his field stool and hoped he'd said enough to satisfy Dlorn's probing. He instantly regretted having gone to the Field Marshal in the hours before the battle of Unchar Pass. Doing so jeopardized all his careful ministrations he'd put in place since leaving the Hierarchy.

"Every kingdom in the Free Lands will lose more, if this army fails," Dlorn said before either royal could comment. The last thing he needed was dissention among his ranks now.

Warrien seemed to take no offense. "Master Theron, I would not jeopardize my life or that of Princess Elsyn, if I did not have the utmost confidence in the Field Marshal. We stand upon a glorious time. All of us. No matter what happens when we reach Meisthelm, the Hierarchy will be forever changed. The High Council will be forced to address radical changes in policy and standing. I would not see Almarin underrepresented."

"That is a conversation for another time," Aron interjected. "We must focus our intentions on the coming battle and what it will take to lift the siege. The army we faced in the north was but a fraction of Imelin's true strength, and that is only what we are aware of. Ute Hai tells us that the Rovers have joined forces with the darklings. Their strength alone is well over ten thousand strong."

"Not exactly encouraging," Karin chimed in.

Aron could only shrug. He'd never been fond of coating the harsh truths. Men going into battle deserved that much, if not more. "Would you have me lie? We need all actionable intelligence, if we are to have a hope of defeating Imelin's main army."

"Long Shadow and I will take care of that," Andolus, the elf prince of Dol'ir, offered. His three hundred elves, the last survivors of the doomed fortress, had been without purpose since engaging the darklings at the Unchar Pass.

Dlorn looked up. "Alone? That is madness."

"No. I'll send a third of my elves out to screen the army. We are faster than your heavy cavalry and can move without being seen," Andolus replied.

His confidence was unquestionable. Thus far, the elves had been one of Dlorn's greatest assets. So much so, he could ill afford to lose them on routine scouting.

"I have units already in the field. Your elves would be better suited to protecting the main army should we become engaged," Dlorn countered.

"Which is why I am leaving the majority here," the elf said. His tone dared any to debate the wisdom of his decision. None did. "We shall depart before dawn. I want to be as far from here as possible before the enemy knows we've gone."

"Will you return before we reach Meisthelm?" Elsyn asked, with genuine concern.

Long Shadow chuckled and finished his ale.

"Unless we are dead, Princess," Andolus told her with a soft smile.

"A fate quite possibly awaiting us all," Dlorn finished the conversation. "As enlightening as this night has been, I must walk the line. No doubt my commanders are already speculating over my whereabouts and what it might mean. Good night, my friends."

Aron waited until the Field Marshal stalked out of the tent before turning back to the elf. "Do you need help? I'd like to get a lay of the land myself."

"Alas, your men will only slow us down. The faster we move, the sooner we may return."

Aron understood but wished the answer was different. He felt as if he'd been behind Imelin for too long. It was time to get ahead and take the offensive. But how? The war was already progressed to the point he no longer felt in control. Compounding his frustrations was the Staff of Life. He cursed the day wizards decided to create the fell totem.

"I'd like another mug of ale," Ute Hai announced. He had a feeling it was going to be his last one for a long time.

Night continued to hold sway over the kingdom of Valadon as Andolus and one hundred elves, breaking into small five-man teams, slipped away from the Galdean army and into the empty countryside. Even on horseback, they went largely unnoticed. Elves were ever the masters of disguise and stealth. Only those men on picket duty marked their passing and they'd been ordered to remain quiet. They stared as grim-faced elves, men and women, rode into the darkness.

Andolus halted what remained of the main group a league out. Snow covered grasslands stretched as far as his enhanced eyes could see. Stands of poplar and elm trees peppered the area, no real forest along their route of march. Andolus knew it gave his elves multiple vantage points to spot the enemy but held equal disadvantages. Elves could hide, but only when there were places to hide in.

"We are a day's ride north of Meisthelm. Each of you take your teams to your objectives and return before dusk. Do not engage the darklings unless there is no way to avoid it. We must be with the main army before nightfall. Am I clear?" he asked.

Heads nodded.

"Good fortune."

They splintered away without further comment. Andolus and Long Shadow watched the twenty-five elves disperse, waiting for them to be well out of sight before departing on their own quest. The elf prince continued to mire under the sting of losing Dol'ir. His thirst for vengeance bordered on obsession but he was seasoned enough not to let that sway his decisions.

Dlorn and the Galdeans needed the best information possible and only his elves had a chance of providing it. Not that the Galdean scouts were talentless. From what he'd seen thus far, the men of Galdea accorded themselves with honor and professionalism. Any benefit he might provide would be blessing for the coming battle.

Andolus looked at the last of the Lords of Teranian, wishing again that Long Shadow would offer his true name and speak. "I make no promises about our chances of success."

The bigger man merely shrugged. Andolus shook his head ruefully. "Just one more time I would like to hear your voice, my friend."

Grinning, Long Shadow spurred his mount forward. The elf had no choice but to follow. Meisthelm lay at the end of their scout. Night faded to morning and then into midday without event. Andolus admitted the silence was oddly comforting, despite his earlier protestations. Too often, clarity was obscured by conversation. He needed all his faculties.

They crested a long, gradual slope and halted beside a copse of pine. His eyes narrowed as he took in the scene laid out before him. The remains of a farmstead were at the bottom of the slope, burned out and forgotten. Wolves and other predators had seen to the family's bodies. The cost of war. Andolus looked beyond the farm, however, at the impossibly big columns of smoke rising up into the sky. Not even he was able to make out the source but the sudden empty feeling in his stomach told enough.

Long Shadow grunted and spat angrily. There was no doubt that Meisthelm lay at the center of the smoke. They were too late.

TWO

Meisthelm

Ruination. The greatest city in the Free Lands was a smoldering wreckage of what had once been. Bodies stretched out from the alabaster walls, the majority being darkling and what Ute Hai identified as his former cohorts. The Rover searched faces for friends, boon companions who had been at his side through numerous struggles since Aragoth fell to the Hierarchy for daring to dream of independence. His hatred deepened.

Andolus and the elves reported with great urgency but there was only so much Dlorn could do. It took mighty effort to move tens of thousands of soldiers and equipment. The army ground on, churning leagues underfoot. When they were within five leagues of Meisthelm, Dlorn had the infantry and cavalry ready for battle. Swords were drawn. Shields secured. Lances holstered and ready to engage.

Commander Lestrin was given command of the vanguard. His five thousand horsemen formed a giant spearhead that moved with impunity across abandoned farmlands. Thus far, they'd met no resistance but none of the commanders expected that to last. Their foe had been too persistent since escaping from their eternal prison of Suroc Tol. Lestrin rode with nearly the entire contingent of Golden Warriors. They were the sole representatives of the Hierarchy and would not be denied this time.

The stench reached them before they were able to see what remained of the city. Burnt bodies and rotting flesh yet to be frozen by winter's kiss. Crows and vultures by the thousand swarmed over the field. Men covered their nostrils lest their stomachs betray their bravery. So much destruction seemed impossible. Hope sagged as the once golden spires of Meisthelm came into view.

Scorch marks covered much of the cityscape. Aron spied numerous buildings that were missing, he presumed them burned to the ground or destroyed through magic. He grew dismayed. The sudden realization of being too late stabbed into his heart. He'd failed. The world was ready to fall because he was unable to perform his duties. The title of lord no longer seemed worthy of his collar.

"What have we done?" he gasped.

Amean glared. He too felt as Aron, but the veteran was savvier. "*We* did nothing. Was that bastard Imelin who did this and no other. Remember that, lad. Turn it into rage and let your sword reap. It is all we can do."

"Doesn't take the sting away, nor the ache," Aron replied through clenched teeth.

"Nor should it. This is total war."

Total war. The concept seemed foreign, despite having been trained in tactics and campaign strategy for years. If Meisthelm was but a fraction of the harm reaped by the darklings, the Free Lands were doomed.

He cleared his throat. "We must get to headquarters, if one still exists."

"No doubt Imelin would have struck at the heart of Hierarchy strength," Amean said. "I'd be surprised if the Knight Marshal was still …"

He let the thought fade. They'd discover the truth soon enough. Lamenting over what might be, served no purpose.

"Commander Lestrin, shall we proceed?" Aron turned to the Galdean.

"I've sent runners back to the Field Marshal. My scouts say the way to the city is clear of enemy forces," Lestrin answered in confirmation.

"That does not mean our enemy is not within the walls," Aron countered. His horse bucked, eager to keep going.

Lestrin flashed a savage grin. "All the more reason to sweep down now and take them unprepared."

"Agreed."

The cavalry thundered down across the plain and to the city walls. Walls, Aron noted, that were largely intact. Was it Imelin's plan to occupy and hold once cleared out? Instincts screamed subtle warnings, yet he refused to heed. Blood hot, Aron ignored caution, knowing prudence would merely slow his efforts. He needed to be among the first in the city.

He urged his horse ahead, ignoring the growing fields of bodies as the prize drew ever nearer. His eyes fell on the city. Walls were burned black. Guard posts along the perimeter were gone. Larger bodies filled the space outside of the gates. Horses bloating from built up gases. Unexpectedly, Aron was forced to rein his horse back to a trot as several figures emerged from the besieged city. Lestrin pulled up beside him, his mouth open.

"Harrin?" he asked.

The Galdean coming out to meet them waved in recognition.

"What is this?" Aron asked, though none had answers.

He waited as Lestrin ordered the vanguard to halt. Horse and rider skidded to complete stops as a small delegation rode forward to meet with those coming from the city.

"I have never seen a more welcome sight!" Harrin Slinmyer practically shouted, as Lestrin and the others dismounted.

"What is going on here?" Aron demanded. His eyes fell on Halvor. He bowed to the priest of the Red Brotherhood. "It does my heart good to see you still alive."

The elf nodded; his face concealed by the shadows of his hood. Burns puckered most of his flesh and kept him secreted within the robes of his order. Though none could see it, Halvor's smile was warm.

"Eh, the little lordling arrives late!" Anni Sickali cackled, with her arms waving wildly.

Aron felt no affinity to the bizarre woman, but it gave him hope to see the trio still alive. How they arrived in Meisthelm was another tale.

"Mage, where is the Black? I see no evidence of siege," Aron said.

Harrin exchanged looks with his counterparts. "Gone, but there is more you need to know. A tale best told when Dlorn and the others arrive. For now, know that the city is secure. What remains of it, leastwise. The darklings reaped a terrible cost among the populace and half the city was destroyed before they pulled out."

He turned to Lestrin, "Commander, I regret to tell you, we've little stable space and almost no barracks left. If you swing your force around toward the south gate, you'll find a swath of land mostly cleared of bodies. The fighting wasn't so bad down there."

"What happened here?" Aron asked. "We were led to believe the enemy was laying siege and prepared to sack the city."

"They damned near did. Worst fighting I ever saw," Harrin replied. His thin face gave him a gaunt look. The look of a man who'd seen too much. "Nor is it a tale

I wish to recount more than once. If you do not mind, I would like to tell you all once Field Marshall Dlorn arrives."

Aron became desperate for answers. His suspicions of the events they'd missed grew the less Harrin relayed. "The High Council?"

The man from Galdea shook his head. "Gone. All of them."

Aron felt gut-punched. Without the Council, the Hierarchy would collapse. The Free Lands would devolve into chaos. A thousand years of progress thrown away with the cast of the dice. He felt lost.

"I will send word to the command staff to arrive with all haste," Lestrin interrupted. His mind already raced ahead to combating the inevitable lawlessness sure to arise in the vacuum of leadership. Looting and riots were only a matter of time once food stores began to dwindle and trade dried up.

Harrin nodded, grateful. "We have grain and water for your mounts. Our scouts reported you were coming fast."

"One question before Dlorn arrives," Aron pressed.

Exasperated, Harrin gestured with a hand.

"Why did the enemy quit the field when victory was assured?"

Harrin's cheeks flushed. "They learned of the Galdean army pushing down from the north and the army of the Hierarchy advancing from the southwest. I can only assume it was a matter of numbers."

Fresh questions emerged. Aron wondered why Conn hadn't been in Valadon to begin with and what kept him from returning in time. He feared that line of thinking led to deeper threats the Free Lands had yet to discover.

"This is him?" Dlorn asked. The lines on his face deepened, or perhaps it was the shadows concealing half of his face.

Halvor folded his hands in front of him. "Yes. This is the Black Imelin."

They stood in mixed disbelief. The man they'd spent months fretting over and planning against, laid out before them on a rock slab. Surprisingly, he'd been laid next to his fellow Council members, those whose bodies remained largely intact.

Dlorn was unimpressed. "This man was the greatest threat to our existence since Ils Kincannon? I've dreaded his name from the beginning of the war, yet now that I look upon his corpse, I am underwhelmed. How could one man come into so much power unchecked?"

Aron knew the answer and feared to elaborate. The truth was High Councilor Zye Terrio's proscriptions against magic use blinded the Free Lands, while pretending to look after their best interests. Imelin had been the last of the great war wizards and played along while secretly building his strength. His betrayal caught the Hierarchy unawares, propelling the world into a vast war that had already claimed thousands of lives.

In truth, Imelin wasn't an imposing man. Tall, yes, but wiry. What he lacked in musculature was more than compensated for by magic. His mind, Aron surmised, was Imelin's most dangerous weapon. How else could one explain how he'd duped the entire world so easily? Aron stared down on the pale flesh with a sense of loss.

He'd anticipated their meeting since Marshal Sevron issued his orders back in Saverin before the war began. Ever a step behind, Aron and his company of Golden Warriors slogged across the northern kingdoms in a vain attempt at stopping the Black. Their paths nearly collided in Galdarath, but Aron managed to slip away with the Staff of Life before the Black swept down into the forgotten dwarven stronghold of Gelum Drol and slaughtered the entire cell of Red Brotherhood priests. All but Halvor, who'd escaped at great cost.

Learning he was the only surviving descendant of Ils Kincannon, a bloodthirsty warlord who'd nearly succeeded in bringing the world to the edge of collapse, extorted terrible mental anguish on Aron. It took the better part of nearly drowning to ease his mind and come to terms with his station in life. Seldom was a man allowed to carve out his own path in life. Aron was bound by centuries of history he was still only vaguely aware of.

The entire quest to reclaim the Staff had been building to an ultimate confrontation against the world's great evil. An evil that was brutally murdered and left for the crows. Aron struggled to find new meaning in his purpose. To make sense of the madness consuming the Hierarchy. Tried, but could not.

Harrin told them it was Arlyn Gert who'd killed Imelin. Arlyn, who then assumed command of the darkling army, and sent it into Meisthelm. Why her? How? He found it difficult to accept that she was the true source of treason. The cancer which had spread down through the ranks, permeating all that was good and healthy. Yet even as he struggled to come to terms with this new knowledge, he knew he was wasting time. Arlyn Gert now controlled an army of monsters ready to sweep across the Free Lands, finishing what Imelin started.

Harrin shrugged. "He had help from inside the Hierarchy. The corruption runs deeper than we've uncovered."

Indeed. The gates to the city had been left open intentionally. Most of the fighting forces were deployed far away from the capital, leaving Meisthelm all but undefended when the darklings arrived.

"Where are the other Councilors?" Aron asked after counting heads.

"One was turned to cinder when the High Council went out to confront Imelin," Harrin explained. "We found the old man in his chambers. Looked like he'd been dead a long time. Those were it. How many are missing?"

Aron ran over the names in his head. "There is one unaccounted for, though I do not recall his name."

"We've a larger issue than a missing Councilor," Dlorn said with concern.

All heads turned his way.

"Who is running the remnants of the Hierarchy now that the High Council is no more?"

It was a question they had no answer for.

Uncomfortable with using the High Council meeting chamber, Dlorn ordered his own council to the remains of the Golden Warrior headquarters. Most of the buildings were burned to the ground. Those remaining had been looted. All found within were murdered with ruthless abandon. More than one Galdean emptied his stomach as they moved the bodies for proper burial.

Aron and Amean strode through what had once been their home. So many friends lost their lives when the darklings struck. Both feared the Golden Warriors were decimated to the point of combat ineffectiveness, much like the Hierarchy. Aron set his fifty men to reconstructing one of the smaller barracks that had suffered the least amount of damage. With the high command dead, Aron was the senior ranking man in Valadon. He decided to send runners west to Saverin to bring Marshal Sevron to Meisthelm to command.

Out of impulse, Dlorn had a pair of soldiers bring in his oversized map table. There was no real need for it, now that they'd reached their target. Dlorn had it out of comfort. He watched as the men painstakingly placed the map in the center of the room, saluted and left. As much as he hated being tied to the map, Dlorn felt a measure of normalcy returning. A quick look around the room showed him all were assembled. He began.

"Ladies and gentlemen, we stand at a dangerous crossroads. The Hierarchy, for all purposes, is defunct. We can no longer look to them for guidance or support. What then is to become of us, here?"

His wolf-like gaze fell on Princess Elsyn. As the crowned ruler of Galdea, she and Prince Warrien of Almarin were the senior rulers in the area. Ironic, considering they were the youngest of the group and had little practical experience ruling. Elsyn only came to power after her father was murdered by one of Imelin's agents. Warrien, while not sharing a similar distressing scenario, had only been in control for less than a year before the war began.

"I have no experience with which to make such decisions, though I caution that Galdea has need of her army. We've done all we pledged to do upon setting out from Galdarath. The enemy army in the north is no more and Meisthelm is once again secure. What more can we do, now that the war has seemingly moved south?" she explained.

A few heads nodded approvingly. The men of Galdea had fought a hard campaign, losing more than their share of troops along the way. A steady string of casualties stretched from Unchar back to the Twins. All were exhausted and ready to return home.

"I agree, however, the only reason Meisthelm is secure is due to our coming. Once we leave, what is to prevent this Arlyn Gert from returning?" Dlorn countered. He knew General Conn by reputation only and was disturbed that the man was nowhere near the city.

Aron supplied his answer. "General Conn is said to be approaching as we speak. He has ten thousand men at arms. More than enough to keep the walls of Meisthelm defended should the darklings come again."

"But?" Dlorn asked. He wanted to go home as much as any of them, but a keen sense of duty prevented him from giving in to temptation.

"Conn has yet to arrive and we have no idea as to what Arlyn intends," Aron explained. "She clearly has designs that have been in place for a long while now. Leaving Valadon now would alleviate the strain on Galdea but leave the rest of the Free Lands exposed."

A manufactured cough brought Warrien attention. "Again, I would remind you all that Almarin has no military stake in this war. At least not yet. That being said, I find merit in what Lord Kryte says. We cannot afford to leave this city, this bastion of all the Free Lands stand for, open and waiting for retribution. Nor can we leave a massive enemy force roaming around the southern kingdoms until they find a place to strike."

"What are you saying, Your Highness?" Amean leaned forward almost aggressively. The more he stayed with the army, the more he wanted to retire and be with his grandchildren.

Warrien swallowed his nerves. "The obvious. We must find the enemy and engage them. Only by defeating Arlyn Gert and her darkling army, will the kingdoms finally be safe again."

As much as the words stung, each of those assembled knew them for truth. Dedication to duty kept them from abandoning the rest of the world. They were the largest friendly fighting force in the kingdoms. The only one capable of combating the darklings.

"The young prince has sound wisdom," Aron began. He chose his words carefully. "Before we can attempt a new campaign, there are supply and logistic issues that must be addressed. Reinforcements would be nice. Perhaps we can conscript men for the duration of the rest of the war."

"Agreed. We must replenish our numbers before attempting to fight our enemies," Dlorn seconded. "I also sense there is more lingering on your mind."

Aron nodded. "Indeed. I would like to know what exactly happened here and how. The more we know about our enemies, the easier it will be to hunt them down."

Heads swiveled to the trio from Galdea. A trio who'd been secretly dispatched by Jent Tariens, Galdea's acting steward, in the hopes of delivering warning to the High Council, as well as the head of the Red Brotherhood. They arrived just in time but were unable to prompt action out of the High Council. Only Dalstrom proved receptive to their warning but the brothers in the Order were few.

It was Harrin who rubbed his aching temples before beginning the tale he swore he'd only tell once.

THREE

The Battle for Meisthelm

They watched in shock. None could believe what they'd witnessed, nor the implications for the future. The High Council lay dead, murdered by their own hands. Streams of darklings and Rovers rushed toward the open city gates. Meisthelm was virtually undefended. The tens of thousands of innocents within the ancient walls would be slaughtered.

"What just happened?" Harrin asked no one in particular.

Halvor's frown went unseen. "We were betrayed."

"Ha! At least that bastard Imelin is dead," Anni cackled from her perch on the wall. The old seer seethed with power, lending her a wild look.

"Imelin? Are you certain?" Harrin pressed.

Arrows began arcing out from the city, slaying scores of darklings.

The priest nodded. "Yes. He was killed by the very same woman now commanding our enemies. This treachery runs deep."

Catapults opened fire. Boulders and flaming balls of pitch screamed overhead. The darklings kept coming, though a hefty portion of the Rovers and mercenaries held back. Men and women, sworn defenders of their city, rushed to the walls with what weapons they could find. Harrin watched the scene unfold, instinctively knowing it wouldn't be enough. Meisthelm was understrength and ill prepared to stop a bloodthirsty army rampaging through the streets.

"We must leave, now! This city can't hold," Harrin panicked.

Anni burst into laughter. "Go where? We're surrounded with no escape route."

Harrin cast a crooked finger at her, while addressing Halvor, "She's mad. Where do your people go in times of duress?"

Sonic waves blew the pair to the floor. Dust and broken bits of stone and plaster rained down on them. Harrin brushed debris from his eyes and was astonished to find Anni Sickali casting bolts of blue fire down into the approaching darklings. *Mad, but more powerful than she lets on.* Defenders nearby cheered, for they were saved by magic! Harrin was amazed that so many took hope in the actions of a single woman. Actions that, unless he was gravely mistaken, wouldn't make much of a difference in the battle's outcome. Picking himself up, the soldier of Galdea searched for a bow. If death had come for him, he intended on meeting it with weapon in hand. The way a warrior should.

Halvor wasn't as convinced. The Red Brotherhood was clandestine but strong. Though Dalstrom hadn't specified how many priests were in the city, the elf suspected there were close to a hundred scattered around the walls. One hundred offered considerable firepower to the defense, but he doubted it would be enough. His untrained eyes looked out upon a field of enemy, tens of thousands at least.

A bolt of wild magic erupted from farther down the wall to his right. Bright green and noxious. Halvor turned in time to see others unleashing their power on the darklings. Bolts of every color poured down from the walls. Darklings and men were burned, melted, and liquefied. Several chasms opened, swallowing darklings by the hundreds before snapping shut again. Still, the enemy advanced.

The lead elements were charging through the open gates when Halvor raised his burn-scarred hands and joined his brethren.

Dalstrom stood on the walls of Meisthelm, far from Halvor and the others, watching the impossible unfold. His plan hinged on Imelin overplaying his hand. Only Imelin had just been murdered by one of the High Council. Any encouragement he might have felt, vanished a moment later when Arlyn Gert assumed command and ordered *her* army into Meisthelm. *Incredible. It appears she has been playing us all for fools all along. Or this is the sharpest twist in politics in recent memory.*

"Kelanvex, send word to the others. They are to attack as soon as the darklings are under catapult range," he told the young woman at his side.

The priest closed her eyes and telepathically connected with the team leaders. "They comply. Where would you like me during the assault?"

"Right where you are, my friend. Try not to get killed."

She wasn't sure if the last was an actual command or a half-hearted joke but Kelanvex gave a firm nod. Apart from being the strongest empath in the Red Brotherhood, Kelanvex was strong with fire magic. That power bristled, rumbling deep within her core as it struggled to burst free. She flexed her hands repeatedly, aching to be turned loose.

Dalstrom noticed this out of the corner of his eye. "Patience. Our foes will soon present themselves. Besides, we have more pressing concerns. Our dear friend

Imelin is no longer among us. We face the uncertain now."

She didn't know what he meant by that. A horde of darklings and traitorous men intent on slaughtering the entire population of Meisthelm was enough of a problem for her. Kelanvex couldn't imagine this new fear gnawing at Dalstrom. Confused, she looked down on the approaching force, noticing for the first time how there were no scaling ladders or other siege equipment. How brazen! The darklings were going to invade through the main gates.

"Now, Kelanvex," Dalstrom said calmly. "Kill them all."

Smiling, the young priest unleashed the full wrath of her power.

"We have to fall back now!" Harrin screamed over the roar of clashing swords and snarling monsters.

Darklings were already pushing through the city. Several streets were aflame. Smoke and screams added to the horror unfolding. Bodies littered the streets. Most were men but that would change soon. Women and children would be exposed, once the last string of defense was broken. Harrin swung down diagonally at an advancing darkling, taking the beast in the neck. The severed head flew down the blood slickened stairs.

Anni was doubled over, exhausted and near death. Halvor fared similarly but still retained a measure of strength. They were in a sorry state. Each had done what they could and more but to no avail. Thousands of enemy soldiers were already within the city. The defenders fought valiantly but in vain. Whole sections of the wall had fallen to the darklings. Several of the Red Brotherhood were dead, killed by Arlyn Gert or being overrun by darklings. Harrin had no intentions of joining that growing list.

Gasping, Halvor managed, "We haven't been given the order yet."

"Orders? I don't need to be told whether I'm about to die or not. We are moving. Now," Harrin snarled and helped the pair up.

Three darklings climbed over the crenellation to his right. Harrin met them. A quick swipe across opened the first darkling's stomach. The second slipped in a pile of spilled intestines, giving Harrin an easy target. His sword plunged down into the beast's heart. The last darkling stabbed his thigh before he managed to pull his sword free. Harrin growled and brought the pommel of his sword down on the soft spot in the darkling's skull. Bone and brain matter sprayed out as he jerked the weapon free.

Out of breath but running on raw adrenalin, Harrin hurried back to his companions. "Which way?"

Only Halvor had any experience in Meisthelm, rendering the other two blind. The elf pointed to the nearest guard tower. Harrin pushed forward. Bodies lay draped in awkward angles around the tower but the interior was empty. Harrin closed the door behind him and breathed deep. The room was large, offering little in the way of defense. A tipped over table and one broken chair were dashed against the wall beside an empty fireplace. The weapons rack was empty, save a dull sword.

"Now what? This is a dead end," Harrin frowned.

Halvor shook his head. "No, press the fourth brick up from the bottom on the right of the fireplace."

Doubtful, he did. There was a hiss. Stale air filled the tower as the fireplace slid aside. Harrin peered into the opening, surprised to find a set of cobweb-encased stairs leading down. He led them down as quickly as they could move. Fear of death held no sway over him. Sword in hand, he brushed the cobwebs aside and headed down.

"Where do these stairs lead?" he asked quietly.

Halvor grunted with each step. Pain racked his body. "To a Brotherhood safehouse deep within the city."

The elf only hoped others of the Order would be there as well. Most of the population didn't know of the underground levels of Meisthelm. Far beneath the catacombs and tombs were layers of the old city from the time before the Hierarchy. Leagues of abandoned halls where a group of people could hide out for a lifetime. Hide or launch an insurrection.

Harrin didn't care. He just needed to get away from the nightmare on the walls. Deep enough and the screams faded. Halvor risked a small light when they reached the bottom. Guiding them as best he could, the elf hurried to find the rendezvous point and hoped Dalstrom would be there waiting.

The murmur of seventy plus priests filled the high ceiling chamber. Dalstrom waited for others to arrive but enough time had passed that those hopes dwindled. It had been six days since the darklings invaded. Six days of unchecked slaughter. All his strength had been deployed on the walls. Any who had yet to return, were presumed lost. So many empty places at the table. So many friends never to be seen again. It was a loss that would be long felt across the Free Lands.

When at last he knew he couldn't keep waiting, Dalstrom held up his hands for silence. Gradually, the priests obeyed. Each looked to him for guidance. Only Kelanvex remained steadfast at his side. Her face was covered in soot and gore. Her diminutive frame remained rigid, yet fragile. She refused to show her true feelings.

No one needed to know just how close to her breaking point she was.

"My friends, you have all fought a valiant battle," Dalstrom began. His voice was soft, while commanding. "No more could be asked from any of you, though I am afraid I must. We must assume Meisthelm has fallen and the darklings are now in control. We can leave the city now, without fear of repercussion. You've earned that much and more, but in doing so, we would be leaving thousands of innocent lives to a horrid fate. I cannot allow that to happen freely."

Many in the crowd nodded and murmured approval. A few did not.

"The only way to find out the truth in your statement is by sending someone back to the surface," Harrin said, suspiciously.

Dalstrom fixed him with an odd stare. Harrin wasn't sure what lay behind the leader of the Red Brotherhood's eyes but felt it was borderline insanity.

"True. I will personally go, though I would not go alone," he admitted.

Kelanvex took a step forward, standing side by side with him. "I shall also go."

"I do not ask you," he said.

Her scowl appeared more menacing under the layers of grime. "You are not going anywhere without me, *sir*."

His smile was genuine. "Very well. Are there any others?"

Already regretting it, Harrin raised a hand. "Aye."

He didn't want to go but needed a firsthand account of the situation to better formulate any sort of plan. Harrin had no illusions about commanding anyone. He'd let Dalstrom handle that. This was his city. Let him spend the hours trying to figure it all out.

"Not going anywhere without me, you fool!" Anni said. Her voice was still weak but the defiance in her tone left Harrin with no doubts as to her abilities. She'd slaughtered hundreds of Rovers and darklings during the battle on the wall.

Halvor, his hood eternally in place, rose to stand beside his friends. "I will go as well. You have earned my loyalty through many hardships. Together, we shall either liberate this city or fall."

Harrin shifted uncomfortably. *These people are all mad. I need to find a way to get back to Galdea. If she still stands*. "Best get it over with, sooner rather than later."

The Galdean was a man used to the open steppe. Being cloistered underground was akin to being entombed. He needed to escape. To breathe the fresh air again. To feel the soft kiss of winter sunlight on his flesh. Dread and fear of what he might find upon reentering the above world, clashed with the instinctive need for freedom.

Dalstrom nodded once and led them down the winding passages crisscrossing beneath Meisthelm. Priests were stationed at the major entry points to the underground world. Minor portals were sealed and kept so with magic wards. The Red Brotherhood designed their trap carefully, creating a funnel with certain avenues of approach down which the enemy had no choice but to come, if they discovered the Order.

They moved for the better part of an hour before arriving at a small alcove at the base of a winding staircase. Two priests emerged from the shadows. They offered a quick report to Dalstrom before being sent back to their post. The immediate area above was clear, for the moment, but with no guarantee it would remain so for long. Dalstrom went up the stairs first.

Harrin wasn't sure about the tactic. There was a time and place for showing leadership, especially the old army adage of leading by example, but trapped in the middle of an occupation, facing a vast host, was not one. Tactically speaking, Harrin would have sent either Halvor or Kelanvex up first. They were more expendable than the leader of the entire Order. Still, he admired the man's audacity.

When Harrin finally got his look at the city, his heart fell. What had once been the crown jewel of the Free Lands, was now a smoldering ruin. Several buildings, former shops and consignment houses barely stood taller than his knees. The wood was charred black and cold. Partially eaten bodies lay here and there. Not as many as he expected to find, but Harrin recalled hearing that darklings were keen on eating fresh meat. His stomach roiled. Every impulse said to return below and wait out the storm.

Dalstrom changed Harrin's mind by pushing forward into the empty street, daring any darkling to attack him. None came. "We must be cautious from here. The battle seems to have moved beyond our immediate area but darklings and other foes may yet lurk nearby."

His deepest fear of confronting Arlyn Gert, made him wary. The head of the Red Brotherhood drew a slender rapier, more for last moment defense than any real protection, as he gathered his magic. Dalstrom wasn't looking for a fight but was prepared for one, nonetheless.

Meisthelm was eerily silent, almost calm in its death. Entire streets were burned to the ground. No doubt, untold hundreds, if not thousands of citizens and refugees thinking to come here for safety, had perished within. An impermeable cloud of sorrow clung to the city as the tiny group moved farther away from their safe haven.

Overturned carts soon littered the street. Broken clay pots and shipping containers turned the cobblestones dangerous. Each step brought crunching they were sure would draw attention. Dalstrom kept going. The stench of burned wood and decaying bodies combined pungently. Vultures hopped about, moving from body to body. Crows lined intact rooftops. Their dark eyes watching everything.

Harrin lost track of how far they'd gone by the time they found the first darkling body. Arrows peppered its chest. *Not nearly enough, if you ask me. Then again, more than one shaft seems a waste*. He resisted the urge to kick the body. A score of men, and a few women, burst from cover suddenly. Each armed with bows knocked. Dalstrom immediately stepped back and raised his hands in a placating gesture.

"Easy now! We are allies," he pleaded, his voice firm and confident.

The obvious leader relaxed his pull but did not lower the weapon. "So you say, but there's a dearth of friends around here of late. Where you coming from?"

"I am Dalstrom. My friends and I have been on the far side of the city, near the old market section," he replied.

He was careful not to give away who he was or their precise location until the men and women proved themselves. They might easily be Rovers or enemy compatriots, given the high level of corruption engulfing the Hierarchy. Six days without an effective form of government to maintain order was enough for looting and total anarchy to begin. Dalstrom guessed that Arlyn wasn't interested in preventing the chaos.

Nervous looks were exchanged.

"Didn't think anyone was left alive over there," the leader said. His eyes shifted across the five arrayed before him.

Dalstrom decided to push a little more. "Got about a hundred people with us. This is the first time we ventured over this way."

A pause, as if deciding whether or not to trust. "Got more than us. Seen any demons on the way?"

Curious. A force so strong should fill at least half of this city. "Not many. How about you?"

"Not since the main army pulled out of here two days ago. City's been right quiet for the most part," came the reply.

Pulled out? The enemy sacked the city only to turn around and leave it? That doesn't make any sense. Dalstrom lowered his hands. "Fair enough. We'll be continuing on, if it's all the same to you."

"Be safe. There's still plenty of these bastards lurking about." He gestured toward the dead darkling.

The two groups separated without another word. Dalstrom decided to lead his toward the Hierarchy palace. He knew the answers he needed would be there, but never imagined what he'd find when he arrived. The Hierarchy, insofar as he was concerned, was dead.

FOUR

Change of Plans

Garin Stonebreaker and the dwarves were huddled together, deep in conversation. They'd done their task but the world had changed greatly since leaving Jerincon two months ago. Two of their ten had died along the convoluted path taken across the Goblin Lands. While none of them bore any ill will toward Sylin Marth or Camden Hern for leading them into danger, Garin couldn't help but feel betrayed by his own kind.

Jerincon was the largest city in the eastern kingdoms and stood on the verge of siege as a combined army of goblins and wylins threatened from the south. Garin and his band volunteered, at the behest of General Dremmin Giles. Only too late did they discover the hidden reasoning behind that decision. Giles viewed Gul Killingstone as a threat to his command of the city and the surrounding areas, going so far as to hire a band of gnome mercenaries to eliminate him. The gnomes, as well as Gul, were now dead.

Still, that wasn't enough to incense them entirely. Garin successfully guided the former member of the High Council to Xulan Lake where they discovered the ancient wizard Elxander. It was Sylin's hope to convince the wizard to return to the Hierarchy and stop the Black Imelin. Hopes seldom lived up to expectation, however.

The dwarves cast suspicious glares over their shoulders to where the two men argued. Life seemed much simpler with an axe and an enemy. The art of politics was often lost on dwarves. Often, but not always. Garin and his cohort wanted vengeance for Gul and only by removing Dremmin Giles from his rule in Jerincon would that be accomplished. Only their quest with Sylin was far from ended and if the old wizard was to be believed, was about to grow more perilous.

"I don't understand. We've come through so much to find you. To get you to return to Meisthelm and defeat Imelin," Sylin protested.

Elxander, seated atop a flattened boulder and looking bored, waited for Sylin to exhaust his list of complaints before responding. "I said I would aid you, if you recall. This is a delicate matter. Imelin, while I can see how you view him as the greatest threat to the Hierarchy, is but a pawn in a longstanding game between good and evil."

"This is just a game to you?" Camden snapped. His cheeks flushed crimson beneath the growth of his travel beard. "Our lives are children's toys to the greatest wizard no one recalls?"

"No one? I've been in exile for that long? Huh, perhaps I should remain so. The Hierarchy has never been grateful for what it's been given. Leaving seems much easier now," the wizard mused. "In certain regards, yes, you are toys. We all are. There are forces at work in this world that neither man nor beast understands. Imelin is just a pawn. We must go south, to Sadith Oom."

"No one goes to the dead land without good cause," Camden said. "It's a barren land, void of life or hope. Only the very worst in this worst land still calls it home."

"Yet it once teemed with life. Ils Kincannon once sought to make Sadith Oom the jewel of the kingdoms, supplanting Meisthelm in stature and glory."

"Which is why the elder wizards established Mordrun Hath there," Sylin suggested.

Elxander nodded approvingly. "Yes. In those days, there was a level of arrogance in the world. Men believed they could do no wrong. How foolish it all seems. The creation of the Staff of Life transformed that arrogance into raw hate. Corruption has ever been a strong force in the weave of the world."

"There must be a way to defeat this evil," Sylin said. His eyes narrowed in thought.

"Defeat? No, never defeat. Good and evil are necessary for each other to exist. It is balance we must strive for."

Camden spat and wiped his mouth with the back of his hand. "How?"

"By destroying the forge of wizards and ensuring the Staff is rendered impotent."

"Better just to destroy the damned thing and have done," Camden retorted.

Elxander grew frustrated. "Have you listened to nothing? The Staff cannot be destroyed by conventional means. It was created by beings far more powerful than any living today. We can only ensure it is never used again."

"One of the Hierarchy's founding principles," Sylin added. He left off the part where they had failed utterly.

"A glorious idea from a better time." Elxander fell silent for a time, allowing his words to sink in. He hoped it was enough to convince them of his need, for how could he adequately explain that the fate of the very world depended on them arriving in Mordrun Hath in time?

"The old man is going to get us all killed."

Garin looked at the dwarf with mild disdain. "Since when does a dwarf fear death? We've been given a task and I am to see it through."

He liked Sylin and Camden enough. A rare thing for a dwarf.

"I didn't say that. I just think we have other priorities."

Maric Trailbreaker wrapped his travel cloak around his broad shoulders. "This is our priority. We were chosen to guard the Councilor."

"And we have," Talrn scoffed. "Hasn't done us much good though, has it?"

"Doesn't matter. We did our job and it's not over yet. Anyone wants to head back to Jerincon can," Garin told his brother.

Despite the fabled dwarven courage, he knew few, if any, would take him up on his offer. Not with the width of the Goblin Lands to cross. Their safest odds were by sticking with Sylin and the cantankerous wizard.

"Says you," Talrn replied. "I won't be satisfied until my axe is in Dremmin's head. Gul was one of the best. Dremmin had no reason to do what he did."

"You are taking the word of a gnome at value," Maric told them with a fixed gaze. Gnomes and dwarves were enemies from old times. "When have dwarves ever been prone to believing another race without investigating first?"

He had a point. They all knew it. Cautious and taciturn by nature, dwarves made their living through detailed negotiations and constant haggling. That Isic the gnome spat poison with each spoken word, there seemed no doubt. His death for killing Gul was in reprisal, but Garin couldn't help but wonder if he had spoken true before his life bled away.

There was a slight, yet real, option that Isic had been hired by another party to turn the dwarves against each other, when they needed unity the most. Devious, but not unfamiliar. Garin held no affection toward

Dremmin Giles. The dwarf was as miserable as they come. But he was the chosen leader of the war band in Jerincon. It would be through his strategy that the city either stood or fell against the coming goblin army. Garin didn't feel right marching back to the city and deposing their leader. Not without concrete proof of treachery.

"Very well. We stay the course," Talrn retreated from his stance. Dwarves were long lived beings with longer memories. There would come a time for retribution. "Brother, we go where you lead."

Garin wished that made him feel better.

Nightfall draped across the grasslands surrounding Xulan Lake. Elxander had disappeared. Fled back to his seclusion in the Tower of Souls to prepare for their departure in the morning. No one complained. A fire was lit and the Stonebreaker brothers managed to set aside their differences long enough to bring down a small plains deer. The company ate good. A filling meal before the trek back west to the Arindl River and the blasted lands of Sadith Oom beyond. It was a long trip, though faster than trying to return to Meisthelm.

Sylin leaned back against a log and rubbed his stomach. He tried, and failed, to recall the last time he'd been so full. Sleep beckoned but his mind was filled with too many thoughts and concerns. The smell of pipe tobacco blew across his face and he turned to see Camden sitting in a similar position, while enjoying a quality smoke. Sylin almost wished he had a habit like that.

As if reading his thoughts, Camden grinned. "You need to find a release. Too much tension will eat you from the inside."

"I used to enjoy sleep," Sylin replied.

They shared a brief laugh. Sleep was yet another on the growing list of items they needed. Sylin recalled hearing soldiers complain that there'd be time enough for sleep after you were dead. He wasn't in a hurry to find out.

"What's that? Do you know what I really miss? A pillow," Camden admitted. "You'd think among our years of experience, one of us would have thought to bring a pillow from Jerincon."

"Your pack isn't good enough?" Sylin quipped.

Camden snorted, choking on the smoke in his lungs. "Too many lumps. My neck aches every morning."

Aches and pains were familiar friends. Boon companions that became inseparable. Callouses hardened their feet, though the occasional blister managed to rise here and there. Muscles bore permanent marks from the straps digging into flesh. Not even the dwarves were immune to the trials of life on the road. They merely masked it through the flagrant consumption of ale.

"Do you think Elxander is going to keep his word?" Camden asked, after a brief moment of silence.

Sylin wanted to say yes. To reaffirm his beliefs but the absent parts of their conversation left him on edge. "I think he is not telling us all he knows. There is strong magic in his tower. I felt it."

"Might be he's had a glimpse of what's going on back in Meisthelm," Camden offered, as he emptied the embers of his pipe onto the palm of his hand before dumping them in the dirt. "Or he's just plain scared."

"I don't think a man with that much experience would be afraid of much," Sylin cautioned.

"Aren't you? Sylin, I'll be honest. There have been times on this quest of yours when I was terrified. For all his quirks and eccentricities, Elxander is still just a man," Camden explained. "He'd have to be insane to march into this without a little concern."

"I'm beginning to think we all are. Get some sleep. We set out early in the morning."

Camden was already nestling into a comfortable position.

Dawn broke to find the already weary band on the road heading west. Elxander was true to his word and arrived just as the dwarves were finishing breaking camp. To avoid potential confrontations with the dwarves, the wizard rode beside Sylin. Camden, deciding to follow suit, rode on ahead with Maric to scout the path ahead. This deep in goblin territory, they could ill afford to run afoul of a patrol.

The wizard made casual conversation with Sylin, ever probing into what Sylin knew of magic and his seemingly growing abilities. The High Council was highly discouraged from using their given powers. It was one of the reasons for Elxander's departure. He'd argued long for the removal of the ban. Wizards were meant to use their gift to help others. What better way to do so than in the service of the Hierarchy?

His pleas fell on deaf ears. Zye Terrio assumed control of the Council and finalized his plans. Magic was, according to him, the bane of existence. A root cause of all the problems in the world. The Free Lands would be better off without the meddling of wizards. Self-exile followed, for Elxander wanted no part of the ignorance plaguing the Hierarchy.

"What will we find when we reach Sadith Oom?" Sylin asked, later in the day.

Elxander made a show of sighing. "I wish I had an answer for you. It was once a green land, but the battle against the Knights of the Seven Manacles and Ils Kincannon left it barren. Rumors have reached me that the goblins and worse have been rebuilding the ancient fortress of Morthus. Great evil is at work here. We must proceed with caution."

"Time is against us," Sylin warned. He went on to detail what he knew of the developing war, admittedly knowing his information was weeks out of date. Enough time had passed that he no longer felt as confident about matters as he had when setting out from Meisthelm.

Elxander kept his opinions private. A gift of the Tower of Souls was the ability to scry into various parts of the world. Checking in on what he saw fit. More than once, the old wizard stopped to see what harm Imelin was causing and the effects of the High Council's incompetence. He feared that if he told Sylin the truth, the young man might lose faith and retreat into himself. Elxander couldn't allow such, for he had need of Sylin, if he were to restore balance and order.

Riding at his side, Sylin frowned but held his tongue. The wizard knew more than he was letting on and it was to the point that being shunned began to irritate Sylin. His policy with his allies was one of open information. None of them could operate effectively if secrets were being kept.

"How familiar are you with Sadith Oom?" Sylin decided to change his approach.

Elxander smiled, approving of the young man's guile. "There was a time when I was very acquainted."

How old are you? Surely you weren't alive during the war against Kincannon. "The Hierarchy has not had an embassy in the kingdom for as long as I know. Certainly not in the generations before my birth."

"No. It hasn't. Sylin, this quest will challenge all you think you know. The world will appear very different once the war is finished. I will not say more, for fear of influencing you, but know that the decisions you make might very well lead to salvation or demise."

Sylin tried to swallow the lump forming in his throat but could only choke on the forewarning. He began to dread his course of action.

"What do you make of all that?" Talrn asked, as they rode ahead of the others.

Camden looked back over his shoulder. Sylin and the others were a few hundred meters behind. Well out of earshot. "I don't trust the wizard. He's not telling us the truth."

The dwarf agreed but failed to see any way out of their current situation without permanently damaging relations between the eastern kingdoms and the Hierarchy. "He's our problem, like it or not. Sylin seems convinced he can help."

"I'm sure he can, though I don't know if that will be beneficial for any of us. We live in queer times, Talrn," Camden said.

The dwarf made a show of clearing his throat and spat heavily. "Said that right."

He glowered over the treachery in Jerincon. It was unfathomable to think a dwarf would betray blood kin. That one dwarf would willingly turn on his brothers in the name of power. Unconscionable. Despite his tepid agreement with his brother, Talrn continued to dream of the day when his axe would set matters right.

"Do you think we need to watch him? It wouldn't do to have the wizard pull one over on us when our guard is down," the dwarf offered.

Camden instantly felt uncomfortable. "Elxander is the man we've come halfway across the world to find. Sylin says we can trust him and that's good enough for me." *To an extent. I haven't gotten this far in life by throwing my trust around.*

Talrn shrugged. "If you say so."

Camden shared the dwarf's doubts but knew better than to express them. Sadith Oom was still many days away. There was at least a little time to prepare for the end of it all.

The goblins crouched, all but hidden in the deep grass. They watched, patient and unmoving, as the party of dwarves began the slow trek west. Curious, three men now joined them. The third appearing at dawn. Suspicions arose among the goblins, for there were rumors among the clans of a great and powerful man dwelling on the island in the center of the lake. A sorcerer some claimed. These goblins knew nothing of that. All that mattered was that a third man was now with the dwarves.

Even more curious, yet sadly inevitable, was the absence of the gnome and the largest of the dwarves. Murder and betrayal choked the lakeshore. Only one of the goblins had witnessed the terrible events of two nights past. Gnomes were seldom a match against a fully armed and aware dwarf, but this one struck wisely in the middle of the night. Cowardly, but effective. The goblins chittered softly when they were certain the dwarves couldn't hear. That the remaining dwarves unceremoniously slew the gnome whispered volumes. Honor only extended so far.

Waiting until the dwarves were out of sight, the goblins rose and scampered into the now empty camp. They rooted through the remains, careful not to disturb the pair of stone covered graves. The dead deserved respect, even among goblins. Satisfied that nothing of value was left behind, the goblins hurried to give their report.

Lost in the soft valleys and rolling hills of the southern part of the Goblin Lands, two hundred goblin exiles gathered in wait. Their purpose was unclear. Their desires confident. Each bore the scars of abandonment by their own people. All were tired of constant warfare. Of lives without purpose other than to die by the blade. Though dwarves and men were inherent enemies, none had suffered by those hands before.

The coming of the dwarf party presented opportunity and challenge. Redemption awaited should the goblins find the merit in confronting their lifelong enemies. Word spread quickly through the two hundred. The time had finally come. Weapons brandished, the goblins collected their gear and struck out after the unsuspecting dwarves. It was a day long awaited.

FIVE

Unexpected Allies

The sun blazed hotly down upon what remained of the Free Rebellion camp. The bodies were all gone now, burned in offering to the next life. Tears were dried up. Hearts hardened. The survivors numbered little over one hundred. A pale offering of what had once been. Poros Pendyier abandoned hope of any others returning. The assassin had done his task expertly. Any who had escaped his blades and not bothered to return, would be well on their way back to friendlier lands.

His meager forces were bolstered by Mard and the Dagger Troll clan. Hundreds of monstrous trolls filled the canyon. They sang, belched, and fought amongst themselves without care or worry of being discovered. They wanted the goblins from Morthus to come. A chance for retribution over the insult delivered upon their confiscated home of Mordrun Hath. Trolls held no fear. Only a dragon was strong enough to kill them singlehandedly and no dragons dwelled within the dead lands.

Hope rekindled in Poros the moment Mard agreed to become an ally. The trolls were an impressive military force. One he hoped might be sufficient to break the power of Morthus. Yet all was not calm. Days after returning to the canyon Poros had called home for three years, a giant of a man appeared, claiming friendship. Horus, he said his name was. The last of his people from generations long forgotten.

Poros found it odd that anyone could survive alone for hundreds of years. His initial questioning of

Horus left him with more doubts and questions than before. When asked where he came from, Horus could only say the mountains to the north. None of the names or land features Poros knew by heart were recognized by the giant. Odd that he should make his way seemingly unerringly to the middle of Sadith Oom.

Alone in his tent, Poros leaned back against a sandstone boulder and closed his eyes. He caught the scent of wildflowers and heard soft whistling coming from nearby. Any other time, he might have smiled in anticipation, but his mind was troubled deeply. Sharna Dal had been rescued from goblins several months ago and used that time to work her way into his inner circles. Poros found her daunting and highly attractive, with hard, yet feminine features and flowing golden locks.

The longer they were together, the more he began to harbor reservations as to her authenticity. She was hiding something. A fact he became increasingly positive about. But what? He couldn't fathom what went on in the dark recesses of her mind and that bothered him more than he cared to admit. Trust was rare these days, yet before he managed to discover the truth of the matter, he and a small group of friends were captured by the trolls. Libek Tug, the rebellion's beloved gnome, was slain outright before Poros and Mard came to an accord.

It was a sad day, but all rebellions were plagued by loss. Libek became just one name in an ever-growing list demanding vengeance. Poros listened to the soft footsteps march up to his tent. He resisted the urge to sigh. Did no one respect his need for privacy?

"Poros, are you in there?" Sharna called, before entering.

Poros wiped some of the sand and crud from the corners of his eyes and smiled. "Where else would I be? This is my home."

"One that needs a woman's touch," she chided.

His smile dimmed, slightly. "I've done well enough on my own. What brings you here, Sharna? I was trying to get some rest."

She made a show of looking to see if anyone was within earshot. "I don't trust these trolls, or that stranger."

What's to trust? We've become trapped in a game none of us are qualified to play. "Mard could have killed us at any point. He didn't need to take us prisoner. The attack by goblins forced Mard into direct actions. He may very well turn on us when this war is finished, but it's a gamble I'm willing to take."

Lips pursed, Sharna placed her tiny hands on her hips. "Says you. How many more must die before you are satisfied? The rebellion is finished. We are all that is left. I … I don't want to see you die, too."

They'd both seen enough to know that death would come when it wanted. Nothing he did would prevent or delay that. All he had to trust in was the strength of his sword until the day arrived.

"Talking like this does nothing to help our situation. You must have faith that we will come out of this for the best," Poros said, but the words sounded empty to his ear.

Horus watched as a trio of trolls threw what he assumed to be bones and broke into raucous laughter. What they found amusing was lost on him, for he had been away from the world for too long. The magic which had contained him in sleep for so many centuries not only kept him alive but rendered him an unnecessary relic without ideations to modern society.

It had all seemed so easy when he first awakened. Horus had travelled far from his mountain retreat, encountering few sentient beings. It wasn't until he entered the canyon of the Free Rebellion, that he realized how much he'd missed socialization. He came from a kind people, but they were never many. Being among these trolls, a species he'd seldom seen before, was anathema to all he'd grown accustomed to.

The slap on his back resonated deep within his flesh, nearly knocking him off his feet. Mard choked a deep laugh as he ambled up beside him. They were almost the same height, though the troll easily outweighed him by several hundred pounds. Horus appeared wiry by comparison.

"It is good to laugh," Mard said, his speech broken and strained.

Horus reluctantly agreed. "It has been a very long time since I last laughed. I'm not sure I remember how."

The troll eyed him warily, suddenly mistrustful. "Why not?"

Horus lacked the strength to explain. To tell the troll how he'd outlasted his race by sheer chance, even as the others were slaughtered in the purge. Some wounds time failed to heal.

"What's going on here? Making friends?" Poros asked, as he strolled up behind them.

Horus turned to look down on the man. "Mard and I were discussing the merits of laughing. It is… foreign to me these days."

"A man must laugh, otherwise we'd go insane," Poros agreed.

Mard nodded his consent.

"We've got plans to finalize," Poros immediately changed the subject. "Our enemies in Morthus continue to strengthen their position, while we dally here. I believe the time has come to strike."

"Good," Mard grumbled. "Trolls are ready to fight. This is no good for us." His meaty hand gestured to his three warriors throwing bones.

Poros recalled an old adage about the unused axe grows rusty or something along those lines. He'd never been one for obscure bits of sage wisdom the older generation was fond of spewing but believed it might just apply to the trolls. Their savagery went beyond anything he'd ever experienced, once again leaving him thankful the two had found common ground.

The trio went on to develop a formulated strategy for dealing with the rising power in Morthus. A daunting task, yet one they must address, if Sadith Oom was ever going to stand a chance at returning to some semblance of normalcy, or at least a measure of freedom. The outcome was in doubt, but Poros imagined that was the way life was meant to be.

"Hey, you listening to that?"

Dom Scimitar, the dour dwarf who continually felt out of place among humans, folded his tattooed arms and turned his ever-present scowl on the former goblin caravan guard. He liked Matis well enough, but the goblin was a traitor, making it difficult for the dwarf to trust him.

"I'm trying not to," Dom grunted. "Doesn't matter who's in charge, we're all going to bleed before this is finished."

"Are all dwarves like you?" Matis asked. His tone was light, almost jovial.

Matis found comfort among the rebellion. A feeling of mattering. Though Dom was incredibly taciturn, Matis felt drawn to him. There was strength in the dwarf that Matis admired.

Dom sensed the humor and replied, "I should hope so. Otherwise, the entire race will be doomed. Don't goblins laugh?"

"It's a new development for me," Matis acknowledged, as memories of the drear life under whip and sword in Morthus resurfaced. "I've never known happiness until now."

Dom made a show of looking around. "This wasteland makes you happy? You're demented!"

They shared a laugh, causing several around them to stop what they were doing and stare. Dwarf and goblin were an odd pair under any circumstances aside from here. Now. Sadith Oom was a land where nothing made sense and the impossible was commonplace. A desperate kingdom lost to nightmares and sheer obscenities. Humanity lacked value. Life became a grueling struggle, with only one way out.

"I don't want to return to Morthus," Matis admitted.

He knew, as did Dom, that should the assault fail, he would be executed as a traitor, his body dismembered and left for the vultures. Daunting, even for a seasoned warrior.

Dom agreed. "I don't want to be in this putrid kingdom any longer, but when were we ever asked what we wanted, eh?"

"The sad life of being a warrior," the goblin added. His head lowered at the thought. Would it be difficult to face his former brood-mates and comrades? He didn't imagine so. Goblins held loyalties to the strongest, not out of friendship. Regardless of whether he showed hesitation or not, Matis knew they would attempt to kill him with ruthless disregard.

"We should find something to eat," Dom unfolded his arms. "Come on, I've a feeling this might be the last time our bellies get full."

Dwarf and goblin ambled away from the brooding leaders of the new rebellion. Let others come up with the planning. All Dom needed was a target and subsequent objective. His axe would do the thinking for him after that. Wars were queer like that. Good men died, while lesser, weaker ones, managed to slither out of the arena to live another day.

Sharna Dal stood quietly in their shadow, watching them with veiled eyes. Her mistrust extended well beyond the trolls, delving deep into those Poros chose to surround himself with. Most of all, she held severe reservations about the integrity of Poros Pendyier. Men like that were dangerous to the future. At least the future she envisioned.

She knew that the combined force, a paltry six hundred in total, would soon depart for the final confrontation against the power in the south. Fates willing, none would return.

If the village had a name, no one knew it. Chonol Distan rode hard to escape the unending plains of Sadith Oom. His purpose was accomplished. The Free Rebellion was crushed beyond salvation. Hundreds of men, women, and even children lay dead at his hands. A master assassin, Chonol slipped through the meager defense of confused rebels. His blades didn't slow. Didn't stop until all resistance was broken, never to rebuild.

Were he a man of conscience, he might have had trouble sleeping. He didn't. Chonol performed the task he'd been handsomely paid to perform. His only regret was having spent so much time among the rebels, pretending to be one of them and sharing their dream of a free Sadith Oom.

Free, he scoffed. There was nothing in the southern kingdom worth saving. It was plain for all to see. Better they died at his hands than the horror lurking farther south. Chonol cared for none of that. He was Gen Haroud. A killer of men. There was a time when the faces haunted him. When he actually felt for his targets. Years passed and with them those days. The dead were naught but casual reminders of how great his wealth had grown.

He sat in an empty common room of what passed for an inn, though in truth, it was little better than a hovel. Dirty men and women shuffled about aimlessly. These were disaffected. The scourge of society, abandoned by all the true powers in the world and broken by hardships unimagined by the majority. Chonol cared little, so long as they gave him wide berth. He sipped the foul brew that passed for ale and began drumming his fingers on the soiled wooden table.

The room wasn't large. Only a handful of small, four seat tables clustered around the middle. With no fireplace and limited natural light coming in from the few windows, the room felt choked. He didn't like it, but this was where he was told to meet.

The dark cloaked figure entered without fanfare. Heads immediately turned away, for none were eager to learn the doings of another in this village. That much Chonol appreciated. His work was best left unnoticed. He waited as the figure took a seat opposite him.

"You're late. I've been here so long, I don't think I will ever wash out the stench," he greeted dourly.

A delicate, feminine hand snaked out from the robes, gloved so as not to befoul her fingers. "I come as I please. Matters in the north have concluded. Where is Bendix Fol?"

"That's his name? Bastard's mad. He's been out in the desert too long," Chonol replied. "He's safe enough. I have him sequestered until you need him."

A stiff nod. "Very good. I have another task for you, assassin."

His eyebrow arched. New jobs were approved by the guild masters. He lacked authority to accept a contract out of hand, yet Chonol found it difficult to say no. Whoever she was, this woman had lined his purse enough to keep him in wealth for the remainder of his days. A handsome sum that he couldn't refuse. "It would have to be extremely lucrative for me to ignore Gen Haroud guidelines."

And it would be. Others would come looking for him when it became known he'd gone against the rules. There was a sense of professionalism among the assassin clans. One he wasn't opposed to but failed to understand. Theirs was the profession of murder. What honor could be made from such vile deeds?

"Do not fear for your pockets, assassin. You will be well compensated. Perform your duties appropriately and the guild masters will leave you alone. You have my assurances," she lied.

Lady, I don't even know who you are. You've more secrets than me, and that's saying something. "What is it?"

He listened as she explained what she needed. Chonol couldn't say he was surprised, but that didn't mean he liked it. Too many variables and far too many opportunities for him to lose his head.

Life alone required a special skill set. Most went mad, while others abandoned the principles almost immediately. Humanity was designed for social interaction. Or so stood conventional reasoning among the kingdoms. Bendix Fol was anything but conventional, however. The wizened old man preferred a life of solitude, far away from the meddling of his fellow men.

He learned early on that there were some people who did not get along well with others. These were the odd, the disenchanted. Those who failed to fit in to societal constructs. His eccentricities made him an outcast, for no other wished to have dealings with a man so odd that he communed with the dead. Ghosts and ghouls.

Bendix once heard the term necromancer cast his way. He scoffed. To his knowledge, there was no way to bring the dead back to life, in any capacity. No. He was far from what others believed. In truth, he only wanted to be alone. By twenty, he'd given up on society. Far later than the various towns and villages he tried to live in managed to last. Driven out, Bendix took to the lower reaches of Eiterland. The decision proved bothersome at first, for he found it odd that no sentient being was anywhere within sight. He had no one to talk to, no one to find comfort in when life pulled too hard. It was a hard burden to bear for the life he wanted.

Decades fled agonizingly slow as age laid heavier claim. Bendix was in his late seventies now. Old and near brittle. Life in the wilds had not been kind but it was precisely what he required to reach his full potential. Unimagined secrets were unlocked as he plowed deeper into the mysteries of life and death.

Rumors spread of the strange man hidden deep in the empty parts of Eiterland. Wicked men came looking, seeking his employ. What need of coin had a man like Bendix? He dismissed their promises of a hefty purse, instead choosing to go a different, unexpected route. Bendix lent his talents to many over the years in exchange for fresh bodies with which to conduct further experiments. Fortunately, his employers weren't men of esteemed conscience. They offered up the bodies, content to keep their coin.

So it made sense to Bendix that the assassin guilds would come for him one last time before death claimed him. He waited for the moment to showcase all his vast knowledge on a grand stage. The assassin arrived for the second and final time not long after his first visit. By this time, Bendix had packed his meager possessions, those he would need for the coming task, and waited idly by a burned-out fire pit.

The Free Lands were about to bear witness to his machinations. The assassin assured him he had but one target to focus his efforts on. One man to assault while the world devolved into madness around them. Bendix laughed with glee, for what was one man compared to the raw power of death itself?

Bendix Fol and Chonol Distan set out for Sadith Oom and whatever destiny fate had decreed.

SIX

Into a New Empire

Guerselleorn was humid. Sweat poured down flesh, clinging shirts and pants to tired bodies. Mosquitos swarmed by the thousands. Disease spread. Dysentery and high fevers ran rampant among the rank and file. Combined with the losses suffered during the perceived defeat of Baron Mron's army, the army of the Hierarchy was at the end of their line. Each day's march was grueling for the already exhausted soldiers.

Normal camp banter was hauntingly absent when halt was called each night. Too many empty spots around the fire or in the tents. Too many men who'd given their lives on Grim Mountain for the survivors, which was, in all fairness, the heavy majority, to be comfortable with.

General Conn stood at the head of the winding column, watching as his weary units pulled into the night's camp. Since leaving Grim Mountain, he decided to take up this position each night until the last unit ceased their march. Grime streaked his face, making the creases and wrinkles more prominent. Already old, Conn felt as if he'd aged considerably since this campaign began. A bead of sweat dripped off his hawkish nose.

"General," a young lieutenant in a filthy and torn uniform walked up and saluted.

"Zin, what have you got for me?"

He handed over a scroll. "The latest sick call numbers."

"I don't imagine I'll be enthused," Conn replied.

The numbers had been increasing daily. Morale consequently dropped.

"About the same as yesterday. We did, however, receive word that a reconstituted infantry unit of roughly five hundred has been cleared from the surgeons' tents at Grim Mountain and are expected to catch up to the main body sometime tomorrow."

Five hundred. We suffered twenty percent casualties. He sighed. "Very good. Let us hope we won't need to press them into the fight too soon."

Zin Doluth winced. While he couldn't have been more pleased to be back in his original role of adjutant, his experiences as the main assault leader on the mountain left him broken inside. Blood stained his uniform. His eyes seemed hollow now. The battle ended three days ago and the army had been on the move for two. Their goal was to relieve the siege of Meisthelm and confront the traitorous Black Imelin.

"Let us hope not," Zin echoed.

"Master Ailwin informs me he received word from Meisthelm. I must admit to being leery about this, considering how long we've gone without any word," Conn admitted.

"You think it might be false?"

He nodded. "Or worse. We must be cautious. Mron's army was beaten, but not destroyed. Some thousands escaped us. Thousands that might prove problematic in our haste."

Zin had no reply. Fatigue had him on the brink of collapse. His mind stumbled through normally easy operations.

Conn noticed this and placed a fatherly hand on young Zin's shoulder. "You should get some sleep. It's been a long campaign and I'll need all my officers in fighting condition when we reach Meisthelm. Go, I'll manage for the rest of the night."

Grateful, Zin saluted and stumbled away.

There goes a good man. Far better than this army deserves. I only hope the mountain hasn't broken him for good. Clasping his hands behind his back, and wincing at the sticky feeling running the length of his spine, Conn wormed his way through the chaos of an army camp to his command tent where most of his commanders awaited.

A quick scan across the tent showed him familiar faces he'd come to appreciate and look to for counsel. The army was fortunate that so many had survived. They would have such need for these men when they battled the last of the Black. Men rose and saluted as he entered. Conn gave a half-hearted reply and bade them sit.

"Gentlemen, good news tonight. Lieutenant Doluth reports that five hundred men have been cleared by the surgeons and are en route to our position as we speak."

Murmurs of approval circulated the crowd.

Conn paused to pour a cup of water and drank half of it. "Conversely, we've received a message from Meisthelm. Before you ask, no, I have not read it. I thought it best for us all to hear at the same time."

He gestured Rhea Ailwin, the former commander of messengers of Meisthelm, forward and gave him the floor.

Rhea cleared his throat. His nerves continued to act up despite months of being among these same men. "The ah, the message is not authenticated but reads as such:

> *Meisthelm has fallen. The High Council is dead, as is the Black Imelin. Arlyn Gert has betrayed the Free Lands and moves south in command of a large army of darklings and Rovers. Hold in place until further orders.*

Golden Warrior Commander A. Kryte.

Rhea fell silent. He'd read the message numerous times and still hadn't been able to come to terms with the content. All he knew and loved was naught but smoldering ruin. The world burned and there was nothing he could do to prevent it. At barely nineteen summers, Rhea hadn't seen much of life. He feared the opportunity to do so was fleeing. Death stalked the Free Lands, an uncaged beast of unquenchable appetite.

Conn's baritone voice broke him out of his thoughts. Bowing curtly, Rhea rolled up the scroll, stepped back, and handed it to the general.

"If this report is to be believed, we have entered an unanticipated phase of this war," Conn went on. Dark bags clung to his eyes, giving him a ghoulish cast. "I want to hear your thoughts on this."

It was the elf, Genessen, who spoke first. "Caution is prudent. We must not overreact to the authenticity of this missive."

"Speak normal for once," Haf Forager, the taciturn dwarf growled from across the tent. The two were fast friends, a bond made stronger during their campaign in Guerselleorn, but respected each other enough to disagree when required.

If Haf's comments caused insult, Genessen showed no signs. He turned to face his friend and companion. "We must not be hasty. The message could be authentic, meaning our entire purpose has changed."

"True or not, the mission has changed. We've beaten down a rebellious dog, only to have another, potentially greater, one in front of us." The dwarf leaned back on his field chair. Wood creaked under the strain. Several of those assembled secretly waited for the chair to give out.

Conn listened to the debate unfold with rapt interest. He appreciated each of their opinions, though was wary of letting this devolve into an argument. Tired men often lagged in judgment. He was guilty of it himself.

The wylin, Ur Oberlon, rose. His iridescent scales flashed in the dim light. "Regardless, we must be prepared to battle another, potentially larger army."

"He's right. The message said this army is pushing south. Perhaps we should cross the Simca River and engage them before they manage to entrench where they are going," Haf suggested.

Genessen clasped his hands together, approving of the suggestion. "I must agree with my dear friend, General. Whoever commands in Meisthelm has no idea what has occurred in the kingdoms while they were besieged. Any army large enough to sack the capital must be dealt with swiftly, convincingly."

"You present a dangerous path," Conn told them. "Professional soldiers, especially leaders, must follow orders. Without rigid discipline, an army will fall apart. You saw this with the Baron's army. The question thus becomes do we throw away our reputations and quite possibly careers to pursue a course of action with the potential of eliminating the last vestige of enemy to the Hierarchy? I, for one, do not yet know."

"What of authentication?" Ur asked. The amphibian was far from his southern home and was the only one comfortable in the high humidity of the western marshes.

Conn nodded. "I've ordered Rhea to draft a response to Commander Kryte. I know of this man. One of the better knights in the Golden Warriors. His bloodline runs deep in the history of the Hierarchy."

"It might be possible he has been subverted," Genessen suggested. "I say this out of caution. If his words are true, the High Council was betrayed by one of their own, again. I will not place my faith or trust in any outside of this army."

"I hear what you all have to say. You've given me much to debate over. Let me stew on this until the morning. We reconvene after sunrise. I believe the army has earned the right to sleep in a little. Order your commands to hold in place and begin recovery operations. I want weapons cleaned. Hygiene conducted, as possible. The cooks will have hot dinner. Regardless of my decision, we do not move for two days."

They rose and saluted. The General had spoken.

Baron Vryce Mron led the remnants of his force east across the southern portion of Guerselleorn. His losses were immense, enough that he had no desire to tangle with any of the army of the Hierarchy for quite some time. Fighting on Grim Mountain had been fierce. Mankind at its most savage. The brutal nature of this war drained his belief in humanity. They were animals at best. Born killers.

Not that he minded. The battle served his purposes. The men in his employ were cutthroats. Pirates and rapists. They deserved what they received from the sharp end of the sword. Looking at it that way, Mron believed he'd done the Free Lands a service. Content with the self-aggrandizement only a maniac could possess, he led his remnants south toward their rendezvous in Sadith Oom.

He found the location odd. The dead kingdom hadn't played a part in the development of the Free Lands in a very long time. Why now would anyone consider attempting restoration of fleeting greatness? Still, the promise of great wealth and power lured him in. The temptation of the future offered much to an opportunist like Mron.

Leagues rolled by at a grueling pace. Weaker men fell out of ranks, many succumbing to wounds suffered during the battle. He didn't care. They needed to reach the Towers of Perdition to secure the bridge before Conn or any other force in fighting strength and still loyal to the Hierarchy, managed to intercede. He figured he'd have close to four thousand able bodied men ready to fight by then.

Days turned to night and back into day and still his army marched. They broke free of the marshes and onto open plains, where they were able to pick up the pace. Mron sent outriders to determine if the way ahead was clear. They crossed into the kingdom of Eiterland without incident. Broken Mountain loomed to the north. A monstrous shadow stretching across half the kingdom. It was, according to Hierarchy historians, the largest mountain in the Free Lands. An imposing figure of raw granite and defiance to time.

Now that Mron looked upon the majesty of the mountain, he felt a kinship with it. Like Broken Mountain, he was too strong and proud to break. Viewing it as a good sign, he spurred his horse ahead. The Arindl River lay not far ahead.

The Nameless Mountains filled his field of vision to the south. The eternal guardians of the fallen kingdom of Sadith Oom. Another day and he'd arrive at the only geographical entrance to the kingdom. He liked the fact that there was but one way in. One way from which an enemy force could approach. The defenders held the advantages. He wondered why Ils Kincannon never secured the border, instead choosing to fight the

Hierarchy on the Plains of Darkpool where his army was eventually overwhelmed and destroyed to the man.

Will I be no different? Is this expedition doomed to a similar fate? He shuddered as the thoughts, unbidden, played havoc in his mind. Mron was a man used to getting his way. An opportunist managing to capitalize on the mistake of others. His barony was given to him from birth. The byproduct of a so-called noble upbringing. The moment his parents were in the grave, was the day he cast off the shackles of expectation and made moves to build an empire.

Now he stood upon the riverbank looking out at the Towers of Perdition. The creation of wizards long ago, each of the four towers loomed fifty meters into the pale blue sky. Some called them guardians. Others said they were made in warning. Mron couldn't care less. As impressive as each was, with intricate carvings of men and deeds, of ancient battles no one cared to remember, and of the broken dreams of an entire people, the towers were naught but relics of a lesser time in his eyes.

It wasn't the towers drawing his attention. It was the imposing figure of Arlyn Gert standing on the bridge. His days of independence drawn to a close, Mron nudged his horse forward. Best to get their long-awaited meeting out of the way so he could settle in and prepare the defenses of Sadith Oom.

For reasons she failed to comprehend, Arlyn Gert often thought of that day when she killed her sister. Just girls at the time, Arlyn was prone to fits of anger and displacement. She'd always wanted more than her lot in life seemed content to give. Joining the Hierarchy and eventually working her way up through the system to earn a place on the High Council seemed her most prudent course of action. Arlyn left her little hamlet as soon as she could.

There was a time, during her hasty retreat — no, withdrawal, retreat signified defeat and she most definitely had scored an impressive victory in the removal of the High Council, the end of Imelin, and the sacking of Meisthelm — when she thought of returning home, only to burn it to the ground and enslave the townsfolk. The war machine growing in Morthus demanded labor at unprecedented rates.

Returning to Sadith Oom hadn't been an immediate consideration for her. She'd intended on occupying Meisthelm, remaking it in her image, while dismantling the entirety of the Hierarchy. What had begun as a grand design for all races, was now a defunct administration burying the very people they claimed to help. She was doing the Free Lands a favor by cleansing the wretched ruling body.

If not for the unanticipated arrival of the Galdean army, she would still be in her palace quarters. Their coming meant the northern half of Imelin's army was defeated. Probably eradicated if she was any judge of Galdean justice. Rumors of a troop of Golden Warriors accompanying the northern army troubled her further, especially if it was true that they possessed the Staff of Life. The combination of both left her with no other option but to move her new army south.

Now she stood on the lonely bridge entering the presumed dead kingdom, watching as another facet of her fledgling empire arrived. At first glimpse, she was unimpressed. The quality of soldier looked bedraggled. As if getting out of their sleeping rolls was problematic. She scowled. Vryce Mron was a man she thought she knew. Seeing the status of his force so denigrated left her with grave reservations.

Still, they'd serve her purposes at least long enough for her to marshal the armies already within Sadith Oom and orchestrate the continued flow of darklings from Suroc Tol in the north. The combined pressure of war on two fronts would crush the remaining life from the Hierarchy. The Free Lands would then be hers to reshape and develop as she saw fit.

She waited, impatient in the strengthening midday sun, as Mron continued at a noticeably slower pace. A lesson was in order. Arlyn couldn't afford to have those under her command openly disobedient. Even if it was one of her more trusted commanders.

"What part of you believes I wish to stand in this damnable heat?" she rasped while he slid from the saddle.

Cheeks crimson, though whether from the rebuke or casual embarrassment remained obscure, Mron offered a half bow. "My apologies but it has been a long road from Grespon. The Hierarchy fights hard."

"Unfortunate for you. I was under the impression you claimed to be able to reduce their numbers more than you actually did," she snapped. Her disappointment with the outcome of the battle of Grim Mountain made her ire barely containable.

He held out his empty hands. "Conn is one of the better generals in the kingdoms. We reduced their numbers and left them mired in the marshlands. More than enough time for you to secure this blighted place and prepare for whatever you have in mind."

She pursed her lips. Mron begged to be slain. The very tone of his voice ached for release. Magic welled within her. Her eyes rolled back momentarily before she regained her composure.

"Do not cross me, *Baron*," her voice was icy. "Where is Conn now?"

Good question. One he lacked a precise answer to. Mron said, “Still in Guerselleorn as far as I know, licking his wounds. I shouldn’t worry about him for a while yet.”

Her fists balled. How dare this man presume to give her instruction! Instincts screamed to remove him now, lest she regret it later. But alas, Arlyn had need of men like Mron. For a while longer at least. “Your men will take up positions around the ruin of Kryn. The space there should be adequate for this rabble you call an army.”

Mron swallowed his rising anger. “What are our orders?”

“Refit and recover as best you can. I am positive the Galdeans will soon be arriving. You will construct defensive positions on the southern riverbank. Defend only. Do not, under any circumstance cross back into Eiterland should our foes present themselves.”

Galdea? What are they doing this far south? She was withholding vital information, enough that he feared the remnants of his army would be naught but a minor delay in the coming war. While he held no affection for the men under his command, Mron was no monster. Dissatisfied, he decided it was in his best interests to enhance the defenses enough to give them the opportunity of a soldier’s death.

Vryce Mron fell in beside her and led his ragtag force into Sadith Oom and what was likely to be their final sights.

SEVEN

Reconstruction

"How much of their tale do you suppose is legitimate?" Jalos Carb asked.

The dwarf, pressed into service with the Golden Warriors after the ill-fated siege in Hyrast when Prince Warrien set matters right, asked as they watched gangs of volunteers working to move piles of rubble. Serviceable items were carted off to the walls. Anything to plug some of the holes and restore the integrity of what remained of Meisthelm. Rebuilding efforts were underway but at an agonizing pace. Too many were dead or missing. The city of thousands was akin to a ghost town.

Ute Hai scratched the side of his upper lip. "Does it matter? We're here and the enemy isn't."

Neither of them imagined their roads would lead to the Hierarchy capital. One was the sworn enemy to all the Hierarchy stood for, the other undecided on the merits of his current predicament.

The dwarf eyed Ute sternly. "Why are you here? Your kind is known among my people. Rovers. Men without a home."

"Traitors?" Ute supplied.

Accusatory confrontations were inevitable. The name Rover was synonymous with being traitors. Those who'd been there at the very beginning, in the aftermath of the war against the Hierarchy, swore they'd not rest until the Hierarchy was defeated and Almarin's sovereignty restored. How naïve they were. Nothing he could do for it, Ute knew the risks from the instant he turned his back on Denes Dron and the men he'd spent two decades with.

It pained him to learn that Denes was also dead. No doubt the Rover leader found his alliance with the Black unfulfilling. Ute felt a pang of regret. He'd tried to convince his friend the move went against their principles. Tried and failed. Remnants of the Rovers were now too deep in the twisted schemes of this Arlyn Gert. There was a slim chance some of them managed to break away as Ute had, but he knew better than to trust to hope. Ute Hai was forced to accept that he was the last of his kind.

"A man I once called friend lay dead," he told Jalos. *Many friends and boon companions through numerous adventures and trials. All dead for what? A madman's greed*? "He was blinded by the lure of what Imelin offered. Little did he guess it was all a lie. The Black used my people as a blunt force instrument. Fitting that we, too, were betrayed."

"By a former agent of the Hierarchy no less," Jalos remarked. "Odd how life twists unbidden."

Odd not being how Ute chose to describe his ordeal; the former Rover went back to watching the downtrodden citizens attempt to rebuild their city.

"How much longer do you plan on waiting here? Every moment we…"

Aron held up a staying hand. "Yes, I know this, my friend. We run the risk of Arlyn strengthening her position. Only we don't know where she's fled to. South is a vast direction."

The older veteran looked at the man he'd once considered a son, proud to see how strong and wise Aron had grown to become. "Not necessarily. There are places we can rule out. The Goblin Lands for one. I can't see them accepting an army of darklings led by a wizard occupying their territory."

"Conn and the army of the Hierarchy are in Guerselleorn. Arlyn fled when she learned of our approach. I doubt she'd run from us, only to get into a fight with Conn," Aron said.

Amean nodded. "Eiterland has no prominent land features other than the Broken Mountain. There's no place to lodge and build a large army."

"That leaves Sadith Oom," Aron finished. Oddly, it made perfect sense, in a morbid style.

All their problems originated in that foul land. Fitting they should end there as well. The longer and more prolonged the war dragged out, the more Aron was growing convinced magic was the source of their problems. Zye Terrio might have had a legitimate argument in banning the use of magic on the Council, though his proscriptions led to their demise.

The Staff of Life, secured within his currently occupied chambers and under guard, was the world's ultimate scar. Thousands died because of a tool envisioned to maintain peace and order. How foolish the ideas of men. History was littered with examples of good intentions falling apart and going awry. The Hierarchy was the latest example Aron could think of.

All the races were meant to benefit from combined leadership with a central military force. For a time, they did. Trade and commerce thrived, even among the warring nations. Greed slipped through the cracks and burrowed into the very foundation of free will. So much was lost as the mighty toppled from power.

"Sadith Oom. We should address this before the others. Asking Dlorn to lead his army even further south when another army of darklings might even now be preparing their assault, feels wrong. Galdea had sacrificed enough," Aron said after some thought.

"This is war. Sacrifices must be made if our way of life is to survive."

Indeed, but who will lead the path into tomorrow? The vacuum of power left after the High Council's murders threatened to leave the Free Lands disunited, vulnerable when strength was required. Aron felt the unity that had once been the Hierarchy slipping away. Already Elsyn and Warrien were contemplating what the future would hold for their kingdoms. Preservation of a way of life, for both northern kingdoms, was paramount for the young rulers. It didn't take much imagination for Aron to see both withdrawing from the shattered remnants the Hierarchy left from its death throes.

Amean regarded his friend with questioning eyes. "How many have already sacrificed in this madness? Valadon is a charred smear of what once was. I fear this kingdom may never recover, or at least not in our lifetimes. Aron, we must find a way to end this war before all of the kingdoms suffer a similar fate."

"What are you really trying to tell me?" Aron asked.

They'd known each other far too long to bandy short words with veiled meaning.

Sighing, Amean explained. "I am old. Tired. My body doesn't respond the way it used to. Aron, I want to retire and move on. I… I don't think I can keep going on at the same rate. This war has taken too much out of me."

Aron closed the gap and placed a comforting hand on Amean's shoulder. "Just a little further. That's all I ask, old friend. We run Arlyn down and finish this nightmare."

"Aye. I can give you that much," the veteran said, with a half-hearted nod.

The pair entered the Galdean army's makeshift council chambers. Absent were Dlorn's senior commanders. Instead, Aron found an eclectic collection of people who looked odd when placed together in such political setting. Elsyn offered a clipped smile that Aron found slightly disturbing. *She knows what is about to happen.*

"Ah, Lord Kryte, good. Now we can begin," Dlorn said and moved to the center of the room. Absent, surprisingly to many of those assembled, was his map table. "First, let me begin by giving the military report. Meisthelm is secure, at least as far as we know. There are rumors of small cells of Rovers and mercenaries continuing to operate within the walls, but as of yet, we have not been able to confirm."

"The potential to cause great damage is high until we are able to ascertain the truth in this," Aron folded his arms and said.

"Agreed. I have companies of infantry scouring the city as we speak but as in most instances, there are no guarantees they will find anything significant," Dlorn added. "In response, I have also ordered heavy mounted patrols around the city for up to five leagues. None have reported any enemy activity. It is my belief, and that of my commanders, that the bulk of the enemy has fled south."

Jod Theron scratched the back of his right hand. "To where? What does Arlyn Gert have in store?"

"No one here can answer that, you fool!" Anni Sickali snorted and threw her hands up.

Jod glared but said no more.

"Please, this is not the time for arguments among friends. We are here to decide what is to become of this great campaign and whether or not Galdea is going to continue its persecution of the enemy further away from our homeland," Dlorn tried to calm them.

Anni pointed a crooked finger at Jod. "Nothing is simple as long as that buzzard is here! I remember you. All too well."

"And I recall your stench as well, false mage," Jod quipped. "You're part of the reason I retired!"

"Ha! Should have shipped you down to the dead kingdom than north," Anni's voice dripped venom. The animosity between them thickened as old wounds were reopened.

"Just who are you, Jod? You've never told us much about your past and I would like to know, if you please," Elsyn partially demanded.

Jod threw Anni another foul look. "This is all your fault! I was just fine until I saw your pruned face again." He turned to the princess, unwilling to continue against the mage. "I was once counted among the senior most representatives of the Hierarchy, well before you were born, young Elsyn. An ambassador of sorts, if you will."

"Ha! You stole me from my home and tried to press me into service," Anni snapped.

Jod's face colored. "Your home was a squalid pit in the middle of Sadith Oom. What fool would want to stay there?"

Dlorn slammed a fist on the table. "Enough! Take your petty squabble outside, but you will not continue to plague my ears with this nonsense here or now. Am I clear?"

Neither replied, though Dlorn took the silence for compliance. "Master Theron, continue."

"There are many levels to the Hierarchy, at least there once was. My job was lost between the cracks. I wasn't meant to be noticed by the ruling bodies of the kingdoms. Clandestine, yes, but with the best of intentions. The High Council sanctioned my missions and I performed as well as able until it was time to part ways," Jod finished.

Aron wondered how much of what he'd learned earlier was true. Whether Jod lost his family as he once said or if there were other, more nefarious experiences in his past. Regardless, Jod Theron was much more than an odd hermit discovered in the Galdean wilds.

Warrien cleared his throat, gently, almost apologetically. "What becomes of the ruling body now that the High Council is… no more?"

"A good question, though not one I feel we, here in this room, are qualified to answer," Dlorn replied. "I suggest, and I do so hesitantly, that we place Meisthelm and the immediate area under martial law until a suitable replacement is installed. Comments?"

"We risk much, especially after what the citizens endured, by putting the military in charge," Warrien warned.

Dlorn spread his hands. "What else can we do? There is no command and control here. How much longer before rioting and crime run rampant? Should that occur, we will lose Meisthelm."

Aron flexed his fingers, noticing a bone deep ache running through several. "We have fifty Golden Warriors to throw into the streets. Disperse them among Galdean infantry on routine patrols throughout the city. That should be enough to calm rising fears and keep looters at bay."

"There is also the possibility of rising angst against the Hierarchy for not being able to protect its own," Elsyn countered.

"Agreed. We are on a very dangerous surface," Dlorn said. When no others spoke up, he continued. "Very well. I will have the documents drafted to institute martial law, until such a time that a ruling body is convened. Lord Kryte, please see to the deployment of your men. If there are no further questions, I suggest we meet at this same time tomorrow."

They dispersed into small groups, discussing how they saw the future playing out. None bothered to speak of how long the Galdean army was going to remain in the south.

Karin rolled over, satisfied to finally be out of the elements and snuggled beneath a bearskin blanket. No princess, she was unused to a life of luxury and found the option of having a working bathhouse almost too much to comprehend. The filth of weeks of fighting and traveling washed away in a brown pool. She'd almost forgotten what her skin looked like, or how her hair felt when she wasn't carrying a winter's worth of grime in it. But like all good things, she knew it wasn't going to last. Life was never that kind to her.

One eye partially open, she studied Aron. He sat with his back to her. Naked from the waist up, the Golden Warrior faced the small fire, lost deep in thought. Frowning, Karin maneuvered beside him and draping the blanket over his shoulders, leaned her head on his back. A calloused hand reached up to cover hers.

"I wish we could disappear," she whispered. "Go away to a far-off kingdom where there is no enemy threat and live out the rest of our days without worry."

Aron found difficulty imagining a land without strife or war. "I fear no such place exists other than in our hearts. Men seem intent on invoking violence against each other."

She responded by burrowing her face deeper into his cool flesh. The tightness of his muscles contrasted her smooth cheek. Karin sighed, fighting back emotional tears as the months of campaign finally burst free. It had been so long since they'd first met that night in Prossin. Violence, she decided, was a part of their relationship. They'd killed several darklings that night, without knowing what it meant for the greater Free Lands. How could any of them have predicted that their entire lives were about to be torn asunder and remade into hardened instruments of warfare.

"Perhaps when this is all finished and naught but a haunting memory, you and I can escape," Aron said quietly. "We've earned the right to do so. Perhaps a quiet home in a field of wildflowers, nestled at the base of a mountain with a stream running beside it."

"I would like that," she said truthfully. "No more swords or armor?"

His smile was genuine, if unseen by her. "No more. I think I am tired of fighting."

The cackle of burning wood was the only sound in the small room for a short while. Golden Warriors were Spartan by nature. Even in Aron's rooms, there was limited accommodations. A hard bed lined one side of the wall. A small desk flanked one side of the fireplace, a wardrobe just large enough for a few sets of uniforms the other. Wool curtains covered the window.

"What if the others decide they need you to help reestablish the Hierarchy?" she asked.

He didn't have the heart to tell her his deepest thoughts. That the Hierarchy was dead, burned to the ground just as half of Meisthelm had been. Aron doubted the ruling body would ever recover and that the kingdoms would be forced to scramble to find a way ahead that didn't result in each of them crashing to the ground.

Unwilling to entertain more thought on it, he slid around into her arms. "No more talk of wars or the Hierarchy. Tonight there is only us."

*

The rooftops were among the safest, most secure places in Meisthelm. Few ventured this far up, making it the perfect meeting spot. Soft winds blew southwesterly across the open plains of Valadon, carrying away some of the burned stench and rot of bodies yet to be recovered and disposed of. Dalstrom always enjoyed the view of the surrounding kingdom from his perch. The Hierarchy watchdogs were gone, giving him free reign of the city. It was a long overdue honor for a man who viewed his life's task as warding the Free Lands from peril.

Footsteps on the clay tiles behind alerted him that his guest had arrived.

"I was delayed."

Dalstrom suspected as much. "What news do you bring me?"

"Conn and his army have been ordered to halt in place in Guerselleorn, though they are not far from the Simca River."

"What of Arlyn?" he asked. His pale eyes absently scanned the rows of missing buildings. How many people were murdered therein? How many begged for their lives before the darklings struck?

The second, smaller figure shifted uncomfortably. "Nothing."

Dalstrom tensed, turning to look Kelanvex in the eyes. "Impossible. An army that size should be easy to track."

The younger priest struggled with trying to defend her answer over reporting what she knew. It was an issue of morality. She chose the truth. "None of our cells have been able to find evidence of their passing. They report that magic was surely used to conceal the enemy."

"Thank you, Kelanvex. You may go now."

Dismissed, she slipped off into the night. The disappearance of an entire army disturbed him greatly. He was no friend of the High Council but took the treason of Arlyn Gert personally. She had once reached out to him, attempting to seduce him into compliance with her bidding. Dalstrom suspected an underlying scheme at the time but lacked sufficient evidence to proceed. Regret serving no purpose now, he pondered his next course of action. Would they be willing to help? Or would he just be inviting further disaster among his ranks?

Night continued to deepen.

EIGHT

From the Ashes

Unbidden, she entered his assigned quarters for reasons still unclear. What was she hoping to accomplish by provoking direct confrontation? They hadn't seen each other in almost two decades. Twenty years was a long time to harbor a grudge or forget past transgressions. Any argument now would be wasted time. Or would it? Her eyes narrowed as she thought back to that day when her life was forced to change. Time and distance clouded the edges, removing the bitterness as well as obscuring select portions of truth. She decided it was enough to proceed.

Jod Theron, for his part, seemed nonplussed over her barging in, as if he'd been expecting her all along. Perhaps he was, for he couldn't deny the renewed emotions boiling in the pit of his stomach. Or his heart.

"It has been a long time," he began.

"Not long enough, you slippery bastard," Anni accused.

With those words, a well of anguish burst free. Her slender body, made fragile by age, trembled beneath the tatters of her winter cloak. She didn't know whether to strike forth and slap him or pull him close in an overdue embrace.

"Why did you do it, Jod?" she asked instead. Her voice was thin, shaky.

"What choice did I have? They would have found you regardless and taken you on their terms. Getting you out of that wretched place was all I could do." *To keep you alive. Can't you see it? I did what I had to for you to live! Why is that so hard for me to say*?

Anni hung her head. Oily strands of grey hair dangled over her face. “They wouldn’t have found me and you know it! Sadith Oom was plenty big enough to hide in.”

“Not from him. Zye wanted all magic users under his thumb. He would have dug you out and turned you over to the Black,” he defended.

Fire burned in her eyes. “Nonsense! Even if he had tried, we could have resisted. The Hierarchy isn’t all powerful, Jod. There was no reason for you to betray all we stood for by joining their ranks. Whether it was for me or not.”

Hands held out at his sides, Jod replied, “I did it for us.”

And a load of good it had done them. They separated not long after, on hostile terms, with more than a few death threats cast from her lips and had not seen each other in all the time between. Finding her waiting in Meisthelm, the source of so much pain and heartbreak, when he arrived nearly proved too much for his old heart to handle.

“Says you. All it did was tear us apart and ruin whatever chance of normal lives we might have had,” Anni moved back to the door. Years of plotting what she’d say when seeing him again proved for naught as her tongue twisted and caught on the words, jumbling them incoherently. Best retreat now and prepare properly.

“I still love you,” he called out.

The door clicking closed was his reply.

The sounds of hammers and chisels echoed across the city as work crews doubled their efforts. Massive burn pits were erected in the centers of where the most damage had been done. Unusable material was burned, while what could be salvaged was taken away to areas in desperate need. Entire neighborhoods, well established over time, were no more. An unfortunate reminder that there was no need to rebuild them, for the inhabitants were dead or captured.

The mood was dour. Thousands of citizens were gone. Innocent lives snuffed out like a candle at dawn. Fears grew rampant that the population might never recover. That the glory that had been Meisthelm was naught but detritus lying forgotten across the plains. Time would heal all wounds, the elder and supposed wiser of those remaining claimed. Those few foolish enough to lay claim to wisdom were quickly, and daftly, beaten back into anonymity.

Amean and his mixed squad of Galdeans and Golden Warriors took their patrols through the areas where activity was highest, despite pleas from Aron to the contrary. He'd proven his dedication to service over a lifetime of soldiering. There was no need to place himself in the center of harm's way should any violence erupt. Amean waved off the concern as only a veteran could and dutifully went about his work.

They halted outside of one of the largest projects and took water. Hundreds of citizens were busily clearing the rubble from one of the larger tenement buildings. What had once been a five-story monstrosity now stood barely twice the height of a grown man. Amean tried, failed, not to think of how many had been trapped inside while it burned.

Nescus, wearing his freshly pinned sergeant chevrons, scanned the work crews before settling in beside his commander. The younger Golden Warrior was no stranger to conflict but maintaining order amid such vast amounts of chaos was entirely new. The Golden Warriors were meant to serve as ambassadors, of sorts, while curbing tendencies of those who would go against the will of the Hierarchy. They were the elite military force in the Free Lands, used sparingly to keep their blades, and reputations, sharp.

"Relax, lad. These folks are worried about taking care of their city. No one is going to loot or start anything while we are here," Amean told him.

A ray of sunlight broke free from the heavy overcast. Amean tilted his head back to enjoy the warmth, pale as it was, striking his weathered face.

Nescus wasn't convinced. "I am not so sure. I've felt as if we've been watched since leaving the compound this morning."

Several heads turned his way. More than one hand dropped to their sword.

"Most likely we have been. The people need something to look to now that the Council is gone." Amean reluctantly tore his gaze from the skies and gave the crowd a quick look. He failed to spy anything out of the ordinary.

Nescus shook his head. "I cannot explain it, but my instincts tell me we are not safe here."

Amean considered what the youth said. He admired Nescus for his actions during the minor scrape in Hyrast. He'd stood his ground and was prepared to defend the inn with his life. Fortunately, it never came to that as Prince Warrien and Aron arrived in time to stop the predations of the former Warden and restore order to the mountain city. Imelin's lackeys were everywhere it seemed. Only they were never truly Imelin's. He was dismayed to learn that another among the Council was the master puppeteer. *How could we have been so blind*?

"Very well," he said after some thought. Though they were in the heart of Meisthelm, there was merit to be found in being on guard. "Take a half squad around the perimeter of this building. No weapons barred unless you are provoked or attacked first."

A satisfied look on his face, Nescus saluted and collected his men.

The dwarf, Jalos Carb, sidled in to take his place beside Amean. Since being pressed into service by Prince Warrien for his crimes against the crown and the Hierarchy, Jalos found himself becoming a fast friend with many of the Golden Warriors. They were prized fighters and men of honor. He viewed them as distant kin.

"That's a good lad," he grumbled with an unnaturally deep voice. "You will need more like him before the end."

"I agree, though I doubt there ever will be an end," Amean replied, reaching into his trousers for his pipe. He began packing it with golden leaf. "Time was, I thought we would only be used as a show of force. The Queen in Aragoth was subdued and peace spreading across the kingdoms. This war took us off guard, though we shouldn't have been surprised. The Black order was always desperate to get into a fight."

"Is there truth in their demise?" Jalos asked.

Amean knew he wasn't referring to Imelin, but to the rumor that the Hierarchy had been responsible for the death of the entire order during the war with Aragoth. He didn't know and he wasn't sure he wanted to. Some secrets were meant to be kept. Replacing his tobacco pouch, Amean gestured for a light. Jalos reached over with a small candle before jerking back as blood splashed his face and hands.

The candle fell away, the flame dying as it dropped. Jalos drew his axe, only to watch as Amean pitched forward. His eyes were rolled up, his body already limp before he struck the ground. Men at arms drew swords and forming a circle around their fallen commander, retreated against the cover of the nearest building. Not that it mattered. Amean Repage held no breath.

"How did this happen?" Aron's voice roared across the courtyard.

Resplendent in freshly shined armor, he knelt beside his friend and mentor's corpse. The company surgeon had already removed the slender arrow piercing his back and confirmed it was poisoned. Jalos exhaled a steadying breath and relayed the events as he recalled them for the third time. Even now, it seemed impossible. Who in Meisthelm would kill one of their most vaunted warriors? The prospect for insurrection heightened.

Aron didn't hear any of what the dwarf said. He knelt beside Amean's body and laid a tender hand upon his still chest. Lifeless eyes stared up at him, as if questioning why? His heart broke. After so many trials, victories and defeats, they wrongfully assumed the end of the war was nigh. How foolish. How naïve. A singular moment of inattention and the war had returned with unmitigated fury.

"Where is he?" he asked suddenly.

Jalos gestured to the guarded door a handful of paces behind them. Aron's face hardened, reminding the dwarf of the cold stone of the mountains.

"Ute Hai, come with me," Aron ordered.

The trio entered the building. Only one was reluctant. Ute didn't know what to expect, or who he would find in the makeshift cell, no doubt beaten and threatened with his life well before any thought was given to summoning Aron or any of the others. The hall was dim. Windows were covered and all exterior doors were sealed. Only the sound of their boot steps echoing down the rubble strewn hall announced their passing.

Jalos led them to a small room that had once been a reception area. Three Golden Warriors surrounded a huddled figure on the floor, knees drawn up and blood-stained arms wrapped around his legs. It took every ounce of morality Aron possessed not to run the man through.

Instead, Aron crouched before the man and forced his head up. Both lips were cracked and swollen. One eyes was black, sealed shut from repeated blows. The awkward twist in his hands told Aron that several of his fingers had been broken. A smear of blood and three teeth at his feet told the Golden Warrior enough.

He turned to give Ute a menacing glare. "Do you know this man?"

Ute stepped into the torchlight and the man's eyes widened, but not with fear. He stared upon Ute with raw, undisguised hatred.

"Traitor!" Blood spat from his broken mouth. "If only my shaft had taken you instead, I might die a hero."

"You, who followed the entire order into betraying our principles would name me traitor? It saddens me to see you like this, Harbou," Ute retorted.

Harbou sneered back at him. "Keep your tears. I have no need of them."

Kneeling before his one-time friend, Ute searched deep for any redeeming quality. Any reason not to proceed. There was none. Frowning, Ute slipped the tiny dagger from his sleeve and plunged it into Harbou's heart before Aron or the others had the chance to react.

NINE

Dol'ir

Felbar, lord of the land between the forked branches of the Simca River on the far eastern border of Galdea known as the Twins, was at the end of his strength. He didn't know what prompted him to take his five thousand men, bolstered with another two thousand accumulated during his march across the kingdom, and attempt to seal off Suroc Tol. Shame from not aiding Dlorn and the army during the battle of the Crimson Fields began it. Resurgent pride in his kingdom and position as one of the nobles kept him going. But now, atop the ruined ramparts of what had once been the elven fortress of Dol'ir, nestled in the Mountains of the Fang and designed to protect the Free Lands from darkling incursions, he felt as if he'd lost his way.

Grey clouds swept across the horizon, leaving him and the soldiers on the wall clear views of the plains of Suroc Tol. A dismal land, void of life for as far as the human eye could see. Though Felbar had yet to set foot in the foul kingdom, and he was rightfully loathe to do so, he recalled the stories jongleurs told of a volcanic land filled with crevices and fields of ash. What limited vegetation there was, grew near the base of the Mountains of the Fang.

Mount Dominion, the seat of the darkling kingdom, was the largest inactive volcano in the Free Lands. Felbar didn't expect to lay eyes on it, for the mountain was deep in Suroc Tol. He had no aspirations beyond rebuilding Dol'ir and keeping the darklings from continuing their invasion of the kingdoms.

Weeks had passed since he and his small army first arrived and constructed a series of defensive redoubts on the Galdea side of the mountains. Their design was intended to hold any sizeable enemy incursions, while offering a fallback position should Felbar's bid to take and hold the elf fortress fail. Thus far, he'd been blessed with limited violence.

Columns of darklings were engaged and destroyed before Felbar was able to secure the fortress. He had no other choice but to advance with as much force as possible, leaving small contingents behind in each redoubt in the event his force failed. Companies lined the walls, waiting for the next wave of darklings, while others rotated through clearing the rubble and reestablishing defensive measures.

A slender man with granite features marched up behind Felbar and gently cleared his throat. The Lord of Twins turned to his adjutant, Captain Stern. While he was not particularly fond of the man, Felbar couldn't deny his efficiency.

"Yes, Captain?" he asked. Lately, each time Stern came to report, it was laden with ill news.

His face reflecting his namesake and his stance rigid, Stern saluted. "The engineer teams have arrived from Galdarath. They will set to work immediately."

"Good. We need this fortress back in operation before the darklings grow wise to our movements."

They'd been fortunate thus far. Every darkling sent east had been found and killed, keeping Felbar's mission in secrecy. But even the most optimistic knew their luck wouldn't last for long. Soon Mount Dominion would learn of the Galdean transgression and respond in force. It was only a matter of time.

"I also have confirmation of our scout teams successfully bypassing the Wood of Ills," Stern finished.

Felbar felt a weight slip away. Aside from the senior leadership in Galdarath, no one knew of their mission, or of their findings. The war may have moved on from Galdea but Felbar learned of another large darkling force marshaling in the aptly named forest situated at the southern base of the mountains, in the kingdom of Coronan. Should that force go uncontested, the entire kingdom stood to fall. Only the Hierarchy command at Saverin was in position to counter the darklings.

Felbar found it necessary, vital, to ensure word reached the southern outpost in time, even while secretly fearing the darklings would return north and attack Dol'ir from behind. He could ill afford to become trapped in the mountains. The elves proved unsuccessful in holding the fortress after hundreds of years. He hoped his own reign would last longer than a moon cycle.

"Excellent. Keep me informed of any incoming messengers." He avoided reiterating how this was the most critical phase of their campaign. *No point in rehashing what everyone already knows. Nerves are high strung enough already*.

Armor scraping against stone drew their attention. Felbar was angered to see two soldiers brawling further down the wall. Weapons were dropped as the men exchanged blows. He spied a trickle of blood staining the right side of one's face.

Felbar whirled on Stern. "End that. Now."

Captain Stern began barking obscenities before he'd taken a step, leaving the Lord of the Twins to wonder what was happening to his men. Tensions were high indeed.

Any hope Felbar held of the rest of the day passing peacefully was crushed before midday. Alarms rose from three separate parts of the wall while he was administering disciplinary actions against the two fighting soldiers. Men rushed to their positions as chaos filtered through Dol'ir. Closing his eyes, Felbar knew the moment would come. He hoped it would have come after his men had more time to repair the fortress. Warfare seldom managed to proceed as men planned.

Already armored and armed, the Lord of the Twins wrapped his bearskin cloak about his shoulders and hurried to the walls. No one within would know the nature of the alarm. His best chance was by finding the senior-most commander on duty, though his suspicions warned that the darklings were pressing in a major assault. His first sights of the ramparts confirmed so.

Archers were firing as rapidly as possible without sacrificing their aim. Torches were lit from stone braziers built into the walls every twenty meters. Sergeants snapped orders to soldiers, while captains and lieutenants formed plans for the inevitable darkling attempt to retake the walls. Should those walls fall…

He found Stern in the middle of the action. The man was pointing out to the plains. Felbar hurried over, careful to avoid getting in his soldiers' way as they hurriedly tried to strike down as many of the foul creatures as possible. His eyes were drawn to the recently fixed portion of the outer wall. Boulders filled the gap, reinforced with fresh cut timber from the Galdean forests. He doubted it would be enough to withstand any sizeable assault. What little he knew of the darklings was enough to suggest the squat, hairy creatures would scamper over the boulders and flood into Dol'ir. Again.

He drew his sword. The familiar weight comforting him as his nerves threatened to get the better of him. He'd purposefully kept out of the Crimson Fields as the two titanic armies turned the ground red, thinking the preservation of his people paramount. Felbar's forces had yet to be proven in combat. A sore topic he was reluctant to address, though from what he was seeing, his men were comporting themselves honorably.

"Lord Felbar, this is no place for you," Stern reprimanded when Felbar drew near. His voice lowered so that only they would hear.

On principle, Felbar might have agreed. Armies needed leaders and he served no purpose should he die here. That didn't preclude him from his responsibilities, both real and perceived. Still, reprimanding Stern in front of the men would be ill advised.

"What is the situation?" he demanded.

Stern resisted the urge to lash out. Instead, he merely pointed out over the wall. Felbar's eyes followed, widening, the deeper into Suroc Tol his view went. Thousands of darklings milled about as hundreds more attempted to scale the walls. Men poured cauldrons of boiling oil down. Darklings screamed and fell away. The stench of burned hair and flesh sickened him. Still the darklings attacked.

A voice shouted, "Fire!"

A score of flaming arrows plunged down into the darklings, igniting scores. Black, oily smoke rose above the walls. Felbar risked a look and was horrified to see darklings scampering over the burning bodies of their comrades, desperate to gain the ramparts. Arrow fire slackened. The darklings drew close. Claws dug into the ancient stone.

"Swords!"

Felbar jerked around, surprised to find Stern was the speaker. His adjutant stood with sword barred and grim determination hardening his face. Impressed, Felbar decided it was time to step back. A moment later, the first darklings reached the crenellations. Soldiers stabbed down. Steel plunged into exposed flesh. Bodies fell away as they were punched, shoved, and kicked off the wall. The darklings continued to attack. An unstoppable tide of hatred turned flesh.

The defenders stepped back in unison and dropped into combat stances. Blood flowed thick as the first wave of darklings was slaughtered. As was the second and third. Stern ordered his men forward again. Swords hacked and slashed. Darklings died. Men fell, as fatigue set in and mistakes were made. Others joined the fight, filling in holes when one opened.

"Lord Felbar! Behind you!" Stern shouted and barreled toward him.

Two darklings ripped their daggers from the dead Galdean and leapt at the suddenly exposed Felbar. Taken off guard, Felbar threw his sword up to block the savages. Claws swiped across his armored shin guards, producing a shower of sparks. The clang of steel reverberated up his arm, stunned by the intensity and raw power of the shorter darklings. Felbar was pressed backwards.

Working together, the darklings managed to topple him. One feigned slipping, instead choosing to trip him by the ankles, and the other leapt on his chest. His breath exploded from his lungs upon impact, sword skittering away. The darkling on his chest reared back, dagger poised to strike. A fast swing and Stern's blade sliced the darkling's head off. Hot blood splashed Felbar's face. He gagged. The second darkling, seeing his partner slain, hissed and rose to attack. It, too, was killed by Stern's plunging sword. He cleaved the darkling from shoulder to stomach and kicked the body away before helping Felbar to his feet.

"My lord, are you harmed?" he asked. His voice rang harsh. The look on his face was one of clear disdain.

Embarrassed, Felbar retrieved his sword. "Yes. Fine."

The taste of darkling blood twisted his stomach. He spat repeatedly to clean out his mouth. Stern was wise enough to keep his amusement private. Cheers arose from behind. The darkling assault stalled. The defenders had won, for the time being.

"Sir, I need you to go below and coordinate our defenses. This will not be the only place the darklings attack. I will keep you informed as developments unfold," Stern ordered. There was no confusion in the command. Felbar was in the way here.

"Very well, Captain. Hold the walls for as long as you can," Felbar prudently retreated.

Stern's voice rang out over the defenders. "Get the wounded below and throw those beasts down. Make room to fight."

Saverin was the busiest it had been in years. The Golden Warrior garrison, under orders from Meisthelm, busily packed and prepared for the long march east in defense of the capital. It was a bold gambit, for the message was already weeks old with its warning of a massive, combined army of darklings and men approaching the city. Even should the entire nine-hundred-man garrison deploy within the week, there was no promise they would arrive in time to assist the beleaguered city.

Marshal Sevron, the longtime commander and senior officer in the western kingdoms, hadn't been so pressed since the war with Aragoth two decades ago. His painfully thin hair, in truth balder than not, clung to his scalp as sweat continued to build. Winter was on the downward side but was still freezing. Justification for the size of the fire he had raging in his office. Age and decades of military service hadn't been kind to Sevron. Where other men would be content with a fire large enough to warm their hands and toes, Sevron needed far more. The cold of winter plunged deep into his bones.

Sounds of men and horses, wagons and carts moving about reminded him of the day Aron Kryte and the others deployed. It seemed like years ago. The war exploded around them, but he was immobilized in Coronan. No one in the Hierarchy seemed to remember the assets they had in Saverin. While he had no desire to go to war again, Sevron found his inability to act demoralizing the entire kingdom.

No one felt safe. Fears were already at frenzied levels. Magistrates and local town leaders petitioned the Golden Warriors daily with pleas for additional patrols and guards along the roads. Sevron wished he could accommodate them, but the sheer numbers requested outmatched his current manpower. Elements of the Coronan defense forces were already deployed across strategic points in the kingdom, largely leaving the area to the west to Sevron.

Dissatisfied with the crown's response, Sevron ordered the formation of several militias to be trained by his best men. They wouldn't be able to repulse a serious threat but would be more than adequate in defending their homes until he or one of his companies managed to arrive. A longshot, but the best chance many of the small communities had. Previous attempts of trying to coerce those in the remotest villages to relocate to Saverin, where he could best protect them, had all failed.

Watching his men brought back memories of Aron and the others. Aron Kryte was his most promising junior commander. A man others instinctively flocked to for guidance. Only a boy when he first gained combat experience, Aron grew to be a fine man with inherent leadership qualities many generals lacked. He, Sevron knew, was the future of the Order. Perhaps the future of the Hierarchy.

The urgent knocking on his office door, more akin to thunder pounding through the mountains in his opinion, tore his mind away from the past. Yesterday did not matter. Only today. Only now and the decisions made that would affect the future. Sevron knew he was going to regret his next words but he bade the man enter regardless. There were times, most times in matter of fact, that a commander's wants seldom mattered.

What entered wasn't what he expected. Instead of one of his men, he looked upon the almost bedraggled figure of a Galdean scout. The man, boy at best, was filthy. His cheeks gaunt from lack of food. No doubt he'd come from Galdea with all possible haste. Sevron waited for him to catch his breath before gesturing for his report.

"Sir, I been told to ask you for assistance," he said between ragged breaths.

An eyebrow peaked. *This is a new twist.* "Assistance with what, lad?"

The youth nodded. "Yessir. Lord Felbar leads an expedition to reclaim that old elf fort. Dolir or some such. We got seven thousand men there right now."

Seven thousand? That size force should be more than adequate to reseal the borders of Suroc Tol and Galdea again. *But what can they possibly want with me*? "I applaud the efforts, but what has this to do with a Hierarchy garrison?"

He swallowed hard, his lips cracked. "Sir, there's a big bunch of darklings somewhere in the Wood of Ills. Or so he believes. No idea their numbers but Galdea don't have any more men to spare to root them out."

Sevron resisted the urge to begin asking amateurish questions. His mind already raced through tactical scenarios and deployment schemes, even as his heart was conflicted with his current set of orders.

"Thank you, lad. Now go and get some hot food and clean up. I will have my answer for you shortly," Sevron told him. Before the lad left, Sevron asked, "You managed to get all the way here on your own?"

"Nosir. Lost Tibbs, Evef, and Ghan along the way."

He saluted and left.

Sevron slumped into his chair, faced with an impossible decision. Logically, he wouldn't be able to arrive in Meisthelm in time to do much of anything. Yet if he disobeyed the Hierarchy's orders, his career was ended. Conversely, should he obey orders and march east, he'd leave all Coronan exposed to an enemy element of unknown size. The west might fold in his absence.

The sun dipped in the horizon by the time he stumbled to a decision. Rationale and dedication to duty were in conflict, but his mind was, reluctantly, set. The Golden Warriors of Saverin were indeed going to war, just not in the direction they assumed. He summoned his commanders and the Galdean messenger. There was much to plan and little time in which to do so.

TEN

Aftermath

Seven assassinations occurred over the following week. Each time it was at the hands of Rovers and mercenaries strategically left behind to disrupt stability operations. Panic and tension rose dramatically as opposition to martial law dissolved. Neither citizen nor soldier felt safe. Patrols were doubled in strength. Efforts were underway to purge Meisthelm of the insurgency but meeting little success.

Aron held a small ceremony for his friend and mentor. The handful of attendees wept and murmured vows of vengeance. He brushed each off. Despite his loss, Aron was unwilling to think ahead. The man responsible for Amean's murder was dead. Tried and convicted by his former peer. While not condoning the spurred execution, Aron found it difficult to grieve, even while knowing they had lost a potential source of inside information of their enemy's plans.

Through it all, Karin stood by his side. She wanted to do more. To hold his hand. To offer comfort as the pain grew too intense. He'd retreated into a shell, leaving her worried. Helpless, she glanced at her love and waited for him to come to her.

"He needs time."

She nodded, trying her best to keep her tears in as Aron stalked off, alone and consumed with anger.

Elsyn slipped beside Karin. Their bonds continued to strengthen now that the competition of affections was removed. The young princess no longer felt guarded around Karin. "We must allow it. He, as well as all the others, have sacrificed so much for the Free Lands. Aron deserves a moment."

"He does, but that makes it so difficult," Karin replied.

She didn't bother explaining that there was no time. That the hour of greatest need had arrived and what little remained of the Hierarchy must once again march to war.

Elsyn's brow knit in troubled thought. "I cannot order my army to go further south. Not while the borders of Suroc Tol remain open."

Karin reached out and gently squeezed Elsyn's forearm. "I know."

"I am to meet with Dlorn shortly. What he wishes to discuss has not been said, though I suspect it has much to do with what we just mentioned." She paused. "My father made this all seem so easy. As if any commoner could perform as the lord of the land. I wish he was still here."

Mention of the late king of Galdea awakened fresh pain. He was responsible for the capture and execution of Karin's father, long ago. That the man had been a Gen Haroud assassin was inconsequential as far as Karin was concerned. Her need for vengeance was what drove her out of Prossin and into Galdea with the Golden Warriors. Little could she have guessed how different reality and desire turned out. She'd forgiven King Elian, only after his passing, and did her best to move on. A life spent dreaming of revenge was no life at all.

"I believe you will be fine. You have a strong support structure and already have more battle experience than most leaders in the kingdoms," Karin said.

"I've never swung a sword."

"Nor should you. If that is not a measure of success, I don't know what is," Karin replied and she, too, walked away.

Cheered, Elsyn hurried down the winding streets of the former Golden Warrior compound to where her escorts waited to get her back to the Hierarchy palace. She rounded the corner and was surprised to find Anni Sickali leaning against a soot smeared wall.

"Hello, Princess."

Elsyn wasn't sure what to make of this. They weren't friends or boon companions. She'd gone to Anni on a dare and now that she had been given time to think, was thrust into the midst of utter carnage since. She began to view the mage as a cancer.

"Anni."

"Dreary times, these days, wouldn't you say?" the mage announced.

Elsyn smoothed the front of her cloak. The crimson color looked out of place among the dark of what Meisthelm had become. "Indeed. War is vexing business. What can I help you with?"

She wasn't sure why she felt cold toward the woman. In point of fact, the mage had gone out of her way to save Elsyn and her handmaidens when the darklings attacked. For her to be here, in Meisthelm along with one of the Galdean army's senior officers and a priest of the Red Brotherhood, either spoke volumes of her dedication or confirmed she was raving. Elsyn feared the truth.

Anni opened her mouth several times before closing it abruptly. What she had to say meant sense in her mind but now she was confronted with having to do so aloud she was… She was what? Reluctant? Hesitant? Why? There was nothing to fear from the young princess. Certainly nothing to fear in the heart of what had been the

Hierarchy. Anni surmised her apprehension stemmed from guilt, deep-rooted and undeniable.

"I wanted you to know that I did not foresee any of this happening," Anni finally managed. "Nor did I see your father's demise. I… I felt it was important you know that before proceeding down this dark journey."

Anni turned and walked away, leaving the princess more confused than she was before.

The army spent so much time in the field of late, Dlorn nearly forgot how comfortable being in garrison could be, aside from the assassinations, poverty, growing starvation and the onset of disease among the poorer sectors. Clean bedding on an actual bed. Hot water to bathe in. The food was army rations his men brought down from Galdea with them, but the cooks at least attempted to make it hot and appear fresh. Their efforts did not go unnoticed among the ranks. If not for the growing concerns over the continuation of the war, he might almost be at peace.

The transition of power proved remarkably easy. With the High Council gone, the Hierarchy command structure collapsed on itself. Dlorn and his growing circle of influential leaders and warriors from across the northern half of the Free Lands found little difficulty in stepping in to restore order and basic services to the war beaten population. Once Meisthelm was secure and free from continued guerrilla style attacks by remnants of the Black's army left behind, he aimed to send units to the outlying villages to begin the reconstruction of Valadon.

Unfortunately, he was no nation builder. All Dlorn's long experience stemmed from the art of war. Politicians and nobles were meant to forge kingdoms and empires, not men versed in the art of the blade. Every mistake made was potentially damning to Meisthelm.

"Ah, Princess, please make yourself comfortable," he perked up, as she swept into the room.

He'd chosen one of the Council's libraries for their meeting. A place of learning and inspiration. Different colored books filled rows across three walls. Detailed wood paneling stretched from waist height down to the faded marble floor. A pair of cushioned chairs, red as her cloak, were set on opposite sides of a globe representing the Free Lands and what the Hierarchy perceived to be the rest of the world. Dlorn found it curious how much more to the world there seemed. Entire continents stretched around the globe. Were each as troubled as his own?

He gestured to the small table with a decanter of northern brandy and two glasses. Though the fire he'd lit to brighten the library was warming, Dlorn figured a little help from the brandy would ease their nerves.

"Field Marshal," Elsyn replied and sat. He seldom addressed her by title when they were alone. In doing so, Dlorn announced the formality of their meeting. She folded her hands and waited as he poured two drinks.

"I wished to speak with you regarding our next moves before we meet with the others," he wasted no time in getting to the heart of the matter.

She accepted the glass and nodded. "Naturally. There is much that needs to be thought out before we move."

"Agreed. My greatest concern is the morale of the army should we decide to march south. Many are in their final month of enlistment. Many more are worried that Galdea stands to fall. I have twenty thousand men here. Men who could be defending their own kingdom. Their homes. Their families."

The words clung heavily to the air. She didn't fault him. How could she? Dlorn merely voiced what every Galdean was feeling.

He continued after noticing the doubt creep across her face. "If we decide to continue prosecuting this war, I will do so to the utmost of my ability, without question. So will the majority of the army. Their loyalty will ensure such, though I suspect a small portion will desert. I do not support abandoning the rest of the kingdoms to selfishly return home, nor do I give credence to charging into a situation we are ill prepared to handle.

"Sadith Oom is naught but a name to many. I think only that cracked mage has been to the foul land. We need more information before we proceed. I say this to you, for the decision of what is to become of the Galdean army will ultimately fall upon your shoulders. I wish times were not so evil but wishes seldom come true. Princess, this is your hour. A chance to show all of the Free Lands the true strength of Galdea and that you rightfully wear the crown."

She made a bitter face as the brandy burned going down her throat. "Are you trying to sway my opinion, Field Marshal?"

He set his empty glass down. "On the contrary, I am keeping my opinion private. When we step into that meeting, all eyes will be looking to you as Galdea's voice."

She wasn't sure what proved more nauseating, the brandy or his admission.

Smoke from the braziers around the massive table formed a thin cloud along the vaulted ceiling. Dlorn and the others mutually decided on using the former High Council meeting chamber, for their course of discussion involved picking up the pieces of the fallen Hierarchy and building a new world. Of course, the Hierarchy hadn't completely dissolved, but without a head, it was only a matter of time.

"My friends, we must decide our next course of action. This war has taken a new twist. All we once assumed has been proven false. The rise of Arlyn Gert as the true power behind the rebellion has… skewed what we once based our tactics upon," Dlorn paused. Despite having spent the better part of winter leading an army across half of the Free Lands, he found it unsettling to address those around the table.

Clearing his throat, he continued with one basic question. "What must we do next?"

"Arlyn must be stopped and her army destroyed. We cannot allow the dark powers in Sadith Oom to rise again."

It was Jod Theron who spoke first. Gone was the half-mad hermit who'd found Aron near dead on the riverbank. In his place sat a poised, well-spoken man of vast experience. Jod bore an almost regal quality, giving Aron more reason to doubt the authenticity of his past.

The Golden Warrior answered. "By now Arlyn will have arrived in Sadith Oom and begun defensive construction. The kingdom has but one entrance. Every moment we delay gives our enemy more time to prepare. It will not be long before the risk will not be worth the effort."

"Bringing us to a separate point. I have twenty thousand fighting men under my command, but we are a very long way from home and already weary. How much more are you willing to ask of the Galdean army?" Dlorn asked.

No one spoke for what felt an eternity. The question was prominent on all of their minds since arriving in Meisthelm. A question all sought to avoid answering. Only now was the severity of this meeting beginning to set in. The handful of men and women seated around the former High Council table -- a table where every major decision made in the name of the Free Lands for almost a millennium -- were about to decide the future of their world.

"The Galdean army has performed admirably from the onset of this war, or so I have been led to believe. You have bled more than any other, save perhaps the people of this once fine city, and it would be ill to demand your continued support," Jod said. "That being said, yours is the largest and most combat ready force capable of halting the darklings."

"There is one other," Dlorn told them. "Conn and the army of the Hierarchy."

From what they knew, the army was located somewhere in Guerselleorn and licking its wounds form a prolonged fight with an army of pirates and mercenaries. Until confirmation was received, the Galdeans were frozen in place.

Dlorn held up his hand, silently asking for quiet. "I understand all of your potential arguments and see two courses of action. The first is that we take the entire army and march south to force our foes into a final battle. Not what I wish to do, all things considered, but viable nonetheless. The second, and perhaps more difficult, would be taking a small force to find Conn and convince him to carry the Hierarchy flag."

"Dicey, for what is to stop Conn from turning rogue now that the Council is dead?" Jod asked. "It is no small test of the imagination to see him becoming a warlord in the aftermath."

Dalstrom, head of the Red Brotherhood and unexpected member of the impromptu council, shook his head. "Conn is an honorable man. He will not betray what he spent a lifetime defending."

Eyes fell on the priest, for none expected him to stand up and defend one of what had previously been an awkward opponent. The Red Brotherhood operated in the shadows for centuries. Always under the Hierarchy's nose and just outside of its reach. Dalstrom was once a strong supporter of leaving for distant shores, but war and necessity took over. Now he sat, trapped in many regards, by the very constructs he sought to avoid.

"If I may," Aron interrupted. "I suggest taking a small force, volunteers only, to find the army. Conn will want revenge for the events in Meisthelm and for the High Council. It is his duty. I will take my company and go."

"You will need a guide who knows Guerselleorn," Jalos Carb, the dwarf, announced. "I spent many years in those marshlands during my youth. I will go."

"As will I," Halvor told them. The burned and scarred priest began his journey in the forgotten corridors of Gelum Drol, far beneath current Galdarath. He alone survived the wrath of the Black Imelin after Aron had absconded with the Staff of Life.

Aron wanted to tell him no. Tell him he didn't have to spend more blood or suffering, but this was war and war demanded from everyone. Others volunteered. Some were told no. Some flew into rage and forced Aron to change his mind. Karin's argument of losing him too many times already struck a nerve and he reluctantly changed his mind. Command staff in place, the council was free to set about deciding their secondary purpose.

Leadership of the Free Lands was gone. Blood continued to spurt from the wound long after the head had been struck. Peace between the kingdoms threatened to dissolve once monarchs and ruling bodies realized what was happening and began to secure their borders. Sad perhaps, but expected, given the tepid history of the kingdoms.

"We must consider the Hierarchy dead if we are to proceed. Even then, I suggest caution in doing so. Not everyone will be on the same side of this issue. Strength is required if we are to have any hope of salvaging any semblance of order from this nightmare," Jod them.

Aron, arms folded and leaning back in his chair, countered, "We are not the High Council. Any attempt of recreating that body might result in catastrophe among the more powerful families."

"I do not propose to fill the High Council, though a council of sorts needs to be enacted until the leaders of the kingdoms can sit down and form a proper body of rule," Jod countered. He gestured to the prince and princess. "Two of which are in attendance. A good start, but they will need more."

"Hold on, I have no intention of remaining in Meisthelm any longer than necessary," Warrien protested.

"Both Almarin and Galdea have strong leadership in place until you return," Jod said. "Two sitting rulers will be enough to garner support among the lesser kingdoms. Add an embarrassingly strong army to give them weight, none will dare challenge or usurp what we are trying to establish here."

"You risk much with this harebrained scheme, dolt," Anni waved him off from across the table.

"More than already at risk?" Jod asked. The precious fire he exhibited around Anni in front of the others was curiously gone. They seemed almost civil.

"Prince Warrien is right. Neither of us can remain in Meisthelm. Galdea is already under siege," Elsyn seconded the prince of Almarin.

"And in good hands. Jent Tariens is one of the best men I've commanded in years," Dlorn told her. "The kingdom will hold."

Dissatisfied, but oddly complacent, Elsyn slumped back into her chair. How she'd gone from a relatively carefree princess to the leader of the kingdom and now a ruling factor in the Hierarchy was a puzzle she struggled to solve. The burden of leadership continued to increase.

By the time nightfall settled across the plains of Valadon, the handful of men and women had reached a consensus of who was to sit on the new council. Warrien and Elsyn were the obvious candidates. As were Jod Theron and Dlorn. Half of the Galdean army was to redeploy home, leaving just enough behind to secure the central kingdom and force a blanket of security out from Meisthelm. The soldiers of Galdea had earned their respite, such as it was.

The rest of the appointees were controversial. Certainly no one the former High Council would have approved of or recognized. Dalstrom was given a seat, as was Anni. Command was deferred to Jod, with Dlorn maintaining control of the army and city defenses. Harrin Slinmyer and Ute Hai elected to go with Aron and the Golden Warriors, each had their reasons and chose to keep them private.

Whatever future the Free Lands had in store was about to be made in the former meeting chamber of the High Council. The Hierarchy was a skeleton, a desiccated corpse upon which tomorrow would be built upon. Good or bad, these men and women were the best hope for survival.

ELEVEN

Invaders

A sandstorm blew westerly across the Plains of Darkpool in central Sadith Oom. The brown wall stretched high into the sky, rivaling the tallest peak of the surrounding mountains separating the southern kingdom from the rest of the Free Lands. Every living being scurried for shelter, lest the storm tear their flesh from their bones and leave their bleached skeletons amidst the other, less fortunate creatures already succumbed to the harsh living conditions.

Sharna Dal stood just inside the lip of a small cave opening halfway up one of the mountains of the canyon walls leading to the remnants of the Free Rebellion's camp. The host of trolls now occupying what had been her temporary home left her deeply troubled. They weren't supposed to be here. Trolls were violent creatures bereft of human decency. Their presence was a stain on her conscience. And they made her life infinitely more complicated.

Lost in thought, she barely noticed the pair of riders charging into the canyon ahead of the storm. Normally, that would have raised alarms, but she recognized the young, blond man and his goblin companion. Eigon and Matis were returning with all possible speed. Sharna supposed it was due to outrunning the storm, but there was a wild flare to their movements that set her nerves on edge. *What now*?

They were already meeting with Poros and Mard, and that odd creature from another age, Horus, by the time Sharna managed to worm her way down through the passages dug into the mountains and into the cavern Mard and his trolls established upon assuming control. The giant beasts were better suited to being underground than in the open, or so Mard bragged as his people dug. Regardless of the reason, Poros and the others were glad to be able to wait out the storm in relative security.

"How large?" Poros asked, glancing up at Sharna as she entered.

Matis hung his head. His mottled grey skin blended too well with the gloom of the cavern. Eigon, his face still beaded with sweat, reported. "Thousands. Tens of thousands. I don't know. I've never seen a force so large."

"Tens of thousands?" Poros gasped. *How are we supposed to hold out or engage a force like that*?

Horus, seated cross legged in the middle of the gathering, looked from Eigon to Poros. He'd learned much from watching these men and women over the past few weeks. Awakening in the middle of a war wasn't his intent, but here he was. Trapped in a foul kingdom that had once been a jewel among the lands, beset by enemies on all sides.

"What sort of army is this?" he asked, a mixture of curiosity and disdain conflicting in his voice. "Why have they come?"

"Some were men, though of a sort I did not recognize," Eigon replied. "The others were creatures from nightmare. Short, hairy bodies with red eyes. They seethed hatred. Wickedest looking creatures I've ever seen."

"Darklings," Horus said, with instant recognition. Ten centuries after he'd entered the long sleep, he awoke to find a familiar enemy, but for them to be so far south could only mean grave implications for the rest of the kingdoms. Much to his surprise, none of the others seemed the least bit concerned with the name.

Poros shrugged his ignorance. “What are darklings?”

“An evil from old times,” Horus supplied. “That were once secured behind the Mountains of the Fang, but it took a great many lives lost before we accomplished that. They… should not be here.”

“They are,” Eigon confirmed. “More than I can count.”

Poros turned to Horus. “How do we handle this? You seem to know them.”

Horus reluctantly nodded. “They are a most persistent foe. Once they smell blood, they will not stop until either their prey is dead or they are. Heartless killing machines that should not have been allowed to live.”

“Will these bastards join forces with the goblins in Morthus?” Dom Scimitar asked. Until now, the dwarf showed no interest in the conversation.

“If they are here, yes,” Horus answered.

“Sounds like a good fight,” Mard chuckled.

Poros, accustomed to the troll’s bravado and only slightly surprised Mard actually believed it, gave his friends a stunned look. “We need more information before we attempt an assault. I want to take a look.”

“You can’t go! Not again!” Sharna blurted out.

His last attempt at gleaning information firsthand resulted in their capture by the trolls at the old ruins of Mordrun Hath. A circumstance she didn’t expect them to escape from.

Poros tensed. His apprehensions against Sharna continued to grow. Something wasn’t right with her. Now that his eyes were open, he found her presence too convenient. *Why now? Why here of all places and times*? Those fears were well grounded. Chonol Distan came to the rebellion claiming to seek vengeance against the goblins. His betrayal and revelation of being an assassin with the Gen Haroud resulted in the slaughter of most rebel fighters. Poros could ill afford to undergo another such event.

But he lacked proof. The thought of killing anyone without hard evidence twisted his stomach. Exile was a viable option but now that a massive army had come down from the north, the only route in or out of Sadith Oom was sealed off. There was a chance the new army would continue moving south, bypassing the canyon the rebellion hid in and giving Poros the chance to escape if necessary. A chance, but he doubted it. Life didn't seem overly excited to cut him a break.

"If not me who?" he replied, as calmly as possible. "Enough have died in my name. I will not have any others if I can help it."

Sharna placed her hands on her hips. "Who will take your place once you are dead? We were fortunate when Mard captured us. Do you truly think we will be so fortunate a second time?"

His smile unnerved her, giving Sharna pause. "Doesn't matter. No one is going anywhere until this storm passes."

Poros pointed to the cave entrance where the wind began to howl a moment before the sky darkened.

"I don't trust her," Eigon said quietly, as he stirred the embers in the fire.

Matis and Dom sat with him. The trio gelled, despite their natural differences. Dwarf and goblin set aside ancient hatreds for the advancement of freedom. Eigon knew little about either race, and had no opinion either way.

Dom Scimitar nodded almost casually. "I haven't trusted her since she first arrived. There's something witchy about that woman."

"Are all human women like her?" Matis asked. Until joining the rebellion, the goblin had had virtually no contact with humans.

"Not in my experience," Eigon replied. "But I come from a very small village. Women are, were less complicated there."

Dom barked a laugh. "Lad, I've walked this world for the better part of a century and I'll be damned if I can figure women out. Regardless, I know trouble when I see it. That one is pure havoc wrapped in an awkward cast."

Both Eigon and Matis risked glances to the opposite side of the cave where Sharna appeared to almost cling to Poros and the rest of the new leadership group. An aura of desperation poured from her. Eigon didn't think she was unattractive, if anything, she had a little too much weight for his particular tastes, a troubling fact all on its own. How could anyone, rumored to have been trapped in one of the goblin slave camps in Morthus maintain any semblance of health? All others coming up from the south were emaciated. Hollow shells of what they had once been.

"She needs to go," Eigon continued.

He said no more. The domed ceiling reverberated sounds in strange patterns. There was no telling what Sharna might have heard, or how she'd respond to it once she was afforded the opportunity. Eigon wished for the return of simpler times. Times when he and his beloved wife dreamed of a better future. Times that no longer existed or would again. She, like his old life, was dead and fading.

The goblin frowned, or perhaps scowled, Eigon still found difficulty in reading his expressions. "That does not seem like our position. She has eyes only for Poros. He must be the one to send her away, should it come to that."

Dom grunted, pausing to reach behind to scratch his left buttock. "I say keep an eye on her. She shows any sign of betrayal and I'll take her head before Poros can act."

They'd already been betrayed once, and by a man Dom called friend. Chonol Distan proved his true nature by murdering the vast majority of the rebels. The dwarf took it upon himself to become the survivors' watcher. Should any foul deed befall, his axe would respond in kind.

What am I doing? I don't know anything about this man and I'm going to ask for advice? Poros shook away the doubts and kept walking. Since leaving his kingdom, his home and all he knew, Poros felt parts of his essence, his core slipping away. He wasn't the man he once was or close to being the man he wanted to be. Life had taken a surreal twist, plunging him down into a well of infinite despair. Loathe as he was to admit it, he felt lost.

"You appear troubled, Poros Pendyier," Horus said, as the rebel leader approached.

Perceptive. Perhaps you can tell me why. "These are troubling times. Mind if I join you?"

Horus gestured to a cut piece of log across from his small fire.

Poros sat, exhaling days of pent up frustration. Only now was he realizing he knew nothing about a man he was placing too much expectation on. "Where did you come from, Horus?"

"Far to the north." If the giant found any misgivings, he kept them private. "We were a mountain people. Seldom coming down to the lowlands, except for trade. At least we were until the war came and consumed the kingdoms. Try as we might, we could not avoid the rising tide of violence."

"Which war?" Poros asked.

Horus gave him a surprised look. "The war against the Knights of Seven Manacles. Do you not know of this?"

The real question Poros wanted to ask was how old Horus was. "That war was over a thousand years ago. I… I wasn't aware of any remnants still alive."

"A thousand years?" Horus whispered. His wife, his people. Gone for ten centuries. The pain of being the sole survivor striking his emotions.

Poros, seeing the consternation his comment caused, quickly followed up, "Did you come from a large people?"

It took a moment before Horus was able to answer. "We were never many. A few hundred at most. Nor were we violent. The war changed that. Forced us to become more than we were meant to be. It is no easy task becoming other than what you are born to be. My wife never adjusted. She was not alone. Many of my people tried to avoid fighting."

"Many of us used to be like that," Poros seconded. "My wife was never interested in fighting either. War makes orphans of us all, my friend. We can only do as we must."

"I wish it were not so. This life is not what we are meant to live," Horus said. "When I first awoke, I was surprised to find how much of the world was changed, yet similar to what I once knew. The mountains and forests. Even the rivers were largely unchanged."

"What brought you here? Why Sadith Oom?" Poros pressed, feeling close to the answers he needed to trust Horus.

Rubbing his hands together, relishing the heat on his calloused flesh, Horus gave him a deadpan look. "There is a confluence approaching. All the major players in the Free Lands will be here. A finality we have all sought. This war, I believe, may be the final war of our kind. Peace, Poros Pendyier. Peace is the final goal."

"Peace is an illusion. There has never been a time in our recorded history where all of the races have gotten along without eventually turning to violence." Poros shook his head. "I fear your dreams may remain just that."

"This is a sad world. Much worse than the one I left." Horus rose, abrupt and oddly frightening. "Know this, Poros, destinies will collide. No matter what happens after this war ends, the world will never be the same again. We are all agents of change. Even our large friend, Mard. Change. Good night, my friend."

Change. Poros couldn't argue the point, though he spent the remainder of the night wondering what the result of that change would be. Fate had the tendency to overcomplicate life.

The winds died down in the middle of the night. Sand and dust settled, leaving the Plains of Darkpool a barren waste of land. Poros held his hand up to block the sun. *Not that much is different. This entire kingdom shouldn't be here. I shouldn't be here. None of this makes sense. Not one damned bit.* Vultures circled high overhead. He wondered if they knew something he didn't.

The mountains surrounding the borders of Sadith Oom were to his left. He and a small band of select individuals were entering the rolling foothills spread out from the base of the tall peaks. They were getting closer to the Towers of Perdition. Eternal watchmen of the southern kingdom. Poros didn't know who had created the monuments or why, though he was beginning to suspect they had much to do with the current status of the Free Lands.

Scouts, Eigon among them, were a league ahead, sweeping the land for traps or ambushes. Poros didn't see many along their route of march. They were deep within the enemy's land. A certain arrogance accompanied the attitude of the goblins this far south. Despite Dom's insistence that the goblins were far from their own kingdom, Poros viewed Sadith Oom as theirs and his rebels the trespassers too insignificant to be bothersome. The advantage was his, for the time being.

Mard and Horus walked at his side. The troll plodded like the most stubborn oxen, while the taller, leaner Horus moved with grace and efficiency. Each step they took was easily matched by Poros' mount. Matis and Sharna rode not far behind. The goblin would not be denied and Poros felt it necessary, and prudent, to keep the mysterious blonde within eyesight. His mistrust deepened through the night. Each time he looked, he caught her staring at him.

"What can you tell me of these darklings?" Poros asked.

Mard glanced over to Horus, curious to learn of his new enemies.

"They are an ancient race, much older than any of us. Legend says they were created at the dawn of time. A force meant to counter and balance the overwhelming forces of good."

"That doesn't make sense. Why would evil be allowed to exist?" Poros failed to grasp.

"I have no answer to that, other than the creators of this world felt it necessary for good and evil to live in balance. Should one side gain dominance over the other, strife and chaos would reign. It is a sad tale," Horus explained, "one I know far too well."

"Are they easy to kill?" Mard demanded, uninterested in their pointless banter.

"Easy enough for one of your stature, friend Mard," Horus admitted. He went on to describe what he knew, which wasn't much, all things considered. His thousand-year slumber left many holes in his memory.

"Scouts ahead," Dom snapped from a handful of paces in front of the group. A pair of well used axes were strapped across his wide back. Their dull silver clashed with his faded and worn leathers.

"Hold here," Poros called.

The group halted. Eigon and three others rode with urgency, suggesting to Poros that danger was imminent. The Towers were still many leagues away.

"What news, Eigon?" he asked.

The young man pointed back toward the mountains. "Thousands of the monsters, and men, are marching south."

"More than the last time you scouted them?"

A nod. Poros felt his heart sink. They were caught in the open with no cover within riding distance. "How far away and are the coming this way?"

"I'd guess a league and possibly. We didn't get a clear look at their route," Eigon admitted.

"The only thing we had going for us was they lacked scouts," another chimed in.

"This is their kingdom. We are little more than a flea in their hides." Poros glanced at his surroundings. A low set of foothills lay not far off to the west, if they could only reach them in time and without kicking up enough residue in their wake to avoid detection. There was no other choice. His handful lacked the strength to defeat any enemy host. It was run or die.

Unless. He turned to Dom. "Lead the others to those hills. Take my horse, I will join you shortly."

"What are you planning?" the dwarf asked suspiciously, as he accepted the reins.

Poros offered his best smile. "I want to get a good look at these bastards and see what we're up against. Hurry along. There is just enough time to get you to safety."

"I will not accept command if you die," Dom snarled.

"I wouldn't expect you to. Now go."

Poros watched them ride off, hoping they managed to avoid the darklings. Waiting until they were but specks on the horizon, Poros began searching for a place to hide. He dropped to his knees and began to dig. Soon the stomp of thousands of feet heading his way trembled the ground.

TWELVE

Cold Indifference

The grasslands of the southern Goblin Lands were largely uninhabited. Sylin found it ironic that such a vile race held some of the most fertile lands in all the kingdoms. Nothing but sweeping waves of lush green for as far as the eye could see stretched before him. Xulan Lake was already days behind them. For the first time since departing Meisthelm, Sylin felt serene. As if nothing could go wrong. It was an illusion at best.

The high walls of the mountains segregating Sadith Oom from the rest of the Free Lands were still out of sight, but fast approaching as the tiny company hurried to meet their fates. Try as he might, Sylin found it increasingly difficult to avoid thoughts of what he hoped would be the final confrontation in his long quest. Months of journeying were finally catching up. His body was perpetually stiff, aching from endless hours in the saddle and myriad of battles fought along the way. Memories of old friends, now in the ground, haunted him, while silently cheering him on from the grave. Sylin Marth was left in a weird place.

"Here, drink," Camden handed over his canteen.

Stirred back to the present, Sylin hesitantly accepted. "Doesn't it seem odd to you that we are in the most beautiful kingdom I've ever seen?"

Camden made a show of looking around, secretly wondering if Sylin was at last cracking. "No, but the fact it's owned by goblins does. If it weren't for that, I might just find a way to retire down here."

"One would have to hate humanity to settle here. There is nothing but silence."

Camden shrugged and replaced the canteen on his saddle horn. "I don't know if you've noticed but humanity isn't all it's cracked up to be. We are living in a time when everyone is focused on killing each other. Not my way of life, Sylin. I was born for better things."

"As if there could be anything better than this!" Sylin forced a laugh.

Camden replied quickly, leading Sylin to believe the answer was already in waiting. "A cold pitcher of ale and a good woman, but not much else, Sylin. Not much else."

The former councilman looked at his companion in new light. Camden was never meant to be more than a guide. A hired hand necessary to get him where he needed to go. Somewhere along the way, they forged bonds of friendship. One Sylin now valued above many others. Men of Camden's quality were rare in a world bent on self-destruction.

"What will you do once this is finished?" he asked. Sylin didn't know why, but he felt as if he didn't want to know. Didn't want to imagine what life might turn out to be once his task was completed.

Camden glanced across the sea of green. His eyes grew misty as a tide of emotions crashed through his psyche. "I don't know. All I know is that we are cast adrift in a storm upon the dawn. No matter what the outcome, the aftermath will not be what any of us are expecting."

Seeing levels of distraught cascade over Sylin's face, he quickly followed with, "What of you? Returning to the High Council?"

No. I don't believe I will. In fact, I think I might just be done with this entire sordid affair. A storm upon the dawn. Will it truly be so bad?

"We need to talk."

Elxander appeared fragile in the flickering firelight. The dominance he exuded back in the Tower of Souls, his source of power, was gone, leaving a brittle shell of a man who should have gone to the grave long ago. What mighty force sustained him, Sylin could not fathom. He only hoped that his own life never devolved so far. A man should know when it was time to lie down for that final time.

The wizard's oddly dull eyes reflected hues of orange and yellow as he regarded the younger man. Brash, with the insane capability of reducing the complex into the trivial. Much like all the current generation, Sylin was a man who lacked knowledge of the importance of past events. Of how the hubris of men led to their downfall. Yet as much as Elxander wished to tell of his involvement in the war against Ils Kincannon and the creation of the Staff of Life, he found his throat constricting each time he opened his mouth. Secrets, the wizard deduced. Secrets he would bear to the grave.

He feigned a smile, tight and thin lipped. "Of course. Please, sit."

Sylin shook his head. "Not here."

The wizard groaned his way to his feet. He decided allowing Sylin the illusion of being in charge was better than provoking unnecessary confrontation so early in their journey. Besides, he reasoned that there was a time fast approaching when all the cards would be revealed and Sylin would be forced to make the ultimate decision.

Once they were safely away from the others, Sylin crossed his arms over his chest and faced the wizard. "I need to know what you aren't telling me."

An eyebrow rose. “Could you be a little more specific?”

“The Staff. The Council. The Hierarchy. All of it,” Sylin demanded. “You know more than you are letting on and it threatens our expedition.”

Elxander slowly exhaled. “It was but a matter of time before you confronted me. I’ve lived one hundred times the amount of an average man. Of course, I know more than you, young Sylin. What would you like me to tell you? That the Hierarchy was created on the premise of every kingdom aiding the others? Or that the High Council lost its way long ago and plunged this world into an unending cycle of violence and bloodshed? Or perhaps you wish to know what your fate will be? Do you have the iron in your blood to stand against the rising darkness? Or will you fall like so many others?”

Suddenly on the defensive, Sylin refused to back down. “I crossed half the Free Lands to find you and now, here in the middle of nowhere, I think your power has fled. We are a long way from Xulan Lake and the magics of the Tower of Souls.”

“Do not be foolish enough to underestimate me,” Elxander warned. “I did not leave my place of solace to bandy words with a fledgling wizard who does not have the foresight to understand his own strength.”

Sylin jerked back. His abilities, such as they were, remained elusive and wild. A talent he struggled to find mastery over. Magic was wildly unpopular in the Zye Terrio regime, leaving Sylin and others with latent abilities to largely ignore inherent properties built into their beings. The result was a dearth of talent, making it no wonder Imelin managed to turn the Free Lands on end with his rebellion. Yet while Sylin acknowledged his power, he never felt strong in it. Not even when using it to save their lives on multiple occasions during this journey.

What do you see that I don't? "This is not about me, Elxander. We go to save the Free Lands and keep the Hierarchy from toppling."

The wizard bit back a laugh. "Perhaps it is time the Hierarchy fell. Tell me, what good has been accomplished just from your generation? Are the kingdoms better off than before? Is this an age of unprecedented wealth and advancement, or are we still mired in petty politics and rendered ineffective by the ruling body? Ask yourself, would this war have happened if the High Council was as strong as your mind seems to think?"

Sylin reeled under the onslaught. His convictions had been strong the day he watched Shali Kolm murdered and decided to leave Meisthelm. They remained strong as he entered the besieged city of Jerincon and as he and his dwarf companions ventured south into the Goblin Lands. Since then, he found his faith decidedly lacking. His mind was confused, conflicted between duty and righteousness. Elxander's assault further devolved his senses, for as much as he wished to see the truth in his actions, Sylin couldn't.

"I have given everything to the Hierarchy since becoming a member," Sylin defended, the words sounding weak to his ears. "Zye and the others may not be the greatest councilors, but they are determined to see the Free Lands thrive."

"Would it pain you to learn the High Council is dead?"

The words hung on the night air. Sylin desperately searched Elxander for signs of duplicity, for deception or subversion. The ancient wizard merely slumped his shoulders, as if the pain of speaking those words aloud robbed parts of his soul. Despite his animosity toward the modern iteration of the Hierarchy, Elxander wanted the best for the kingdoms. He feared his wishes were naught but shattered dreams.

"How can you know this?" Sylin asked. The question choked him, lodging in his throat before worming free.

"I have seen it."

Confused, Sylin asked, "What do you mean seen it? How could you possibly see anything from here? Speak plainly, Elxander."

"What does the High Council mean to you?" the wizard asked instead.

Sylin paused. The question resonated with his core principles. The Council, in itself, meant little aside from being the governing body of every living being in the Free Lands. They were replaceable. Each chosen from different kingdoms and meant to serve until they either lost interest or effectiveness or died on duty. It was not a glamorous lifestyle, yet the possibility of doing and creating good was abundant. Many on the Council were his friends, the rest being loose acquaintances.

"The roots of betrayal run deep," Elxander continued after seeing Sylin struggling while trying to process the information. "Many are the powers hidden within the Tower of Souls. I was able to ascertain the foul events in Meisthelm, prompting me to alter our journey south. While I was unable to bear witness to specific events, I can confirm that the High Council is dead. All but you, and one other."

"Imelin," Sylin hissed.

"Perhaps," Elxander shrugged. "That remains to be seen. I will tell you that the enemy is moving south to consolidate their forces in Sadith Oom. It is there the fate of the Free Lands will be decided. There we must go, for our destinies will be fulfilled deep in that cursed land."

Nothing coherent to say, Sylin stumbled off. Shock collided with reality. Sylin no longer felt confident about any of his decisions or plans. All had gone awry since entering the Goblin Lands. He wondered if perhaps the world would be better off if he had died with his friends.

Unbeknownst to the wizards and dwarves, one hundred goblins lurked in the night, within earshot but out of sight. They'd been tracking the dwarves since leaving Fallon Run over a week ago. The goblins, uncharacteristically, made a point of staying out of sight. Dwarves and goblins were natural foes, making the possibility of violence erupting a foregone conclusion. An act the goblins were not willing to engage in. So they tracked the dwarves and their human companions down to Xulan Lake.

Days and nights bled into each other until time had no meaning. The goblins edged closer to their prey each night. They overheard private conversations and tried to understand the motives of their blood enemies. The mention of Sadith Oom gave them pause. Many of their kind had already gone to that fell kingdom. The promise of violence propelled them, but caused controversy as well, considering the main push was north to Jerincon.

Their route was leading closer to Eleran, the seat of goblin power in the kingdom. What fool purpose drove a handful of dwarves so close to the city was beyond any of the hundred. Urgency forced their actions, however, it was suddenly imperative that the goblins intervene. They readied their weapons and moved into positions behind rock and into ditches. Sunrise was not far off. The wait would not be long.

When dawn came, a trio of goblins, unarmed and with empty hands raised, marched into the dwarf camp. They were quickly surrounded and threatened. Surprisingly, it was the humans who addressed them. The dwarves deferred without protest.

"What is the meaning of this? Who are you and why are you here?" Sylin demanded. His experience with goblins thus far had been violent, merciless. For three to come into camp unarmed, whispered madness. The dwarves waited for the trap to spring.

The lead goblin, hands behind his head and shoved down to his knees, spoke. "We do not seek hostility. We come with a warning, and an offer."

"I've an offer. The flat of my axe," Maric snarled from the armed circle ringing the goblins. Other dwarves seconded with growls and curses. Ancient oaths sworn before their gods.

Sylin held up a hand. "Speak plainly. What could a goblin offer us that we would believe? We've been harried and attacked by goblins since crossing the Arzen River."

"I have one hundred warriors not far off. If we wanted you dead, it would have already happened," the goblin remarked.

Heads perked up, scanning the grass and rolling terrain for signs of the enemy.

"I don't believe you," Sylin countered.

The goblin whistled, shrill and piercing. Dwarves stiffened as his words proved true. One hundred goblins surrounded the handful of dwarves and men. None had weapons barred.

"As I said, we have come with an offer."

Sylin swallowed the lump in his throat. "Go on."

"Our people are going to war on two fronts. We have no quarrel with the dwarves to the north and none with the people in the dead kingdom," the goblin said.

Sylin risked a look to Elxander, who remained impassive. "What is it you want exactly?"

"We offer you safe passage out of our kingdom and will assist you in your journey to the dead kingdom."

"Who said we are going to Sadith Oom?" Sylin demanded.

Garin Stonebreaker bristled with insult. "What does a dwarf need with goblins? Give me a reason not to kill you."

"Other than you dying as well?" the goblin sneered. "My warriors and I no longer wish to serve in the goblin army. We… we are defecting."

"I don't trust him. There's nothing to keep him from stabbing us in the back, same as Isic did to Gul," Talrn called out. The dwarf glared down, arms folded and axe leaning against his hip.

"Answer him," Sylin warned the goblin.

Insulted, the goblin barely maintained his composure as he gave Talrn a stern glare. "You may keep our weapons until such a time comes when you do. You will see."

"Will you fight when we do?" Garin's question came as more of a demand.

The goblin nodded aggressively. "It is not that we lack the desire to fight. It is that we wish to fight the proper enemy. I am Yerg. You have my word."

"That will have to be enough," Sylin extended a gloved hand and helped Yerg to his feet. "Any attempt of betrayal and there will be blood."

Reluctantly, the dwarves lowered their axes. A new phase of their journey was about to begin. One none of them could anticipate.

*

The journey across the rest of the Goblin Lands proved uneventful. Several goblin patrols passed near without discovering them, thanks in large part to Yerg and his warriors. Discussions continued among Sylin and the dwarves. Tensions remained high. The two groups kept to themselves for the most part. Neither seemed thrilled with the prospect of fighting alongside the other. Sylin didn't care, so long as tensions didn't boil over to fighting.

Elxander continued developing an unsteady relationship with Sylin, offering to teach him various aspects of magic use and other critical areas needing improvement. The going was difficult, but Sylin felt growth after each session. Time, Elxander warned, was just as much of an enemy as what awaited in Sadith Oom.

The foul smell of the southern reaches of the Croom River struck them before any came within sight of it. Gulls and geese swarmed over the banks, picking away at shellfish and grass. The dwarves trudged on, unimpressed with the sight. Soon the party wound north, where they halted.

"Behold, the Towers of Perdition," Elxander announced and pointed at the massive structures still in the distance. "Guardians of the ancient kingdom. They were once the most potent totems in all the lands, though their power has long since faded. Now they stand alone, forgotten by most of the world. Sad really."

"Looks like there's more than that," Garin pointed to the northern shore where hundreds of dark shapes were busy constructing barricades and defensive positions. "The way in is being guarded."

"You said there's only one way in."

Camden scowled. Thoughts of abandoning them and heading back into the open plains once again emerged. “There is, and we can’t take it. Any attempt to break through that mess is suicide.”

“There is another way,” Elxander offered.

Dwarf and man looked to him and listened as he outlined a secret path through the mountains and into Sadith Oom.

Garin tugged on the ends of his beard. “Finally, tunnels. It will feel good to be underground again, as long as there are no dragons to contend with.”

“Dragons? You’re not referring to Tragalon, are you? That old beast couldn’t chew you unless making you into a nice soup first,” Elxander chuckled.

Garin glowered but said nothing.

“What’s to say those tunnels won’t be equally guarded?” Sylin asked. He felt gut punched.

“Nothing, but that is life,” the wizard replied. “Come, we have work to do.”

Reluctantly, the unlikely group stalked back to where the others waited and set about the tasks the wizard Elxander had in mind. Sylin still had his doubts.

THIRTEEN

The End of the Beginning

Meisthelm was oddly quiet, despite the hundreds of workers attempting to rebuild. Spot fires continued to spring up but were extinguished in short order. The insurrection Aron and the others feared had yet to mature. Those left behind to cause damage were scarce, uncoordinated. Any attack thus far was met with equal force. Retribution was swift as the soldiers of the Galdean army conducted thorough sweeps of the city, ousting hidden cells of enemy fighters. As a result, friendly casualties dropped.

None of that mattered to the bitter Aron Kryte. Each morning he went to visit Amean's grave and offer his condolences. The wound of losing his closest friend refused to close. Some pains, he concluded, went too deep to heal. No words provided solace. No amount of care or consideration shown by Karin and the others penetrated the thick layer of callous over his heart.

The cold disassociation with friends and comrades allowed him to focus on his task. War had left Valadon only to permeate in the south. A new cycle of violence consuming more people. Aron was tired. Twenty years of wearing the golden armor turned him into more of a machine than a man. Giving the rebuilding city a final look, he gave himself a deeper one.

Aron's fears, he accepted after much deliberation, centered on his inability to control the eldritch power laced within the Staff of Life. He still lacked knowledge, making him dangerous. That he destroyed an entire army of darklings, without knowing how, settled ill upon his shoulders. While not averse to killing when there was no other option, Aron found his actions reprehensible on deep levels.

Ghosts followed in his wake, burdening him without remorse. More would come. This was the harsh reality of warfare. Aron felt weighted down. Each step harder to take. The only way out of his downward spiral was to learn how to use the Staff effectively. He owed all of those who'd fallen along the way at least that much, if not more.

A crow landed on the broken remains of a gargoyle to his right. Wind rippled through the coal black feathers. The bird cocked its head and stared at Aron, unblinking. *Even the beasts offer judgment. Am I condemned or is this the beginning of something better*? The caw was crisp, penetrating his psyche. Oddly, Aron felt his confidence bolstered. Fresh strength seeped into his veins, filling his tired muscles and invigorating his mind. He had work to do.

Swords clashed as the Golden Warriors occupied the training pits. Sparks fell as steel struck. Practice drills honed over the course of years were enacted for the first time since the company deployed from Saverin. For the most part, each of the men welcomed the opportunity to stretch and exercise their martial skills. The Golden Warriors taught that warfare was an art form, just as much as a painter's strokes or writer's words. When done properly, the dance between warriors was graceful and inspired.

Covered in sweat, Jou Amn raised his sword in salute to his partner and stepped away. His body was sore. Too many weeks spent in the saddle and filled with worry, weakened him more than he could have guessed. Practicing his sword skills again after so long was akin to greeting a long-forgotten friend. He dipped his head into the wooden barrel filled with melted snow and rainwater and wrapped a heavy, golden cloak around his shoulders.

"You don't expect others to drink from that after shoving your head in there, do you?"

Jou finished wiping his face with a towel that had seen better days and laughed. "These dogs have drunk worse, Commander."

He and Aron clasped forearms. "How are the men?"

Jou joined him in watching the others go through their drills. "Well enough. There've been a few nicks and scrapes, a little bruising here and there, but otherwise, they seem to recall their training."

"They'll need it," Aron confirmed.

Final preparations were underway to depart. Aron and his compliment of Golden Warriors were ready to set off in search of Conn and the army of the Hierarchy and begin what he hoped was to be the last stage of the war. He considered leaving a small contingent behind to assist with the fledgling Council of Delegates but Dlorn would hear none of it. The prosecution of the war in the south was paramount.

Jou nodded. "They'll be ready. These are good lads."

He still felt awkward being named as Amean's replacement, but professionalism dictated his actions. The only area he vowed to never seek entrance was as Aron's mentor and trusted confidant. Jou respected the memory of Amean far too much to desecrate him in death.

Aron had no doubts. The Golden Warriors were utmost professionals. The very best in the Free Lands. Aron's greater concern came from readying the Galdean half of his party. Volunteers all, they were already war weary and about to move farther from their homeland.

Every man had a breaking point. Aron wondered how many of the Galdeans, or even his own men, were about to reach the end of their ropes.

A dangerous thought, as it led him to the unknown that was Conn's army. He knew nothing of their state, whether they remained combat ready or were lying broken on a forgotten field in a place with no name. They were placing the future of the kingdoms in the unknown.

"When do we depart?" Jou asked.

"At dawn. Every hour we delay allows Arlyn's army the opportunity to strengthen. Sadith Oom has but one entrance. We cannot afford to let the enemy establish permanent defenses. How goes the collection of supplies and weapons?

"We've weapons aplenty. The armories are filled. Supplies are proving trickier. There's a large portion of the population on the verge of starving. How much can we legitimately expect to steal away for the campaign before anarchy consumes what remains of order in this city?" Jou reported.

Aron feared similar scenarios were playing out across the kingdoms already afflicted by the war. Resources were stretched perilously thin. "This war could not have come at a less opportune time. Winter's severity has weakened us considerably."

"The skies are breaking. Spring is not long off," Jou explained.

"True, but without enough people to plant and sow crops, there will be famine on unprecedented levels. Chaos will consume the kingdoms unless we can end the darkling threat and restore a sense of confidence to the people."

Aron knew none of that mattered now, nor was it under his control to ensure the people were taken care of. His focus was on, and had to be, the campaign in the south. Only by ending the war and freeing the armies of Galdea and the ruins of the Hierarchy, would he be able to restore any semblance of order.

The burlier Jou rolled his shoulders, exercising some of the tension out. "Dlorn is capable enough of handling problems here. Leastwise, he has proven himself on the battlefield. Meisthelm will be in good hands with us gone."

Aron found difficulty arguing the point. The field marshal was one of the better leaders he'd encountered during his twenty years of service. Men like Dlorn were rare, for they placed more emphasis on their men than themselves. It was an example Aron strove to follow, for soldiers always fought better when they thought their leaders were one of them.

"I shall leave you to this. Have the men ready to ride at dawn."

They clasped again and Aron left Jou barking what any good noncommissioned officer considered encouragement to the others.

Nightfall swept away the troubles of the day, while paving the way for other, clandestine business. Dalstrom, alone on his abandoned rooftop, watched the wall of clouds sweep over the different colored tiles of the buildings untouched by the flames. His gaze occasionally rose to the mighty spires Meisthelm was famous for. Their golden domes reached high into the sky. The once proud beacons of liberty and justice for a hundred generations. Their luster was lost on a man such as he. What use were golden monuments only a handful enjoyed, while the world burned around you?

Pebbles trickled down the clay tiles to his right. Dalstrom tensed, magic flaring to life in his fingertips. "You are late."

"I was delayed. It is getting harder to avoid being seen while I sneak off."

The leader of the Red Brotherhood was thankful the darkness kept his face hidden. "This city is once again becoming occupied. Life returns. It is the natural order."

Kelanvex tugged her gloves tighter and halted. "Why do you come up here? There is too much desolation to be seen from this vantage point."

"It reminds me of better times," Dalstrom replied. "Was your quest successful?"

She paused, careful not to mince her words. "The Gen Haroud assassins are not to be trusted, my lord."

"So you did meet with them," he concluded.

"I did. They are reprehensible people who justify their crimes by the currency lining their coffers. We should not use them."

Dalstrom enjoyed seeing this spark of defiance in her. She didn't know, but he was grooming her for greater positions in the Order. "What is done, is done. Are they willing to accept the contract?"

"There was division among them. Half were willing to take our coin, while the others feared retribution from Arlyn," Kelanvex replied with bitterness. Her disdain for the assassins clearly demonstrated.

"Division is a good thing," Dalstrom said. "The more dissent among their ranks, the better our chances of not being betrayed. Will they accept the contract?"

"Yes."

Mixed emotions troubled him, despite this being his idea. What had seemed a safe bet was proving worrisome for reasons he couldn't quite place a finger on. Dalstrom looked to the massive structure of the Hierarchy palace complex. A permanent seat awaited within, leading him to question his decisions.

"Thank you, Kelanvex. That will be all."

Dismissed, she left him. Dalstrom wasn't the same man as he'd been before the siege. A central piece was missing. One Kelanvex worried might never return. Should her suspicions prove correct, the Red Brotherhood was in store for what might be radical change.

"Kelanvex," he called over his shoulder. "Same time tomorrow night. I will have the coin at that time."

Odd, she again forgot to ask why they met on the rooftops, especially now he was part of the new Council of Delegates. There was no secret of his being the head of the Red Brotherhood, nor should there be shame associated with such. His power rose with his appointment and the Order given credence among the new Council. Kelanvex couldn't help but wonder if there were other, more sinister reasons for his having her contact the assassin guilds.

"I thought I'd find you here," Karin smiled as she entered the largely abandoned dining hall on the main floor of the palace.

Elsyn nearly dropped her half-eaten biscuit before regaining her composure. The redness in her cheeks turned to a smile. She rose. "Good evening, Karin. I had hoped to speak with you a final time before you left."

There was never any doubt of Karin going south to find the army. Her attachment and love for Aron continued to strengthen daily. It was a testament to the goodness of the heart in times of pure duress. Elsyn once despised the woman, viewing her as a rival for Aron's love. Only, and she recognized this now, she and Aron never had anything other than a fantasy. The princess of Galdea was never meant to consort with a lord in the Golden Warriors. At first it stung, but Elsyn adapted and found in Prince Warrien what she once assumed had been there in Aron. The animosity between the women subsided as each developed their relationships.

"Ghastly business, and I regret having to go, but one of us needs to keep Aron safe," Karin smiled and sat opposite of Elsyn.

The princess shoved a plate of half eaten yellow cheese slices and day old dark bread closer to Karin. "I wish I were going with you."

"No, you don't. Nor would I, if our roles reversed," Karin corrected, selecting a small chunk of cheese and popping it into her mouth. "There is much for you to do here. The Hierarchy may be in its death throes, but order must be restored. The Council of Delegates is our best hope."

She empathized with Elsyn. The princess was torn by emotion and duty. She needed to return to war-torn Galdea to rebuild all that had been lost since her father's murder, but her station as princess made her invaluable to what the fledgling Council was hoping to achieve. It was a double edged sword she couldn't avoid.

Elsyn doubted anyone as young as she, and Warrien, was capable of making rational, informed decisions, but resigned herself to doing her best with what she had. "I can think of better deeds on which to spend my time. The throne of Galdea…"

"Is in good hands with Captain Tariens," Karin finished. "Half of your army is about to depart for home and there are no other large bodies of enemy forces ranging in the north. Galdea will recover and lead the Free Lands into a more prosperous time."

Or so I believe. Oh, Elsyn, you have no idea what lies in wait for you.

"Kind words but they fall short of offering comfort," Elsyn replied.

Karin swallowed and smiled, thin lipped and tight. "Comfort is a forgotten dream. We live in perilous times. I go south with the army and I am not certain I will return."

"How can you speak like that?"

The princess failed to find intelligence in whispers of death. Any thought less than of total success allowed negative aspects to enter.

Elsyn held up her hand before Karin could reply. "Listen to me, Karin. You go to find salvation, not just for humanity but for all the races in the Free Lands. Our lives are in your hands. The army of the Hierarchy is renowned for bravery and skill. If any force in the kingdoms can defeat this Arlyn Gert and her darklings, it is they. Besides," she added with a wry grin. "You have Aron and the Staff of Life. What other weapons do you need?"

She didn't know why but mention of the Staff left Karin ill. Thoughts of an entire darkling army evaporating as the Staff's power destroyed them, twisted her stomach. Did a similar fate await her at the end of the road? Was this quest yet another pointless endeavor being played out across the span of history? An unending legacy of the violence programmed at genetic levels? She hoped not. Hopes mattered little. It was with the cold steel tempered in impossible heat and the iron in men's hearts that this war would be decided.

They continued to eat in silence.

"Are you certain you have enough men? We've no idea what condition the army of the Hierarchy is in. How many men they have left or if they are still an intact fighting force," Dlorn looked up wistfully from beneath his bushy eyebrows.

Aron adjusted his sword belt. "I do not know what to expect, but five hundred Galdean veterans accompanying fifty Golden Warriors should be more than sufficient enough to scare away any darkling or mercenary force along our path."

The commanders of the Galdean army had gathered to send off their soldiers. Hundred more lined the main avenue through the heart of Meisthelm and on to the western gate. This was history in the making and perhaps hopefully, the beginning of the last campaign in the worst war in recent years. Pennants and flags waved, proud and stern in the morning winds. The colors of three kingdoms were represented as the heroes readied to depart.

"Bring my men home, Lord Kryte. It will be difficult enough explaining to their families after word spreads across Galdea that I *let* them go," Dlorn chided.

Aron's eyes flashed with mirth. Both men knew they were forced to turn away thousands more, settling on men with no wives or children. At least that way, only mothers and fathers would mourn. The Golden Warrior felt either possibility was dour in the best of times. A company of light infantry marched by with grim looks on their faces and pride in their steps. A barked order and they saluted both Dlorn and Aron.

"Galdea!" Dlorn shouted, as he snapped to attention.

A roar went up from those lining the road. The time for speeches was gone. All that remained was the order to march. Aron offered his hand to Dlorn. "Field Marshal, it's been an honor. Until our return."

"Farewell, Commander. Safe travels," the older Dlorn replied.

He walked alongside the Golden Warrior without speaking, each lost in private thoughts. Before long, Aron arrived at the head of the column where he climbed into the saddle. His friends, boon companions who'd shed blood and given more than any had the right to ask for, were already saddled and ready to ride for the army. Despite knowing each name and face, it still managed to surprise Dlorn that Harrin Slinmyer volunteered to accompany the quest. His respect and closeness to the burned elf, Halvor, lured him in.

Dlorn went to each of the command group and offered his well wishes. They were among the bravest men, and women, he'd had the pleasure of serving with. True heroes the Hierarchy deserved. His faith that they were strong enough to see the army on to victory grew the more he thought on it. They were what all should strive to become.

Aron drew his sword and raised it high above his head. "Forward… march!"

The column lurched ahead. The quest to find General Conn and end this horrible war had at last begun.

FOURTEEN

Into the West

The western plains of Valadon were largely untrodden and untouched by the war. They were also largely clear of snow, the plague of armies in the north. With winter ebbing, open roads were critical to Aron's success. Time was as much of an enemy as Arlyn Gert. His battalion moved with as much urgency as possible, given most of his men were afoot. Horses were reserved for the scouts and his Golden Warriors, forming the heavy cavalry part of the combined command.

Scouts ranged a thousand meters away from the road, sweeping the lands from Meisthelm down toward the border with Guerselleorn. In addition to the five hundred Galdeans, Aron's forced was amplified by the addition of Andolus and his three hundred elves. Previous arguments among themselves resulted in a mixed vote. Many wished to return home for the battle to retake Dol'ir from the darklings. Others felt it was their duty to see the war to conclusion. Andolus opted for carrying on. Dol'ir was a ruin best left forgotten until a better time, when hearts were given time to heal.

He, the ever-silent Long Shadow, and Jerns Palic rode ahead of the main body. The elves shared theories and tactics which might be necessary once they reached the Towers of Perdition. It had been several mortal lifetimes since either one had ventured so far south, leaving gaps in their knowledge of the modern world. Detrimental, but not life threatening. Or so Andolus hoped.

"Are we on the right course of action, Andolus?" Jerns asked, after looking around to ensure they were out of earshot from the rest of the column.

Andolus' face remained passive, emotionless. "As much as can be. What possible good could we do by returning to the ruins of Dol'ir?"

"An entire kingdom of darklings may already be flooding through the pass."

Andolus shook his head. His long hair swishing across his shoulders. "The Mountains of the Fang are riddled with passages and tunnels. If the darklings truly wished to escape into the Free Lands, they could."

"But our alliance with the throne of Galdea?" Jerns questioned. The younger, though not by much, elf was unused to being this high in the chain of command. He secretly longed to return to the ranks where all he had to be concerned about was whether his arrows flew true.

"Will stand. We have the support of the crown princess and the general of their armies. Our focus must center on this task. Anything less is complete disservice to the men at our backs."

Long Shadow grunted agreement, prompting both elves to wonder when or if he would ever speak. The massive man, twin swords strapped behind his back, rode with impunity. He could read their thoughts, for they were clear upon their faces. Long ago he learned that true men spoke little, while letting their deeds speak for them. His vow of silence remained and would for as long as the campaign to rid the Free Lands of evil remained. Only occasionally did he find the pull of comradeship almost enough to break his vows. Almost.

Andolus eyed him with suspicion but returned to his conversation. "I believe that Dlorn will keep his word by sending a contingent of forces to Dol'ir."

Galdean steel and engineering would defend and rebuild their fortress, no doubt better than before, but it would never be home again.

"Where shall we go once that is complete? Once the darklings are again sealed within their borders?" Jerns asked.

Andolus pondered a moment, for the question was the cause of many hours of restlessness and consternation. With their fortress of Dol'ir gone, reduced to rubble by a mindless foe, the surviving elves had no home. There was nothing left of their once proud race. Naught but fading memories and tales of better times.

"I believe it is time to return to Dreamhaven. Our time in this land is drawing to an end. Inevitable, yet sad all the same," the elf lord told him. "Perhaps we should restore a measure of old glory before setting off across the shore."

Mention of the legendary sanctuary of the elves, famous for stands of silver trees, sent ripples of gooseflesh over Jerns. Some whispered it was the birthplace of all elves. A home Jerns longed for. "It has been long since I last gazed upon the Druinna Calar. Will the others follow our lead?"

"If enough survive, though I will not demand obedience or compliance. All the elves have endured has earned them the right to decide as they see fit. Regardless, I will not seek to retain command once this war is ended," Andolus continued.

Jerns struggled not to rein his horse in as the statement shocked him. "You cannot be serious. We have been under your command for centuries. What will we do? Where will you go?"

Andolus smiled and looked at Long Shadow. "I am thinking a long trip overseas. Though he has not told us of it, the kingdom of Teranian intrigues me. Perhaps

Long Shadow and I will explore his kingdom before my heart settles enough to calm my soul."

True to his bond, Long Shadow remained silent. His eyebrow rose with curiosity.

Before either elf could comment further, a scout came riding back to the column at full speed. The shraak of steel being drawn told Andolus his silent companion was already prepared to face any coming threat.

"Wait here," Andolus ordered. "I go to Lord Kryte."

The scout was already delivering his report by the time the elf lord managed to catch up.

"… more than we could avoid, sir," finished the scout.

Scowling, Andolus smashed a fist into his open palm. "Too soon. We've barely ridden a day out from Meisthelm."

Harrin cleared his throat. "Can we go around?"

They had the combat power to fight whatever sized force lay in wait, but Aron was loathe to commit his force to a pitched engagement. Deviating off the main road was equally foul, for it would lengthen his journey, and potentially, cause him to miss his rendezvous with the army of the Hierarchy. If they still existed. Aron was living in a world of too many ifs. He needed to find a way to mitigate that and proceed forward.

"No. The delay would be too severe."

"Leaving our one choice to fight," Andolus ventured.

Aron turned back to the scout. "Is the road clear at least?"

"You're thinking we can punch through with cavalry and the infantry to clean up?" Harrin theorized. His mind was already racing through various scenarios. Tactics was a hobby of his, having studied all the greatest military minds in the north. King Elian. Olag the Red. Fentris the Dour and his band of fifty. All accomplished soldiers and leaders of men. Harrin once held aspirations of joining their ranks, of standing side by side with those long dead heroes in the halls of their forefathers. His path to glory was anything but spectacular, leaving him in the unenviable position of struggling to find action.

Aron nodded. “The old ways work best. Command the infantry and I will lead the cavalry.”

Not the words Harrin wanted to hear, but what he expected as the majority of cavalry belonged to the Golden Warriors.

“What of my people? Where shall we be during this engagement?” Andolus asked, already dreading the answer.

“Out of the way for the time being. We have no idea what size force, or what composition, we are facing. Should the ambush prove larger than anticipated, we will have need of your long bows to pull us out of trouble,” Aron told him.

Displeased, Andolus accepted his assignment. “We shall be ready when you call.”

Satisfied with the order of battle, Aron looked at his commanders. “Form up and prepare to advance. We hit them hard and without mercy. Cavalry, keep pushing through the ambush and give the infantry room to clean up the mess. Questions?”

There were none.

“Good. We attack on my signal.”

The Golden Warriors smashed through the hastily erected barrier of felled trees, killing their way through a mixture of darklings and Rovers. Ute Hai, his initial reservations toward fighting his people, smashed, swung his sword with the best of Aron’s men. Vengeance seemed petty, so much so, that he viewed his actions as being morally righteous. The battle ended quickly. What remained of the enemy once the Golden Warriors tore through their ranks were cut down with ruthless efficiency by Harrin and the Galdea infantry. Only a handful managed to escape the elf sharpshooters. Three Galdeans and one Golden Warrior mount were slain.

Aron ordered them to regroup and reorganize while funerary rites were conducted on the dead. It was a hasty service, for Aron refused to delay any longer than necessary. Men sharpened swords and saw to their mounts. Others chided the knight reluctantly turned infantryman, as his gear was transferred to one of the baggage horses at the rear of the column. Rather than marching in full golden armor, the knight donned boiled leather plate and changed his boots.

His penance did not last long, for the second ambush was sprung a short time later.

Aron ripped his sword out of the darkling's chest and watched as the light left its eyes. Gore dripped from the steel, mixed with ropes of putrid flesh. The stench of rancid blood gagged him. Sweat beading his face, Aron scanned the killing ground. Scores of bodies filled the small ravine, others floating in the shallow creek. Only a handful belonged to his battalion.

Arrows littered the western slope. Aron hated having the elves engage so soon but there was little choice. A secondary, larger force of darklings attacked once the Galdeans were drawn into the engagement. Andolus and his elves were the only thing preventing a total slaughter. Dusk was beginning to set by the time the last darkling died.

"We cannot continue on this pace," Harrin said from his knees. Blood stained his armor, only a little of it his. "The ambushes are growing more complex."

Meaning the enemy knows how to fight us. I fear you may be righter than you believe. "Agreed. Jou Amn, take a detachment north and find a bivouac site. The rest of the battalion will be along as soon as we can clear this area and see to the casualties."

"Sir." The burly senior sergeant went to collect his men.

Andolus approached with a handful of bloodied arrows. "It appears the way forward is not as clear as we were led to believe. We estimate over three hundred enemy soldiers in this ambush, another hundred in the previous one."

"We cannot delay," Aron insisted.

"It is clear our foes have been careful in their preparations. These attacks are not in the style of the darklings. My guess would be a man of some military intelligence is coordinating their efforts."

"A Rover," Ute said.

"Or mercenary. Or possibly someone among the traitors' ranks," Andolus finished. "There are too many variables to be certain until we manage to close with them and force an actual confrontation with a positive outcome."

"The delay could cost us the war," Aron said, sterner than he wished.

"We are already in a no-win scenario, Aron. It is up to us to choose the best course of action from what we are given," Andolus saw the anguish behind Aron's eyes. He surmised it was the pain of losing his closest confidant and friend that edged him closer to madness. The elf knew all too well how deep the grieving stretched, for he had suffered from those same effects many years prior.

Aron shook his head. "I cannot fight with a target. We continue riding for the army and Conn."

"Even if the entire design of these attacks is to drive us to exhaustion before breaking us in one final act of defiance? Will you risk the lives of these eight hundred men for vain glory? No amount of slain foe will bring Amean back, Lord Kryte. Do not throw away our opportunity to end this war."

Aron's mouth snapped shut before he stormed off. Andolus and Harrin stared after, wondering how much more the young Golden Warrior could take before shattering.

"That didn't work," Harrin commented, as he, too, slipped back to his men. As before, there were dead to bury and wounded to see to.

Andolus stood, frowning. His fear of their expedition falling to pieces grew. He had to find a way to placate Aron before the man doomed them all.

That way presented itself in the forms of Karin and Halvor. Andolus rarely had dealings with the priests of the Red Brotherhood but Halvor was of his blood. Reasoning with another elf was by far an easier task than trying to barge through the walls humans tended to throw up for self-preservation. His best chance stood with him and should that fail, he would risk invoking the relationship developing between Aron and Karin. At this point, he was willing to attempt anything to save their quest. New determination strengthening his bones, the elf lord went in search of his quarry.

Aron despised sitting in the middle of unfriendly and mostly unknown territory with an undetermined enemy force lurking nearby in the darkness. The horses were corralled in the center of camp, pushing the infantry around the perimeter where they took turns pulling guard duty and trying to sleep. Only the old hands found sleep an easy target, for they'd been conditioned to sleep on any terrain and in any circumstance. The younger, less experienced soldiers jumped at the strange sounds of the night, half expecting darklings to rush soon after.

To counter the effects of exhaustion and anticipation, Andolus deployed half of his elves to an outer picket ring one hundred meters from the camp. Their keen eyes were better adapted to seeing at night and they needed less rest than humans. Small fires were built, knowing that the enemy already knew where they were, so hiding would have been wasted effort. Soon the smell of roasting meat filled the clearing, thanks to the hunters who'd managed to run down a pair of stags just before dark. It was a most welcome meal.

"How far away do you think we are from the army?" Karin asked, after finishing her last bite of venison and swallowing it down with a mouthful of water.

Andolus poked the fire, amazed even after all his long years at how the flames ever hungered. "Still some days. I don't expect us to reach them soon." *Especially with the darklings obstructing our way.*

Shivering, Karin wrapped her riding cloak around her shoulders. "There must be an easier course."

"Perhaps there is, but we do not know precisely where General Conn is located. Guerselleorn is a vast kingdom. The largest in the Free Lands, I believe. He might be anywhere," Halvor said from within the prison of his cowl. Since being burned by wizard fire, he seldom lowered the crimson hood.

"It all seems so pointless," Karin shook her head.

"You invite despair with negative thoughts," Andolus interjected. "Guerselleorn may in fact be large, though I have never been here, but it is not endless. There are only so many places between here and the Port of Grespon where an army of ten thousand may wait. Regardless, I have sent three scouting teams ahead to find Conn. With a little good fortune, our paths will cross soon. All you need is faith, Karin."

"I find faith difficult to come easily after all we have been through," she told him.

He found no debate in him, for her words echoed strongly with what he and the others from Dol'ir suffered since being forced from their home. So long as the war raged unchecked, others would suffer and fall. The pride felt from knowing he was willing to risk everything, including his life, for the betterment of others, eased his riding into another battle.

"There have been similar times when I felt similar," he admitted.

"How did you overcome that?" she asked.

"Who says I did?" he smiled and said no more.

"I like it in the south. The nights seem less cold here," Karin said, after setting her leather armor beside her bedroll and lying down. "Where are we going to settle down after this war?"

Aron glanced back over his shoulder, contemplating her question. He wasn't ready to give an answer, for the war still had far to go and there was no promise of survival in their future. Better to avoid dreams of tomorrow until they were forced into yesterday.

"You should sleep. We've another long day ahead," he told her.

She was glad he couldn't see her scowl, though he must have felt it boring into his back. "It doesn't hurt to take your mind off the present, even in this situation, Aron."

"We are at war. Any moment taken away from the task at hand might result in less than desired consequences," came his reply.

She resisted the urge to throw something at him. "Do you want to talk? About Amean?"

He tensed. The muscles on his back rippling beneath the sweat-stained tunic. "No. Get some sleep. We move out at first light."

Rebuked, she decided nothing more was going to come of it and burrowed into her sleeping bag. Tomorrow she would give her report to Andolus and tell him she failed. Not the way any of them wanted to enter this new phase of the campaign. A pack of wild dogs brayed somewhere in the night, no doubt alerting others of the meal of corpses piled in the ravine a league away. She shivered, but even mongrels needed to eat.

FIFTEEN

Dol'ir

Thick snowfall blinded the defenders as what they hoped was the final winter storm slashed into the Mountains of the Fang and the slowly reconstructed elven fortress of Dol'ir. Equally, the darklings were forced to seek shelter and wait out the fury ravaging their kingdom. Most campaigns suspended during the deep winter, but not the defense of Galdea. Felbar and his commanders recognized the necessity of continuing the war when most of the population huddled before fires and tried to find their next meal. The continued existence of humanity relied on his men.

Less than ten thousand strong, Felbar funneled most of his combat forces into the ruined fortress, while engineers and pressed work crews labored day and night to repair the damaged walls. He ordered the addition of spikes atop the roofs and walls to deter another potential aerial assault. The lessons of the elves were to be displayed in the reconstruction.

Captain Stern, having been recalled from the initial redoubts on the eastern side of the mountains and recovered from the first true battle since the Galdeans occupied the fortress, warmed his hands over the fire in the central guard tower. Captains and sergeants of the guard came and went as guard shifts rotated out. A full company of infantry manned the walls, with another three held in reserve. There was never less than two hundred men standing watch against another darkling threat at all times. Stern was thankful the wall was less than three hundred meters wide, spanning from one mountain flank to the next to block the entire pass. So long as the darklings remained on the ground, Stern did not fear being overrun.

"Captain Stern, I thought I would find you here."

Concealing his frown, the captain stiffened. "Lord Felbar. You should not be here. We have had this discussion."

"There is no threat at the moment. The snow is as detrimental to them as it is to us." Ignoring the concern, Felbar joined him at the fire. "I have word from Galdarath."

Stern waited, seeing no point in speaking. Words should not be thrown about casually.

"A messenger rode in before dusk. Jent Tariens has received word that the army is returning home," Felbar continued, once it became apparent Stern wasn't going to rise to the occasion.

"Good. We will be able to hold this fortress indefinitely. How soon can they deploy here?"

Felbar winced. "They are not."

"My lord, why waste my time with information I cannot use when I have a very real war to prosecute on my hands?" Stern asked. His voice darkened, undertones of hostility seeping through.

Felbar's hands went up, desperate to placate his second in command. "Do not forget who you serve, *Captain*. The army is still far from Galdea, and to be correct, only at half strength. It seems their campaign against the darklings and the rogue wizard has taken a heavy toll. More so, Field Marshal Dlorn and the Princess have remained in Meisthelm along with the second half of the army."

"Why would they do that? The Hierarchy has an army."

"Perhaps not. The message was decidedly short but I gleaned that the Hierarchy is on the verge of utter collapse. No one seems to know where their army is, forcing Dlorn to remain behind and secure the central kingdoms. The acting Regent informs me that he will dispatch a quality task force to aide us once they have been given the opportunity to recover. I doubt they will arrive before winter's end."

Stern nodded, understanding the reasoning behind the tactics, even while feelings of abandonment surfaced. "I have five thousand combat-ready men here. We can hold for that long, if not more. The kingdom must come first."

"I expected no less," Felbar confirmed. "What is the status of weapons and supplies?"

"Arrows are running short, though we try to reclaim as many as we can from the dead. I also have fletchers working through the night to build a stockpile. Weapon smiths are busy repairing damaged swords and shields. We have enough men to hold, but our weapons are being punished at a rapid pace," Stern said, the figures at the top of his thoughts. "Rations will become an issue the longer we stay in place."

Felbar nodded. "I've already apprised Galdarath of the situation. We should expect the first supply train within the next few days."

"Good enough. Is there anything else, my lord?"

Felbar considered forcing the issue, of discovering the truth behind the disparagement from his senior captain. That was a battle he wasn't willing to fight at the moment. The strain of the last few days was beginning to wear on him. Only now, here at the end of the world, was he beginning to understand what it meant to defend the people.

He felt old, spread thin. Wrinkles and age lines filled the shadowed corners of his face. His eyes were constantly sore. Heavy bags crowded under each. More grey hairs than he liked now streaked his head. He wasn't ready to be old. Nor was he willing to remain in Dol'ir for the rest of his life. The concept of rebuilding the fortress was contingent on Galdea and the other kingdoms in the Hierarchy, and was noble and perhaps necessary, but keeping his force in the mountains indefinitely was impossible.

"How long can we hold before the men lose heart?" he asked, catching Stern off guard.

"I… I do not know. The men remain in good spirits. Our victory over the darklings bolstered their mood. It helped them see the truth in what we are doing," Stern replied. "But it will not last indefinitely. Balance must be struck or we shall burn out faster than a candle. Maintain communications with Galdarath. I will ensure the men remain in fighting conditions. My lord."

The admission was all Felbar could hope for. So long as the men kept heart, they would defend the fortress and their kingdom. His major concern stemmed from coming from a land so far from the mountains. Sooner or later, rot would settle among his soldiers. The desire to return home to protect their loved ones would grow until it threatened to dissolve all he'd sought to build.

Not that he blamed them. His own desire to look upon the fertile valley of the Twins grew daily. Staying in Dol'ir was a matter of honor. He'd already let the kingdom down once and would be damned to do so again. He bid Stern a good night and returned to the main keep where his staff had cleared rooms for him.

The second assault came in the middle of the night. Snow blind, the Galdeans failed to spy the darklings until the first ranks were already over the wall. Dozens fell under the fury of the initial onslaught before Stern rallied a defense. The captain bellowed orders to those sergeants nearest him as he strode into the midst of the fighting with sword drawn.

Two darklings charged him immediately. His blade took the top half of the first's skull, spilling brains and blood across his lower trousers and boots. Maximizing his motion, Stern brought his sword back around and slashed diagonally across the second darkling. It died grasping his legs. Hatred etched upon his face, Stern kicked the corpse aside and continued forward.

It began to snow harder, obscuring his vision. A soldier fell before him. His throat was slashed through. Another screamed as he was pitched over the wall, down to the waiting darkling ranks below. Stern killed the darkling responsible by severing the back of his neck. Now in the middle of the fighting, he had a better view, and understanding, of the action.

Everywhere he looked, men and darklings were locked in bitter embrace as they tried to kill each other. Bodies already covered the top of the wall. Rivulets of blood and gore ran beneath his boots. Steam escaping from the bodies melted snowflakes. Initially, the darklings held the advantage but the defenders slowly reorganized and pushed back. Entire sections of the wall were reclaimed by the Galdean through sword and spear.

Stern grabbed the nearest man by the lip of his armor and dragged him close. "I want a shield wall established. Have oil and torches brought up. We drive these beasts back to what pits they came from."

"Sir!" the soldier hurried through the morass.

Satisfied, Stern searched for his next target. There were still many darklings left to kill and his blade thirsted. He didn't wait long. A pair of darklings had one of his men trapped against the wall, stabbing him repeatedly in the chest and arms. Stern grabbed the nearest darkling by the throat and with a bestial roar, heaved its body over the wall. His sword plunged into the other darkling's back with a sickening crunch. Stern pushed with all his strength and was rewarded with watching the blade burst through the darkling's chest. He shook the body free and knelt before the soldier.

The Galdean raised a bloodied hand, touching Stern on his gauntlet, and died. Mixed emotions raging across his gore stained face, Stern closed the man's eyes and returned to the fight. It was close to dawn before the enemy was thoroughly repulsed.

The western part of Coronan was largely uninhabited, much to Marshal Sevron's relief. Rumors of the darkling force gathering in the Wood of Ills troubled him, giving him doubt of his ability to combat the threat. He had just under one thousand Golden Warriors and another two thousand retainers and support personnel. Saverin was the single largest Hierarchy garrison in the western kingdoms. Sevron debated whether it was enough.

Everything he had learned and heard of the darklings thus far, gnawed at his stomach. Implacable killing machines from a foul kingdom akin to demons from the old world, the darklings were anathema to all the Free Lands represented. Sevron shook the thoughts away, for they served no purpose other than to destabilize his command. Moreover, it led him to thoughts of Aron and the others.

Were they still alive? Had they fallen to the enemy and even now lay buried under the snows on some forgotten battlefield? Was that to be his fate, an inglorious death at the hands of beasts who should not exist? Sevron liked to think his legacy would survive beyond that. The Hierarchy demanded obedience and he was sworn to serve.

Closing the door to his private quarters for the final time, Marshal Sevron pulled his riding gloves on and hurried to the stables. Most of horses were gone, already marshalled on the training fields outside of the garrison. Commanders and senior sergeants busied with final pre-deployment checks, while the staff officers finalized their route of march and potential tactics for kinetic responses to the darklings. The Wood of Ills was many days ride north, but war was often unpredictable.

He accepted the reins to his favored grey mare. "Thank you, Dorhman. You have been a most capable squire."

"My lord," the young, mousey looking boy blushed and bowed.

Sevron climbed into the saddle. "Alas, I cannot bring you with me. There is the real threat none of us may return and I will not be held accountable to your parents should any harm befall you. I learned long ago not to induce a mother's scorn."

"But, my lord …"

"Go home, Dorhman. Enjoy your time with family. Should I return, I will summon you to fulfill your duties once again." Saying no more, Sevron gently tapped his heel to his mare's flank and exited the stables.

A disheartened Dorhman watched as feelings of failure dragged his shoulders down.

The task force was assembled and in ranks by the time Sevron arrived, pleasing the aging Marshal who expected discipline above all else. An army without discipline invited disaster. His tired eyes looked over his men, resplendent in their shining armor. They were the pride of the Free Lands. The very best warriors from every kingdom. No other force known to the Hierarchy was capable of besting them on the field of battle. Or so he hoped.

Sevron took his rightful place at the head of the formation and looked into the faces, young and old, of his soldiers. Friends and strangers, they were all family. *How many will not return? Am I to be the last marshal in the storied history of our order?* Drawing a deep breath, Sevron felt decades of latent fears spring forth within his chest. Retirement had never been more attractive.

"My friends," he began, his deep voice carrying on the wind. "Today we embark upon the great crusade! This is the hour the Golden Warriors were created for. Our reason for existing. The dark powers of our foe have spread their cancer across the Free Lands, consuming kingdoms whole. Others have bled and sacrificed while we remained here, protecting this county.

"The days when the Golden Warriors avoided the battlefield are over! War threatens us all with a fate darker than at any point in the last thousand years. You are trained for this. You've been selected over all others as possessing of the qualities and attributes of the greatest warriors. Today, we go to war!"

Sevron's heart skipped and his flesh pimpled as a mighty roar went up from his soldiers. Banners waved. Swords and spears were drawn and thrust into the sky. Veteran or apprentice, each joined their voice to the collective. Pride filled the Marshal. The Golden Warriors were at last going back to war.

Villagers and townsfolk from the surrounding area flocked to line the main avenue out of Saverin. They cast winter flowers down on the road before the first riders. Children waved. The eldest saluted. Mothers and wives struggled to keep their tears from spilling.

Numerous hands stretched out to grasp at passing riders. A chant was raised, praising the Golden Warriors even as well wishes and shouts of approval spread among those gathered.

The Golden Warriors sat straighter in the saddle, taller, prouder. A bugle belted out a marching cadence from the middle of the column. Sevron drew his sword and saluted the civilians. They deserved that much, if not more. Soon the village was behind them, naught but ghosts lost in the rising mists burning off the ground. Pomp and circumstance finished, Sevron deployed his task force into combat formation. It was a mighty golden spear marching into a den of enemy forces.

"We are still some days from the Wood of Ills," Captain Thorp told the company commanders as he withdrew the maps from their wooden container.

A light snow fell, speckling their armor and cloaks before melting. The handful of captains and lieutenants crowded around the hastily erected field table as Thorp went on to detail their movement schedule. Sevron stood in the background. He knew the route by heart, freeing his mind to worry over the daily trials of command in the field. Supplies, replacements, maintaining a clear egress route back to Saverin in the event of defeat, or massacre.

His clear dislike of Thorp made staying out of mundane affairs easier for the aging marshal. The time was fast approaching when he would at last step down from command. Thorp was trite and difficult to deal with, but the man was competent and more than capable of leading a troop of Golden Warriors. Once, Saverin might have considered sending Thorp on to a different assignment before the war began.

"Marshal, have you anything to add?"

Startled, Sevron jerked back to the present and cleared his throat. "No. I have said enough. You all know your jobs. Follow on orders will be issued once we are within sight of the forest. I want scouts vigilant. As of this moment, we are in enemy territory. Expect an assault at any time. Questions?"

There were none. Dismissed, the leaders returned to their companies, leaving Thorp alone with Sevron. The look of disappointment, an almost permanent fixture on the younger captain's face, offered little insight into what Thorp felt. Sevron clasped his hands behind his back and gestured with his chin. "Out with it, Captain."

"Marshal, you cannot expect to have the men maintain heightened vigilance for the duration of our campaign. Tensions will rise and nerves will fray," Thorp protested after checking to ensure he was quiet enough not to be overheard. "You risk burning out this command before they have the opportunity to cross swords."

"What would you have me do? Allow the company to blindly march into the forest and get slaughtered?" Sevron defended. "This is not my first war, Captain, unlike you. Vigilance might be the only factor keeping us alive long enough to engage the darklings."

Thorp's arms flew wide. "We do not even know what they look like other than a few old passages from the histories. Demons and mythological beasts. The prospect of fighting an unknown enemy does not bode well for us."

Glowering, Sevron stalked off. Thorp stood in the falling snow, confused and frustrated. The sound of man and beast readying to continue their march echoed behind him. Sevron's words stung, as much as he wished otherwise. It was not his fault he lacked combat experience. Peace had reigned over the Hierarchy for the entirety of his career. To be cast adrift in the madness of the current war, a war without modern conventions or rules, left him at a severe disadvantage.

More than anything, Thorp found himself seething with jealousy. He wanted what Sevron had. The prestige. The experience. The power and respect. Until this war began, Thorp was lost in self-doubt. The Hierarchy machine lumbered on without regard for the men and women locked within. Thorp saw the war as his best opportunity to redeem his character's failings and propel his career to infamy. All he needed was to find a way to remove his final obstacle: Marshal Sevron.

SIXTEEN

Sadith Oom Arises

A lifetime of constantly wanting more than life deemed willing to deliver, made Arlyn Gert a bitter woman. She fought and clawed her way, first into the Hierarchy as a menial neophyte, and then up through the ranks to the esteemed position on the High Council. It was never enough. She wanted more and stopped at nothing to get it. Convincing Imelin of his righteous path, was but the first step.

Men like Imelin were fundamentally weak. She'd seen it a thousand times. So haughty in their power, they were terrified of being misremembered. Arlyn twisted Imelin's mind to do her bidding. Not that it proved difficult. The last of the Black seethed deep inside over the loss of his entire order during the war with Aragoth. That betrayal, cleverly constructed through misdirection and natural fears she helped instill among the senior council members, was the catalyst to all that had happened in the twenty years since.

Now she stood in the heart of her new kingdom. A bitter wasteland deprived of former glory by the very forces once claiming to defend the righteous. She scoffed at the audacity the Hierarchy infused in people. History spoke of Sadith Oom being green, a paradise at the bottom of the world. A glance in any direction showed that none of that glory remained. Ils Kincannon and his ill-fated Knights of the Seven Manacles ensured the kingdom would never recover during that final battle on the Plains of Darkpool.

Fitting, she supposed, for what more appropriate place was there for Arlyn to begin her new empire? Retinue at her back, she rode ever closer to the newly reconstructed fortress of Morthus. Dark spires jutted into the pale sky. Obscene. Perverse. They took on the look and feel of a graceful demise. The inevitability of the end of all things. Arlyn was no princess. Her drive and ambition propelled her to commit the unspeakable to achieve what she wanted.

Her fingertips tapped incessantly on the saddle horn. Arlyn's mind raced toward the collision of dreams and reality. Sadith Oom. The kingdom of wizards long dead. Her kingdom. The birthplace of an empire. She knew it was but a matter of time before her enemies, great as they were, massed and turned south. An unprecedented convergence was coming. One the Free Lands would never recover from.

She'd already seen to decapitating the Hierarchy. That outdated mode of leadership was responsible for the crippling of all life and deserved the fate befallen it. None among the High Council were fit to rule. They'd grown decrepit, lethargic. Zye Terrio's ban on magic proved his undoing. By denying the Free Lands use of a natural occurrence, he ensured his own demise through the same.

Foolish, by all accounts. Arlyn was the strongest on the Council, more powerful than even Imelin. The sheer arrogance of that man offended her on multiple levels. Disposing of him was her best course of action. One she needed to see to before continuing with her plan. With him dead, alongside the rest of the Council, Arlyn had but one remnant left to deal with. Imelin's attendant, Barathis.

The man was a worm by her reckoning. Whispers suggested he'd been a soldier once. A knight. Why any man would abandon his rightful place in the ranks to serve a delusional wizard was beyond her. The murder of his master no doubt left him seething. Betrayal was the coin of the realm of late. How much longer would Barathis wait for his opportunity to strike, despite his professed allegiance to Arlyn?

She broke into smile. This was a game she knew far too well. A dust cloud announced the arrival of a company of goblins. Her escorts to Morthus. Arlyn dismissed the urge to reflect upon the paths taking her to lead a combined army of less than desirable creatures. Goblins. Darklings. Usurpers and traitors. Not the army she wanted, but General Conn was too loyal to sway. Arlyn was forced to make due. Not that it mattered. Soon the entire world would be aflame and she the cause.

"I thought the marshlands were miserable. This is beyond intolerable."

Baron Vryce Mron wiped his face of sweat for the hundredth time this day. His deployment to the gates of Sadith Oom saw the end of Guerselleorn's miserable humidity and the drastic, almost fiendish, rise in temperature. The crippling heat was already responsible for putting several of his staff in their cots. Dysentery and heat exhaustion spread through the ranks, reducing his ability to defend the bridge crossing.

Across from him, with a boot propped up on an old crate used for a chair, the mercenary Hurst picked his fingernails clean with his dagger. He was dissatisfied with his position. Killing the former general Gulnick Baach was meant to be his catalyst into power and for a time, it was. The Black rewarded his ruthlessness by placing him in command of the armies. Glory untold was within his grasp before the ultimate betrayal rendered him back to a mere mercenary. Now he served as a hound, that rabid beast struggling to break its chains, at the discretion of Arlyn Gert.

"Quit bitching and accept where we are," he snarled and wiped his dagger on his sleeve.

Mron glared at the man. "Remember your place, Hurst. You are but a mercenary. An honorless man, only necessary when there is killing to be done."

Instead of retorting, Hurst offered a savage grin. "That's right. You'd do well to remember that fact, Baron. Gert wants men who lack compunction."

Slapping the dagger back in its hidden sheath up his sleeve, Hurst left the command tent with Mron contemplating what he'd just said. Worse, the Baron worried of taking a knife, that dagger to be precise, in his spine. His life grew that much more complicated, as if he needed it. Nothing he'd done since leaving Guerselleorn mattered. His allegiance was sworn to Arlyn, though for reasons even he was unsure of. The promise of gaining his own kingdom in the aftermath of the war lured him into her service but left him stranded in a sea of abject cruelty. He needed to find an exit strategy, before the dagger fell.

In need of peace of mind, Mron strapped on his sword belt and went to inspect the defensive preparations. Thousands of already haggard men busied shoring up the southern riverbank to repel potential water crossings. Sharpened stakes and barbed wire concealed beneath the surface would catch any boat, stranding the soldiers packed aboard and making them easy targets for his archers.

A contingent of darklings were deployed on the far side to slow the enemy advance. They were meant for sacrifice. A lamb for the slaughter. Mron had no reservations against using them so. They were beasts and deserved no better. He squinted to make out their squat, hairy forms as they settled into the mud and scrub brush to wait. Mron silently wished they all fell in the coming fight.

The bridge spanning the river was roughly fifty meters long and ten wide. A substantial passing, capable of funneling thousands of soldiers across, as well as any artillery or siege engines the army of the Hierarchy brought. Thankfully, Mron hadn't been exposed to Hierarchy engineers while he battled them in Guerselleorn. No. This was going to be a standup fight, infantry and cavalry and it worked in Mron's favor.

Without artillery, Conn would be forced to funnel his entire force onto the bridge. The cost in lives would be severe. Even with his depleted force, Mron knew he'd be able to hold the bridge long enough for Arlyn to muster her entire compliment. Conn's army was all that stood between them and conquering the Free Lands. A ragged force of less than ten thousand who were already tired from the earlier campaign. Victory was assured.

A sharp sting caused Mron to slap the side of his neck. Three tiny, black insects were plastered across his palm. They were reaping a terrible toll on the army, spreading fever and in extreme cases, worse. Mron cursed. A hundred bites covered his neck and hands. Thus far, he'd avoided any potential disease but the odds were against him. He almost couldn't wait for Conn to arrive. At least that way, he'd have an adequate distraction from the biting insects.

Mron slipped back into the tent, frowning at the lack of wind blowing through. The only reason he'd ordered the sides rolled up was to facilitate the wind cooling him off. A week since establishing his command, Mron swore the wind had only blown once. He almost missed the seedy undercurrent of the Port of Grespon. Crime and piracy he could manage. The perils of Sadith

Oom were meant only for the hardiest of men. Ones lacking the intelligence to make something of their lives. This was a dead kingdom and he had no interest in adding his own sun-bleached bones to the list of victims.

Poros Pendyier collapsed his battered looking glass, hanging his head. Whatever ideations he once had of finding a way to best the enemy forces arrayed in the entrance to the kingdom, dashed the moment he laid eyes on them. Men and monsters swarmed in the thousands. Even with Mard's trolls, there was no way his diminished rebellion could win through. The cause was lost.

"Grim," Horus said from a meter away. The giant lay in the burning sand amidst patches of dry grass, his brow furrowed in concentration. "This was not here when I entered the dead kingdom."

Scowling, Poros slid down the back slope of the hillside they were perched on. The others followed suit. All his dreams, the hopes of leading his disenfranchised people to liberation and eventual prosperity, dashed upon the mountains. Broken, beaten, and scarred, Poros was finally beginning to succumb to the pressure of leadership.

"What do we do now?" Dom Scimitar asked, brushing his trousers off. "I am all for a good fight but charging into that mess is suicide."

Poros hung his head. "I know. I am afraid it has all been in vain. The rebellion is finished."

Two days ago, he lay in the dirt, half buried to avoid being spotted as half of the darkling army marched south to Morthus. The sun baked him, pushing him to dehydration as rank after rank of darklings flowed past. His eyes widened with shock upon noticing the pale, heavyset woman riding at their head. A human? Was she prisoner or leader? He did not know.

Horus promised a way to defeat that army and bring the rising power in Morthus crashing down. Now, after looking upon the second, almost equal sized force, Poros knew it to be untrue. The logical assumption was the rest of the Free Lands had fallen. The Hierarchy broken in defeat. He fought not to weep.

"Do not be so fast to abandon hope, Poros," Horus encouraged. "There are always paths to victory, even when the hour grows so dark we cannot see them."

Mard broke into laughter, prompting the others to regard him oddly. If the troll felt discomfort, he didn't show it. "These puny creatures are no match for troll steel."

"In small units perhaps but there are thousands warding the Towers of Perdition," Poros debated. "Your trolls would tire and fall eventually."

Scratching a line in the dirt with the toe of his boot, Dom looked up and asked, "What are they guarding?"

"What?" Poros asked, confused.

"That bridge is the only way into Sadith Oom. Any army would be forced to come through here. There are close to five thousand fighters down below and enough static defenses to repel a dragon. Why?" he explained.

Horus nodded.

Matis, the goblin renegade, gestured with a gnarled finger. "They are expecting a battle."

Dom grinned. "A damned big one, if I am to judge correctly. We are not alone. War is coming to this blasted land and we are in good position to take our foes by the back of the neck when they least expect it."

"But we cannot!" Sharna Dal protested, much too vehemently for Poros' liking.

"What choice have we?" he replied. "We are here for one purpose. Live or die, we are going to stand and fight against these monsters. Even if it costs us our lives."

Fuming, Sharna pointed her finger at his chest. "You will be the death of us all! How many, Poros? How many more need to die before you feel justified with your crimes?"

"What would you have me do? Throw down my sword and walk into their camp in surrender?" Poros asked.

"Anything is better than suicide," she spat.

"This one is feisty," Mard rumbled with approval.

More like treasonous. What is your game, Sharna? He decided to push a little more. "What would you do if you were in charge?"

She looked about the group, desperate for an ally. "Not die here. We can take to the caves and wait out the coming war."

"Coward," Mard accused.

"Call me what you will, but my bones will not be forgotten on these plains," she sneered, suddenly unafraid of the massive troll.

His greyish skin darkened, turning a sickly shade of green-black. Poros was impressed the troll didn't crush her outright.

"What of the assassin, Chonol Distan? You do not believe his work is finished here, do you? The assassin only killed most of the rebellion, but our ranks have replenished," Poros told her. "Our enemy will come for us once they are done with whatever army comes. Nowhere is safe, Sharna."

"The assassin is gone. He…" she snapped her mouth shut, realizing what she had said.

The others crowded in around her, some drawing weapons. Sharna tried to step back and bumped into

Draeden. Panicked, she reached back and fumbled around his waist before jerking his two-foot short-sword free. She spun faster than any of them could react and ripped the blade across Draeden's exposed stomach. The man screamed and fell back.

Sharna had a sliver of room to try her escape. She made it a few steps before a burning sensation spread up her spine. Sharna blinked as pain, raw and visceral, gripped her. She fell to her knees. Darkness crowded the edges of her vision. Breathing became difficult. Sharna raised a hand to her chest and was surprised to find an arrowhead projecting through her leather armor. Her eyes rolled back into her head and she pitched over dead.

Poros watched his shot speed true and was rewarded when Sharna toppled over. His stomach rebelled, and he vomited. There had been a time when he found himself attracted to her. A point where love was almost in question. That all ended when he began to realize the truth of her duplicitous nature.

Doing what Poros couldn't, Dom stomped up to the body and searched it. He grunted as his fingers curled around a small pendant concealed in her robes. It was a sword wrapped in black cloth. Gen Haroud.

"A damned assassin," he accused.

Wiping his mouth, Poros managed to shake his head. "No, not an assassin. Something worse. A spy. She must have been in league with Chonol the entire time."

He looked down at Draeden, who had fallen silent. Blood stained hands desperately clutching his stomach to keep his innards from spilling out, but no more. Eigon knelt beside him and shook his head. Draeden was dead.

"Hot. Hot. Hot!"

Chonol winced, fist balling as anger flooded his senses. They were a day into Sadith Oom and he already struggled with the urge to kill his ward. The crazed hermit was bereft of sanity, often talking to himself while babbling inanely over some obscure bit of alchemic lore. None of what he said made sense or difference to the assassin. Arlyn hired him to get him to Morthus, not bandy pointless conversation. The trouble was, Chonol doubted he'd be able to get Bendix all the way to Morthus without cutting out his tongue.

"Did you not hear me, young man! This blasted land is blasted hot! I think I can feel my skin melting off my bones!"

Chonol kept riding, knowing his limit of control was fast approaching.

Bendix either did not care or took the silence as encouragement. "Sand and dust. No cloud in sight and here I am, me, trapped on a ghastly beast without rhyme or reason. Let us not forget the murderous, sinister figure who rides before me! More likely to knife me in my back than offer me a sip of water."

The sound of Chonol's teeth grinding was louder than each footstep of both horses combined.

"He hears but does not listen. No one listens to poor Bendix Fol. Broken. Twisted and foolish. Ha! That's what they say when they think I am not listening. All madness."

Chonol reined in and turned on the old man. His sword was in hand and pointed at Bendix's throat before the alchemist could blink. "Listen to me now, old fool. We are going to continue to Morthus and you are not going to speak another word. Arlyn Gert wants you alive, but she did not specify if you needed to be in one piece. Irritate me further and I'll cut your tongue out and feed it to you. Understand?"

Bendix swallowed the sudden lump in his throat and vigorously nodded. The instant placation left Chonol unsatisfied and considering whether to push his blade a little harder, but there was no telling what the old fool would tell Arlyn once he was delivered to her. Choosing wisdom over gratification, the assassin sheathed his weapon and continued riding. Morthus was but two days away and with it, the end of his sordid affair in the dead kingdom. He hadn't fully realized it until now, but Chonol despised Sadith Oom.

Deliver the package and ride north to collect his spy and they would be done with the south for good. Thoughts of reuniting with his partner and sometimes lover entertained him enough that he began to whistle. Perhaps life wasn't so foul after all.

SEVENTEEN

Into the Marshes

The meager, yet obscenely powerful, force crossed into Guerselleorn three days after departing Meisthelm. Aron kept a firm pace, while being careful not to burn out the already sore and spent Galdean infantry. Wagons would have been better to transport their armor and extra kit, but there was a shortage in the city and surrounding farmlands. Supplies were equally sparse, forcing the battalion to forage as they went. It was a delicate game, for they could not afford to take too much from the villagers along their route.

A full day into the southwestern kingdom and Aron was forced to slow the pace. Any more without standing down to recover lost strength, would render their infantry useless and he had the nagging feeling that he was going to need every sword before long. They made camp just off the road before sending hunting parties out to look for meat. Successful, the hunting parties returned with three banded deer and a brace of snow rabbits. The aroma of roasting meat tempted stomachs as the sun began to set.

Aron made his rounds through the camp, inquiring on this soldier or that. He paid special focus on those who appeared more haggard than the others. Men with that faraway look in their eyes he associated with being too long on campaign. After all they'd been through since leaving Galdarath, Aron couldn't help but wonder how much more they had left to give. Many, he knew, would not make the journey to Sadith Oom.

Andolus found him alone at the edge of camp well after the sun set. “This is not a secure kingdom, Aron. You should be back in camp, not exposing yourself to potential foes.”

“After all we’ve been through, do you really expect me to fear the night?” he scoffed lightheartedly. “Your elves ward us. I have utter faith in their skillsets.”

“True enough, but there are other dangers in the night,” the elf replied.

Aron was almost afraid to ask for an explanation. Elves were among the eldest races and far more cryptic than he had the imagination for. Whatever secret torments of the night Andolus referred to only increased Aron’s unease.

A scream, high-pitched, broke the uncomfortable silence between them. His hand grabbed for his sword. Andolus did the same. The scream echoed again, sending chills through both men.

“A woman,” Aron whispered.

Andolus squinted, attempting to peer deeper into the night. He picked up a faint, pale green glow in the distance. He pointed. “The screams are coming from there.”

Without delay, Aron drew his sword and took off into the night. More innocent lives were in danger. More victims of this impossible war.

“Aron, wait!” Andolus called out, only to be ignored. Scowling, he hurried to catch up. “We should not be doing this.”

“There are people in danger, Andolus. It is our sworn duty.”

He shook his head. Aron’s pace was grueling, but easily enough matched by the long strides of the elf. “That is not what I mean. Remember what I said about the denizens of the night?”

Another scream ripped the darkness, followed quickly by another. And then another. A chorus of wails rose from the night, filling the air with their wretched sound. Aron hesitated, resolve wavering just enough for doubt to creep in. Mists swirled around his ankles. It was cold, impossibly so.

"What is this?" he hissed through clenched teeth.

The elf lord halted at his side. His face was impassive, yet almost sad. "What I feared. We can go no farther tonight. Anyone who walks into that will never return."

"Walks into what, dammit?" Aron grew angry. The elf's refusal to deliver a straight answer left him at a tactical disadvantage. He couldn't effectively fight what he didn't understand. "What is making those sounds?"

"I have only heard rumors of such beings, though their lore has been passed down by my people for centuries," Andolus relented. "They are known as the *droghi*. They are trapped souls. Doomed to wander these marshes in search of fresh souls. A great many must have been killed nearby for them to manifest so."

"*Droghi*," Aron echoed in disbelief.

The elf nodded. "Vile creatures caught between worlds. The only way to destroy them is by starving them. We cannot win a battle with them, Aron."

They watched as skeletal arms reached up from the mist. Flesh sloughed off the bones in ragged, putrid strips. The screaming intensified, forcing man and elf to cover their ears.

"We must warn the others not to come near," Aron shouted over the cacophony.

Andolus agreed. The *droghi* would attempt to lure the unwary in with their screams. Any man or elf entering the mists would forever be damned. Together, they hurried back to the camp and began issuing instructions to the commanders of the watch. More than one curious soul was forced back into his tent throughout the course of the night.

Roll call showed that a handful of soldiers were missing. Aron refused to allow search parties, instinctively knowing what had become of them. A quick conference with Andolus and his closest confidants and advisors and the battalion was once again on the march. The elf confessed that the *droghi* would not be an issue in daylight. Their powers only manifested at night, rendering them incapable of affecting the soldiers. Leery, Aron led the combined force forward into the area the mist occluded the night prior.

His relief did not come until long after the last infantryman was well clear of the area and they were back on the road to wherever Conn and his army awaited. Humidity and high temperatures slowed their pace. Water intake became extremely important, for these were men unused to the heat. Winter's grip was weak this far south, adding yet another danger to Aron's ever-growing list.

Shortly after midday, he summoned the Red Brotherhood priest to his side and together, they rode ahead of the main body. Halvor remained hidden beneath his hood, despite the swarming heat. The elf curiously chose to avoid speaking with his kin, a fact not lost on Aron, though he was wise enough not to mention it. Until now, he assumed the close-knit kinship of elves extended to all of their race. Was Halvor considered rogue? An outsider for betraying his people to join the Order?

"This kingdom is not to my specific tastes," Halvor said in answer to Aron's unspoken question. "Too humid for my skin, even before the burns."

"At least you don't have fur," Aron quipped. Sweat already beaded on the back of his neck in that sliver of space between his armor and his tunic.

Halvor reached forward to pat his horse's neck. "True. We must take into account for our companions. What is it you wish to discuss, Commander?"

Aron drew a deep breath, still unsure how he wanted to approach the subject. Ultimately, there was no debate. He needed to know what to do if any of them were going to end Arlyn's threat and restore peace to the kingdoms. Any lingering torment or horrors the scarred elf continued to suffer needed to be made secondary, if Aron was going to gain the knowledge he required.

"The Staff, Halvor. How do I use it?" he asked, his voice shaky.

The crimson hood dipped. "A simple question with a complicated answer. What do you think you know of it?"

"A weapon created by wizards during the war against the Seven Manacles," Aron recited the common lore taught. "It cannot be destroyed or controlled."

"Fabricated niceties designed to make us awe and respect such power, and not entirely true. The Staff was indeed forged by wizards, but with the design of enhancing all life, not destroying it. A hundred magic users, the most powerful in the kingdoms, gathered in Sadith Oom at the forge citadel of Mordrun Hath. Those were… less convoluted times."

"Peaceful? I was under the impression the kingdoms were in constant struggle against each other," Aron said.

"Not peaceful, just less confusing. Political alliances and disputes contributed to most of armed conflicts. In retrospect, it is a wonder we are alive to have this conversation," Halvor replied. "The southern kingdom was once considered a crown jewel among the kingdoms. A green land of immense beauty and natural grandeur. The wizards maintained balance between life and the world we occupied. The Staff of Life was going to be their crowning achievement. A tool intended to preserve life by ending warfare."

"A lie," Aron whispered.

"Indeed, though not one of malicious design. Ils Kincannon, your ancestor, took his army across the kingdoms, waging a war of unification under his banner. He knew that he could not claim the throne to the land without subjugating Sadith Oom and the wizard cadre, so he marched his Knights of the Seven Manacles south."

Aron shook his head. "Wait, how did he obtain the Staff? You said the wizards had it."

"A young wizard whose name has been stricken from history betrayed his Order and absconded with the Staff. He delivered it to Ils and set events in motion that we continue to deal with to this day," Halvor explained. "Staff in hand, Ils assaulted Sadith Oom. It was only on the Plains of Darkpool, after several days of combat, that he changed his mind. The sight of tens of thousands of dead and wounded soldiers must have affected him, for he bade a young priest name Traic to take the Staff north and bury it where it would never be found."

"Gelum Drol," Aron finished.

The elf nodded. "Aye. The ancient dwarf stronghold seemed the perfect place for the world to forget the Staff of Life."

"The histories say the Staff cannot be controlled, nor destroyed."

"Truths for the most part. A theory has formed that Ils managed to coerce the magic kept in the Staff and that only one of his bloodline could replicate his results. You, Aron Kryte, are the last of that bloodline. You can master the Staff and use it to destroy the threat posed by Arlyn Gert and her armies."

Aron mused on this. Ending the war, in favor of the Free Lands, was his ultimate goal and challenge but his trials would not end there. "We can win the war, but I need to know if the Staff can be destroyed. Such power should not be allowed in the hands of one man, or a council of many."

"I wonder if the wars would end once this totem is removed." Halvor asked no one. "The Staff can be destroyed, but only in the forges under Mordrun Hath."

Satisfied the impossible was, in fact, possible, Aron shifted back to his original question. "Fair enough. Can you show me how to use it?"

"Specifically? No, that is a task only your blood can accomplish. However, within each of us is a spark. The source of our lives. The very breath we desire. You must center your mind and heart by looking inward. Find that spark and concentrate. Your mind should be able to grasp it, control the wellspring of power."

"How am I supposed to do that?" Aron asked in confusion.

Halvor appeared to shrug. "Again, only you can know that answer. Once you link with that spark, however, you will be able to channel all of your energies and desires into the Staff. The two of you will become one. Or so the histories explain."

Frowning, Aron felt no closer to his answers. Adding to his frustrations, he had no way to practice until the battalion stopped at nightfall. Hours spent idle in the saddle, while his foe grew stronger. There being no point in lamenting matters out of his control, Aron decided to focus on Halvor's spark.

He closed his eyes, clearing his mind. Images of friends and fallen companions attempted to prevent him from reaching deep inside his mind and it was only through extreme mental effort he managed to break through. Barrier after barrier fell in slow, methodic order until he thought he saw a flicker. A glowing brightness threatening to burn out his mind's eye. Aron shied away, retreating back to the surface before halting and trying again.

Aron surged deeper, daring to look at that one commonality all men share and few are ever graced to witness. Tentatively, he reached out to grasp the spark. Darkness took him. When he awoke, what he assumed was moments later, he was on the ground flat on his back. Halvor slid down from his saddle to help him up.

"Wha… what happened?" Aron groaned.

The vibration of several riders approaching at speed told him the others were catching up.

"There was a flash and you were thrown out of your saddle," Halvor explained. His bright eyes widened from within the shadows of his hood. "You attempted to reach your spark."

Aron reached up to accept Halvor's hand, groaning as he was dragged to his feet. "I don't think it wants me messing around in there."

He swore he heard the elf chuckling softly.

"How do I get past the shock?" Aron followed up. "I can't use what I don't understand."

"Patience and practice will show you the path to obtainment. Do not lament your initial attempt. I am certain you will endure additional failure before succeeding."

"Not reassuring," Aron told him.

He busied brushing the dirt and debris from his clothes, while the others caught up. Karin was the first, sliding recklessly from her saddle to grasp him by the shoulders. She studied him with a worried glare, as if undecided whether to be angry or not.

"I am fine," he tried to reassure her.

"Somehow I doubt that," Karin growled. "What happened?"

He deferred to the elf, trusting in his discretion to keep certain aspects of the truth from them. Only Andolus cast doubtful eyes upon the priest. The commotion died down and they were able to get moving again. Somewhere ahead lie the last general in the Hierarchy and for once, Aron wasn't in a rush to reach him. He closed his eyes and reached deep within. The spark was within his grasp.

"What do you suppose that was about?" Sari asked.

Nescus wasn't one to comment on matters he didn't have knowledge about, but there was no denying Lord Kryte had been acting weird since leaving Meisthelm. The combination of anger over Amean's loss and whatever trauma he suffered in silence, was taking a toll. "None of my business. All we need is to watch our squads."

Sari looked back at his men. He wondered if he was in equally bad condition. "I don't know about you, but I'm ready for this campaign to end. I need a vacation."

"Vacation?" Nescus snorted. "You just got done seeing half of the Free Lands. What more can you ask?"

"Less bodies and no fighting," the younger Sari replied.

Nescus nodded. "Agreed."

Jalos Carb listened to their banter and suddenly longed to be among his own people. Dwarves were volatile people, so unlike men and elves. For the first time since leaving Hyrast, he wondered what his family was doing. It had been so long since he left the Wilderlands.

"You shouldn't stare."

Disturbed, Jalos glared at the traitor, Ute Hai. "You should mind your tongue."

"We have more in common than you might think," Ute said, unperturbed.

Sunlight glittered off the jewels braided in his beard. "I did not betray my people. The burden of shame rests heavy on your shoulders."

"Do you have any idea what it feels like to walk away from men who depended on you for two decades? From beliefs that formed the core of all I am? Who I am? You may be far from your home but you can return. That option no longer exists for me."

The dwarf regarded him, quietly judging him. "Your people will be ready to kill you without compassion. Are you prepared to face that?"

"I already have," Ute whispered. "Killing a friend is no easy thing."

"Nor should it be," Jalos reminded him. "You have passed but the first in a string of trials. Keep your steel sharp and your mind centered. Many more will fall before this war ends."

The dwarf failed to reassure him, doing little to relieve the anguish tormenting him when the others were fast asleep. Ute Hai allowed his thoughts to drift. He went over the chain of events leading him to this point. It all began with a poorly executed ambush. Aron Kryte and his warriors stormed into the Rover trap, reaping a horrid toll. Revenge drove Ute straight back to Denes Dron, only to find his leader had already sold the Rovers to wickedness. How many had fallen between that day and now?

Now he rode in the company of the very man he once swore to kill. A companion who was willing, albeit reluctantly, to stand side by side with him. Life, Ute mused, was fickle that way. The armored column marched step after step deeper into Guerselleorn. There had been a time when he would have stolen away into the night, never to be seen again. Ute couldn't shake the feeling that he and Aron's fates were intertwined until the end of the campaign.

Ute swatted at the gnats biting his hands. He missed Aragoth and her frozen steppes. The mountains and rivers. Freedom awaited in the forests and valleys of home. Sadly, Ute was reasonably certain he was never going to see home again. "This war is going to be the death of us all."

Jalos caught his whisper and agreed. But what a glorious end it was going to make.

EIGHTEEN

The Army of the Hierarchy

They encountered outlying scouts a day later and were escorted to the heart of the army's camp. It was a sprawling mess of tents and reek. Latrines and burn pits ripened the air, compounded by the natural stench of the dead and wounded. The army of the Hierarchy gave off the appearance of a battered and thoroughly demoralized force.

Aron kept his opinions to himself as they rode deeper into the camp. That he was unimpressed was an understatement. Conn and the other commanders had let their army fall into disarray, as if it held no purpose when the Free Lands needed it the most. It was an unforgivable travesty. Even so, soldiers perked up as the Golden Warriors marched past. Curious onlookers, perhaps embarrassed by their own state of disrepair, rose in witness. The iron will of the Hierarchy had come at last.

A grizzled man looking far older than his young age was waiting outside of the main command tent structure. He bore a sunken look, complimented by weeks' worth of ragged beard growth. Blood stained his uniform dark brown and his boots were borderline unserviceable.

"Commander Kryte, I am Lieutenant Zin Doluth, adjutant to the general. If you will dismount, I will lead you and your staff in to see him. Your mounts and the remainder of your force will be seen to."

"Sergeant Amn, see to getting our people an area to camp for the night," Aron ordered.

"Sir," the newly appointed senior enlisted man snapped and wheeled off to the rest of the battalion.

Doluth watched them for a bit, unimpressed by their golden armor.

Pulling off his riding gloves, Aron asked, "What happened to this army, Lieutenant?"

"Grim Mountain."

Doluth led them into the tent without another word. Enormous braziers in each corner of the main chamber provided enough warmth and light for the dozens of minor staff officers pouring over maps and the latest intelligence reports. Few stopped what they were doing long enough to acknowledge the newcomers, as Doluth took them straight into Conn's private quarters.

"Lord Commander Aron Kryte, General Conn. A pleasure," the old general said without rising from his chair.

Aron took in the room. Aside from a small cot in the far corner, Conn only had a chair with a field table for a desk. His armor and weapons were stowed off to the side. Pipe smoke clung to the ceiling and a half empty mug of what he assumed to be water sat beside the never-ending stack of reports needing to be read.

"General, my force and I arrived as quickly as we could. We have news," Aron said.

"The battle is long finished, Commander. What use have I of your men now?" Bitterness edged his voice. Conn winced as he took a drink from the mug. Definitely not water.

Suddenly uncomfortable, Aron continued, "We are only briefly aware of your campaign, though it is not the reason we have come."

"Meisthelm should have apprised you before sending you to this godless kingdom," Conn snorted. "Did they not receive my messages?"

"You don't know?" Harrin Slinmyer ventured.

Conn eyed the Galdean wearily. "I am in no mood for guessing games."

"Meisthelm was besieged. Half of the city was occupied and razed before the Galdean host managed to retake it," Aron explained. "The High Council is no more and the Hierarchy collapses around us."

Conn's face paled. Rumors, no more than raw whispers had reached him of troubles befalling the crown city, but without Ailwin's messenger birds, there was no way of accurately knowing just how bad the situation was.

"Dead?" he uttered and thought twice of taking a second drink. "How can this be?"

Aron launched into an abbreviated version of the greater war, leaving out key facts Conn didn't need to worry over. Beginning with the treason of the Black and ending with the treason of Arlyn Gert, he covered numerous kingdoms and the rise of the darklings; an enemy Conn had yet to encounter.

"I never cared for that bitch. Too condescending and smug in her ivory tower," Conn snarled at the mention of Arlyn's betrayal. "Who commands the Hierarchy now?"

"A mixed council of men and women from across the kingdoms. I am willing to bet that many kingdoms still have not been apprised of the current situation," Aron told him. "Field Marshal Dlorn secures Valadon with half of the Galdean army."

"You bring ill tidings, Kryte. I have less than ten thousand men under my command. They are not enough to restore order to all the kingdoms and fight the enemy. What would you have us do?"

"We must march on Sadith Oom and force the confrontation," Aron replied. "Most of our enemies have retreated south, though for what purpose, we have not been able to gather. We must take our full strength and end their threat for good."

Conn wet his lips, choosing his words carefully. "These men, my men, have been involved in a harsh campaign against a worthy foe. We are battered, bloodied, and on the verge of morale exhaustion. How much more would you expect us to give?

"You are the sworn defenders of the Hierarchy! It is your duty to continue fighting!" Karin exclaimed. She drew Conn's ire in the process.

"According to you people, there is no Hierarchy. Haven't these men served enough? Each of them deserves the right to go home to their families, if they still live, yet you want them to pack up and march into the dead kingdom to face what? Monsters from children's tales? What you bring me is… implausible."

"Implausible or not, that is our mission," Aron interjected, as he sensed the conversation getting out of control."

"You are dismissed. I must think on this," Conn waved them out.

"If you will follow me," Doluth announced from the tent flap. He gestured toward the exit.

Angered and frustrated, Aron wheeled about and stormed off. The others filed behind. Only Harrin Slinmyer hesitated. The Galdean fixed Conn with a murderous glare. "My people have bled for the Hierarchy. Thousands have died between Galdarath and Meisthelm. What gives you the right to abandon your oaths?"

He, too, stormed off, leaving a weary general in his solitude.

Harrin kicked the nearest pack, sending an unsecured helmet rolling away. "Stupid bastard! He's going to get us all killed."

"He is doing what he thinks is right. Do not be so fast to judge, my friend."

Harrin glared at Andolus, wondering where the elf's allegiance rested. Long Shadow's imposing presence loomed behind him, prompting the Galdean to back down.

Aron folded his arms. "As much as I do not want to admit it, I believe what Andolus said to be true. We all saw the haggard state of the army upon entering the camp. They teeter on the edge. Conn is rightfully concerned about pushing them too hard. Fear drives our actions, Harrin."

"We cannot afford any more delays," Karin seconded the Galdean.

Shaking his head, Aron said, "We are outnumbered. If we push, Conn could easily have us arrested. I will not risk fighting a loyal army."

"Aron is correct. We must give him time to accept that the world he left behind no longer exists. All accounts of Conn suggest he is a good man, else the High Council would not have placed him in such esteemed position. He will see the merit in our needs," Andolus cautioned.

"Time is against us," Karin reiterated. "Every moment we delay gives our enemies that much more time to prepare."

"What happens will happen, whether we manipulate the scenario or not. I suggest refitting and seeing to our soldiers," Halvor told them, his voice calm.

"He's right," Aron seconded. "You saw the looks these men gave us when they spied the golden armor. Their morale will improve just from our presence. Jou, have the men form squads and begin working through the camp. I want to know how low morale is and what we can do to improve it."

"I'm sure the boys will be glad to share war stories," Jou Amn told them. Soldiers the world over formed bonds, not only over shared experiences but from the deeds of others.

"I will go as well. There is another I must speak with," Andolus told them. He left without waiting for questions. Curiously, Long Shadow remained behind.

Aron slumped down and rubbed the back of his right leg. Weeks and days of being in the saddle, combined with what he assumed was going to be a difficult process ahead, left him drained. Sleep beckoned and it was all he could do to ward it off. He forced a tight smile when Karin sat beside him and rested her head on his shoulder.

"Why does it feel as if the entire world is against us?" she whispered.

He wished he had an answer.

Andolus worked through the army of the Hierarchy. The vast majority of soldiers ignored him. They'd seen elves before, confirming he was heading in the right direction. Once or twice he asked for assistance. The soldiers were helpful, without being conversational. He expected no less. Their war consumed more than mere stamina. The psychological effects reached deep into each of them.

He kept walking, entering the supply area. Smiths busied sharpening swords and spear points. Armorers hammered out dents and did their best to repair badly damaged armor and helmets. Fletchers crafted arrows by the hundreds. Wagons pulled by oxen teams moved basic food stores to staging areas throughout the camp in preparation for the nightly meal. Andolus was both impressed and appalled at the levels humans would go to wage war against each other.

"I thought I would find you here eventually."

His smile was genuine, for the first time since leaving Dol'ir. Andolus turned to face his confronter. "Genessen. You look well."

The elf commander tilted his head in acknowledgement. "Well enough for the slaughter we've endured. You should be fortunate you were not here."

"I have been through torments enough since Dol'ir fell, brother," Andolus replied.

His voice was haunted. Empty.

"Word reached me shortly after we departed for Guerselleorn," his older brother admitted. "Are there many of us left?"

"Three hundred."

Genessen's eyes widened. "So few?"

"This war is far worse than you can imagine," Andolus said.

"No doubt Conn will relay your tale to us at the nightly commanders meeting. Have you come alone?"

"No. They have all come with me. Winning this war is the only way our people will be free again. Right now, we are trapped without a home," Andolus said.

The elves walked, suddenly eager to be away from the casual prying ear. Conversation floated around the inconsequential, neither excited about telling the other of their misadventures in the Free Lands. They laughed and shed tears. Memories of friends and fallen comrades brought the brothers closer. Dusk began to crawl across the land by the time they finally got down to the heart of their dilemma.

"What must we do next? To say this is not our war feels wrong," Genessen admitted. The pain of losing their fortress home bit harshly. There was the feeling of guilt underlying his decision making process. A compulsion to carry on until the end.

"I agree. Aron and his group are good people. He is the only one capable of ending the enemy threat." He chose not to reveal that Aron bore the Staff of Life. Andolus trusted his brother, but Genessen was just one among thousands. "I have already spoken at length with Jerns Palic."

"He still lives? I always assumed he would die in Dol'ir, as attached to those miserable rocks as he was," Genessen laughed.

"You can tell him yourself. We will take what remains of our people and occupy Dreamhaven. Will you join us?"

He hesitated. Until now, Genessen had given the future little thought. He'd served as ambassador for his people for decades. Meisthelm and the Hierarchy were his home, just as much as Dol'ir once was. His loyalties were torn. "I… do not know. That is a matter to be resolved only after the war."

"I understand," Andolus lied.

They parted when Genessen was forced to report to Conn's tent for the nightly briefing. Andolus watched his brother go, concerned over the radical changes burned into him since they last stood the wall at Dol'ir. He was forced to conclude that they were all different. Wars had the tendency to lay low even the greatest.

Not all reunions were filled with joy. For some, the prospect of seeing the face of those long shoved to the back of memory inspired conflict. Old feelings of hatred and animosity that time could not soothe. So it was Jalos Carb stumbled upon his blood-kin, Haf Forager. There were no tones of brotherhood or comradeship. Haf, upon recognizing Jalos beneath the grime of days of traveling and more than one skirmish, connected a mighty right hook on the other dwarf's chin, throwing him to the ground.

"You stone eating bastard!" Haf roared.

The commotion froze scores of soldiers. Never before had any witnessed a pair of dwarves mauling one another. They stared wide-eyed, with open mouths but only long enough for one or the other dwarf to fix them with bloodfire eyes. The crowds parted, leaving the dwarves alone to settle their dispute.

Jalos rolled to his knees and crouched, waiting for the opportune moment. "A sucker punch, how like you."

Haf pointed a stubby finger and growled. "You should be in irons, never to be allowed to roam free again, after what you did."

Jalos lurched forward but was met by Haf's boot. The kick sent him sprawling. Dust billowed around him. Haf was on him before he could blink away the dust. Punch after punch slammed into his face. Haf grabbed him by the collar and twisted as his assault bloodied Jalos' lips and nose. Haf did not stop until his arm grew tired.

Knuckles bloody, Haf stepped back to give Jalos room to rise.

Spitting a mouthful of blood, Jalos laughed. "Is that the best you can do? All these years and naught but a bloodied nose to show for it?"

"Keep mouthing off and you'll swallow teeth. I've wanted to kill you for decades."

"It wasn't my fault," Jalos protested. "I told her not to follow us. She didn't listen."

"My sister was not to blame for her death," Haf bellowed. "It was you! You led her to her doom and dare walk in my presence! Were it not for the General's orders, I would split you in two."

"Haf," Jalos attempted but was cut off by an angry wave.

"I do not ever want to see you again. Cross my path again and I will murder you, kin-slayer."

Haf Forager left him there, covered in dust and bloodied. Reunions, Jalos Carb discovered, were not always worth looking forward to.

Aron and what had become his command staff were summoned to General Conn's tents shortly after dawn. Bellies full of bowls of steaming oats and cut up apples, they attempted to clean their clothing and equipment before obeying. Conn may be the commanding general of the army of the Hierarchy, but he had no authority over the Galdeans or Golden Warriors. The general could wait, just as he forced them to wait overnight.

"Welcome friends. It is good to see you again," Conn announced.

Aron grew suspicious, for the man addressing them was not the same defeated man as the day before. Conn appeared almost regal. A man worthy of his rank and station.

"General," he replied emotionlessly.

Conn's eyes narrowed. "Allow me to present my staff. You have already met Lieutenant Doluth. He led the main assault up Grim Mountain and broke Baron Mron's spine. The wylin is Ur Oberlon. With him are Genessen the elf and Haf Forager, his dwarven counterpart. All are proven battlefield leaders and have provided me with the best possible counsel under the worst possible conditions."

Aron was obligated to do likewise. "This is Lord Andolus, formerly of Dol'ir. His silent companion is the last of the lords of Teranian, from across the seas, or so I am assured."

Long Shadow nodded.

"This is Halvor, priest of the Red Brotherhood and my closest advisor. With him is my personal seer, Karin Ilth. We have been together since the city of Galdarath. It is a pleasure to meet with all of you," he finished.

Formalities completed, Conn settled in to the heart of the matter. "My staff and I have spent half of the night debating the merits of your scenario, and not without much argument among friends. This army has been in the field for the better part of a year now. Many of my soldiers were conscripts and even now approach the end of their enlistments. You ask them to abandon their contracts, forcing them to continue fighting a war many of them no longer hold faith in."

Aron tensed. The idea of deposing Conn and his staff was also discussed. It was a plan he had no desire to enact but was prepared to do so, should the general forget his vows.

"That being said, this is still an army in the service of the Hierarchy. The High Council's death holds no bearing or sway over our orders. We will deploy south to Sadith Oom and meet this enemy of yours."

Relief flooded through him. Aron managed not to smile. "My thanks for your participation, General. I know that this was no easy decision to make, even with your oaths of service to the Hierarchy."

"It is the... proper course of action."

Spoken like a man who doesn't want to lose his head or go down in history as yet another in a long list of traitors. "Of course. Now that we have reached an accord, it is time to discuss our plans. The enemy is strong and Sadith Oom has but one, miniscule entry point."

The captains of both forces did not leave the tent for a day and a half. By then the army was ready, once again, to go to war.

NINETEEN

Morthus

Regrets often became the cornerstones upon which lives develop, regrettably. Many succumbed to the grief inspired within, ending their lives before the regrets grew too strong. Once birthed, the roots sink deep into the soul and refused to let go without causing deep tears in the fabric of mind and spirit. A vicious end to a tormented life.

Poros languished under the knowledge of his deeds. His arrow was responsible for murdering Sharna Dal. A despicable act of violence he should have found a way to avoid. Not that he was averse to killing, many bodies lie in his wake since forming the Free Rebellion. None of them belonged to women he was developing feelings for, even if she had turned out to be a spy. His mind was fractured.

"You should let the past go," Horus said, after slowing his stride to walk beside Poros. "Holding on to so much grief does naught but break our spirits. I know this more than most."

Poros considered his words, for the giant of a man had lived long enough to see his entire race vanished from the world. Any suffering Poros felt was miniscule in comparison. "How do you fight that feeling? How do you manage to keep the past behind you?"

"By looking forward to the future. The man responsible for killing my people, my wife, still lives. I can feel it. I believe this is the reason for my reawakening," Horus concluded. "Otherwise, what purpose have I in this new world?"

Purpose. The driving question all men struggle to discover an answer to. Some died without out ever learning why they'd been born. Others chose to turn from their paths, dissatisfied with their lot in life. Poros felt trapped somewhere in between. Every direction he turned offered trial and tribulation. But which way was his destiny? He verged on becoming lost.

"You miss her?"

Poros almost said yes but stopped. *Do I? She would have cut off my head if I didn't stop her. How can one miss a killer*? "I do not know. She was trying to work her way into my heart, and for my part, I was starting to give it to her. She was not without her charms, Horus. The revealing of her treachery skews all of my beliefs, even though I knew she was not who she claimed to be."

"Trust is the real victim. Once truth fails, innocence is next. The two are inexorably twined. Lose one and we lose the second."

Poros chuckled. "My innocence has been lost for a very long time."

"I profess to not understanding human emotions. Was that truth or sarcasm?" Horus asked, his head cocked.

"Humor, Horus. It was a joke."

"I do not understand," Horus admitted.

Shaking his head, Poros turned his attentions back to the mismatched force around him. Trolls, humans, a dwarf, and a troll comprised the ranks. All were battle tested. The proven survivors of the worst the world had to offer. He admired them all, knowing them to be among the best in the Free Lands, but would they be enough to break the control of Morthus?

The promise of battle filled the Dagger Trolls with levity. They laughed and snarled in their own language, exposing boisterous claims of who would kill the most.

Poros found them only slightly odder than Dom's views on warfare. He'd already witnessed their capacity for brutality when a goblin force attempted to assault Mordrun Hath. Poros had never been more thankful to have such brutes as allies. No army in the Free Lands was strong enough to defeat a large army of trolls.

Their scouting mission to the Towers of Perdition provided enough intelligence for Poros and the rebellion to plan their next phase of the insurrection. Sadith Oom was a land in turmoil. Fresh armies were marching south toward Morthus, armies of monsters with, curiously enough, a woman at their head. Poros saw so many moving pieces, he judged he'd be able to slide his force east to collect the remainder of Mard's trolls before pushing south. Timing was everything. They knew war was coming, else why would the bridge at the kingdom's entrance be so heavily fortified? All he needed to do was wait just long enough for the northern armies to strike and use that distraction to make his move toward the heart of the goblin occupation.

The first sign of trouble came at dusk when they walked into a company strength goblin patrol. Caught off guard, the rebels were forced back on the defensive, as cruel arrows felled several, including a pair of trolls. Neither side could risk withdrawing without incurring massive casualties, as well as the threat of reprisal should goblin reinforcements get summoned.

Mard drew his war bar from over a shoulder and bellowed. Ranks of trolls formed on either side with shields lowered and interlocked. He forewent donning a helmet. The night winds blew his black hair wildly. The trolls marched, in-step, toward the waiting goblin formation.

Poros watched with awe and more than a little terror. The ground trembled. Heavy footsteps crushed small rocks, while kicking up clouds of dust. Spears and swords were lowered. Many of the trolls took up an ancient war chant. The words were harsh, volatile to the ear. Poros gave the goblins credit. They were either very brave or excessively ignorant. He doubted any other race would stand the line against the tide of malevolence about to crash into them.

"Dom! Get the others and ride north. We must cut off their escape route back to the bridge," Poros shouted over the din of battle as troll and goblin closed.

The dwarf reacted immediately and rode with speed. One hundred rebels rode at his back. Poros remained behind with Horus and a score of guardians. The notion that the goblins would win through Mard's trolls was ridiculous but better men were killed for lesser lapses in judgment. The Free Rebellion had already been gutted and left for dead once.

He needn't have worried. The battle ended almost as quickly as it began. Mard stomped through the field, crushing the skulls of those goblins unfortunate enough to only be wounded. There would be no prisoners. Poros sheathed his sword when Dom and the rebels returned. He hadn't needed to use it. It was an odd sensation, for he was unused to standing by as battles played out.

"A handful attempted to flee. We killed them all," Dom had blood splashed across the left side of his face and down into his beard.

Poros grimaced. "The commotion will have traveled far on the night air. Others will come."

"Does this change our plans?" Dom asked. The possibility of additional patrols in this vicinity increased based on this engagement. They could not afford to face continued delays.

Poros heard laughter coming from what had turned into a slaughter ground. The trolls were enjoying their work. "No, but we must hurry. There will no doubt be more patrols, or worse, throughout the night."

His fears stretched beyond the immediate. Endless possibilities arose. The enemy could easily be reinforcing the defenses. More companies might already be crossing into Sadith Oom. Supply trains from Morthus were being dispatched north in support of the war effort. His mind ached as they sorted through each. The worst feeling any field commander could have was confronting the unknown.

"We must hurry. Have the lads search the dead for weapons or supplies and make it quick," Poros told him.

He gazed upward, at the vast sky filled with stars. Night was so pure here. Without cities or civilization to mar the skyline or occlude the darkness, he was able to see deep into space. *How many thousands of worlds are there like ours? Are we the only one? Are those bright stars naught but a sea of destruction beyond our own world*? He closed his eyes. *Do wars ever have an end?*

It was a question he knew he was never going to live long enough to find out.

Morthus was under a constant strain of activity. Thousands of slaves continued to ferry blocks of stone quarried from the pits west of the city while construction crews built the city of Arlyn Gert's dreams. Her ruling seat in a fledgling empire. Dreams of returning Sadith Oom to its former glory inspired her, though she was conflicted. The southern kingdom meant much to Arlyn, for it had produced the greatest weapon of the modern age.

The Black Imelin's failure in retrieving the Staff of Life was one of the main reasons she saw fit to eliminate him. She brokered no incompetence. So long as the Staff remained in play, her plans were in jeopardy. Tens of thousands of goblins and darklings occupied the southern half of the kingdom. They were an impossible barrier the remnants of the Hierarchy's finest forces would break upon.

She stood on the balcony of her still unfinished tower in the main castle. So high up the slaves building her legacy seemed little more than insects. Dark specks scurrying to and fro. Hundreds died daily and were cast into the burn pits or given to the darklings. She reviled at the thought of devouring human flesh, without halting the practice. The darklings originally swore allegiance to Imelin. They now followed her, but that dynamic could change if she failed to follow through on promises.

The city sprawled for a league in every direction. Stone structures comprised the central core, while massive storage buildings and slave pens were situated off to the western quadrant. Barracks lie north and east, for it was easier to deploy should any enemy reach this far. Hovels with families and the young, as well as merchants, what few there were, were in the south. Morthus was developing from the ruins it had once been, but it was a far cry from the luxury she enjoyed during her time in Meisthelm.

Arlyn wanted more. Her patience, while one of her strongest characteristics, was far from infinite. She'd already spent decades cultivating her plans. A few more years would not hurt. One of the secrets of the old order of wizards was long lasting life. She'd already extensively researched what the Hierarchy libraries contained and was convinced that all the answers lay in the ruins of Mordrun Hath. Unfortunately, the Forge of Wizards had a rather nasty troll infestation that needed purging first.

They could wait, at least until she broke Conn and with any good fortune, those pesky Galdeans. She had incorrectly assumed that murdering King Elian would reduce their will to fight. Instead they mustered close to their full strength and turned the northern half of her army into ruins. Arlyn could only assume that they would continue south in pursuit. It was of no matter. She had enough strength marshaled to break all the armies of the Free Lands.

She pursed her lips. Still, it wouldn't hurt to increase her odds of success. Arlyn strode back to her desk and rang the tiny golden hand bell. All the furnishings had been taken from her chambers in Meisthelm, along with various other important artefacts and decorations she eyed possessively during her tenure on the High Council. A slave appeared, unkempt and dressed in a tattered shift hanging down to his knees.

"Summon Duoth N'nclogbar at once," she ordered, her voice harsh.

The slave bowed and hurried away.

Arlyn busied herself with arranging her desk and office while she waited. Sadith Oom may be a miserable land, but there was no reason she needed to suffer. She was, after all, the future empress of the Free Lands.

Some creatures should have never been birthed. Races so vile the very kiss of sunlight was enough to boil their flesh. Beings whose utter malevolence and hatred for all life permeated through others around them. Common human lore suggested they were meant to be the dominant species. Few knew it was a bold-faced lie. What might was there in man, when demons like the grohls roamed the dark places of the world?

Finished with the darkling leader, Arlyn hurried to confront one such creature. Her stomach churned at the thought of standing in its presence again. Hume Feralin was the most terrifying creature she'd ever encountered. A monster with the unquenchable lust for blood. How many hundreds had already been devoured? Arlyn shuddered at the thought.

Misconceptions perpetuated the grohl legend. Ones she helped emplace. The beasts were rumored to have been created by wizards in the time before the Hierarchy. The truth was much worse, for they were born of the elemental darkness at the dawn of time by the great evil from beyond the veil of stars. For whatever purpose, grohls were the antithesis of the other races. How many ranged the world was unknown, though a great crusade was begun during the early years of the Hierarchy to eradicate the species. Records claimed the endeavor was highly successful, but not total.

Arlyn entered the grohl's chambers deep within the heart of Morthus. Void of light, the creature thrived on darkness. She sensed him. Caught the heavy rasp of breath. The fetid stench of diseased and necrotic flesh. Arlyn nearly gagged. A hulking shadow pushed deeper into the shadows to avoid being struck by the glare of torchlight she'd brought. Only the barbed tip of his tail remained in sight.

"I was not to be disturbed," Hume ground out with a sound akin to rocks being ground to powder.

"Do not make the mistake of thinking you are in command here, Hume. You never were, merely holding the position until I returned," Arlyn defied him.

The low growl made her nervous. Planting both feet shoulder width apart, Arlyn stood her ground. She struggled to understand Hume's speech, for it was an alien sound and violent to hear. The tail flicked.

"Morthus is mine," Hume said.

"No. This kingdom belongs to me. You run the city at my discretion," Arlyn pressed. "War is coming, Hume. How much longer will you take to finish construction?"

"Not long," the grohl said after an unnatural pause. "Many slaves must die."

"Their lives are not my concern. Work them until they expire. This city and the surrounding defenses must be completed within the next month."

"As you command," Hume ground out. "Leave me before I kill you."

Arlyn glared, summoning her magic. It wouldn't take much to incinerate everything in the chamber, herself included, but she needed Hume. His iron will was the driving force behind the reconstruction efforts. Once the city was finished, however, she had no qualms against sending the monster to his demise. There was no room for opposition in her schemes for the future.

Gathering her skirts, Arlyn slid from the chamber before succumbing to her rage. The clink-ching of hammer and chisel echoed deep within the castle's bowels. Progress. She was reshaping the world in her image. A lifetime of patience finally reaching fruition. She regretted having to abandon Meisthelm, but the Galdean army was too strong and well prepared for her to maintain her position. Rather than think of it as retreat, Arlyn chose strategic withdrawal.

Not that it mattered. Much of the kingdom of Valadon was shattered, a charred husk of what once was, and the northern kingdoms languished under a constant series of assaults from the darkling army Imelin left north of the Unchar Pass. By withdrawing to Sadith Oom, she ensured what remained of the northern armies would follow to continue prosecuting what they assumed to be the end of the war. Little could they know they were marching into a trap. Torchlight lent her grin a feral look. All her plans were steadily falling into place.

TWENTY

Into the Tunnels

"This isn't going to work," Camden said. Disappointment crossed his face as he watched the dwarves and goblins finish building the rafts that would take them across the river. "We've got just as much chance of drowning than not."

Sylin tried, and failed, to ignore the journeyman. He was growing increasingly more certain Camden was almost at his breaking point. Any time a man began to think hard on retiring or what he was going to do next, before the current task was complete, signaled the beginning of the end. Not that he blamed him. Camden had only signed on as a guide for the former Councilman. There was the unwritten understanding of getting into a minor scrape or two, but not a full invasion into the dead kingdom. It was easy to see death beckoning.

"Our dwarf allies are more than capable engineers," he chose his words carefully.

"It's not the dwarves I worry about," Camden said without taking his eyes off of the goblins.

They hacked and slashed at the wood in contrast to the elegance of the dwarves, who demonstrated an almost loving approach to crafting their rafts. Sylin remained wary of the goblins. Duplicity wasn't against their nature. Outnumbered, he and the handful of dwarves would be hard pressed to fight if the goblins turned on them.

The conflict disturbed him. He was a member of the High Council of the Hierarchy. His mandate was to help others, all others, regardless of race or proven hostility against the other races. These goblins had done nothing to him, nor had they shown any form of aggression. Sylin should be giving them the benefit of the doubt, but his heart remained troubled. Perhaps Camden wasn't the only one reaching the end of his tether.

Construction continued into the night. Dwarves were avid perfectionists, much to Camden's lament. The Croom River flowed by, dark waters lapping against the shore. Unnerved, Camden stepped back from the water. Nothing they were doing felt right. Working hand in hand with goblins, who might well have been among the ones chasing them across the entire kingdom, attempting to breach an enemy kingdom while avoiding being spotted by thousands of enemy soldiers not far away, and then marching into the heart of Sadith Oom, chilled his soul.

Camden constantly peered north to where the combined defenses into the kingdom were being fortified. Torches turned the sky sickly orange, for whoever commanded the defense held no fear of being attacked. That fact worried him more than he was willing to admit aloud. Sylin needed his full support, but he found it difficult to give, the longer the quest dragged on.

It was supposed to end when they reached Xulan Lake. The decrepit wizard proved more problematic than either of them guessed. His presence forced the quest to continue, only not in the direction Camden hoped. They were heading deeper into danger instead of back to the comforts of Meisthelm. He couldn't shake the feeling that one or more of them weren't going to be returning.

"These rafts have a better chance of drowning us than getting us across," Camden continued. "Do we have any idea where to go once we land?"

"You need to make your mind up. Are we going to drown or traverse the mountains?"

Camden glowered at Talrn, despite knowing the comment was meant in jest.

"Relax, you are letting your nerves get the best of you," Sylin cautioned. "We have gotten this far. We will make it the rest."

"Alive?" Camden asked.

Sylin had no answer.

"That's it. We're finished," Garin announced a short while later.

The dwarves busied packing away their tools while the goblins milled almost aimlessly. Sylin noticed the disparity between the two, knowing there was no amount of peacemaking possible for reconciliation. Hatred ran deep between them. Sylin paused to wonder how their already fragile alliance would hold up when it came time for axe and sword.

Elxander chose that moment to return. His habit of distancing himself from the others at inopportune times continued to irritate many of the others. The ancient wizard was supposed to be looked up to, a banner for all races to gather behind. Instead he chose to remain apart, as if being near so many after so long spent in isolation would contaminate him. Sylin's respect for the man continued to fade.

"Wizard, we are ready to cross," he was unable to keep the disappointment out of his tone.

Elxander clasped his hands. Veins stuck out like thick blue snakes crossing the desert. "Good. Good. The sooner we enter the tunnels, the better for all of us. It would not do for our enemies to catch us."

Maric and a pair of goblins burst into the work area from the north. All were out of breath. Worried.

"What is it?" Sylin asked. He reached for his sword.

The dwarf pointed behind him. "A company sized force heading this way. We've not long before they reach this point."

Sylin looked to Garin who shrugged and said, "Fight or flee. We can handle a company of goblins."

"Not goblins. Something… else," one of the goblins said. His tusks reached his nostrils and were covered with slime.

Elxander faced the north, whispering words of power. He stiffened as his enhanced sight showed him everything. "Darklings."

The dwarves perked up.

"Quickly, put the rafts in the water," Garin urged.

Dwarf and goblin hurried.

"What are darklings?" Camden asked.

"An evil from the old world," Elxander explained. "Garin is correct. We must leave, now."

Feeling control slipping, Sylin reached for his pack. He turned to Thork Ironrock. "Get the horses and ponies out of here. With luck we will see you back in Jerincon."

The dwarf had volunteered to lead their mounts back across the Goblin Lands to safety. It was a difficult choice, but one needing to be made. Each of the rafts were too small to ferry any of the animals. Garin and the others harbored severe reservations about having to continue through the dead kingdom on foot.

Thork wasted no time on words. The dwarf hurried to escape before being cut off. A pair of goblins went with him. Many of the dwarves were against it, for Thork was outnumbered, but Garin calmed them. Any dwarf was more than a match for a pair of goblins. Besides which, moving as a combined force was the only way they were going to escape the goblin kingdom unnoticed. Every decision was a risk. Sylin waited just long enough to watch Thork and his companions disappear into the night.

The rafts slipped into the hungry river. The current threatened to drag each down river before dwarves and goblins plied their oars with enough strength to cross the hundred meters. None knew their ultimate destination, only that they needed to reach the far shore as quickly as possible. The dwarves reached land first, if barely. All the goblin rafts landed a stroke or two behind the stouter dwarves.

"Garin, get a head count," Sylin ordered. He then faced Elxander. "Did we escape undetected?"

"As far as I can tell, though the darklings are a vicious foe. Certainly more cunning than either of our traveling companions," Elxander said. "Still, we must not tarry. The sooner we are into the mountains, the safer I will feel."

"What aren't you telling me?" Sylin demanded. His suspicions on what the old man's true motives might be worsened.

Elxander gave him an approving nod but said nothing. Cursing under his breath, Sylin hurried to help his friends. Night continued to deepen but they did not have much time. Sunrise and their enemies were both near.

"What do we do with the rafts?" Camden asked.

"Cover them with sand and hope they are not discovered come the dawn."

They lacked the time necessary to dismantle them and in Sylin's mind, might very well need them again should their foray into the dead kingdom turn sour. The last thing he wanted was to be trapped in Sadith Oom without an exit strategy. He'd finished burying one corner of his raft when Elxander pulled him away.

"I need you with me. The path into the mountains is treacherous and I will have need of your talents before we emerge on the opposite side," he explained. Elxander held up a hand when he saw Sylin about to question him. "There is no time for explanations. We must hurry and I need you at my side."

"Not until you explain what is going on," Sylin demanded.

Elxander, much to Sylin's surprise, did not sigh or exaggerate being annoyed. Instead he offered a thin smile. "There are many foul creatures in this world. Creatures who reject the light of day. I fear we are going to encounter some on the next phase of our journey."

Another test? Sylin looked at the grey-stone mountain wall directly ahead. "What awaits us?"

"I cannot say for certain, though it is rumored a colony of stroghoi dwell deep in the mountains." He continued upon seeing the confusion on Sylin's face. "Earth eaters. They are remnants from the dawn of time. Prehistoric monstrosities best left forgotten, and undisturbed."

He went on to describe them, but Sylin had already stopped listening. Whatever these stroghoi were, they couldn't be as bad as a dragon.

Elxander gripped his forearm. "Be ready. This will not be easy."

Camden walked up. "We're ready."

"Let's go."

Sylin, with the ancient wizard at his side, led the way into the mountains. They followed a game trail into the slopes. Mountain sheep and cave bears lived high above, along with a rare breed of big cat seldom seen. Boots crunched on the scree as they slowly began the climb to the tunnel mouth. Sylin felt as if he was being watched, yet every time he paused to look around, he found nothing. That emptiness crawled across his flesh. Was this the legacy of Sadith Oom?

Several goblins and a few dwarves slipped during the ascent. Heavy packs, for they were forced to carry all of their supplies, weighted them down enough to make the climb miserable for the heartiest. Hands reached out to help others. Bodies were pushed as the climb became steeper. Finally, at several hundred meters up, Elxander guided them to the tunnel mouth.

Talrn and another dwarf shed their heavy packs and marched into the opening with weapons bared. Others picked up their gear. Sylin waited, counting in his head until he was sure the dwarves were far enough ahead to warn them of potential threats. Elxander entered the tunnel next, without pause or concern for the others. His focus centered on the stroghoi.

"I will take the rear guard. Move at speed and do not stop until we reach the other side," Garin told him.

Sylin hadn't felt so out of touch with his surroundings in a very long time. Worse was the lack of control he suffered from. He wasn't sure what was going to happen once he reached Xulan Lake. Wasn't sure if Elxander still lived. All his focus and drive ended with finding the wizard. Thinking ahead served no purpose. That lack of judgment now proved detrimental, for they were marching deeper south instead of back to Meisthelm, where he once believed he could make the most impact on the Black's betrayal.

The darkness of the tunnel was suffocating, cutting off all thoughts of what might have been. Sylin reached unsteadily for the nearest wall. Blinded, he could feel the walls closing in, collapsing, without the ability to save himself. Sparks assaulted his night vision. Sparks that burst into open flame as the dwarves lit torches.

Sylin studied their surroundings once his eyes adjusted. The tunnel was wide enough for three to walk abreast and tall enough he didn't have to stoop. This led him to question if the tunnels were natural or crafted. Asking Elxander seemed pointless. No doubt the wizard would offer a riddled answer, while deftly avoiding a solid explanation. Sylin began to think the old man might not know as much as he was leading on.

"How long will it take to reach the other side?" he asked, wincing at the weight his echo carried.

"Less than half a day, providing we are not accosted. I imagine we should find Sadith Oom with the rising sun."

Sylin frowned. "What of the stroghoi?"

"Less of a threat, the more we go unnoticed."

The company began to move. Sylin's doubts rode upon his shoulders as each weary step dragged him deeper into the unknown.

The first sign of trouble came some time later. A small rockslide in one of the smaller offshoots forced the goblins to pack together. Panic threatened to ensue as fears of being buried alive arose. Unseen through the dust clouds choking the tunnel, great gaps formed in the walls. A scream was abruptly cut off. Swords were drawn. A second scream echoed deep in the heart of the mountains.

Camden drew his sword. His eyes were wild, endlessly scanning the tunnel for signs of attack. "What is it?"

"Keep moving! Hurry, we must flee this place," Elxander all but shouted.

Dwarves and goblins picked up the pace.

Sylin stood his ground. "What of those screams?"

"We cannot help them. The stroghoi!"

Frustrated and fighting the urge to go back to the pack of goblins to offer aid, Sylin needed to see their enemy. Needed to have a legitimate target. The combination of intense emotions gripping him caused his magic to flare to life. He ignored Elxander and fought his way through the rushing goblins.

Of the stroghoi there was no sign. Scraps of flesh and pools of dark blood lined the walls and floor in splotches. Sylin halted. He was alone. Garin and a few others were still on their way unless they had been attacked as well. A weapons belt lay in the middle of the tunnel. Sylin crouched to examine the teeth marks on it. Massive, cutting it in two in some places. What manner of beasts are these stroghoi?

Rumbling in the ground drew his attention. He rose and took a defensive position. The tremors stopped, abrupt and worrying. Garin and a trio of goblins arrived suddenly. Their confused looks suggested none knew what had happened. Sylin raised his hand when the ground beneath the lead goblin dropped away. A sluggish creature lurched up from the dark. Razor sharp teeth bit and tore into flesh as the stroghoi swallowed the goblin.

Through many adventures and harrowing moments Sylin's quest ranged half of the Free Lands, but he had never imagined a creature so reprehensible. The stroghoi were beyond primitive. Their worm-like bodies were impossibly thick and mottled brown. Hundreds of teeth filled the mouth capable of devouring victims whole.

Sylin's study was interrupted when Garin swung his double headed axe into the stroghoi's body. Blood and ichor erupted. Chunks of flesh ripped away with the blade. The dwarf swung again and the worm let loose a mournful wail. The remaining goblins roared and attacked. Steel bit flesh but the worm's flesh was thick and difficult to pierce. Sylin closed his eyes and directed his energies toward the worm. A blinding flash and the stench of roasted flesh filled the tunnel.

Garin stumbled away, choking on dust and acrid fumes. The goblins followed. It occurred to Sylin that he'd never seen a goblin cry until now. They snarled and glared accusingly. Garin waved them off. This was not the time for questions.

"Catch up with the others," Sylin said. He reached out to help the second goblin to his feet. "The others are not far ahead."

"What was that thing?" a goblin demanded.

"Hungry," Garin answered. "What of the rear guard?"

Sylin shook his head. "To risky. We must stick together before more of the worms come."

"How many did we lose?" Garin asked, as his eyes took in the blood and gore around them.

Sylin hesitated, unsure if the answer served any positive purpose. Ultimately, he knew keeping the information from his allies might prove detrimental. "Two goblins insofar as we can tell. Hopefully, the others have not been assaulted while we've been here."

Anger simmering, the goblins pushed past him. Any confrontation needing to be had would come after they escaped the mountains. If they escaped.

Camden ripped his sword from the dead worm and had to lean against the tunnel wall to keep from collapsing. Three of the monsters lay dead, but only after reaping a wicked toll. One dwarf and seven goblins had either been consumed or were among the bodies filling the tunnel. That was how Sylin found him a short time later. He offered a quick report before Sylin motivated them to get moving again. Dawn was not far off and he had no desire to remain in the tunnels any longer than necessary.

Fright provided urgency and the war party abandoned all caution. Dwarf, man, and goblin barreled through the tunnel with the impunity of a conquering army. Elxander was secured in the middle of the group, for Sylin wasn't taking unnecessary chances. Whatever the wizard schemed for them in the dead kingdom, Sylin knew Elxander was going to play an intricate part. He, before any of the others, needed to survive.

He allowed his relief to show only when the faint light of day began to creep deep into the tunnel. They'd reached the other side but at terrible cost. One tenth of their strength would not reach Sadith Oom. A horrible waste of life Sylin accepted personal responsibility for. Nothing for it, he bade Talrn and the scouts to find a way down out of the mountains. The others struggled to catch their breath.

Sylin pulled his canteen and took his first look into the dead kingdom. His first instinct suggested it was, indeed, a desolate land. Endless plains of sand and dirt stretched away from the jagged mountain slopes. No forests, limited brush, and not a blade of grass in sight. Nor could he discern any natural water source.

"The journey will be perilous, for Sadith Oom is a wretched place."

Sylin wasn't sure when Elxander came to stand beside him. "We will need water to cross that. And food. None of us have packed enough to get us where you want us to go."

Leaving the statement open ended, Sylin hoped to pry more information from the taciturn wizard. There was none. Elxander was content to leave him in the dark. It proved too much for the former Councilor.

"We are not leaving these tunnels until you tell me where we are going and what our purpose is," Sylin rounded on him. "Eleven of us are dead because of you, Elxander. Being a wizard does not absolve you from responsibility. Why are we in Sadith Oom?"

Elxander studied him, searching for latent weaknesses or hidden agendas. "You are finally becoming the leader the kingdoms have need of, young Sylin. I am impressed. We are heading south and east, to the ancient forge of Mordrun Hath. I have already told you the war is coming here, and with it the fabled Staff of Life. We must prepare the forge in order to destroy the Staff and end this long running conflict. As for your concerns of food and water. The Plains of Darkpool provide. Have your people conserve their water. There is an oasis less than a day south of here. Fig trees and other fruits will be found as well. Does that satisfy your questions?"

"For now," Sylin answered. He hadn't expected that much and felt uneasy now that Elxander had spoken.

Talrn returned with news of finding an adequate place to rest and refit halfway down the slopes. Relieved, Sylin knew a meal and the chance to get their grievances off their minds would do much to improve morale as they prepared for the final stage of their journey. He took his first step into Sadith Oom and struggled to fight off feelings of impending doom.

TWENTY-ONE

The Wood of Ills

The Wood of Ills was considered one of the most naturally sinister places in the Free Lands. Named for the vast amount of foul beasts and negative events emanating from deep within the wood, the forest spread from the ocean and the lower reaches of the Mountains of the Fang in the west, to a third of the way into Coronan in the south and east. Over one hundred leagues wide and twenty deep, the forest provided ruffians and brigands with ample room to escape authority.

Marshal Sevron stared at the forest with reservations. Mist clung to the snow-covered trees, giving the illusion of wicked deeds about to occur. Of monsters too foul for the imagination to conjure, bursting from the mist to devour his force. He shivered beneath his bearskin cloak. A stiff wind blew through, knocking a wall of snow from the intertwined branches. He had the impression of walking into a graveyard.

"Marshal, the force is arrayed in battle order."

Sevron nodded, barely listening to Thorp's report. He trusted his officers and men to do what they'd been trained for. His concerns stemmed from the forest itself. Not even the Hierarchy ordered patrols into this fell place. Sensing the hesitation in Thorp's tone, Sevron gave him an imploring look.

"Sir, this is a very large section of land. There is no way we can sweep and secure the Wood," Thorp continued.

"I appreciate your concern, Captain, though I doubt these darklings are interested in avoiding contact.

If reports are correct, they will most likely engage us the moment we are spotted," he said.

Three thousand soldiers, one third dressed in shining golden armor, were arrayed in distinct formations fifty meters away. Cavalry, which would soon be rendered ineffective by entering the Wood, formed two ranks deep in front of squares of infantry. These would provide the bulk of the fighting force and all his muscle once battle was engaged.

His knowledge of the Wood of Ills was limited, hampered by the lack of actual patrols over the last ten years. Tree density, slopes and ravines, natural water features. All were unknown strategy changers and that left him frightened. Sevron hadn't used his sword since the Aragoth rebellion. He had a feeling that was going to end soon. The trees began to sway as the winds picked up.

"We are wasting time here," Sevron said.

"There is little daylight left. I advise doing a reconnaissance along a broad flank."

"I agree," Sevron surprised him. "Deploy two full companies. No patrol is to be smaller than platoon strength and they must be back before dark."

"Yes, sir."

Sevron stopped him after he went a few steps. "Captain. We do not see eye to eye on a great many issues, but I have regards for your tactical genius. Never hesitate to offer suggestions that might improve our chances of success. We attack at dawn."

Thorp nodded. "Yes, sir."

Sevron continued to watch, the younger officer catching his interest. He knew Thorp's ambitions and was prepared to deal with them accordingly. Men like Thorp were useful in combat, but cancerous without an enemy to fight. Fortunately for Sevron, they were almost always transparent in their actions.

Sergeant Laris had been a platoon sergeant for a little less than a year. Saverin was his fifth duty posting over the course of his career and if all went according to plan, his last. Retirement beckoned and the brutal winter helped force his decision. The Hierarchy had been good to him for the better part of two decades but a man had to know his limitations. The body slowed down. Aches and pains were daily, where they were once occasional. Laris loved the Golden Warrior corps, but knew it was time to hang his armor up.

Too many grey hairs decorated his once coal black beard. Lines and wrinkles covered the backs of his hands. Tiny lines creased his forehead and the corners of his suddenly dulled eyes. Callouses clung to his hands and feet. He grew tired quicker.

None of that hindered his performance. Laris was a consummate professional. He drilled his platoon harder than most of those in the garrison. Having already seen combat on numerous fields and kingdoms, he had lived through the best and worst men had to offer. Too many former comrades never returned home. Many others were broken shells of what once was. Laris had killed too many to recall over the course of his career, but none had been monsters of legend. As tired and worn down as he was, he couldn't wait to sink his sword into darkling flesh.

He led his platoon into the Wood of Ills, just as any leader worthy of the title should. Laris learned long ago that respect was earned through the quality of his actions, not his ability to boss others around. The platoon moved through the gnarled trees three abreast in squads of ten. Squad leaders followed his example by marching ahead of their men.

Notches were cut in trees, small arrows to mark their passing and the direction back to the safety of the army. Thick canopy, despite the lack of leaves, occluded much of the already faint sunlight. Pockets of shadows grew deep and dark. Ample room for lurking monsters. Despite their latent fears, the Golden Warriors made as much of a trail as possible. Laris did not want to be the man responsible for getting his platoon lost. He'd never hear the end of it from his peers.

Intent on the way ahead, none of them spotted the abnormal lumps clinging to the tree trunks high up in the branches or the red eyes blinking as the soldiers passed beneath. No one saw the darklings until they were dropping down atop them. Men cried out as fangs and daggers sank into the exposed flesh of their necks.

Laris whirled, unclasping his heavy cloak to have better movement, and watched in horror as several of his men fell. Their blood stained the snow in obscene patterns. Many more struggled with throwing their attackers off, lest they suffer similar fates. Laris looked down into the terrified eyes of one of his newer soldiers as the boy desperately tried to stop the arterial bleeding from the side of his neck. The boy died without Laris being able to remember his name.

Enraged, Laris hefted his sword and charged into the fray. The first darkling to spy him was hewn in half. Laris grunted as he ripped his blade free from the darkling's stomach. A raw stench assaulted his senses. He grew dizzy and fought off the urge to vomit. Laris forced the fact that these monsters were worse than what mothers frightened their disobedient children with and considered them naught but animals. Those he could face and slaughter at will.

His sword whipped through every darkling unfortunate enough to come within reach. He killed without pause or consideration. Gore covered his armor as escaping heat from the corpses turned to steam. The battle ended quickly. Laris stomped down with all his strength and crushed the head of a wounded darkling and paused to catch his breath and recover his bearings.

No living foe stood the field, though he spied numerous dark shapes hurrying off. Laris, ever so reluctantly, began to take head count as the squads busied seeing to wounded and verifying the dead. He went into the Wood of Ills with fifty battle ready men. He was walking out with twenty-three.

Sevron wanted to bellow his frustration to the skies. Initial losses for what was supposed to be a simple reconnaissance were unacceptably high. Hundreds of men went into the forest. Less than half walked out again. Fifty percent casualties without gaining any actionable intelligence. He was just as blind now as when they first reached the forest edge. He wanted to bellow, and rage to whatever deity deigned to listen, but in doing so, he reduced his level of command. Sevron bit his tongue and vowed to prevent similar results come the dawn.

His captains awaited. Many stole furtive glances at the forests, unable to help themselves. Half expected a full-blown assault in the middle of the night and the mood in camp reflected as much. Golden Warriors, the pride of the Free Lands, were supposed to be better than today. Myths of invincibility crumbled to ash as the bodies were prepared for funeral pyres. Those bodies that were recovered. Several remained missing but were presumed dead.

"Gentlemen, report," Sevron said, after storming into the small circle.

He was in no mood for banter or hyperbole. Traditional attitudes were shelved to facilitate a quality battle plan. Thorp cleared his throat and began.

"The pyres are set to be lit. All bodies have been identified and recorded. Services will be conducted upon completion of this meeting."

Sevron nodded, his mind wandering to how he was going to convey his condolences to so many, so very many, families. His heart felt weighted down. "Numbers?"

An uneasiness rippled through the captains. Casualty counts were not often mentioned in such company. Thorp licked his cracked lower lip before answering. "One hundred and seven dead. Eight more are missing."

"One hundred and fifteen men dead," Sevron snapped. The intensity of his gaze caused several men to step back. "Because we underestimated our opponents. We marched into that forest with impunity, thinking our golden armor would protect us from the very worst the Free Land has to throw at us."

"Sir, I do no…"

Sevron cut Thorp off. "How else would you explain this defeat? And make no mistake, gentlemen, this was a staggering defeat. Tomorrow, when we march en masse, we will do so with such authority, the very roots of the Fang will tremble. I have half a mind to burn this Wood to the ground, though I suspect the filth grown within would beat us back."

Nods and grunts of approval circled the group.

"Tomorrow, we strike swiftly. Rip out the heart of these damned monsters and push all the way to the Galdean border. Questions?"

A young captain, barely old enough to shave in Sevron's estimation, asked, "Sir, what is the order of march?"

"Skirmishers in front, followed by the heavy infantry. Cavalry brings up the rear. I will take position with the heavies. Sergeant Laris," Sevron waited for the battered sergeant to stand beside him. "In your opinion, is our armor help or hindrance?"

Laris looked to each of the captains in turn. Many expected to see a broken man, but instead were greeted by a steeled veteran with hatred burning deep in his eyes. "It helps. Not a man was wounded by their claws, fangs, or blades where the armor was strong, but the darklings focused their attacks where we weren't wearing armor. Almost as if they knew our weaknesses."

"Which very well may be possible, considering the high level the Black Imelin attained before betraying us all," Thorp concluded.

Sevron added the comment to his growing list of reasons to transfer the man as soon as this campaign ended. "Be that as it may, you heard him. I want all units in armor. Look to the trees and take nothing for granted. The young Galdean scout assures us a large force is securing the pass out of Suroc Tol. With luck, the only darklings we are going to fight are already within these cursed woods.

"I want triple security tonight. Torches and large fires to enlarge our field of vision. All captains and senior sergeants will walk the perimeter at least twice before dawn. Am I understood?" he asked.

He could tell from their concerned looks that none viewed his leadership style approvingly. The campaign was just beginning and he was already recklessly risking his life like a newly commissioned lieutenant. Thorp's smug look told Sevron he was doing the proper thing.

Word of the slaughter in the forest was already circulating the camp, threatening to tear the army apart. He needed to stop it before too much damage was done. Going into the midst of battle and pulling routine guard duty expected of fresh recruits was the best way he knew how.

He dismissed them all but Laris. The sergeant felt out of place but followed orders. Sevron waited until they were alone, casting a sour look at Thorp who lingered just beyond the edge of the firelight.

"Sergeant Laris, I need the truth. Can we beat these beasts?" Sevron asked, laying a gloved hand on his shoulder.

Laris shifted uncomfortably. Being summoned by senior leadership normally meant for a long night of unpleasant circumstances. "They are savage, and rely on underhanded tactics, but I believe we can best them. It will take all of our might, probably more, though."

"I suspected as much. We are going to have to give more on this mission than in any of the past," Sevron admitted. "I want you and your men to remain here while we deploy. You've given enough already."

Anger flared in Laris's eyes. "Marshal, with all respect, my men and I will rejoin the line. We've been bloodied, but that is no reason to cower while our friends go forth. We will fight, as men of the Hierarchy are sworn to do. This is our war."

Sevron smiled grimly and nodded. Men like Laris gave him hope. Perhaps his meager force was strong enough to destroy the darkling threat after all. He dismissed Laris and prepared to make his rounds of the perimeter. The night was cold and long, but it was armed with steel and the iron will of the men of the Free Lands.

Jent Tariens could not recall the last time he felt such immense relief. Soon, all his troubles would be gone, erased under a flurry of banners and marching boots. Today, the army of Galdea returned and with it the rightful heir to the throne and ruler of the kingdom. His long trial was coming to an end. Jent relished the notion of returning to being just the captain of the guard.

The nobility and all their inherent issues could be forgotten, left for others better suited to dealing with politics and policy. He'd never wanted the position, nor the responsibility. Jent was a soldier and that is where he belonged. Yet as excited as he was to see the army return, he languished under feelings of not having been part of the greatest campaign in modern history. A soldier who had not seen battle since the very first action of the war.

Would they accept him as they once had? Was it possible to command respect from men who were seasoned veterans? He frowned thinking of the sidelong glances from those who looked down upon him. But that was war. Few were afforded the opportunity to choose their fates. Jent was personally selected by the crowned princess to represent the kingdom, and the throne.

There was no shame in this, though he struggled with his emotions as he was nearly at the city's main gates. Squads of polished guards and freshly enlisted soldiers lined the boulevard. Dressed in their finest uniforms, they were proud representatives of Galdea. Jent frowned. What message did this send to the battered and beaten men returning from war?

Dagil Orn, matching him stride for stride, noticed the consternation and asked, "What is it? We've rebuilt and prepared this city for war as best as possible. The princess will approve, as I am certain Field Marshal Dlorn will as well."

"It is not that," Jent said. "The army has spent weeks on campaign, no doubt fighting hard the entire way. How would you feel returning home to find spit and polished men greeting you? It twists my stomach, Dagil."

"You know we cannot dismiss them. Protocol demands a proper honor guard upon the return of the ruling body."

"I understand, but it does little to diminish the feelings of inadequacy I suffer," Jent said.

Dagil was correct. They could not dismiss the honor guard. It was their sole purpose and would also take insult if told to disperse. Jent hated feeling trapped, though he imagined none of those men lining the road were thrilled with being placed in their position.

The gates of Galdarath were thrown open, inviting their warriors home. Warm sunlight bathed the entrance to the greatest city in the north. As if cooperating, the skies cleared but for a handful of fat clouds. It was the first day the men of Galdea gazed up at the sun in a very long time. The day was perfect.

Jent should have known that to be an ominous sign. Marching outside of the city, his group waited as the impossibly long column eased into view. He'd already spied the army from atop the walls and was mortified to see so many missing. Tens of thousands not returning. He could not imagine suffering through such loses.

"There is no royal sigil," Dagil said.

Jent scowled. "That might be a tactical decision. Dlorn is wiser than to announce the royal heir rides with the army."

He felt the lie even as the words slipped from his lips. If further proof was needed, it came quickly. Dlorn was missing, as were many of the senior aides and captains. Old friends he longed to speak with. Jent waited, impatiently, as the army ground to a halt. Commander Lestrin and Daril Perryman dismounted and approached.

"Captain Tariens," Lestrin saluted. "You have no idea how good it feels to be home."

Jent swallowed. "Commander. Where is the princess and the Field Marshal?"

He feared them both dead, along with so many others missing from the ranks.

Perryman pulled off his heavy riding gloves. "That is a different tale. I am quite afraid you are not yet relieved. This city, and the kingdom, remain in your capable hands for the foreseeable future."

Jent was sure he heard Dagil cut off a lighthearted laugh.

TWENTY-TWO

To the Dead Kingdom

The army of the Hierarchy awoke with the ravenous hunger of an insatiable beast. Swords sharpened, shields repaired, the ten thousand men representing all the Free Lands packed what meager belongings they took on campaign and readied for the long march to Sadith Oom. It was an ominous day, yet one filled with anticipation. The end of a long war was drawing nigh. An opportunity to return home and put down their swords for good. That, more than any speech from their commanders, provided ample inspiration.

Banners from every kingdom waved in the morning breeze coming off the marshes. Aron took in the sight with renewed vigor. Doubts continued to plague him, but they were considerably less than before reaching Meisthelm. He worked on mastering the Staff of Life when he thought others weren't paying attention. The magic was ancient, hostile. Aron found it resisting his efforts.

Aron fought back twice as hard. They lessened, as did most of the ill effects from linking his core to the Staff. Slowly, oh so slowly, he began to explore the depths of his connection with the infernal totem. He felt invigorated. Raw energy trickled into him, bolstering his weakened systems. Aron quickly learned how a man such as Ils Kincannon, his ancestor, might fall prey to the lures of power whispered in the cold, dark hours of the night.

The Staff did not belong in the mortal world.

"I've always enjoyed the morning a campaign begins. There is clarity of purpose. The focus of thousands of men, all driven toward achieving the same result," he said.

Karin struggled to keep from insulting him as a massive yawn took her spontaneously.

"There is harmony in it," he continued, unaware of her ordeal.

"If you insist, though I see only men ready to go home," she replied.

He eyed her quizzically. "Is that not the objective of every campaign? I do not believe that any man wishes to raise arms against another. There are bad souls here and there, tyrants and warlords intent on accumulating power, but to find true evil is a rare event. All the men around us pick up the sword to defend what they hold dear. Their families and homes. Not a one wishes to fall on a battlefield, but they will, if needs be. It is an honor to be among them."

Karin cocked her head in thought. "Would it not also be a burden? Knowing that your actions will lead to countless deaths?"

He held out his hands in a sympathetic gesture. "Such is the hardship of leadership. I may have survived this long, but I have not done so without suffering grievous wounds upon my psyche. Too many friends are no longer among us. The hurt never goes away."

Karin opened her mouth when a violent jolt threw her to the ground. She writhed, her body cramping. Aron shouted her name and dropped down to steady her before Karin managed serious harm. He heard footsteps of several others coming near. Finally, after tense moments, he felt her relax.

"What happened?" he asked after she locked eyes on him.

Sweat dappled her brow. "A vision. Aron, I am able to *see* again!"

Her ability to scry the future had been hampered almost since the onset of their journey out of Galdarath. Dark magic blinded her to larger events happening across the kingdoms. She assumed that those powers would return with the death of the Black Imelin. Only he had been dead for the better part of weeks and she still hadn't had any visions.

It was a cost she'd come to accept as days stretched into weeks and then months. Karin, who once relied on the visions to guide her, steadily grew accustomed to the handicap. For it to rush back into her in a flood of energies, left her drained.

"We must hurry. Arlyn Gert is about to make her play for dominance," she warned.

Aron rocked on his heels. "How? We have her penned in Sadith Oom."

"The Forge of Wizards. She is going to attempt to unlock the secrets of the ancient wizards. Aron, if she is successful, we will all die."

Her tone left little doubt. Aron pulled her up and together they went to confer with General Conn.

Senior commanders were consulted and a rapid decision made. Aron and his combined force of Golden Warriors and Galdeans, augmented with the vanguard of Conn's army, would push ahead with the objective of securing the bridge crossing into the dead kingdom. Conn and the bulk of the main army would follow at best possible speed. Andolus and the elves would accompany Aron, screening the flanks from any potential enemies lying in wait.

Horses saddled and ready to ride, Aron signaled his force to deploy. He was stopped by the dour looking Ute Hai. The Rover appeared much changed from their first encounter in Coronan. Gone was his hatred, that burning flame propelling him into an endless series of actions that defined his life. In its place was newfound purpose. Ute had spent many nights since killing one of his former friends locked deep in thought.

"What is it?" Aron asked.

Ute did not hesitate. His mind was made up. "I have thought long on what I must do in order to survive the coming days." He held up a hand to prevent Aron from interrupting. "No, let me speak. You and I have been foes for many years. Our paths continued to cross from the moment the war in Aragoth ended. I can longer go home. I realize this, nor can I consider myself a Rover. I am… kingdomless."

"The Queen repented and rejoined the Hierarchy. Aragoth is once again with us," Aron said.

"Would she be lenient and accept a traitor into her ranks? No. I cast adrift from kin and kingdom. There is but one destination left to me. I… I wish to enlist in the army of the Hierarchy," Ute concluded. Regret filled his eyes, reflecting the pain felt in his heart.

Aron was shocked. The men of Aragoth were talented fighters, capable of battling the Golden Warriors to standstill. Their betrayal sent ripples through the kingdoms. For Ute to admit acceptance of what he'd spent the better part of two decades ignoring, took immense courage. Still, the lord of the Golden Warriors found it difficult to put his trust in a lifelong foe.

"Are you certain this is what you want?" he asked.

Ute shrugged. "It is time for change when your enemies become your allies. Where else have I to go?"

Aron slid from the saddle and drew his sword. "Kneel."

Hesitant, Ute obeyed. He bowed his head, unable to look into the eyes of the man he'd long ago sworn to kill. The touch of steel on his shoulder made him flinch.

"Ute Hai, I commission you in the army of the Hierarchy. You will serve as a lieutenant, holding all authority under rank and title. Rise, Lieutenant Hai," Aron commanded.

He did and was surprised at the strength a mere sentence offered. Ute Hai felt like a new man. One with purpose again. Looking Aron in the eye, he said, "Thank you, but do not make the mistake of believing this changes our relationship. I will never think of you as a friend, Commander."

"I did not think you would, Lieutenant," Aron said.

A curt nod and Ute was on his way back to his horse, leaving a very confused and oddly relieved Aron.

"That was interesting," Jou Amn commented from his saddle.

Aron climbed back onto his mount. "Damned peculiar, if you ask me."

"Do you think he will hold to that oath?"

Aron hoped so. "I do not know, but there is a strong sense of honor in the man. The time is fast approaching when we will all be put to the test. Let us hope he remains true. He is a good sword and a capable veteran. Something this army desperately needs."

Jou remained unconvinced. "Are you going to tell the General?"

Should I? It is the proper course of action. Conn needs to know who is in his chain of command. Yet if I did so, what would happen to Ute? "I think I shall keep this an internal matter. Regardless of where we stand now, Ute Hai was once a senior leader of the Rovers. I cannot see Conn or any of the others in the upper command will look highly upon what I did."

Jou laughed. "From Rover to Golden Warrior! What wonders the world works."

"Do not grow overconfident, Jou. Ute is commissioned, but he has a very long way to go before he can expect to earn the golden armor. We are wasting time here. There is a war to fight," Aron said.

A quick look and the bugler bleated out the call to march. The dead kingdom was at least a week away. The Hierarchy war machine ground into action once more.

Leagues rolled by. Aron made a point of choosing a different road from the one his force used to find Conn. When asked why, he merely replied 'let the dead remain dead'. None but those who had accompanied him knew what he was referring to. The matter faded quickly as Conn was forced to trust in Aron's judgment.

Aron continued to converse with Halvor. The priest of the Red Brotherhood offered helpful bits of knowledge previously unknown to the warrior. Imelin had been the last war wizard in the kingdoms. While Aron had no desire to resurrect the title, he knew he would need better command of both the power of the Staff and the power within him, if he was going to find a way to defeat Arlyn Gert and destroy the Staff.

During lulls in the training and conversation, Aron felt his attention pulled to the empty place Amean left. He'd known the man practically all his life, owing much of his success to the wily veteran. Amean Repage was one of the finest men, and valued advisor Aron had ever known. Only now he was dead. Murdered by traitorous filth who lacked vision. Men who once served with Ute Hai.

The vicious circle, Aron realized, needed to be broken if any of them were going to escape. To do so, he needed to be able to forgive. Amean's loss would be felt for a long time. Jou Amn was one of the better men left in the Order, but he was gruff and almost standoffish. The men needed leaders to look up to. Aron knew that Jou would mold into a better leader given time, but how much did they have remaining? The war continued without regards to their needs or wishes.

His focus returned to Ute. He wasn't responsible for Amean's murder. In fact, he acted out of character by murdering one of his own men. Former men, Aron corrected. The Rover part of Ute's life was ended. If he could find it within to move on, so too, could Aron. He owed Amean that much at least. The road to Sadith Oom left him with far too much opportunity for his mind to wander down aimless trails.

"What do you make of this Lord Kryte?" Conn asked his senior leaders as the main army began to move.

A massive armored snake winding across the open flats of Guerselleorn. Sounds of man and beast ranged far and wide as the army of the Hierarchy recovered a measure of lost glory. With newfound purpose, they marched to avenge their losses on Grim Mountain, the virtual dissolution of the Hierarchy, and for the preservation of loved ones. More than mere freedom was at stake, it was the continuation of a way of life.

Genessen the elf spoke first. "Capable. Competent. A good man to have on our side. If my people are with him, there is little cause for doubt."

"Hmmph, says you," his dwarven counterpart replied. "I trust a man based on actions, not the company he keeps."

"Do you know of him, General?" Zin Doluth asked. His voice was the strange combination of timidity and awe.

Conn nodded thoughtfully. "I do. He is headstrong and too sure of himself. A common flaw among many of the Golden Warriors. They believe they are the very best fighters in all the kingdoms. Warriors without equal. I have worked with their Order many times and always came away unimpressed."

His harsh criticism rippled through the officers. Each knew the reputation, and authority, the Golden Warriors held. To suggest they were anything but the very best was ridiculous.

"Still, we are fortunate to have them," Conn followed up, lest his subordinates begin to think he had hidden motives. "Lord Kryte is young, but experienced. His troop has been engaged in a seemingly impossible campaign since the end of autumn. They understand this new enemy better than any of us, for now."

His grin was predatory and spread through the others. Thoughts of confronting a new enemy and in doing so, restoring peace to the Free Lands inspired each. Many long days of marching stretched between redemption and now. The army ground on. Step after step.

Genessen yawned and stretched out his shoulders. They were sore from sitting in the saddle for so long. He reluctantly admitted that he was getting old. Worse, he began to feel it; an uncommon characteristic among elves. Contrary to popular belief, his people were far from being immortal. They could be killed, that much was common knowledge, but they also suffered from disease and time. That they had an exaggerated lifespan worked both in their favor and against them on occasion.

He always appreciated the night, for it felt like a comforting blanket. Genessen walked through the heart of the camp, speaking with this soldier or that. He was well liked and respected among the men. Many viewed him as a good luck charm, for wherever the elf went, good things followed.

Finishing his rounds, the elf turned for the command area and his waiting cot. Genessen didn't enjoy feeling fatigued. It clouded his thoughts, leaving him uncertain with decisions that would otherwise be simplistic to make. He paused as a strange sound caught his attention. The elf scanned the surrounding area but found nothing out of the ordinary.

His gaze went skyward. Genessen's mouth dropped. He drew his sword. A flight of scrathes edged into view. Monsters from the old world and forgotten by virtually all. He knew them too well, for his time in Dol'ir was spent in constant battle. It was not the winged monsters that bothered him so much as what they carried.

"To arms! To arms!" he shouted.

His cries of alarm were already too late. Genessen watched as scores of darklings dropped down into the sleeping camp. The slaughter began almost at once. Hefting his rapier, the elf plunged into his ancient foes. His blade took the first across the back of the neck, nearly severing it. Genessen stormed past, pausing to look at the obscene way the darkling's head hung by a few tendons.

A jolt and shower of sparks danced off his shin guard. Genessen slashed down and was rewarded with a spray of blood as his sword sliced through the darkling's neck and into his heart. Growling, the elf cursed his lack of attention. Many darklings were already on the ground, crawling through the camp to murder men in their sleep. There would be time for feeling foolish for not having remembered the enemy's tactics when Lord Kryte first mentioned the return of the darklings. Right now, he needed to refocus and kill as many of the beasts as possible.

A soldier was pinned to the ground and brutally stabbed to death while he was too far away to help. Had he his bow, both darklings would already be dead, but he had fallen prey to the false security of being in the middle of a sprawling army camp. Genessen charged the darklings, who met the challenge with guttural roars. The engagement was fast and furious. Sword clashed with short daggers. When it ended both darklings lay dead.

A wall of armored infantry hove into view. The monsters were an unknown foe, but battle was what these men were bred for. They hacked and slashed through the darklings with unparalleled fervor. Genessen wisely stepped aside, lest he be caught between the opposing forces. He watched in awe, and more than a little horror, as the men of the Hierarchy fought their first engagement against the darklings. The slaughter was impressive.

Bodies piled up. Some were soldiers, but the clear majority were darklings. Genessen correctly judged that all the enemy on the ground had abandoned their task of sweeping through the tents in order to combat the wall of steel challenging them. He'd almost forgotten the raw hostility the beasts displayed. They fought without regard for safety. Focused on murdering all within their reach.

The battle raged far longer than he imagined. When it was ended, Genessen counted over two hundred darklings. Not a mighty force by any means, but they'd done their duty. The entire army now looked to the skies for follow on assaults. Sleep was slow in coming. Men remained on guard deep into the night. Harassment tactics were common among the darklings, for they successfully disrupted the way an army performed.

Genessen stayed in the area long enough to ensure no other darklings remained in hiding before heading off to find Conn. It was past time they discussed the perils of the enemy awaiting them in Sadith Oom.

TWENTY-THREE

At the Towers of Perdition

"Damned fool. He is jeopardizing the mission," Harrin cursed.

Aron shook his head. "He is doing what he feels is best for his men. Unfortunately, he cannot see beyond the reach of his army."

"Meaning what?" Karin asked. She sat across from him at the small fire pit.

The elves confirmed there was no enemy presence within leagues, so the vanguard was able to enjoy what, in all probability, would be one of their last hot meals.

"Meaning he is basing all of his decisions on the last attack," Aron replied.

Since learning of the darkling attack on the main army the night prior, Aron and his unit had been forced to halt in place until the army drew closer. Valuable time lost because of an overcautious attitude.

Standing just outside of the light, Andolus said, "Perhaps he is right to do so. This is not the first encounter with scrathes, yet we have not encountered any since leaving Galdea. Imagine being assaulted in the deep of night by thousands of darklings, all born by the winged demons. The war might very well end here instead of the dead kingdom."

"The threat is only substantial at night. Archers would be able to pick the scrathes off at distance in daylight," Jou countered. His eyes remained locked on the rabbit he was turning over the fire.

"These are all well founded points, but the argument is pointless," Aron said. "Conn will move the army as fast or slow as he wants, despite any protestations, thus leaving us in a unique position. We are three days ride from the Towers of Perdition. Do we linger and continue forward at a handicapped pace or do we move to secure the river crossing with all haste? I may command the expedition, but I value your opinions. What should we do?"

Jou replied first. "The longer we delay, gives the enemy more time to prepare defenses. Breaking into the dead kingdom might take a dragon before this is finished."

"Do not speak of such creatures lightheartedly, my friend. They have exceptional hearing and often take interest in the affairs of men," Andolus cautioned. "I do, however, tend to agree with you. We destroyed the northern half of Imelin's army, but do not know the full strength awaiting us. The army of the Hierarchy might not be strong enough to break through should we delay overlong."

"Agreed. Speed is paramount to our success," Harrin seconded. The Galdean continued to grow more anxious, the deeper south they rode. He'd once held visions of seeing all the Free Lands before he died. Those were dreams of childhood fancy, for the world was not at all what he'd envisioned. More than anything, Harrin wanted to go home.

Long Shadow grunted. The eternally silent man stood like a statue, his eyes betraying his emotion. Aron was afraid to look into those steel grey eyes. Afraid that the pain lurking deep within was too much to bear.

"Anyone else?" he looked around.

Ute Hai cleared his throat before saying, "I do not say this lightly, for I know what awaits me. My people, what is left of them, will be waiting for us at the bridge. Denes Dron once thought Imelin to be the key to our revenge against the Hierarchy. His contract with the Black was to be our rise to glory, but we were never more than pawns. A few of the others felt as I did, and were wise enough to walk away in the middle of the night. I believe many more wish to do so but fear for their lives. The Rovers will be on the bridge."

"Will they fight?" Aron asked.

"I do not know. My heart wants to believe no, but the fanatics left in Meisthelm tell me otherwise. Regardless, it is their blood that will be spent first," Ute said.

Aron lamented for the man, while questioning whether Ute was going to be able to face those he once named friend. He secretly decided to have Sari and Nescus watch after him, with orders to eliminate the former Rover at the first sign of betrayal.

"Bringing us to another issue," Andolus said. "We have a sizeable force, most capable in many regards, but we do not have the strength to seize that bridge. Not without siege equipment."

"Conn has engineers and an artillery unit. There are plenty of forests along our path," Jou suggested.

"Aye, but how much time will it take to construct a battery of ballista? We cannot afford to broker many delays before our mission is rendered pointless."

Hidden beneath his hood, Halvor raised his head. "I suggest we ride to the bridge and begin a series of feints and raids to weaken the defenses. We must get into Sadith Oom with haste."

Few in Aron's battalion knew the truth of the priest. Of how he'd been savaged by dark magic, the only survivor of his cell. Of his sworn quest to see the end of the Staff of Life and the fulfillment of the Red Brotherhood's purpose. He remained a mystery to all but those who had been with Aron in the hidden catacombs of Gelum Drol.

Aron trusted him implicitly. “Agreed. Get the men ready to march. Conn can take his time, but we must be willing to engage the enemy as soon as possible.”

“What of the artillery?” Jou asked.

“We let Conn deal with that, but only after we get actionable intelligence. Andolus, can you send a detachment forward to scout?” Aron asked.

“I will lead them personally. Being around these filthy soldiers crinkles my nose,” the elf joked.

Aron wanted to question the judgment in his decision but needed someone he could trust. With options limited, he acquiesced. “Jou, I need a squad to return to Conn with our intent. Also, inform the General that there is need for siege engines.”

Besides, by the time Conn gets word from us, we will be too far forward to be recalled. The future belongs to me. What am I to do with it?

“Sir,” the burly Jou replied as he excused himself.

One by one, the group broke up. Missions needed planning and all needed rest. Aron sat alone for half of the night, staring into the fire until it died. His first thoughts were of the empty space where Amean should have been. Realizing they only served to hold him back, he closed his eyes and reached down to the spark of power in his soul.

The air lost humidity the closer they rode to Sadith Oom. Southern Eiterland was mostly void of settlements, though they passed numerous empty villages and homesteads. Aron frowned as he failed to recollect many details of this kingdom. He attributed many of the abandoned structures to the rise of Arlyn Gert, prompting him to question how long she and Imelin had been planning their revolution and perhaps more importantly, why the Hierarchy turned a blind eye to the goings on this far south.

Curiously, many of the buildings were not ransacked or burned. They remained largely intact, suggesting that the inhabitants were either given ample time to escape the tides of war, or were captured and taken south for whatever nefarious purpose Arlyn envisioned. Yet another failing of the Hierarchy. Was the problem systemic and largely ignored? He began to think so.

"Look!" Karin uttered.

He followed where she pointed and was greeted with the grey-red of the mountain wall separating Sadith Oom from the rest of the Free Lands. Haze clung to the peaks, blurring the image he knew would last until his dying day. The dead kingdom. The source of so many problems the Free Lands faced for over one thousand years. It had taken the better part of half a year and perils throughout numerous kingdoms for Aron to reach this point. He felt the dread pouring off the mountains.

"At last," he said. "We have come to the final showdown. I do not know if I am up to the task."

Karin felt the sting in his admission. She had no idea how much it took out of him to finally release that tension. Stretching out to grasp his hand, she said, "There is no one else in all of the kingdoms who can stop the evil growing here. You are the last descendant of Ils Kincannon. Who else to finish what he began?"

"That was not reassuring," he told her. The wry grin said otherwise.

"What can I say?" she said with a smile. "I am here for moral support."

"Nescus! I want all patrols and scouts brought in. Form ranks and expect an attack," he ordered.

Nescus clasped his fist to his chest and rode forward. The time for secrecy was ending. No doubt the enemy knew of their presence by now and were taking steps to counter any advance. Aron decided to pull in and continue their march with the expectations of impending combat. He reached down to pat his horse, calming both of their nerves.

It was an old, familiar tick. One he felt before every major engagement. Aron resisted the impulse to reach for the Staff of Life. He'd formed a bond with the totem. A silent call whispered to him. The Staff wanted to be used. Wanted to be unleashed again. Aron fought against the desire, knowing that if he gave in, his moral compass would be compromised. Should that occur he'd be no better than his ill-fated ancestor. Aron did not want to be remembered as the man who ended all life.

"Do you expect an attack?" Karin asked. She tried, and failed to find any material threat in the immediate future.

"I am unwilling to take chances. We have come too far to become lackadaisical," he replied.

The mountain wall loomed across the horizon, yet it was still nearly a day away. More than enough time for Arlyn to spring any trap. Thankfully, Aron had more than enough soldiers with him to prompt such a fight. Enough that he almost felt sorry for any Rovers sent to confront them. The vanguard marched on.

Andolus seldom felt comfortable in large crowds. People bothered him, with their pettiness and the incessant need to cloister together. He snorted. As if that gave them strength. All one needed was to look inward to find the true measure of personal strength. He much preferred being atop the walls of their fortress home of Dol'ir, with kin and friends.

He by no means viewed elves as superior. They were but one of many races in the world. His comfort level among them was at issue. Most of his people stayed among their own kind. The world continued without their influence and they were satisfied with the results. Others, like Genessen, were dissatisfied with remaining hidden from the world. Their desire to become more than what they might otherwise be, propelled them to greater levels of interaction.

Andolus often felt envious of their ability to forge ahead without looking back. This, he concluded, was as close as he was going to come to being alone and free. Twenty-five elves, and his boon companion Long Shadow, were the only living beings for a score of leagues. The desolation of the southern kingdoms was an affront to all his people held dear. Horse and rider continued to ride.

Jerns Palic rode on his right. The elf wiped the sweat from his brow and drank deeply from his water skin. "A foul land. I can feel the very world weeping."

"Great evil has been allowed to grow, thrive even. We must be cautious, for I, too, feel the grievance," Andolus said.

Thin, wispy clouds peppered the sky.

"Were we wrong to leave Dol'ir?" Jerns asked.

Once, Andolus would have found such a question offensive. There was a time when the elves were better than their current station. A true power among the greatest in the Free Lands. Humanity's rise left little room for the elves. The vast majority traveled to far kingdoms on different continents. Only a thousand remained behind, for their sacred oaths would not be undone. Those oaths left seven hundred corpses in the all but forgotten Mountains of the Fang.

"We once swore to defend these kingdoms. How can any turn away from commitment?"

Jerns scowled. His high cheeks pulled taunt. "Those oaths are no more. We suffered dearly for them, Andolus. We've been given freedom, to go where we wish and to do as we please."

"Is that much of a life when the one purpose we chose ended in failure?" Andolus asked.

"I do not question the morality of what we are doing, only the wisdom behind it," Jerns replied after a brief pause. "There is the very real possibility we will all die here."

"Death comes for us all. Does it matter where?"

Jerns shook his head. "Not so long as we stand side by side."

Satisfied, the elves drew closer to the mountains. The smell of the Croom River, ancient and dusty, reached them. Many covered their noses, for it was a stench unlike any they'd encountered in the north. Scrub brushes peppered the landscape. Ravines deep enough to conceal mounted riders stretched back to the river. The ground was coarse. It forced the elves to slow their pace.

Long Shadow stiffened suddenly, rising to scan the area more intensely. His right hand reached back for one of his swords. The elves halted in place, many going for their bows. Nothing stirred. Andolus did not see any cause for alarm.

"What is it?" he asked, wincing at the foolishness of it. Long Shadow hadn't spoken since he first reached this land.

He followed where his silent companion pointed but failed to spy anything significant. Frustrated, he was about to ride forward when Long Shadow halted him and put a finger to his ear. The elf closed his eyes and listened. On the wind, the slight pitch of voices locked in argument. How many he could not tell, though the residual noise suggested many.

The elves formed a crescent. Archers drew and waited as swordsmen slipped ahead at a slow walk. Andolus and Long Shadow rode at the center. Each expected to engage whatever foe lay in wait. They crept along the serried edge of the nearest ravine, eventually falling into single file. The argument grew louder, more intense.

The elves rounded a bend and stopped abruptly. A score of men dressed in leathers and armor that had seen better days filled the ravine. Two were on the verge of throwing blows. A watch party, Andolus surmised. He was about to order his troop back when the elf behind him pitched out of the saddle and hit the ground, lifeless. Three darts, no doubt poisoned, jutted from his chest and neck.

Mercenaries, their bickering ended, roared and began to climb out of the ravine. The easy slopes did not provide much challenge, forcing the elves to retreat and regather their effectiveness. Mercenaries poured after them.

"Now!" Andolus shouted.

Arrows sped between the riders. He felt the brush of feathers as one shaft barely missed his right cheek. Cries and grunts of pain rose from their pursuers. The elf waited until all his people were safely behind the row of archers before wheeling about and charging. Andolus took only a moment to scan the number of bodies on the ground compared to those still rising from the ravine.

His small force had the advantage. Time wasting as his mind swirled through various tactics and angles of approach, Andolus ordered an attack. Long Shadow burst ahead of the others, his larger charger relishing the opportunity to enter battle once more. The elf envied his silent friend. To be at peace with what came naturally, was a rare gift.

The mercenaries struggled to form ranks before the elves crashed into them. Arrows continued to fell enemies, but to their credit, they held firm. Long Shadow crashed into them. His mount slammed a hoof down atop a mercenary's thigh. Bone snapped in two as the man screamed and fell with Long Shadow's sword piercing his throat.

Not wanting to miss the opportunity to test his mettle, the silent warrior slid from the saddle and waded into the middle of the fight. His swords danced on the wind. Sweat soon covered his bare arms. He ripped through a man's stomach charging from the right, dropped to one knee and hacked downward to cleave a second man from shoulder to ribs with his left hand.

Long Shadow rolled forward and plunged his swords into the belly of the onrushing mercenary. With a mighty roar, he ripped his swords outward, severing the man in half. Blood rained like a curtain, splashing the silent warrior. Seeing such savage fury, the surviving mercenaries broke. Elves raced past the scene to hunt them down, lest any return to the bridge.

Andolus stared, mouth agape. Never in all his years or experience had he witnessed such savagery. Long Shadow butchered the last man without remorse. His respect for the man from across the sea went deep, but this presented a new challenge. How could anyone kill with such passion? The elf bordered on despair, for he, at last, came to understand just how much this war was changing them all.

Those elves who'd hunted the surviving mercenaries returned a short while later. Disappointment clouded their features and Andolus knew. At least one of the mercenaries had escaped back to Sadith Oom. The enemy would soon learn of their coming. They would be prepared by the time Aron arrived. *How much more slaughter can we take before our souls are forever lost?*

He feared the answer even while knowing he had no choice but to continue the advance. The confluence was about to begin. One way or another, the Free Lands and all within were never going to be the same again.

TWENTY-FOUR

The Bridge

Meisthelm continued to rebuild at a remarkable pace. Survivors emerged, slow at first — as if deciding whether the current occupation was akin to the fallen Hierarchy — before realizing their city was not going to be fixed unless they assisted. Armed patrols increased and the amount of enemy activity dropped. Scores of Rovers and mercenary cells were rooted out and eliminated. Justice resumed at a slow pace.

Winter broke without fanfare. What little snows remained melted and were absorbed back into the earth. Temperatures rose. Dalstrom enjoyed this time of year. Not hot, yet not cold either. There was no need for wearing his heavy robes of office. He wore them for comfort's sake. That and they made him feel safe. Odd, that one of the most powerful men in the Free Lands should need the childish comforts of an old robe.

His meeting with Kelanvex began much as it always did. She berated him for dragging her up to the rooftops, while he sighed and ignored her. Kelanvex was one of the brightest priests he'd seen during his time in the Order. Gifted with magic and natural insights made her a powerful rising figure. He toyed with the notion of grooming her to replace him when the time came to step down. Fortunately, that was a day long off.

She sensed his melancholy and changed her approach. "Are you certain we are doing the right thing?"

"What else would you have us do? The purpose of our Order is to ensure the Staff of Life is never unleashed again," he replied. "We cannot have a second Ils Kincannon."

Kelanvex frowned. The Black Imelin once provided that threat. His timely demise should have left the Red Brotherhood content in the knowledge they'd performed their jobs. Dalstrom remained unconvinced. Or perhaps he wasn't willing to risk any chances. She wished she could figure him out. The leader of the Order remained an enigma to her.

"The assassins have left the city."

His eyebrow rose. "You saw them?"

"I followed them for a league before returning to Meisthelm," she confirmed. "Has the Council of Delegates been informed?"

"No." He paused before answering.

Kelanvex sensed his duplicity. "You risk ruining all we have striven for. Dlorn will not sit idle once he learns of this… betrayal."

He turned, surprise on his face. "Betrayal? I serve the Order and we serve the Free Lands. Is it betrayal to ensure the Staff returns to obscurity? I think not!"

"Others will not view it so," she defended.

"Perhaps not. We must be cautious. History stands upon a crossroads. Vigilance is required if we are to guide our people into a new, better age. Has there been word from any of the southern cells?" he asked.

She nodded, still unsure of his true motivation. "Several are already moving. The sleeper has awakened and is already in Sadith Oom."

"What of the wizard?" Dalstrom asked.

"On his way. It appears the former Councilor Marth was successful."

All major pieces were in play. Dalstrom exhaled a heavy breath. He'd done all that was required of him since the development of the war. The fulfillment of purpose was exhausting yet satisfying. *So why am I terrified of what might come*?

"Thank you, Kelanvex. You have done all I asked and more. I … could not have accomplished this without your aid. I am indebted to you," Dalstrom said.

Dismissed, Kelanvex slipped away. Her mind raced and it was with reservation she arrived at the one inescapable conclusion. Dalstrom needed to be watched.

He watched her go before returning his attention to the city of his birth. Meisthelm. City of kings and the ruling elite. He looked forward to seeing the results of this transformation as the city struggled to regain a sense of self. Satisfied his work was done for the night, Dalstrom returned to his chambers. Despite coming to acceptance of his position, he continued to find it odd, almost uncomfortable, that he now resided in one of the former High Councilor's chambers.

Closing the gold filigreed door behind him, Dalstrom brushed through the antechamber and private office to enter his bedroom. The giant bed was large enough to fit four abreast. Plush blankets and pillows were surrounded by four carved pillars connected with iron bars overhead. A room fit for a king. He shed his robes and froze as the hair on the backs of his arms rose.

"Who is there?" he demanded.

Bright blue electricity cackled from the plush chair in the far corner. "You and I need to talk."

He squinted, readying his own magic. "Who is that? Anni? What are you doing here?"

"I could ask you the same, priest. What game are you playing at behind our backs?" she demanded.

"Release your magic, old woman. I am no threat to you," he protested.

Her blast sizzled inches from him as he made to leave. "You're not going anywhere until you explain to me why you've contracted Gen Haroud to go to Sadith Oom. Your answers depend on whether I kill you or not."

Dalstrom slumped in defeat. There were some days when nothing went according to plan.

Every attempt to draw out the defenders of Sadith Oom ended in failure. Aron tried sending small groups forward and when that didn't work, he mustered his entire force. Not a single Rover or darkling moved to counter. Frustrated, the lord of the Golden Warriors withdrew his force and established a defensive perimeter for the night.

"A most persistent foe," Andolus remarked, once his inspection of the lines was complete

Aron folded his arms. "I don't understand. Every other time the darklings have attacked on impulse. They should be swarming us by now."

"Clear evidence that another commands them."

"Who? We saw Denes Dron's body. Imelin is dead, as is Gulnick Baach. Who is left?" Aron asked.

"We must assume Arlyn Gert has collected her own command staff. Darklings are beasts, naught but minions, and the Rovers have proven capable allies. Do not forget the mercenaries we encountered yesterday," the elf explained. "An entire host of potential foes might await us on the far side of that bridge."

"It would be wise to brace for the possibility of senior army leaders who might have defected when Arlyn announced her bid for power," Ute suggested.

The Rover's gaze was locked on the Towers of Perdition. What remained of his people waited in the shadows.

Aron winced. "He is correct. This rebellion has been long in the making. There is no telling how many within the Hierarchy have turned traitor. We cannot plan our assault accordingly, however, for there are far too many possibilities confronting us."

"How do we overcome that obstacle?" Harrin asked. The Galdean, tired from traveling and missing every major engagement of the war thus far, wanted to close with the enemy.

"Did Conn give any indication of constructing siege engines?" Aron asked the younger Golden Warrior at his side.

"He did not, though I was under the impression he was not overly enthused to do so. The General seems most persistent in his ways," Sari reported.

"We are on our own for at least two more days," Andolus said.

Aron punched a fist into his open palm and began pacing. "Attacking the bridge full on will only result in getting us killed, even though I suspect they would not expect anything so foolish."

"The bards would certainly appreciate it," Jou grumbled from atop the tree stump he'd adopted as a chair.

"Wonderful but let us not give them reason for song just yet," Aron said. "I have an idea."

Mist covered the ground on both shores. Sunrise was still far off, though the sky was growing lighter already. Reeds and waist high grass rippled in the pre-dawn breeze. Out of range of the torches lighting both ends of the bridge, five hundred elves and men crawled agonizingly slow. They halted in line once they were within bow range and waited. Aron knew the elves could see clear enough in the murk, but his soldiers needed more to strike their targets accurately.

Aron rose just high enough to get a good look at the bridge. What he saw left him feeling worse than before. The enemy reinforced their defenses on the northern shore, adding a full company of Rovers to accent the darklings lurking behind sandbag walls and fortified positions. Elves and darklings were ancient enemies who knew each other well enough, but the addition of the Rovers changed the dynamic.

He held the advantage in numbers, but only until the enemy reorganized and reacted to send reinforcements across the bridge. Aron secretly hoped for such, knowing it was the only way he was going to be able to get any notion of the enemy's true strength. Darkness obscured his vision, even through the looking glass. Despite that, he was able to discern four individual barricaded fighting positions behind a narrow trench. The trench being filled remained a mystery, but one he was willing to explore before committing.

Andolus moved with the stealth of a viper, stopping beside Aron. The elf made mental notes of the defenses before lowering back into the grass. Aron did likewise.

"Several hundred, but a manageable enough number," Andolus whispered.

Aron agreed. "Bring up the others. We attack just before dawn."

The combined force slid into position. Men with their crossbows edged closer, as their weapons were more powerful and dangerously effective at close range. Elven longbows would begin the assault with the intent of drawing the enemy in where the Golden Warriors could wield their crossbows. Aron had every intention of killing the enemy garrison and securing the northern shore. Holding it for two days was a matter for another time.

The first rays of pale sunlight edged across the horizon. As one, three hundred elves rose from the tall grass and fired. Darklings and men pitched over, many falling into the river and were swept away. Confusion gripping them, the survivors milled about as another salvo dropped scores more.

"In the grass!" a Rover bellowed.

Swords were drawn. Men hurried into formation and charged. Scurrying around their feet, darklings brandished their daggers and joined the attack. The elves loosed a third salvo before giving the illusion of retreating. Bolstered by their apparent cowardice, the Rovers pushed harder. Two hundred men rose less than ten meters away and fired. The crossbow bolts punched through armor and knocked several off their feet. Men and darklings fell dead. Red blood painted the fat blades of grass.

The Rover charge faltered, giving the elves — who'd already stowed their bows and drawn swords — the opportunity to attack. Aron, Long Shadow, and Andolus led their warriors into the slaughter. Elves and men clashed but there was never doubt to the contest. A handful of Rovers attempted to retreat across the bridge but were cut down by crossbowmen.

Aron kicked an oncoming darkling in the face before swinging down to take the top half of his head. Less than a hundred enemy soldiers remained to halt the elves and they were slaughtered with almost reckless aggression. Long Shadow was the first to reach the bridge. His broadswords were covered in gore, each dripping blood, but the big man wasn't even breathing hard. Elves and a handful of men soon joined him.

The battle ended without fanfare. One elf and two men died. Acceptable losses considering the entire defensive garrison was slaughtered. Aron crouched beside the trench and dipped a gloved finger into the murky fluid.

"Pitch," he said, looking up at Andolus.

"They meant to burn us out. A pity we cannot use this for our purposes."

"No, but it will give us a small measure of delay should we be forced to retreat in a hurry," Aron said.

Nescus joined them. "Commander, we've secured the bridgehead and are ready to move the rear elements up."

"Do so."

The sooner Aron had his full force in position, the better he'd feel. Sunlight grew stronger, banishing the darkness for another night. Soon the enemy would be able to see them. Sergeants issued orders and a great effort was begun to shift the stationary defenses around to face the southern shore. The men moved quickly.

"How long do you think?" Andolus asked.

Aron hadn't stopped looking at the far side since the battle ended. He couldn't understand why the enemy refused to send additional troops to investigate. Clearly they were expecting an attack, but to abandon their carefully established position on the northern shore without effort made no tactical sense.

"Under normal circumstances, I would venture they should have already come, but this is most odd," Aron said.

"We could always send a foray halfway across." The elf suggested.

Aron didn't think many would volunteer for that. "A suicide mission?"

"An attempt to discern what our enemy is thinking," Andolus countered.

"I wouldn't mind stretching my legs a little," Nescus announced, "Sir."

The Golden Warriors exchanged a look only men in combat understood. Executing the mission wasn't about who wanted to do it, or even why. It was about doing what needed to be done to ensure the safety and in the most extreme conditions, survival of the men to the left and right.

"Very well, but I will go with you," Aron said. He held up a hand before Nescus could protest. "What better way to provoke a response from our silent friends across the river than by presenting them with one of the most recognizable figures on our side?"

"Providing those across the river are educated enough to understand the importance of said man taunting them," Andolus countered.

"Was that humor?"

The elf splayed out his hands. "A modest attempt. We are far too serious of late."

Aron placed a hand on the taller elf's shoulder and laughed. "One day I will teach you the finer points of human interaction. If I live long enough, that is."

"I would be remiss if I did not accompany you across the river. I would not want to rob you of the opportunity."

"Great. We're all going to get killed together," Nescus muttered.

The trio waited only long enough to ensure the defenses were emplaced before setting across the aged wooden structure. Several planks were missing. Others were broken or jagged. Time and disuse destabilized the span, leaving Aron to question if it would support the weight of an entire army.

"Not entirely stable," Aron remarked.

Andolus resisted the impulse to stomp his foot on one of the weaker looking boards. The river flowed fast and reminded him of a foul stew often found in off the road taverns. Far from being a masterpiece of engineering, the bridge should have collapsed long ago.

"Why is this structure left to rot with time when the Towers of Perdition are magically protected?" Andolus asked. His suspicions continued to grow.

They were a quarter of the way across. Heads were popping up from the far side. A few score at first that quickly grew into hundreds and then thousands. The entrance to Sadith Oom was well defended.

"There are concealed catapult emplacements to the left and right," the elf pointed out.

Aron focused on the chest high wall blocking the passage into the dead kingdom. His mind, tactically trained, raced through possibilities unseen. How many rows of barriers were there? Were there more trenches filled with pitch, or worse?

He would have companies of archers emplaced on the mountainsides. Any enemy assault would be met with heavy casualties. Aron spied the open beaches flanking the bridge. Not overly wide, but several hundred meters long and partially sheltered from the entrance.

"Commander! What is that?"

Aron snapped around to see where Nescus pointed. His heart lurched. A pair of thin ropes ran the length of the bridge for as far as they could see. Hardly concealed beneath and around the rotted edges, the ropes made his heart beat faster. Aron hurried to the edge of the bridge and bent down. He was horrified with what he saw. They weren't ropes at all. They were fuses.

"Get off the bridge, now!"

Nescus turned to sprint away without second thought. Andolus waited for Aron to catch up.

"What is it?" he asked.

"The bridge is rigged to detonate."

"Which explains why they haven't seemed willing to cross," the elf concluded. He skidded to a halt and gave a final glance back across the river. The tiny flicker of flame confirmed his worst fears. The enemy had lit the fuse. "It is going to explode!"

He and Aron sprinted. Stride after stride the pair hurried to escape death. Yet no matter how fast they ran, the fuse burned faster. Each boot step echoed like thunder. Aron began shouting for those soldiers nearest the edge to get back. He failed to see Andolus stop and hurry back to the edge.

Dagger in hand, Andolus knelt beside the fuse and began to cut. The cord was thick and difficult to cut, forcing him to saw harder. Sweat dripped down into his eyes. His muscles strained and was at last rewarded by his blade slicing through the fuse. Andolus rose to leave when the first drum of pitch exploded.

Flame and debris showered over the immediate area. Several of the defenders were knocked off their feet, blown back by the concussive force. Aron was among the first to pick himself back up. Tears in his eyes, his face stained with soot and blood, he desperately searched for any sign of the elf. Smoke and debris obscured his vision. When it cleared, he saw the amount of devastation. Most of the bridge was either gone or burning. Andolus was gone.

"NO!"

He turned to see Long Shadow bellowing his grief.

TWENTY-FIVE

The Dead Kingdom

Sadith Oom was unlike any other kingdom in the Free Lands. A contradiction of senses leaving many confused. Legends said the land was once ripe and fertile. It was long considered the jewel of the kingdoms. Ambassadors and royalty from across the seas often visited to form bonds of trade and friendship. For a time, the kingdom was one of the richest and most peaceful in the known world.

Then war happened and the glory of Sadith Oom burned in the rage of wizard fire. Tens of thousands were killed in the largest instance of genocide in recorded history. The transgressions of a relative few were played out across the entire land. Truth of how the war began was lost, though many of the brightest scholars theorized it began as most human travesties: with jealousy.

Men, of all the races, never seemed content with what he had. The desire for more propelled the race to levels of greatness, advancing society often at unprecedented levels. It also served as the harbinger for war and unmitigated violence. Ils Kincannon, for whatever reasons now lost to time and the natural human condition, sought to reshape the world in his image. His armies swept across the Free Lands, offering each with the option of joining him or perish.

Much like now, his war carried on until reaching the far south. It was long theorized that his original intent was to destroy Mordrun Hath, thus freeing the people to live according to their personal beliefs, instead of the almost fanatic control of the wizards responsible for creating the Staff of Life. A trail of corpses decorated the lands in his wake.

The end arrived most unexpectedly. A great poisoning was begun, some say by the wizards themselves, for they had grown desperate to halt the army of the Seven Manacles. Every living thing in the southern kingdom withered and died, until naught but an ocean of sand and dirt remained. Whole tribes were eradicated. Survivors were few, tending to burrow deep into the mountains to escape the tide of violence.

Perhaps that helped stop Ils Kincannon, for the mortal spirit can only handle so much before it breaks. The senseless slaughter of innocents halted his army on the Plains of Darkpool. He realized that his actions were among the root causes of so much suffering and wanted no part of that legacy. Ils allowed his army to become trapped and eventually, wiped out to the last man by the armies of the fledgling Hierarchy. To facilitate the peaceful transition out of the war, he refused to surrender. Ils Kincannon died with his men.

Sylin recited what he knew of the conflict and still could not figure out how such utter desolation had come to Sadith Oom. Too many gaps in the recorded histories remained to get an accurate picture. He now wondered if they were deliberately left out. Did Kincannon's followers intend for a second revival of hostilities long after his death? The possibilities frightened him.

Dust devils raced across the plains. Out there, lost to time and progress, lay the remains of arguably the most famous man in history. Sylin recalled that there was no official ceremony to lay those souls to rest. Their bodies were left to rot in the sun, while the victors returned north to rebuild what was lost. Sylin found the callousness mildly disturbing. Soldiers deserved better, even if they held opposing ideations.

"Stare too hard and you'll burn your eyes. Damn, but this is a hot land and we are not even in it yet," Camden said.

The journeyman sat beside him and stared. Each new sight helped him realize that he needed a major life change. His ways, while they'd served him well for the first part of his life, were largely unfulfilling. Camden longed for a day when he no longer needed to wear a sword. The thought left a smile on his face.

Noting this, Sylin said, "You're in a good mood today."

"I'm still alive. Considering all we have been through, that is cause enough for celebration," he replied.

"Indeed. Are the others ready to move?" Sylin asked.

"As far as I know. Some seem fairly shaken up after our fight in the tunnel."

The former Councilman nodded. "I have been giving that some thought. Those worms only attacked after we made our presence known, suggesting they are not overtly aggressive."

"Seemed aggressive to me when they were killing us."

"What if they were placed there as a defense mechanism?" Sylin asked.

"How do you mean?"

He gestured to the plains. "This kingdom holds many secrets worth killing for. Secrets the old orders would want to keep buried from the general population. Wizards are fickle sorts…"

"Not the word I would use," Camden sneered.

"Indeed, but they are not fools. They had already lost control of the Staff of Life and were murdering their own land. It is not inconceivable to think they created the worms to defend the less known entrances into the kingdom in the event of a second revolution," Sylin concluded.

"Wouldn't the worms have died long ago without the magic to sustain them?"

"I do not profess to understand the ways of wizards," Sylin said. *Though I am on the way to becoming one*.

The growth of magic within him left Sylin with mixed emotions. He found the power an unwelcome necessity. More than once on his journey, it had saved their lives, but he failed to come to terms with the need to continue developing his powers. Meeting Elxander certainly did not help his attitude. The ancient wizard was more hassle than either Sylin or Camden cared to deal with, yet Sylin couldn't help but feel a time of closure was fast approaching and Elxander was meant to play a pivotal role before the dust settled.

"At least we don't have to go back through those tunnels on the way out," Camden tried to sound jovial. He doubted there was going to be a return trip but knew better than to voice his concerns. Enough ill had already befallen them. Adding more stress to the situation served no purpose.

"We should get moving. I have a feeling the heat is only going to get worse," Sylin suggested. "Rouse the others."

Mordrun Hath, according to the frayed and decidedly outdated map Elxander provided, was still many days south. The terrain was relatively flat once they climbed out of the mountains but the lack of vegetation and a natural water source added peril. Not to mention the untold numbers of enemy soldiers already secured within the kingdom. The journey was potentially going to be the most arduous since leaving Meisthelm all those months ago.

Elxander provided no additional support during their descent. He'd grown increasingly introverted, as if being assailed by a plague of faded memories suddenly returning in force. Sylin couldn't begin to imagine, if his suspicions were correct, what it must be like returning to the scene of one of the greatest crimes in history. He also secretly wondered how much Elxander had had to do with the desolation of the kingdom.

Awkward silence mired the group. Though they'd shed blood together, the dwarves and goblins continued to maintain their standoffish differences. Sylin wished there was more he could do to bridge the gap, but some hatreds ran deep. He made a note of pulling Yerg, the goblin leader, to the side the next time they halted.

The sun was barely above the mountaintops and the heat was obscene. Sylin felt as if his eyes were burning. Whatever sweat had accumulated, evaporated in an instant. He had never felt such intensity before, leading the fledgling wizard, questioning why the Hierarchy practically never sent envoys or patrols this far south. Perhaps the Free Lands would not be in such a predicament if policy was different.

He faulted Zye Terrio for this. Their friendship was tepid at best. A loose bond of commonality in serving the lands. Zye's policies led the kingdoms to total war. It was a failing Sylin could never forgive. Resigning his position seemed the most prudent act at the time, only now he wasn't sure. The High Council needed to move in a new direction if the Hierarchy was going to survive to its next iteration.

Mind wandering, Sylin failed to notice the sudden shift in the goblins. They fanned out, forming a semi-circle around and behind the dwarves. Weapons were drawn, understandably so, considering the dangers inherent around them. The dwarves did the same, though they marched in double file.

Dust rose above the shimmer on the plains. Too large to be anything but an enemy patrol, Sylin cursed his carelessness for leading them too near the Towers of Perdition and the main avenue leading down to Morthus. The dust cloud was moving in their direction. He looked back. The mountains were too far away. They'd never make it in time. Nor were there places to hide. They were trapped in the open with only one option. Fight. He was about to issue commands when the goblins quickly surrounded them.

Swords were leveled at the dwarves. The dwarves and men were stripped of their weapons. Dwarves were valiant fighters, but even they knew when the odds were too much. Goblins snarled in their foul language, while Yerg went to the head of the column and ordered them to continue marching. Magic sprang to life. Sylin readied to attack his betrayers. A pained look from Yerg prevented him from unleashing his might.

"What is happening?" Camden whispered.

"I… I don't know," was all Sylin managed.

That look. Why was Yerg almost pleading with him not to attack? Clearly the goblin intended on passing the dwarves over to the enemy. Sylin doubted the goblins had ever been on their side and cursed his inability to see matters before they happened. Strangely, Elxander remained passive. The ancient man hobbled on with a faint smile.

Dark shapes emerged from the dust. Goblins. What looked to be an entire company, possibly battalion. Sylin's heart sank. Even with his magic, there was no way the nine of them were going to win free from the sheer size of the enemy force. His quest was ended. He'd failed.

Both goblin forces ground to a halt twenty meters apart. Yerg stepped forward to meet with his counterpart. What was said was beyond Sylin. Languages held no place for him, though he wished otherwise. Snapping and snarling, the goblins soon broke out in raucous laughter. Sylin felt the dwarves tense. Garin was knocked to his knees by a pair of goblins guarding him. The other goblin troop laughed as they continued heading toward the Towers of Perdition. Soon, they were naught but distant specks.

Yerg stopped his goblins and snapped an order. They immediately handed the dwarves their weapons. Some going so far as to apologize for the rough treatment. Garin laughed and brushed off his trousers.

Sylin confronted Yerg. "Explain, now."

"Relax, Sylin. Yerg here did us a favor," Garin intervened.

Camden, face a harsh shade of crimson, almost shouted, "A favor how?"

"Those goblins were heading for the bridge. Seems an army is approaching. It looks like war is following us down here," the dwarf explained. "More so, he told his kin that we were captured and being brought to the masters in Morthus for questioning. Yerg saved our skins."

"You speak their tongue?" Sylin asked.

Garin shrugged. "You learn your enemies after a time."

Yerg nodded in agreement. "They believed me, but others will come. A great battle approaches. Many units are heading to the front. We must hurry away."

Satisfied, but still wary, Sylin resumed the lead of their expedition. He was impressed with the quick thinking Yerg showed and dismayed that none of them had considered the possibility ahead of time. The goblins were proving to be an incredible benefit. He hoped that luck continued, for Sylin had a suspicion that the journey to Mordrun Hath was going to get worse. He hoped he was wrong.

The company halted at dusk, though Sylin was loath to do so. Without cover or proper concealment, they were prey for whatever predators roamed the dead kingdom. They hadn't spotted any animal life yet, so that meant goblins, or worse. He ordered a double perimeter set and posted roving guards. The Forge of Wizards was too close to allow for mistakes.

Animals of enormous size passed nearby during the middle of the night. So large, Sylin had trouble making out their shadows in the deeper darkness. Elxander told him they were ghosts from long ago. Tusked herbivores that once roamed these plains in abundance. Sylin had no idea whether this was true or not, but the creatures passed without incident.

The dwarves broke camp after a quick travel meal of dried meat and the last of their biscuits. Garin even went so far as to offer Yerg and the other goblins sergeants places in their circle. Animosity would never fade, but the two sides were steadily becoming allies. Respect, never given, had been earned earlier. It was a start.

The first sign of trouble occurred shortly after midday. A large body of forces was spotted moving in their general direction. Though distance was difficult to gauge, Sylin had no doubt that the shadow signature of this group was much larger than the goblins who had confronted them earlier. Not even Yerg or his goblins would be adequate force to stop whatever was coming.

"We should wait," Elxander suggested, though his tone left little doubt of his assumed authority.

Garin pointed back. “For that? To do what, kill us without effort? Whatever they are, we must assume them hostile.”

“He’s right. This is enemy territory. There are no friendlies this far south,” Sylin added.

Elxander merely smiled. Soft, yet deceiving. It was the look a father gave a son who thought he knew better. Sylin felt as if he’d just been scolded.

The dark blurs neared without picking up their pace, eventually turning into shapes and then massive figures that made the dwarves and goblins recoil. Weapons were reached for, formations made.

Sylin snatched Camden by the shoulder as the journeyman went to join the lines. “What is this?”

The look of horror on Camden’s face told him enough. “Trolls.”

Sylin drew his sword and reached deep within for his magic. He passed a quick glance at Elxander and was surprised to find the ancient wizard standing with his hands clasped patiently behind his back.

Mind swirling with seemingly impossible scenarios, Sylin struggled with the concept of the trolls not being enemies. Everything he read of them suggested they were brutal creatures, butchers of many races. He failed to see any way his meager band, though bolstered considerably by the goblins, would be able to adequately defend against a troll horde. Still, Sylin couldn’t resign himself to accepting a fight was about to break out.

Camden saw the look and whispered, “You realize they are going to kill us? Even with that crotchety old wizard, we do not have enough strength to hold a line.”

“We don’t know that, Camden,” Sylin insisted. “Yerg and his company turned out to be friendly. What is to say these trolls aren’t similar?”

"Have you ever seen a troll fight?"

"No," he admitted.

"This can only end in slaughter. Ours," Camden fell silent as the dark figures emerged as individuals.

They were terrifying to behold. Nine, some ten, feet tall and heavily muscled. They were beasts with jutting tusks and sloping, heavy foreheads that made their eyes appear small. Each was armored with boiled leather plate and a variety of weapons capable of rendering the dwarves into naught but pulverized meat. Sylin felt fear for the first time since encountering the dragon in the Grimstone Mountains.

The trolls ground to a halt and waited. Sylin considered moving forward to confront them but paused when several humans emerged from within their ranks. At their side was a giant of man, though with less evolved features common in the modern era. He sucked in his breath as he studied the giant. Bronzed from a lifetime of being in the sun, the man was thin and wiry with thick eyebrows and tufts of hair on his arms and legs. His garb was old but sown animal hides that had clearly seen better times.

"Who's in charge here?" a burly man with many scars and a tired look demanded.

Sylin didn't hesitate. "I am Councilman Sylin Marth of the High Council. To whom do I speak?"

"Poros Pendyier, leader of the Free Rebellion."

Though he'd never heard of such, Sylin couldn't debate the authority with which Poros introduced himself. They studied each other, both clearly thinking the other a threat.

The giant broke the silence by stepping forward and pointing a crooked finger at Elxander. "You!"

His bark echoed over the otherwise empty plains. Dwarves, goblins, and a handful of trolls readied to attack as Horus stepped toward the wizard with more open hostility than any of them had ever seen.

"Hold! What is the meaning of this?" Sylin demanded, though his voice came out weak, broken.

Enraged, Horus continued. "This man is responsible for the death of my people! He killed my kin! Slaughtered my bloodline until only I remain! This man I will kill with pleasure!"

Sylin saw the magic in Elxander's barred fists. He couldn't allow both sides to be slaughtered as the wizard unleashed his full power. Simmering anger reflected in the wizard's eyes. Closing his eyes, Sylin saw the end claim them all and he was powerless to stop it. His meager powers were not enough to stop one of the most storied wizards in the history of the Free Lands.

TWENTY-SIX

Cleansing Flames

Flames burned on either side of the advancing Golden Warriors. A wake of darkling corpses lay behind them as the army forged deeper into the Wood of Ills. Gone was the luster and mystery of the forest. The dangers became corporeal, manifested by creatures from a forgotten age. The men of the Free Lands aimed to send them all back into the irrelevance of memory.

Embarrassed by the severity of the initial engagement, Marshal Sevron deployed his men with ruthless efficiency. They plunged into the forest in golden armored wedges, stopping for nothing. Casualties were highest in the beginning. Slowly, almost too gradually, Sevron's men grasped their enemy's tactics and responded in kind. Thousands now lay dead in the ash and melting snow.

Supply trains constantly shuttled fresh supplies into the advance, while ferrying out those too wounded to continue fighting. It was an efficient operation. Sevron, having retired from spending two full days at the tip of the spear, now directed the army. He regretted burning the forest but there were times when needs must. Each loss of life propelled his actions to the edge of becoming drastic.

Acres of the forest were already charred ruins. Without any place to hide, the darklings were forced to fight or flee. Many chose the only way they understood and were slaughtered by vengeful men with sharp iron. It almost wasn't fair. Sevron viewed a stack of corpses dispassionately. Killing them became easier once he accepted they were naught but beasts, savage killers without compassion or inspiration.

With so much burned acreage, Sevron was forced to adjust his tactics. He drew his forces in, almost forming a line separated by a few hundred meters to give them room to fight without being atop each other. The forest burned on either side. He didn't care if the entire place burned to the ground. The darklings would find no purchase to carry out their reign of terror in this part of the Free Lands.

"Sir, I have the latest intelligence reports."

Scowling, Sevron reluctantly took his eyes from his foes, "Go on, Captain."

Thorp struggled to conceal his disappointment. The glory in this battle was meant to be his. Sevron already had his time to bask in the glory of victory. Now he was a relic best left to be put out to pasture with the other greybeards. How was he ever going to advance by standing in Sevron's shadow?

"Forward scouting units have reached what they believe to be the main darkling stronghold. There are some hundreds milling about and…"

"Yes?"

Thorp swallowed. "We have reason to believe that a great many are underground. The army is going to have to go down to get them out."

Thus costing us untold lives in the process. Sevron's look turned grim. As successful as the campaign had turned out, he wasn't willing to risk his men on a whim. "I need more than an assumption before committing our forces like that, Thorp. Has it been confirmed?"

"I am working on that, Sir," Thorp replied.

Sevron nodded. “Get me answers, Captain and fast. The tide has shifted against these creatures. Now is the time to break them.”

“Yes, Marshal,” Thorp saluted, despite standing protocol for units in the field, and left.

Sevron had hoped their issues, while strikingly obvious, were cleared after his last conversation, yet Thorp insisted on his infantile reservations. The man was a growing problem. He briefly considered ordering Thorp to the frontlines. No doubt the junior officer would relish the opportunity to demonstrate how he was meant for greatness, while being the future of the Golden Warriors. Disturbed, the Marshal returned to his solitude.

Sergeant Laris returned to the front with those survivors of his ill-fated patrol. They hungered for the opportunity to repay the darkling’s generosity and were given the chance not long after reentering the forest. The darklings were frightening, and attacked without warning or mercy, but he was wise to them now. His blade hewed heads and limbs, as if it were sport.

Flames spreading through the treetops, the conflagration helped drive his foes into his waiting sword. After three days, Laris was exhausted. His men were likewise, but none requested to be relieved. This was their battle as much as anyone’s. He couldn’t have been prouder.

“Sergeant, this clears out the last batch,” a blood-stained trooper said with a goofy grin.

Laris stepped down on the back of a darkling’s head and leaned forward to wipe his sword free of the grime and gore. “A good day’s work but this wretched forest is not cleared yet. How many did we lose?”

“Phelbin.”

Laris cocked an eyebrow. “That’s it?”

"Yes, Sergeant."

"I'll be damned. The lads are getting better at this!" He was encouraged. Learning how to combat the specialized tactics the darklings employed proved challenging at first but his men were gradually getting the better of them. They were, after all, just beasts with rudimentary knowledge of iron weapons. He'd killed enough animals over the course of his life to grow comfortable with fighting the darklings.

Grinning, he said, "What say we go and find another batch to kill? My arm still has strength left in it."

The soldier matched his grinned. "Aye, Sergeant. I will round up the boys."

"Good lad," Laris nodded.

He watched the man go, pausing to think of what Marshal Sevron and the others would think of him now. There was no way they could continue to view his earlier failure in the same manner as before. He might even get a medal out of it. Pleased with his actions, Laris went to find the rest of his platoon. There was still much left to do before the campaign ended.

Two more days of hard fighting brought the Golden Warriors within fifty meters of the rumored underground hive. Sevron continued to develop a plan as the army marched, burned, and fought for every meter of ground. Ranks of soldiers fanned out to form a perimeter around the tunnels. Access points were uncovered and guarded to prevent darklings from escaping. They could hear breathing underground. A good sign.

Engineers worked tirelessly to establish a rudimentary road through the remains of the forest. Great wagons pulled by teams of oxen rumbled over hewn logs and gravel pulled from the nearby riverbed. Each carried barrels of pitch and oil. Captains, already in position, directed the wagons to where they were needed. All was in place by nightfall of the third day.

Nervous with anticipation, Sevron paced through the muck. His boots and lower leggings were coated in mud but he cared not. The campaign to rid the Wood of Ills was drawing to a close. Why was it he did not feel at ease? Sevron couldn't help but feel he was missing a key element. But what? The frustration left him locked in place, suddenly fearful of making the wrong decision.

He spied Thorp stomping through the muck to reach him and soured. The man had a habit of arriving precisely when Sevron did not need him. "What is it, Captain?"

"The Quartermaster reports all barrels are in place and ready to be deployed. Company commanders are prepared to assault the enemy position. They await your word," Thorp said, taken off guard by being confronted first.

"What don't we see, Thorp?" he asked.

Thorp hesitated. "I do not understand what you mean."

Sevron gestured to where the nearest wagons sat. "The enemy has proven to be cunning throughout our engagement. Why should they allow themselves to become trapped underground as we approach?"

"Sir, we have killed thousands during our march north. There cannot be many remaining."

"I wonder…"

As if in answer to his doubts, hundreds of darklings burst from the cover of the unburned forest to the north. Many soldiers were swarmed and killed before they had the opportunity to react. Many others were wounded while rallying. Pitched battle ensued.

Sevron drew his sword. "Maintain watch on the other directions! Order all captains to drop their barrels while there is yet time!"

Panicked, Thorp forgot his animosities and hurried about his orders. A great cacophony erupted, drowning out all other sounds as pitched battle spread across the immediate area. Men and darklings fell. Arrows flit here and there sporadically. Fields of fire were greatly reduced and largely ineffective. To their credit, the Golden Warriors responded with speed and decisiveness.

Sevron plunged his sword through a darkling's chest and kicked the body away. A second was run through by a pike and left writhing upon the stake. The Marshal of the Golden Warriors bordered on despair until he saw men bearing torches race toward the open tunnels. Barrels were cracked open, their contents pouring down to where the others waited. One of his men was tackled by three darklings and murdered. His torch skittered away.

Arcs of flames plunging into the ground told him all was not lost. His soldiers were rallying. Gouts of flame erupted from underground. Explosions followed as trails of fire reached the intact barrels of pitch. Those closest to the tunnels were thrown from their feet. Several darklings and more than one soldier collapsed as flames swallowed them. Shrill screams pierced Sevron's mind. Sounds he would relive to his dying days.

Secondary blasts ripped the ground apart, collapsing the center of the tunnel complex. An inferno emerged, devouring all within reach as fresh oxygen fueled the flames. Sevron braced as the ground shifted and groaned beneath him. He stepped, twisted his ankle and fell. Without a helmet, his head struck a thick tree root and Sevron knew only darkness.

Thick, black smoke curled between the remaining treetops, turning the canopy slick with residue from the flames. Darkling bodies were collected and thrown into the still burning pit. The area stank of burned flesh and hair. Triage areas were set up to the south. Many of the walking wounded had already been treated and returned to their companies. Those more severely injured were placed in order of severity for treatment. Wet weather ponchos covered too many from head to toe.

Sevron watched his army securing the area. He felt foolish with a bloodstained bandage wrapped around his head but the surgeons were adamant about it. There was an almost nostalgic air about the makeshift camp. There'd been no sign of darklings for two days. Most of the flames had burned out, leaving the landscape a charred ruin for as far as the eye could see.

Tired of being idle, Sevron pushed himself up and went to the hospital tents. There he found a morose Thorp. Gone was the feeling of self-importance. The young captain was a greatly changed man, and for good reason, Sevron thought, as he looked down on the stump of Thorp's left arm.

"Captain, how fare you?" he asked.

Dried tears streaked his face through the grime. Thorp was reluctant to look up, to meet the judging gaze of a man he once assumed inferior and past his prime. "The doctors say I should be retired."

Sevron nodded. It was a fact they all must face. That day when a lifetime suddenly grinds to a halt and all that remained were the memories of. "You will be well looked after."

Unable to stop the tears, Thorp broke down and hid his face. Sevron reached out to squeeze his shoulder before wandering off to give the man the space he needed.

Some lessons taught did not need further exploration. Sevron walked for what felt like hours. His mind gradually turned from thoughts of loss and regrets to the future and what must be done next. The Wood of Ills had been cleared of darkling presence but there was still much left to do. First on his list was to inform the newly established garrison at Dol'ir. The Galdeans, no longer needing to worry over watching their backs, would now be able to focus the fullness of their wrath on Suroc Tol.

TWENTY-SEVEN

Crossings

Catapults launched massive boulders into the static defenses. Sun-dried mud walls burst apart or collapsed into dust with each strike. Men and darklings were crushed. Elves, enraged by the loss of Andolus, arced flaming arrows down into the wooden guard towers. The well-developed defenses of Sadith Oom were systematically reduced to ash and rubble, but would it be enough?

Under the joint direction of Haf Forager and Jalos Carb, thousands of soldiers foraged across the countryside for logs large enough to form the base of rafts. The army of the Hierarchy was not equipped for river crossings or siege but was adapting with rapid fluidity. A sense of urgency claimed them. Many felt that the war was coming to a close. Others wanted only to go home but knew the only way to do so was by crushing the enemy in Sadith Oom.

For some, especially the Galdeans who had crossed half of the Free Lands and fought in continuous campaigns from the Crimson Fields to Unchar Pass, it was the culmination of a defining series of events. The depths of war stretched across the kingdoms in unfathomable horrors. Though many would die before the enemy was either destroyed or begged for surrender, the end was greatly anticipated. To the man, they were tired of war.

Jerns Palic stepped forward, reluctantly, to assume command of the elves. They followed his commands with fervor, for the need for revenge over the loss of Andolus burned hotly. Jerns struggled with similar desires and conserving resources. Each shaft became precious and they would have need of as many as possible when the time came for the final battle. Fletchers and armorers busied filling quivers but it was never enough. The dark eyed elf watched the far side of the river with undisguised violence. The army needed to cross to smash the defenses and enter the dead kingdom. He vowed to be at the head of that push.

Conn gestured to a series of boulders lining the opposite shore to the right of where the remains of the bridge were pillared into the ground. "We must send many men across with ropes to guide the rafts."

"The current is strong. Many could drown in the attempt," Aron cautioned. Memories of his own disaster in the Simca River made him shiver. "The dangers may outweigh the results."

"What else can we do? There is no other crossing into Sadith Oom. Whatever god designed this part of the world did so to spite men," Conn said.

"I will lead," Ur Oberlon offered. The wylin was the logical choice, for he was equally at home on land and in water. Being amphibian had advantages.

Conn nodded, having already arrived at that conclusion. "How many do you suppose you'll need?"

Ur studied the rocks. "How many rafts will cross at once?"

"As many as we can get, though I would caution no more than six," Conn told him.

His army lacked an official engineer command, but the men responded well enough to the harsh barking of the dwarves. Conn contemplated rebuilding the bridge, but that would have to wait. Establishing a beachhead was priority.

"Those first rafts will be vulnerable for quite a while," Jou Amn said. The Golden Warrior scowled as he imagined the slaughter. "They've nowhere to retreat to and will be exposed to every devilry the enemy possesses."

"An unavoidable risk, I am afraid," Conn said. "Their one advantage will be that our foe cannot come at them in force. There is a chance, albeit slim, that whoever we send across first will be able to hold long enough for reinforcements to arrive."

Jou immediately looked to Aron and felt some of his fury abate as he correctly guessed his commander's thoughts. "Commander, no."

"What else are we here for?" Aron replied. "We are the defenders of the Free Lands. Any danger should be confronted by us."

"Haven't we been through enough?" Karin interrupted.

They had, him more than others, but that was no reason to stand down. Aron faced her. "Karin, this war will not end until we make it end."

"But you have…"

A hand gesture stopped her in mid-sentence. While Conn and a handful of others knew Aron bore the Staff of Life, it was not common knowledge. Aron wasn't willing to divulge that one secret. Treachery already ran rampant among the kingdoms. They'd seen it as far north as the mountain city of Hyrast. If Imelin and Arlyn managed to spread their influence that far, it was only fair to assume several officers and senior sergeants might also be reserve agents waiting for the right moment to strike.

Conn seemed to share, at least partially, her view and expressed it. "Are your men in condition to swim the river?"

"For the most part, regardless, what choice have we?" Aron replied.

Jerns quickly added, "I will take a third of my people. We can cover you better by scaling the rocks and waiting until the enemy strikes."

"I do not like risking a third of my best archers," Conn said. If the initial landing force was cut off, they would be overrun and lost. Placing so many of his best in the advance wasn't tactically sound considering how long of a time it would take for the second wave to land. Those few soldiers were going to be stranded.

Aron folded his arms. "I would feel more comfortable with archers covering us from up high. They might just give our enemy pause. My men can hold off any assault, at least long enough to land the second wave."

"It will take days before we get enough men across to break through those defenses," Harrin Slinmyer commented. The Galdean had been aching to get into the fight, only now that one had arrived, his stomach threatened to betray him.

"There is no option but to rebuild the bridge," Haf suggested, though his gruff voice made it sound more like an order.

Conn wiped the sweat from his forehead with an old rag. He recognized the need to ferry as many troops across the river as possible, but so many tasks proved almost daunting. "Ur, select your men, as many as you need. You will depart at dusk. Haf, have a contingent get to work on that bridge. I want the enemy position bombarded nonstop. Do not give them pause or the chance to regroup. The longer we press our attack, the more strength we can get across the river. Questions?"

There were many, covering virtually every angle he could think of. Conn sighed. There were times when a general felt overwhelmed and underprepared. This was one of them.

The Croom River was the foulest of all rivers in the Free Lands. Some claimed it was residue from the great poisoning of Sadith Oom over a thousand years ago. Aron did not know. What he did know, was the waters were cold and the current was strong, though neither anywhere near either of his previous experience. It took all his strength to span the river. Hands finding purchase in the muck and sand, Aron had never been gladder than to be on land.

He picked up sounds to his left and right as others joined him. Ragged breathing dominated the beach. No time to lament, Aron rose on shaky legs and drew his sword before turning to help the others. Darkness dropped on the lands, leaving him almost blind, save for the flames roaring in the mouth of the pass. Nerves got the better of him and Aron began to scan the rock walls for signs of life.

The Golden Warriors arrived in the third group. Jerns and the elves were already across and climbing into position high above. In theory, they would be able to cover the landings and deter any organized resistance. The elves were good at what they did and the stealthiest people Aron had ever met, but they were only a hundred.

Ur Oberlon and his select crew were busy anchoring the ropes that would ferry the rafts. Going back and forth would become taxing on the men operating the rafts but there was little other option. Conn assured him that the men would be rotated out after each crossing. It was the best they could do, given what they had to work with.

Aron cursed his lack of foresight in checking to see if the bridge had been rigged with demolitions.

Explosives were a relatively new concept for modern warfare and terrified him. Sword and spear were one thing, but to die by being blown to pieces was inhumane. As much as he wanted to attribute the explosion to Arlyn's magic, Aron knew men were responsible. He'd been privileged to witness testing a little over a year ago and wanted nothing to do with it since.

Ninety-seven of the one hundred men under his command made it to shore. Aron hoped the other three would turn up further downriver and make their way back to the marshalling area. Logically, he prepared his mind for their deaths, however. War was brutal in the most extreme measures. No time to linger on them, Aron ordered his men into squads and darted forward of where Ur's group finished their task.

The catapult barrage was doing its job. Thus far, no Rovers or darklings showed their faces. Aron was too experienced to think they'd achieved total surprise. Ropes were pulled taut and the wylin signaled across the river. The first rafts were loaded with light infantry and began the harrowing journey across.

Aron pulled his squad leaders together and whispered, "No enemy gets through us. We cannot afford to lose those ropes."

Nods returned to him. Satisfied, Aron edged closer to the pass. Resisting the urge to keep glancing up at the rocks was harder than he thought, for the need to know he was adequately protected from above weighed heavily. Aron pointed left and right and his men fanned out in a twenty man front, five rows deep. He anchored the center and waited.

The darklings obliged them quickly, springing forth from hidden crevices in the mountainside. Most were cut down mercilessly. Aron strode through them, exorcising all the pain and suffering felt since entering

Meisthelm. Amean's face flashed before him when he blinked. A darkling died. He almost grinned in savage glee. It felt *good* to slaughter the enemy.

The last darkling fell as a series of catapult rounds crashed into the enemy defenses. Aron jerked his blade from a darkling's chest and ordered, "Hold the line! Reform ranks. Second rank to the front!"

Those tired soldiers who'd already engaged the enemy, gratefully retired to become the last rank. Aron needed to find a way to secure the beachhead. One side, his side, of the former bridge was secured and held fast, but there was another avenue of approach being underutilized. He wished there'd been time for Conn to plan for a double crossing, but the maneuver threatened to prove too risky for the reward.

Arrows plunged down from the rocks, slaying scores of approaching darklings and a handful of unsuspecting Rovers who were trying to use stealth to approach the invaders. Aron felt odd thinking of his men as such. They were the sworn defenders of the kingdoms. What twist of fate left them as invaders!

The darklings continued to attack, though Aron spied most of the surviving Rovers retreating. He took that as a good sign, one signifying the enemy was fractured, possibly ready to break. No doubt they were shell shocked from being bombarded throughout the day. He wondered how much of that he would be able to stand before breaking.

Rafts ground onto shore and the following wave rushed across the sand and rocks where Aron directed them to form up. His men still hadn't exhausted themselves and were good for more of the fight. A fact he was thankful for. Every moment they lasted brought another wave closer. The rafts plied back into the river where the handful of men manning them pulled back across the Croom.

Just when Aron thought there was a lull in the fighting, hundreds of Rovers, darklings, and goblins rushed through the barrage to assault his lines. Outnumbered, the Golden Warriors fought like demons. Many grew tired of killing the darklings and itched to lock blades with their long-hated foes, the Rovers.

It took all his discipline not to wade into the fray. Perhaps it was Ute Hai's seeming return to the Hierarchy that tempered him, or perhaps it was that too many had already died. Regardless, he felt conflicted. Rovers loyal to Imelin killed Amean, but they were just as trapped in their current situation as he. Ultimately, there was no lack of conscience on his part. The Golden Warriors met their hated foes in a tremendous clash of steel and aggression.

Elven arrows slew several, prompting confusion among the ranks, but not before a handful of Golden Warriors were slain. The others used the confusion and pushed their attack dangerously close to where the catapults rained destruction. Those Rovers forced back were caught in a withering crossfire and slaughtered to the last.

Aron lost track of time. When next he turned, he saw close to seven hundred soldiers standing behind him. How did that happen? Jerns climbed down from his perch. His look was calm, uncanny with placidity.

"There is something you need to see," he told Aron.

The elf looked at the amount of bodies littering the beach.

Aron grabbed Jou and said, "Hold the line here. Get the army into the fight."

He followed Jerns up the mountain, suddenly realizing how exhausted he was. His body ached from head to toe and he wanted to crawl into his sleeping sack and forget all of this. Life was not so kind. He groaned as Jerns helped him over the last rise. They passed scores of elves along the way. Aron assumed the others were deployed higher up. Jerns and his elves proved most capable warriors.

"There, behind what remains of that barricade," Jerns pointed.

Aron squinted in the semi-darkness, unsure what he was supposed to see. Mild destruction filled the pass. Bodies lay everywhere. What else? He knew he was missing the point. "What am I looking for, Jerns?"

"Look closer. There are few defenders considering how developed their position is. I think they have pulled back and await us further south."

"A ruse? That makes no sense," Aron said. "Why go through all the trouble to keep us out, only to fold as soon we apply pressure?"

Jerns nodded. "What know you of Sadith Oom?"

"Just what the legends tell. I have never had the need to travel here," Aron admitted.

"I believe the enemy means to draw us south, to the Plains of Darkpool."

It was Darkpool where the final battle in the first war ended. Where Ils Kincannon betrayed all of those sworn to his cause. Aron understood the symmetry of it and was appalled. The implications of such a move were staggering. He had no idea how many soldiers the enemy had. Should the army of the Hierarchy advance onto those open plains, they stood the very real chance of being surrounded and destroyed. *Just as my ancestor*.

"We must warn Conn," he said.

Another salvo of boulders slammed into the poorly defended pass. Jerns flashed a grin. "First we must get that barrage lifted. I do not fancy being crushed by our own engines."

Conn and his command staff made the crossing when a third of the army was across. Bridge construction was already underway. Haf and Jalos combined their wits and knowledge and had the pressed engineers building as quickly as they could get fresh materials. Thankfully most piers were undamaged by the explosion. Without the threat of being attacked, the dwarves had the bridge framed and ready to lay cross timbers by dawn.

Rafts continued to ferry fresh troops into the fight. It took little convincing from Jerns and Aron before Conn committed those already across to securing the enemy defensive positions. Rafts of supplies brought fresh water, food, and armor. Aron ordered his men into full battle dress. The sight of golden armor shining in the morning sun had been witnessed on hundreds of battlefields throughout the course of history. Once more they would stride into the enemy while instilling fear.

The rest of the elves raced across the gap to scale the walls on the opposite side of the pass. Aron's men formed ranks behind him, as did several companies of the regular army. Marching in step, they entered the mouth of Sadith Oom and advanced through the wreckage of the enemy defenses. A handful of Rovers too severely wounded to survive were put down as the army passed but there was no sign of additional units.

Aron surveyed the area suspiciously but found no enemy living. Companies spread out behind him in rehearsed movements until the entire pass was filled with soldiers. If the enemy had trickery in store, now was the moment, yet nothing happened. The pass was abandoned. He wanted to continue into the dead kingdom. Wanted to find Arlyn Gert and end this war. He glanced up to where

Jerns waited and saw the elf shaking his head. The enemy was gone. The way into Sadith Oom was open, inviting them in with malicious intent. The Towers of Perdition stood watch of the battle, impassive and judging in eternal silence.

The war in the north was ended. All their hopes and dreams rested on the ten thousand men behind him. Together, they would either defeat their foes in a singular contest or meet their fate the way Ils Kincannon had one thousand years earlier. The weight on Aron's shoulders pushed him down even more.

TWENTY-EIGHT

The Dead Kingdom

Sergeant Volm, native of the mountainous kingdom of Trimlon, had never seen such sights in any of his previous travels. The mountain range separating Sadith Oom from the rest of the Free Lands was beyond impressive, stretching high into the sky like the broken teeth of some ancient beast. Foreboding, impassable, the mountains proved an effective barrier. So taken with the stone heights, Volm all but ignored the Towers of Perdition as he passed between them.

His company marched behind him. They kicked up so much dust, there was no way to conceal their movements. Volm knew the enemy was watching. He felt it. Their experiences assaulting Grim Mountain changed his perception of war. Regardless of who comprised their enemies, each campaign promised to be as unique as it was violent. Volm would just as soon not kill another living being but had no qualms in doing so. At this point, he was fighting for his way of life and the opportunity to return home.

He was surprised when Lieutenant Doluth returned. The younger man turned out to be a solid officer and more than capable in a fight. He was also reduced to a shell of the man he'd been before leading the main assault against Baron Mron's forces. Volm shrugged it off. Wars changed men. It was a simple fact all needed to accept if they were to move forward and leave the past behind. He'd seen more than one man succumb to nightmares of foul deeds past.

Volm didn't mind Doluth accompanying him on the march. Neither of them knew precisely where they were going, only that the trail led south. Nor could General Conn or any of his ranking officers explain how many soldiers awaited. One senior commander suggested there might be a dragon waiting for them, for all they knew. Volm, like everyone else, knew stories of dragons. Great winged serpents who plagued the skies, devouring all. He found the idea intriguing and couldn't stop wondering what it would be like to see one.

His confidence in the army's ability to wage an effective campaign increased as soon as the Golden Warriors arrived. Volm revered them, having already signed up for their ranks before the war began. They were consummate professionals in his eyes, worthy of every accolade they received. Being selected to march with them in the vanguard and make the river crossing in the first wave, was an honor he'd never imagined.

And they came with elves! He'd never seen an elf up close, other than the one assigned to Conn's command staff, but that was from a distance. They were the best bowmen he'd ever watched in action and fairly decent to converse with, despite the obvious cultural differences. With such an awe-inspiring coalition, Volm did not see any way they could fail.

"This is a depressing land."

Stirred from his thoughts, Volm glanced at the burly Golden Warrior to his right. Jou something or other. He was almost embarrassed to have forgotten. The Towers of Perdition were behind them now, mere specks on the northern horizon. His legs ached, telling him they had marched for the better part of a day and that sundown was fast approaching.

"Rumors say it will be like this the entire way," Volm said, unsure why he bothered to state the obvious.

Jou grunted and pulled deep from his canteen. The water was warm, almost tepid. “Makes me almost miss the snow.”

“You fought in the north?”

“Aye. A nasty affair it was, too, but at least we could warm up by the fire at night. There is no escaping this heat,” Jou told him.

Golden Warriors! Volm walked in utter fascination, trying hard to imagine all they’d gone through in Galdea. If even a portion of the stories were true … “I applied for entrance into the Golden Warrior program before the war.”

Stupid. Why would he care? The man has seen more fighting in the last half year than I have over the course of my career.

Jou grunted again. “There will be plenty of open positions once this mess is finished. Survive and you just might make it.”

Volm heard nothing else. He was a seasoned veteran acting completely out of character in front of one of his idols. The embarrassment flushed his cheeks, making him thankful for the intensity of the sun. That much at least, he could conceal. They continued marching. All Volm could think about was what he would look like in a suit of golden armor.

Nightfall offered respite from the blistering heat. The army ground to a gradual halt. It took almost an hour for the last elements to march into the perimeter and retire for the night. No fires were lit, despite everyone reckoning the enemy knew exactly where they were and could launch an attack at any moment. Conn insisted on field discipline. Should that begin to crack or breakdown, the army would be lost and they had come too far to fail.

He walked into the hastily erected command tent and was pleased to see he was the last to arrive. That was how it should be. This meeting was for only the senior-most commanders and detachment leaders.

"Let us begin," he said without pause. "Master Forager."

The dwarf rose, pausing to spit a wad of dark juice. Some of it dribbled into his beard. "The bridge is framed and planked halfway. If we work through the night, it should be completed enough to get the infantry units and horses across in the morning."

"What of the siege engines?" Conn asked.

Haf laughed. "That will take some time and a more permanent structure. We are building to expedite the deployment of the army, General. We never planned on having catapults in the first place."

"Understood, but war is fluid. We must adapt to every situation, and with ease. Do what you can," Conn said. "We must also be prepared to guard the bridge. It would not do to have our enemies sneak in behind us and demolish it again."

He left out the obvious fact that there were no natural resources to exploit in Sadith Oom. Any raw materials would have to come from across the river. The army would be trapped should the enemy attack the bridge. It was a risk to leave a small company, but one he felt justified in taking. Their objective was Arlyn's main army. Failure likely constituted being decimated and there would be no need of an escape route.

"We need actionable intelligence," he continued. "This kingdom, while long turned into legend, has been largely unexplored by the Hierarchy for centuries. We are blind."

"There are rumors of small indigenous tribes living here. Could it be possible to seek them out and offer terms?" Aron suggested.

The sordid love affair of Jod Theron and Anni Sickali immediately came to mind. Her anger at being taken away from this fell place opened new trains of thought. Aron doubted she was the only living being from Sadith Oom. Where there was one, others must follow. Finding them might prove an impossibility, however.

Conn seemed to be thinking along the same lines. "I cannot risk the movement of this army on rumors, Commander Kryte. Give me something more substantial."

That was the problem. No one had any confirmed source with which to work. The entire kingdom might just as well be a blank slate.

"How far do you want the vanguard to push ahead tomorrow, sir?" Doluth asked.

Conn appraised the man. Some of the weariness was gone, replaced by an almost cagey need to return to the field. He'd seen it many times over the course of his career. Some men, once having a taste of the adrenalin born of combat, held on to an unhealthy craving for more. Zin Doluth was a good man and a valuable officer, but that might change should he give in to desire and become one of the beasts they battled.

"No more than a league. I cannot stress the importance of not knowing where we are going or what we are looking for. Until someone can produce a map or some such, we are effectively blind. The army will continue to move to contact where we will engage and defeat the enemy. I do not expect this war to last much longer. We have our foes cornered. That makes them more dangerous in my opinion."

"I will take my men and ride with the van," Aron said.

It wasn't a request. The Golden Warriors did not fall under the authority of the regular army, thus he was technically free to do as he pleased. Aron was experienced enough to know better than to turn the ranking officer against him. It was a delicate balance to maintain.

Conn had issues with placing his very best in the front but knew he lacked the authority to countermand the decision. The Golden Warriors may be the Hierarchy's chosen, but they were a pain to work with. Still, Aron and his men had performed admirably thus far and their golden armor was worth the cost of losing a few hairs. He conceded.

"Very well. Will you accept command of the vanguard?" he asked.

Aron hesitated. He had no problem with command but felt that the time was fast approaching when he would be pulled in a different direction. "That is acceptable. I request Lieutenant Doluth be assigned as my second."

Keeping integrity with the regulars was important. Especially should he be forced to leave abruptly. The army could deal with the enemy. He needed to find and eliminate Arlyn Gert. Only then could peace become possible.

Conn almost sighed with relief. "Done. I want you to deploy before dawn. We continue to strike south until something changes. Dismissed."

"We should have brought Anni with us," Karin said.

Aron had returned a short while ago and they sat huddled in their field tent. As the ranking officer, he was entitled to a tent almost as large as Conn's but he lacked the hubris. Aron settled for the same living conditions his men shared. He might command, but he was no better or worse than the others.

He did not disagree with her, though doubted what good Anni would produce had she been forced to return to her homeland. The mage made a habit, a very loud one, of letting all know of her displeasure from being stolen by Jod that never felt right to Aron. Outspoken, he listened to her prattle. He'd been in Sadith Oom for less than a day and could not figure out why anyone in their right mind would ever want to return.

"She would prove more burden than boon," Aron said. "I wish she had given us an actual map rather than the simple drawings I have."

Conn's frustrations over not having detailed maps were felt by many, no more so than Aron. He, who felt destiny forcing his hand by propelling him to the end. Aron immediately shared what he had with the others but Conn was hesitant to trust the scribblings of what was purported to be a madwoman. Aron didn't blame him.

Karin wasn't convinced. "Aron, you know just by being from here, Anni would prove invaluable. No one has been in the dead kingdom for generations. The Hierarchy ignored this place, and for good reason."

"The ignorance of a handful may be the damnation of us all," he replied, and immediately regretted it. "Karin, I am sorry. I did not mean it. I… I am exhausted. This war drains me and the Staff demands my attention."

She stiffened. "What do you mean? What has the Staff done to you?"

He tried to wave off her concerns. "That is not how I meant it. The power of the Staff grows the farther south we get. I can feel it humming, vibrating almost. It wants to be used."

"And you are the only one who can do so," she concluded. "Aron, are we sure about this? The Staff drove your ancestor mad and nearly destroyed the world. What is to say the same will not happen to you?"

He didn't have an answer. How could he? The Staff of Life was against every natural law. It did not belong in the natural world. Aron wanted nothing more than to destroy the foul instrument, thus lifting the curse associated with those unfortunate enough to possess it.

"Let us think of other, happier things. I do not want to spend my night in this wretched place mired in thoughts of despair," he said.

"What did you have in mind?" she asked, teasingly.

Aron leaned forward and placed his lips on hers. Dawn was not far off and he aimed to make the most of every moment.

Ute Hai stared up at the endless blanket of stars cascading across the skies. He'd never seen a purer night sky. There was serenity up there. A void of strife. How could such a scene languish under the painful constraints of man? The former Rover suddenly felt homesick. He was tired of fighting, tired of war. Ute wanted to return to Aragoth and forget the past twenty years.

Mounted, and thankful that the bridge was completed as fast as it was, Ute waited for Aron and the others. Fresh blisters covered his heels. He was never shy of walking long distances, but it had been far too long since he last endured a forced march with full pack, and in such intense heat. Why anyone would willingly come to this kingdom made no sense to him. He missed the snow and windswept steppes of his home.

Now that they were officially attached to the main army Ute was forced to wear the insignia of his new rank. He never imagined being part of the army of the Hierarchy, or riding side by side with the man he'd once sworn to kill. The world shifted in unimaginable ways. Movement drew his attention. He watched Aron approach.

"A good morning for a ride," Aron said in greeting.

Ute cocked an eyebrow. "If you insist, though I suggest we are riding in the wrong direction."

Aron chuckled. There was no disputing that. "Be that as it may, we have a job to do somewhere ahead. Is your sword up to the task?"

"You should know better than to ask such," Ute replied. "How far will our path take us, I wonder? The enemy is ahead, but where? Too many questions plague my mind, Aron Kryte."

"I do not know what lies ahead, nor can I promise that your Rovers won't be among the first we encounter," Aron cautioned. His doubts of Ute's loyalties remained strong. A man willing to turn his back on sworn oaths once, would do so again.

"All is as it will be," Ute said. "We ride for the enemy then?"

Aron paused, he wished he had better answers, for his own peace of mind more than any other. The Staff began to exude control, almost pulling him to the west. Was that where the fabled Forge of Wizards waited? He didn't know.

"We ride where the battle takes us."

It was the best answer he could come up with. They were joined by Zin Doluth and his staff. Aron was relieved that he did not have to continue the conversation.

"Commander, the vanguard is assembled," Doluth announced.

With the bridge being finished ahead of schedule, Haf was able to shuttle the horses across and to the army's bivouac during the middle of the night. It was a welcome relief to many. Most of the army remained afoot, but the heavy mounted element was returned, giving Conn an armored punch the enemy could not counter.

"Very good. Let us begin," Aron said.

"Which direction?" There were no roads in Sadith Oom, though passing troop formations left enough of a trail for the Hierarchy to follow.

"South for now. We follow the tracks. Have the companies spread out in an arrowhead formation. We take the center."

Doluth nodded. "Yes, sir. Where would you like my staff?"

"With me. Should anything befall me, you will need to assume command." *That and I think you will be taking command sooner rather than later.*

Doluth accepted this with relief, though he found the cryptic hidden meaning behind Aron's words troubling. "Sergeant Volm! Let us move out."

"Sir! My squad has point," Volm barked and began the long ride south.

Aron watched the soldiers around him. Quiet professionals who performed their duties to the best of their abilities, with limited knowledge or resources. He felt new hope awaken. Perhaps the campaign against evil was going to succeed better than any of them suspected.

Two thousand men rode out of the army camp and into the late night. Goblins and darklings might be anywhere. It was a calculated risk Aron felt comfortable taking. He secretly wanted as many of the enemy to come out and strike as possible. While they lacked intelligence of the enemy's strength, he figured their resources and manpower were not unlimited.

Karin followed a step behind Aron. There'd been discussion of assigning her to Conn's staff for her ability to *see*. She had none of it. Wherever Aron went, she was going to be at his side, be it to demise or salvation. Their love continued to strengthen. She'd come to view him as an unbreakable link in her life. One she could not live without.

Her horse snickered, prompting Karin to reach down to pat its neck. What did the animal know that she didn't? She was afraid to ask. Her magic would flare when necessary, hopefully before it was too late. Karin suddenly felt very small as darkness swarmed in around her. Sadith Oom truly was a land of nightmares come to life.

TWENTY-NINE

The Serpent Returns

Chonol Distan crinkled his nose. Their adopted yurt stank of bat shit and rancid materials Bendix Fol assured were 'chemicals'. The assassin didn't know what chemicals were but there was little he'd seen in this life that suggest refuse from any animal was beneficial. This further reinforced his belief that the old man was half again as crazy as the nonsense he messed with.

"How much longer are you going to be? The whole tent reeks of shit," Chonol growled.

Bendix cackled what might have been a laugh as he continued to grind and mash the wooden bowl filled with shit and other things. Since arriving in the dead kingdom, he'd been immersed in his task. A specialty few in the kingdoms possessed, if Chonol was any judge. Already thinking the old man well beyond the boundaries of madness, the assassin watched from a distance. His hand never straying from the hilt of a blade.

Chonol wiped the sweat from his forehead with a stained rag. He couldn't stop sweating. Even in the relative darkness the yurt provided, he found Sadith Oom most inhospitable. Killing off the majority of the Free Rebellion should have been the end of it. The Guilds were supposed to award him payment and send him off to other parts of the world. How he wound up returning to the south was beyond him. The only conclusion making sense was that someone higher than him either wanted him dead or out of the way for whatever was coming.

Cursing, he wiped a fresh sheen of sweat away and picked idly at the lichen growing up one of the yurt walls. Most of his life was veiled. He had no knowledge of his parents or where he was from, though enclosed spaces always left him feeling haunted. As if some bad memory lurked beyond the edge of his grasp. Childhood? Parents? Chonol didn't know, though he couldn't deny the level of discomfort he suddenly felt.

Of course, it could always be the obnoxious mixture Bendix continued to develop. Each time he blew his nose, Chonol was positive the last of his nose hairs had fallen out. "What is the concoction you're brewing old man?"

Bendix paused to give him a queer glare. "A most violent mixture our friends will not expect."

"Magic?" Chonol asked.

Bendix looked as if he was about to assault him. "Ha! Fools! Always blathering about what they know nothing of. As if magic was the sole defining power in this world! No, fool. Not magic. This is something much more potent."

"You try my patience. Out with it already," Chonol warned.

Bendix threw down the small wooden pestle caked in drying shit. "Alchemy."

The assassin threw up his hands in disgust and stormed from the tent and into the ravaging sunlight. A trade he willingly accepted to escape the madman's drivel. Chonol didn't know what alchemy was, though he'd heard rumors of powerful men comparable to sorcerers with the knowledge of the elements. Perhaps it was his antiquity whispering in the corners of his mind or it could have been fatigue. Regardless, Chonol decided he wanted nothing to do with Bendix Fol and his alchemy. There wasn't a problem in the world that couldn't be solved with a sharp blade.

"What do you make of our new friends?" Camden asked Sylin once they were far enough away from the others to avoid being overheard.

Sylin contemplated this. While he certainly didn't expect to find allies this far south, the presence of the trolls enhanced his odds of success. An entire clan of trolls, if Mard was correct. Sylin couldn't help but feel encouraged by their willingness to fight the enemy farther south. That an army of goblins, men, and darklings, not to mention them being led by a grohl, of unknown strength waited somewhere on the Plains of Darkpool eroded his fledgling confidence.

"I think we have become very small players in a much larger game," Sylin said.

Camden shifted uncomfortably. He missed his horse and the ease of riding. Walking through the accursed kingdom left his feet sore and his muscles aching. Worse, he continued to fight feelings of abandoning everything to find that quiet place in the world where life would pass him by. There were times he hated loyalty.

The journeyman glanced over his shoulder to where the giant loped. "What about him? Seemed ready to take off Elxander's head when we met." *Not that I blame him. The old codger is more of a pain in the ass than any I've met in a while.*

"That is a subject I do not think I want to know. At least not now," Sylin said cautiously.

His own emotions relative to the wizard remained in flux. Too many variables swirled through his mind, often dead ending without resolution. Sylin didn't trust Elxander but knew that the only way to succeed was with him at their side. Any confrontation between Elxander and Horus threatened to rip their already fragile alliance apart.

Sylin blew out a long, deep breath and reflected on the choices that had propelled him into his current situation. He doubted leaving Meisthelm now but seeing the aftermath of Shali Kolm's death spurred emotions he didn't know he had. He'd never been one to feel at ease among his fellow councilors. They were quarrelsome on the best days, intolerable on the worst. That didn't mean he wished them ill and knowing they were all gone but him and Arlyn left him scarred.

Without the High Council to rule the Free Lands, would devolve into anarchy. Making it even more important he complete his self-appointed mission and end the threat in Sadith Oom forever. It was the only way he could see a path into the future where the world didn't burn down around him.

"Have you realized our position continues to deteriorate the longer we are on this journey?" Camden asked. He didn't want to call it an adventure, because those often-held moments of entertainment. This quest was an unending ride of misery, from the rogue storm while aboard the *Gallant,* to the dragon in the Grimstone Mountains.

Sylin nodded, though his eyes were on the horizon and centered on events yet to play out. "There seems to be little choice. We are almost at the end of the journey. As long as we hold faith in one another, we should be all right."

Camden snorted, laughed. "You don't expect me to believe that?"

The laugh proved contagious, for Sylin couldn't keep from following.

Murmurs spread through the dwarves. Despite being uncomfortable among so many of their ancient foes, they managed to maintain composure, with only a few harsh words traded. The goblin contingent remained wary of the trolls, even as they'd grown somewhat accustomed to being among the dwarves. Their battle in the tunnels entering Sadith Oom helped erase some of the old hatreds but Sylin feared the addition of the trolls would ruin it all.

"I do not like this, brother," Talrn whispered.

Normally ranging far ahead of the others, the gruff dwarf felt odd among so many. He much preferred being alone in the field.

Garin's expression was masked beneath the grime of several days travel and his copper moustache and beard that, for reasons Sylin couldn't fathom, seemed to have grown into one complicated mess. "Goblins and now trolls. Our great-fathers must be turning in their graves!"

"Bards will sing of this for generations, though whether from shame or glory, remains to be seen," Talrn suggested.

"If we survive," his brother added.

The younger dwarf shrugged. "We've been in tougher situations. Though not with an entire clan of trolls at our side."

"Will they turn on us, do you think?"

It was Garin's turn to shrug. "One cannot say. I think we are about the same purpose for the moment. Should they decide to turn, there will be little we few can do."

His words were sobering. Counted among the greatest fighters in the Free Lands, a handful of dwarves were no match for an entire clan of the much larger, and meaner beasts. Any battle would be fierce and bloody, and last but a few moments. Not even the promise of eternal glory was enough to help the dwarves overcome being heavily outnumbered.

They were bolstered by the presence of Dom Scimitar. The elder dwarf was a legend among the people of Jerincon. His disappearance years ago prompted many to believe him dead. A travesty really, for at one time, he'd been rumored to be next in line to assume leadership of the border city. Garin would never admit this, but he always viewed Dom as an idol.

"Lord Scimitar, what can you tell us of these trolls?" Garin asked the perpetually angry dwarf marching at his side.

Dom scowled and spit a mouthful of phlegm. "There's no lord here, lad. I'm just Dom. The old life is well behind me. This is where I made my bed."

The Stonebreaker brothers exchanged wary looks but held their tongues. Every man had his own reasons for doing what they did. Whatever issues Dom faced in Jerincon or earlier in the Drear Hills, was severe enough to make him want to abandon civilization and to their dismay, his own people.

"The trolls? What can one say? They are formidable fighters and a great asset," Dom admitted.

"Can they be trusted?" Talrn asked.

Dom shrugged. "Can anyone? We are at war and if what you tell us is true, the entire world is crashing down around us. We might be the only fighting force left in the kingdoms capable of stopping the enemy. Puts things into perspective, eh?"

"I think I need some ale," Garin mumbled and kept walking. Sometimes legends didn't live up to expectations.

A day and a half later, the mixed company arrived at the ruins of Mordrun Hath. Elxander halted in mid-stride, for it had been so very long since he last looked upon his former home. The wizard felt mixed emotions threaten to tear him apart, for it was both boon and bane. Gone was the majesty, the splendor of towers and crenellations once filled with the brightest minds across the world.

His heart sagged as he recalled days when Mordrun Hath was considered a jewel, rival only to Meisthelm. Marbled halls lined with statues and priceless artifacts now lost to ruin. Elxander suddenly realized he had become a relic, an abandoned part of history best left to faded memory and whispers among the librarians.

Sylin, who had finished the march alongside Poros, looked from the wizard to where Horus waited. Animosity smoldered in his aged eyes and Sylin knew it was but a matter of time before Horus made his move.

"Not much to look at," Poros told him.

Sylin didn't know what to say. The legends of Mordrun Hath suggested this was once a pristine place worthy of praise. He felt disappointed. "What can we expect?"

"More trolls. It smells wretched," Poros said. His memories of being locked in the dungeons produced a foul taste. "Mard is intelligent enough, for a troll mind you, but his clan didn't appear to do too much damage from the limited parts we were able to see before being interned."

"A pleasant way of saying you were a prisoner," Sylin said.

"This is the dead kingdom," Poros replied. "Modern civilization conventions do not apply to any part of this place. My party and I were captured by trolls while we were following a goblin across the plains. Turns out Mard has no love for goblins either."

"Yet one walks among your group."

"Matis is a good enough sort. He's proven handy in a fight and harbors no love for those bastards down in Morthus," Poros said. "You're one to talk. You've brought enough with you to get into a fairly decent fight, and win."

"They found us. Seems they are equally tired of how matters are run in Eleran," Sylin told him. *In fact, anarchy is ripe across most of the kingdoms. This place may just be the sanest in any of the Free Lands*.

"Part of the reason I left the upper kingdoms," Poros admitted.

The column, now close to a thousand strong, began the slow descent down to the adopted entrance of the ruins. A half squad of trolls ambled out from the shadows. All were armed and wary, despite seeing Mard and the others marching toward the head of the column. The Dagger Clan were wise to be cautious with so many supposed enemies alongside Mard.

"Hai! We are home," Mard bellowed. His words echoed off the sand dunes.

Several trolls milled about, unsure of the wisdom of accepting his word out of hand. That pause proved fateful, as the first explosion blew two off their feet, while bathing a third in flames that wouldn't extinguish. Goblins and men screamed and shouted. A second and third explosion ripped the ground around the entrance to the ruins.

Mard watched in horror as the burning troll finally fell dead to the sand. "Move! Inside!"

Poros led the column as much around the engagement area as the terrain permitted. Whatever was making the flames was wickedly lethal and had the ability to slaughter them all, but those chances were higher the longer they were caught in the open.

"Elxander! There is a wizard here," Sylin shouted as he snatched the old man's bony arm. "We have to neutralize him!"

The ancient wizard shook him off. "This is not sorcery."

Suddenly spry, Elxander stormed into the fire and cast out his arms. Blue-green bolts of energy flared from his fingertips. Many struck dirt and sand with no effect, but a handful managed to detonate hidden bombs that would have shredded the column. Several men dropped to their knees to hold their ears, as the awful noise tore into eardrums and trembled bones.

"Move! Everyone inside!" Poros bellowed above the roar, as successive explosions rippled outward.

Elxander strode as a man possessed. Gone was his painfully aged persona. He'd grown strong, filled with renewed purpose. Sylin was suddenly afraid. He looked up to see three fist sized orbs sail over the nearest dune. Each exploded mere moments after striking the ground. He watched as a goblin was shredded by tiny shards of metal.

The blast knocked Sylin down. Sand blew in his eyes. All he could see were the vague outlines of various boots rushing past to get into the relative safety of Mordrun Hath. Gruff hands reached down to help him up and half pushed, half dragged him down.

"Hold still," he heard right before water flushed his eyes.

Sylin blinked rapidly and used a rag to wipe his face. "Is everyone inside?"

An unnatural pause worried him. "Hard to say. There was a lot of confusion out there and the area is occluded by smoke. Sylin, what was that?"

"Who is still outside?" he asked and got back on his feet.

"That crazy old wizard, the troll, and a few others." Camden said.

"Casualties?"

"More than we can afford," Poros snarled. "That bitch has found us out."

"Who? Arlyn? Why would she come here? For us?" Camden rattled off questions.

Sylin gestured at the walls surrounding them. "This place holds magic. You heard Elxander say it. The way to defeat Arlyn is by awakening and controlling this structure."

Another explosion, this one much larger, knocked dust and small chunks of stone from the ceiling.

"I don't think we got here in time," Camden said, almost woefully. "We need to find whoever is attacking us and stop them."

"Can you fight these demon flames?" Poros asked. "I've seen much in my day, but never seen a troll burn to death. Their hides are near impervious to flame. Whatever is out there has immense power. What about that old man of yours?"

"If he still lives," Sylin suggested.

Smaller explosions rocked the dune slope to the north. If he still lives.

Smoke stained his face and hands, charring his robes. His hair, normally greasy and stringy, whipped about as subsequent blasts continued to tear the immediate area apart. Elxander stalked across the burning sands without fear. He knew all too well the truth of what he faced and though it bothered him to learn a practitioner of the arcane arts lived, knew precisely how to combat it.

Alchemy was banned by the Hierarchy many centuries ago for the very reasons he now faced. Bodies littered the downward slope. A loss, to be sure, yet not as severe as it might have otherwise been. Shockwaves from the blasts battered his frail body, but they were weak. This alchemist had gifts but did not know how to use them. A fatal error.

"Come to me, little man! Let me give you the wizard's justice!" Elxander taunted, using magic to project his voice.

A pair of orbs chucked in his direction was his answer. Elxander lashed out, destroying each before they had the chance to hit the ground. Moving swiftly across the shifting ground, the wizard crested the dune and funneled the full rage of his strength downslope. A crossbow shaft turned to cinder inches from his heart.

He squinted through the green flames, hungry to find his attacker. He spied an object and felt exhilarated. Uttering a spell unheard for generations, Elxander blew away the wizard fire and smoke and was able to stare down on the bleached bones of who could only be the alchemist. The awkward pose suggested he hadn't expected a counterassault. Elxander managed to cull the threat with near complete surprise. Despite the ease of victory, the wizard remained unsettled.

Too many questions plagued his victory. Who was lobbing the spheres and just who had fired the crossbow bolt? The alchemist may be dead, but a very real threat, probably one of the Gen Haroud assassins, remained. Elxander found it prudent to withdraw inside Mordrun Hath. The others could handle an assassin. He had higher business to attend to.

THIRTY

Retribution

Daril Perryman and Lestrin rode at the head of one thousand bitter, battle hardened men who dearly wished to return to their loved ones. Instead, they were forced to scour the minor duchies of Galdea to cull the mild rebellion and bring all nobles back under the banner of the princess. Daril looked upon the snow and ice-covered walls of Lord Beren's Greyhawk Keep with open disdain.

There was no love lost between them. A grudge dating back to their grandfathers. Rumor said that it was Daril's family who were the rightful heirs to the keep. Beren's family usurped the lands and title, thus casting the Perryman's into military service to retain their right to have a voice. True or not, Daril would like nothing better than to place the tip of his sword to Beren's throat.

"Perhaps you should stay back and allow me to handle this," Lestrin offered upon seeing the anger smoldering in his friend's eyes.

Daril waved him away. "No, Lestrin. This is the repayment of a debt long in the making."

"The princess will not look kindly on you slaying one of her nobles, even if he is a royal prick," Lestrin said.

"No blood, my friend. On my honor," Daril promised.

Lestrin almost breathed relief until Daril quickly added, "Unless I somehow trip."

The cavalry commander chuckled despite himself. With anyone else, he might have been cautious, but the pair had been through far too many trials since first deploying from Galdarath at the onset of winter. He snorted. So long ago, it felt a lifetime, though in truth was but a handful of weeks. As good as it felt to be home again, Lestrin couldn't help but feel changed on a fundamental level.

He was no longer the thoughtful, carefree man he'd once been. That visage was replaced by a hard man with little tolerance for foolishness and the natural, over-aggressiveness that came from being on campaign. Wars were not for the faint of heart, nor should any be entered lightly for the sake of all who suffered. Lestrin didn't mind fighting. He merely wondered when it was going to end and what life might be like in the tepid aftermath.

"We are wasting daylight and Lord Beren has already waited out the war and the winter with relative comfort. Let us invite ourselves in," he growled.

Daril grinned and followed his friend down the small slope to where a handful of retainers guarded the gates. They spotted the hard glares under fur rimmed helmets. The dented armor and haggard looking men at arms marching on their keep. Shame quickly spread from man to man, for each knew that they should have gone to war with the rest of their kingdom.

"Open the gates," the captain of the guard ordered.

Chains rattled as men pulled the heavy wooden gates open. None of the guards looked into the eyes of the force entering as Lestrin's force funneled into the keep. Staff and servants scurried out of the way as one hundred armored men swept into the keep with swords bare.

"What is the meaning of this!" Beren demanded as he stormed down the hall to meet them.

Lestrin blocked Daril and took the lead. "Lord Beren, we are here at the behest of the throne. You will either join ranks with the army or we shall remove you from all titles and properties."

"Immediately," Daril added.

"I thought I sniffed you, Perryman. Is this some ploy for revenge? Come to rob me of what's rightfully mine at last?" Beren asked.

Lestrin placed the back of his hand on Daril's chest. "No, Beren. We are here on the Princess's orders. Surrender your men and return to Galdarath with us and you will be allowed to retain your title."

"I have committed no crime," Beren defended.

"Surrender your men and follow my instructions."

"If I choose not to?"

Lestrin sighed. "My orders neglected to specify whether she wanted you alive or not."

The unveiled threat stole Beren's defiance. As much as he wanted to spit in their faces, he was no fool. Going against the crown now that most of the army had returned was tantamount to suicide. Besides, the men who'd so blatantly invaded his home harbored no reservations against using violence to achieve their goals.

Self-preservation running strong, Beren sagged as his false bravado left him. "Very well. You will allow me the opportunity to dress for the journey?"

Lestrin gave a clipped nod. "We ride before sundown. Captain Suerv, detail and escort to assist the Lord."

A snap of fingers and a squad of decidedly fierce soldiers surrounded Lord Beren. The look of despair he gave as he realized his world was being torn down, was one Daril would relish for years to come.

"Are you certain he was the last? There are so damned many nobles in this kingdom, I can scarcely remember who is who."

Dagil snorted a laugh. "Relax. Your harmless insurrection has come to an end. Lestrin brought Beren in not long ago. Even if he isn't the last, none of the others will dare go against the throne with him in custody."

Jent Tariens, unwilling steward of Galdea, felt like punching the wall. The position had been nothing but raw chaos and as much as he was relieved to have most of the army home, it still wasn't ended.

"With Dlorn and the Princess in Meisthelm, we continue to lack a strong leader," he said. "Fear will only keep the nobles in check for so long."

"Fear and the fact that nearly fifteen thousand soldiers, fresh off campaign, have returned and now occupy the major army fortresses in the kingdom."

All save one. Jent automatically looked westward, to the distant Mountains of the Fang, where Lord Felbar and his few thousand were attempting to seal off Suroc Tol and trap the darklings within. Should the Lord of the Twins succeed, he would effectively end the war in the north.

It was a grand plan. One Jent found far too many issues with to feel comfortable. Yet he'd acquiesced without hesitation. The only way to cleanse Galdea was by plugging the hole ruined Dol'ir created. He absently wondered if the elves were going to return to their home or would they wander off like so many of their kin in the past? Strange, but he felt sorrow at the thought of their kind no longer walking the forests of the world.

"I wish Lestrin would assume command," he said, without prompt.

Dagil jerked back in surprise. "He is needed to maintain command over the army. I am afraid the days when you were a mere captain of the guard are long gone, my friend. You are a leader now. Men look to you to keep them safe, hoping that your decisions will continue to better the kingdom as the war draws to a close."

"Have I?" he asked.

Confused, Dagil asked, "Have you what?"

"Made the correct decisions?"

"That is a matter only time will solve. All you can do is the best with what you have been given. There is no room for doubt in your position, Jent."

"I know, but it would be far easier if I knew what was happening in Dol'ir. Felbar's entire force could have been wiped out, for all we know. Even with Lestrin back, they would be hard pressed to exert control over the mountains."

A dispatch rider had arrived earlier in the day with news that Felbar was engaged by a heavy enemy force after securing the ruins and sealing off the pass. All accounts suggested the fighting was fierce and might go either way. Jent couldn't afford to let Felbar fail.

"Have Lestrin see me after he gets something to eat."

Dagil knew the tone meant Jent was scheming. He also knew men usually were asked to perform above expectations when schemes were enacted. He concealed his grin. It was about time Jent started acting like a leader again.

Felbar crumpled the parchment and tossed it into the fire. Winter was ebbing but maintained a healthy grip in the Mountains of the Fang. He constantly shivered beneath his heavy cloak, and that was only when he wasn't on the wall fighting alongside his men. Which, against his desires, wasn't all too often. Not since he'd been forcibly removed from the center of fighting by Captain Stern.

"Bad news?" Stern asked, as his eyes lingered on the flames catching the edges of the parchment. Green and blue, but not red or orange. He found fire, for reasons he'd never understand, fascinating.

"On the contrary. That was probably the best news I've received since leaving the Twins," Felbar countered.

"I don't understand."

"Reinforcements are en route, Captain. Five thousand of Commander Lestrin's best infantry, fresh off campaign, are coming to assist us in ending this debauchery," Felbar announced. "The end of the war is finally in sight."

Stern wanted to cry. Additional combat power meant they would finally be able to devote the full complement of engineers to begin rebuilding the fortress in earnest and better than before. Galdea would once again be the strength of the north and Dol'ir would return to glory and prominence as the iron spear of the west.

Horns blared from both ends of the wall. Alarms cried out over the keep. Felbar and Stern hurried out of the makeshift office and made their way through the confusion and throngs of soldiers trying to take up their predesignated fighting positions. Ranks of infantry and archers were already in place by the time Felbar arrived.

"What is it?"

A sergeant pointed down into Suroc Tol. His face was pale, ashen. "My lord, an entire army of darklings approaches."

"An *army*?" Stern asked. His tone suggested disbelief.

There was no way an enemy force that large was capable of sneaking upon the fortress since Felbar ordered a field of fire cleared for one hundred meters. Surely the sergeant was exaggerating.

"Thousands of them. They crawl across the land like bugs under a torch. We'll be overrun!" His voice cracked.

Felbar reached out to grab him by the shoulders. "Calm yourself, sergeant! You are a leader in this army.

The men are looking at you for guidance. Be the example."

Felbar's words slapped sense into the rattled sergeant. Recognition entered his eyes and he steadily began to remember where he was and what he was about. Drawing his sword, he said, "My apologies, my Lord. I will return to the line, if it pleases you."

"Fight well, sergeant," Felbar said with a nod.

"That was inspiring," Stern remarked after the man walked away.

Felbar glared at him before turning his attention to the open area between Suroc Tol and Dol'ir. Dark figures swarmed over the land, true to the sergeant's word. He couldn't tell how many, only that his men were in for a fight.

"Bring every available archer to the wall and order them to begin firing immediately," Felbar ordered.

Stern questioned the decision. "Is that wise? If the walls are taken …"

"If the walls are taken, it will not matter. Do it, now!"

Hundreds of darklings began to climb the scored and battered walls. Felbar felt warm suddenly and wondered why he was already sweating.

"Rider approaching!"

Daril Perryman and those around him drew swords and fell into defensive formations. The Mountains of the Fang loomed high in the mid-morning sky, all but dominating the skyline. The sun was at his back, thankfully, making it easier to march west. They hadn't encountered any resistance or sign of enemy activity yet. *Or at least we hadn't until now*.

The rider entering view, dressed in stained and dirtied golden armor, was the last thing Daril expected to see in this part of Galdea. He raised a gloved fist and the order to halt was passed back through the column. The Galdean war machine ground to a halt. Many spied the golden armor with a sense of relief. The combat intensity the Golden Warriors provided helped many of them through dark days during the campaign to liberate Meisthelm. That others were operating close to Suroc Tol was a good sign.

"Who commands here?" the Golden Warrior asked.

Daril bristled, while taking little umbrage. "I do. Commander Daril Perryman."

A curt nod. "Commander, I come with word from my lord, Marshal Sevron. The Wood of Ills has been cleansed of darklings and we are pressing north to the Mountains of the Fang to assist the Galdean force already under attack."

"Attack? I was led to believe that Lord Felbar had already secured Dol'ir from the enemy," Daril said.

"Near as we c'n tell he did, but a runner came in last night. Looks like the fortress will fall if we don't arrive soon."

Damnation. All we need is one small break. A chance to catch our breaths. Will this war never end? "Very well, inform the Marshal I have two thousand men with me. We will ride with all haste, hopefully combining our force with yours."

"Yes, sir!" the Golden Warrior clasped his mailed fist to his chest and wheeled about to return to his command.

Daril watched him with thinly veiled envy. If his men only had half of the iron discipline the Hierarchy's backbone held, this war would have ended long ago. Feeling nostalgic, Daril summoned his captains and passed down the order. The force was to move with all dispatch and arrive expecting to get into a fight.

Felbar swung through, wincing as the impact of steel and bone jarred the length of his arm. His reward was watching the darkling's head roll away. Tired, spent, his sword already dull from overuse, the Lord of the Twins felt his hopes of success slipping away. His men only had so much to give and a great many were already dead or wounded.

Compounding his frustrations was the natural terrain of the pass. Felbar was only able to commit a small amount, in relation to his total strength, of combat power to the walls. The majority of his five thousand warfighters were stuck either in the fortress or the pass behind, unable to get through the throngs of men already fighting or waiting to get into the fight. There was no greater feeling than not being able to act, while comrades were in harm's way.

Felbar felt their frustration but there was little he could do to change the situation. He lacked the mounted force necessary to turn the assault back on the darkling horde and give them the armored punch required to sweep the enemy from the field. He knew there was no way to drive the enemy back with infantry alone and was resigned to falling into a strictly defensive role. A role he was well suited for, all things considered, but one he despised with a passion.

The desire to fight, to reclaim his lost honor, ran deep. He needed this victory for personal salvation, as much as to rescue Galdea from the nightmare it was entrenched in. Anything less, threatened to leave a tarnished legacy. Time for rumination passed and Felbar was forced to place his concentration back to the battle, as a fresh wave of darklings scaled the walls on the corpses of their kin.

Captain Stern was the first to hear the baleful horns blaring from the east. Hope buoyed in him, for they were Galdean horns. Help had finally arrived. Stern hurried to the eastern parapet and took in the massive column of Galdean soldiers and Golden Warriors crawling through the fortress defenders.

"Clear the way, damnit! Let them through!" Stern roared.

Men began to move faster. The eastern gates were opened to allow the reinforcements entrance. Men cheered and waved their swords in the air. The sight of so many countrymen refilled their hopes but it was the mighty golden column that inspired them. All doubt was cast aside, for never had so many Golden Warriors been summoned to Galdea under flags of war. It was a sight all would remember to their dying day.

Stern slumped against the rough chunk of stone freshly placed atop the wall and sighed. They were no longer alone.

Daril and Sevron fought side by side. Their mounted columns drove deep into the darklings. Thousands were trampled and hacked down. Any pretense of mercy had long abandoned the men of the eastern kingdoms. Every darkling was part of a greater disease that needed to be expunged from the world. By the time the battle ended the slaughter ranged for the better part of a league.

Felbar rode out to meet his fellow commanders and was surprised to see the flint grey, close cropped hair Sevron wore beneath his helm.

"You arrived just in time," he said with thanks.

Sevron offered his hand. "An unfortunate delay, but one with good tidings. The enemy has been driven from the field here and the Wood of Ills has been cleansed. Galdea is no longer in immediate danger, my Lord."

"Felbar, Marshal, please. I am just Felbar at this moment."

Sevron's eyes narrowed, as if considering the authenticity of his statement. "Very well, I am Sevron."

"Well met, Sevron," Felbar said. "What are your orders now?"

His gaze on distant Dol'ir, Sevron said, "If it is all the same to you, I believe I will take up command, or at least partial command, of this fortress for a time. You and your people did well. They are to be commended for holding the scourge at bay. Your actions may have saved what remains of the Hierarchy and the Free Lands."

Felbar's gaze fell before shifting to Daril. He remembered the brash commander from the battle of Crimson Fields.

"That is a tale best told over a tankard of ale and a warm fire," Daril said. The sorrow in his voice was undisguised.

The commanders retired from the field, as captains and sergeants began clearing the area. An outer defense line was established several hundred meters into Suroc Tol, while the dead and wounded were returned to safety for care. Regardless of what men privately thought, the war in Galdea was over. It was time to rebuild.

THIRTY-ONE

A Serpent's Touch

Arlyn unleashed her full fury into the Rover captain as he finished his report. The man was turned to cinder and collapsed into a heap of ash, even as bolts of magic scored the walls and ceiling in her newly appointed throne room. Chunks of stone and plaster shattered on the marble floor. She spit when she talked.

"How is this possible? The bridge was destroyed! Someone explain to me how an entire army was able to breech our defenses?"

She spun, taking in those few remaining in the chamber. All cowered. Any other time, she might have found that amusing, for the majority of men were naught but bluster and puffed chests in her mind. Now they wilted under her gaze. All but one. She respected that, if while struggling with the desire to lash out at him next.

Hurst, the mercenary captain elevated to commander after his directed assassination of General Gulnick Baach in Galdea, folded his arms and dared meet her gaze. "Treachery, my Lady. The enemy used elves and an ingenious ferry system to take advantage of our arrogance in the defense."

"I directed those defenses, Hurst," she seethed.

He shrugged. "Like it or not, they were ill conceived. The commanders on the ground were overconfident in their positions and failed to anticipate that Golden Warrior brat."

"Where is Mron?" she demanded. "Why has that snake not delivered this message personally?"

"Would you?" Hurst snorted.

She pointed an accusing finger. "You were supposed to watch him. I should have you flayed for incompetence."

"I fail to see how that would help your position," Hurst defied. "We need leaders going with the army."

Arlyn paused. "Go where? This is Sadith Oom, dolt!"

"There is an enemy army advancing south. We must deploy to meet them, or stand to lose all you've sought to build," Hurst replied.

Killing Hurst would be so easy, so satisfying, but he was correct. Arlyn needed true leaders, if her army was to salvage her dreams and defeat her hated enemy. Mron was incompetent, the Rover leader naught but ashes, and Hurst remained. That alone was enough for her to question his loyalty.

"Very well. You shall lead, Hurst. Only you have proved your allegiance, though I suspect there is more benefit to you than me," she said. "Deploy as many forces as you need. Stop the army of the Hierarchy."

"What about reserves?"

Her glare was answer enough. Hurst bowed and walked off. The time had finally come to prove his indispensable worth to the world.

Arlyn watched her freshly appointed leader of the army go with extreme reservation. He was far from the best but the best she had available. How had it all gone wrong? Sacking Meisthelm was meant to be the crowning achievement of her life. Instead the Galdeans arrived, forcing her south. Though the Hierarchy was all but deposed, Arlyn lacked the reach to exert total control over the Free Lands. She needed the strength hidden in Sadith Oom to do so. Conn beat her to the punch.

Conn. A detestable man she'd despised for many years. Mron was supposed to destroy his army, thus preventing him from being capable of mounting any sort of coherent offensive against her. Hurst was right in mentioning the young lord Aron Kryte. He was proving more of a problem than anticipated and if rumors were correct, he now carried the Staff of Life. As much as she wanted to go with the army to handle the situation personally, Arlyn decided the staff bearer was more of a priority.

There was the very real possibility that Kryte lacked knowledge of the Staff's true power, but it wasn't strong enough for Arlyn to rest her tactical strategy on. Her magic was strong but was it enough to defeat a bearer of the Staff of Life? She doubted it. Options limited, Arlyn needed to abandon her army and advance her plans for reopening Mordrun Hath. The ancient secrets of the original magic user orders were ready to be awakened. Once completed, she would be unstoppable.

Arlyn gathered her robes in her left hand and hurried to find a select group of escorts to see her to the Forge of Wizards. After that, she must once again visit the creature, Hume Feralin, in his lair. She detested the arrogance of the grohl. His gaze left her feeling naked, bare. Making her initial bargain with the creature was a calculated risk she'd been eager to take when she first made her bid for power.

Hume was a nightmare made manifest. A most foul monster from the darkest pits of depravity. Since arriving in Morthus, Arlyn decided that killing the creature when his task was complete, was her best course of action. He had much work to complete first. As usual, he was expecting her.

The grohl remained on the edge of shadow, a roiling mass of poisoned flesh without form or definition. Arlyn knew from the texts what grohls looked like, though he refused to show her more than his eyes. She had yet to see him in the open.

"Ever you come unbidden," he snarled.

Arlyn ignored the barb. "There is work to be done. The time has come, Hume."

"There is magic at play in Sadith Oom," Hume replied. "An ancient foe has returned home. One I did not expect to find again."

"What are you talking about?" she demanded. "If there was magic at work, I would know."

Was that a grin? "You think you are wise, yet for all of your strengths, there is much weakness. The confluence has arrived. Mordrun Hath is important once more."

Arlyn watched him fade back into the darkness. "Wait! You have a task to perform! I command it."

Red eyes glowed bright. "Speak."

"Kill every slave. I want Morthus cleansed of all nonbelievers. The time has come to reshape the world in my image," she seethed.

Hume said nothing. His thoughts already on the bloodbath to come.

Baron Vryce Mron paused to watch the dark columns of smoke billow above the mountaintops. He couldn't help but feel satisfaction in knowing most of his men had escaped before Conn managed to ferry his assault force across the river. The move was sudden, inexplicably fierce for men who'd so recently been at the end of their ropes. What changed?

Mron had seen the Golden Warriors himself, before withdrawing. They were a new addition, possibly what the army of the Hierarchy needed to recover and find new purpose. He had little doubt about who led the assault. The Golden Warriors were fierce beyond measure. Even with limited strength, they were the premier power in the kingdoms. Every moment they continued to serve among Conn's men, was one in which Mron felt defeat edge nearer.

The remnants of his army were several leagues south of the Towers by now. They'd been expected to stand and die. Retreat wasn't an option, at least according to Arlyn Gert. The madwoman seemed intent on getting all his people killed. Tactically, it made sense. Mron was a threat to her upstart reign, should he decide to make a move for control. What she didn't know was that was never his intention. Nor was dying for no cause.

Mron harbored deep, unending grudges against the Hierarchy and wished to see their power broken forever. He'd already wounded Conn at Grim Mountain. Dying at the gates of Sadith Oom served little purpose. Leaving a token force alongside the darklings and Rovers and other unfortunate souls caught in Arlyn's war machine, Mron hastily withdrew to hide among the foothills of the western border. Once the army of the Hierarchy passed south, he had every intention of returning north, to Guerselleorn.

There wasn't any reason to continue his suicidal quest this far south. All the Free Lands now lay open to his will. He need only reach out his hand and the world would begin to fall. Besides, he didn't figure Arlyn was going to hold out against Conn. Rovers and darklings were fodder, not line soldiers necessary to defend a kingdom, and the gates had already been breached. Reinforcements were bound to arrive.

He planned on being long gone before they did. The greatest obstacle, in his limited observations, had been evading Hurst. Fortunately, the mercenary was more concerned with increasing his standing among the army, not babysitting Mron. Slipping away at the onset of battle hadn't proved very difficult at all. Grinning at his wits, Mron continued to watch the smoke. It wouldn't be long now.

"Are we trapped?"

Mard glared at Karin.

Poros shook his head. "No. I do not think there were many assailants. Certainly not enough to pen close to two thousand armed warriors in these ruins."

"This my home," Mard growled in warning.

Holding up his hands, Poros said, "I meant no offense, my friend. We are all tired and stressed. Forgive me."

Snorting, the Dagger Troll leader hefted his war bar and stalked away. The indignity of being caught unawares in his stronghold stung.

"I killed the alchemist but not his guard." Elxander hadn't spoken since entering Mordrun Hath. His eyes never stopped wandering, as if remembering the glory of days long past.

"Who is to say there aren't more?" Aron demanded. For all they knew, an entire army could be converging on the ruins. An army with more of those bomb makers.

Elxander regarded him flatly. "I would know."

"How about you tell us where the killer is so we can eliminate him?" Jou asked. "This waiting only buys our foe time we cannot afford to give."

Whatever his thoughts, the ancient wizard fell silent once more and resumed his studies of a place he once called home. Sylin watched the exchange, feeling utterly helpless. Elxander wasn't anything like he'd imagined when first conceiving the idea of finding him. Zye Terrio once warned that the old wizard was best left alone, a forgotten relic of lesser times. Sylin hadn't been convinced and only now began to see the truth in the concern.

He was beginning to think dragging Elxander out of his imposed exile might do more harm than good. The others were already in agreeance, leaving only him. Then there was the giant Horus. A man without a race or kingdom. Whatever evil once befell his people, Horus refused to say. He merely glowered at Elxander. There was a time of blood approaching and Sylin wanted no part of it. He only hoped it happened once the war was ended and the Free Lands were safe once more.

"We cannot sit here doing nothing," Jou pressed.

"What are we supposed to be doing?" Camden asked.

The question, while serious in nature, came out partially humorous enough to make several of them chuckle. Camden seldom considered himself a funny man, but decided it was the right moment for levity.

Eyes slowly turned to Aron, and he felt their weight threaten to pull him down. What were they supposed to be doing? He hadn't a clue. All he knew was that the Staff of Life needed to return to Mordrun Hath and the forge from which it had been cast. Everything after that was unknown.

"The answer to ending this war is locked within these walls, and the staff Aron carries. Legends say, he alone has the power to unlock the true power and destroy this weapon."

Halvor spoke with surety, a rare thing, all matters considered. The scarred elf priest was a broken shell of who he'd once been but the time had finally come for him to prove the worth of his knowledge and training. He alone knew they needed Elxander to unlock the secrets of the forge. Unfortunately, the wizard was indisposed.

Aron's hand drifted to the Staff, taking comfort in the feel of old cloth wrapping the ancient wood. "Halvor, can you guide me to where I need to be?"

"I can," the elf replied after some consideration, "Though we will need the wizard's assistance to succeed."

"Leave that to me," Sylin offered.

"Councilman, are you sure you can influence the wizard? He seems… most disagreeable," Aron said.

Sylin waved softly. "Please, I no longer serve on the High Council, nor, if what you have told me is correct, does the Council exist. I am Sylin only, and yes, I believe I can get Elxander to help us."

Horus, knees drawn up around his chest, coughed and spit. His disdain for Elxander and wizards in general evident. "That man knows treachery and will not hesitate to betray you once he figures he has achieved his objectives. The bones of my people are testament to that."

"That was a long time ago, Horus," Aron said. "You cannot expect him to remain the same after centuries."

"What else would he be? A snake never changes colors."

The giant fell silent, leaving them to ponder his meaning. Enough had already been spoken, any further words of his would prove meaningless. Horus rose and went off in the opposite direction of Elxander.

"Follow him. Ensure he does nothing rash," Aron ordered Jou.

The Golden Warrior wanted to debate the wisdom in Aron's decision but was a professional. Sword at his hip, Jou hurried to catch up to the long strides of Horus.

"That will become a problem before too long," Aron said, once they'd gone.

Sylin agreed. "There is time yet. We must get Elxander to unlock the forges. If what the priest claims is true, we should be able to destroy the Staff and end Arlyn's threat."

"There is still an army out there wanting to kill us. Destroying the Staff has been important since the Red Brotherhood led us to it in Galdarath, but why? Imelin is dead. There are no magic users in the Free Lands, at least none we know of other than Arlyn. How is destroying the Staff going to stop her aggressions?"

"All magic is tied to the Staff. In theory, you should be able to direct the unleashed energies of the destroyed Staff in Arlyn's life stream, thus ending them both," Halvor supplied. Even he admitted the answer, while the best he could muster, was flimsy.

"This keeps getting better," Aron muttered. "Let us go find the wizard and end our war."

"About time," Camden muttered and fell in line.

Haggard, body aching and nearly drowned, the elf pulled himself out of the Croom River and collapsed in the sand and mud. Each breath was labored. An act rival to fighting a battle against an impossible foe. His head pounded. His eyes burned. Everything hurt, yet he was alive, and that was a wonder.

Andolus gradually lifted his head from the ground. Sand caked the left side of his face. He reached a hand up to brush it clean and stopped as a wave of intense pain spread across his face. Wincing, Andolus felt the tips of splinters peppering his flesh. Pieces of the bridge were embedded in him and proved difficult to remove. Fresh blood mixed with the dirty water as he painstakingly pulled each sliver out. His face was a tattered mess by the time he finished.

No time for lament, Andolus forced himself to rise and assess his situation. Daylight was breaking and he was on the southern shore. A look back across the river showed him an army of men working to rebuild the bridge. *So the others survived*. He took that as a good omen. Finding them might prove more problematic.

Andolus looked around and was dismayed to find numerous bodies littering the beach. Some were his brethren. A battle had occurred. Who were the victors? A quick search showed him the number of darkling and Rover bodies far outweighed the men of the Hierarchy. Some of the strength returning to his legs, Andolus staggered into Sadith Oom.

The once elaborate enemy defenses were shattered into smoldering hulks. Hundreds of bodies stretched out as far as he could see. Nestled against the mountains was a string of tents. He recognized Conn's command tent and felt relief. The allies had won the opening battle and were preparing to march south.

Scouts found him and helped him to Conn. The general looked him over, impressed the elf still lived. "Lord Andolus. We thought you were..."

"I feel dead, if that is any consolation," the elf said.

"We have been through many trials thus far, though I am afraid many more await."

"General, where is Aron?" Andolus asked. He had no time for random banter. All campaigns were beset with difficulties. This one should prove no different.

Conn licked his lower lip. It was cracked and dry. "He took the vanguard south less than a day ago. The campaign has begun in earnest."

"How were you able to ferry so much strength across the river without a bridge?" he asked.

Conn explained all that had happened since the bridge was destroyed, making sure to point out most elves went forward with the Golden Warriors. Andolus couldn't blame them. He would have done similar. Still addled, the elf lord needed to reach his people. He didn't know why, but a strange voice pulled him deeper south. It whispered how necessary he was to the end of the war. The fulfillment of a lifetime. Andolus explained his needs to Conn. The General was hardly surprised.

THIRTY-TWO

The Plains of Darkpool

A week passed before Conn had enough strength across the river to begin the final march south. Tired and ready for it all to end, soldiers hefted their packs, sharpened their weapons a final time, and formed ranks. Conn made the decision to wear light armor only, much to their relief. The boiled leather was crude and wouldn't hold up long in pitched battle, but it was better than marching across Sadith Oom in full metal. He counted on there being enough time from the moment initial contact was made to order second echelon forces into full armor so they could engage.

Haf and the engineers worked much quicker than any expected and a replacement bridge was in place by the time the army began to move. Wagon trains carrying supplies were hurried across. Empty barrels were filled at the river and loaded onto specialized wagons. Others carried armor by specific companies, thus making it easier to react when the fog of war settled in.

Fresh hope was kindled among the men. Knowing the end was near, and that they would have artillery support and as many supplies as the army had available, bolstered spirits more than any inspirational speech a commander might give. The feeling spread through the army with uncanny speed, reaching the command staff a league into the march. Conn felt years shed from his conscience. He almost felt confidence, inspiration again. Almost.

Rhea Ailwin rode at his side. Communications had been reestablished with Meisthelm, giving him purpose again. The young Master of Messengers had only one bird left by the time Kryte and the Golden Warriors arrived with news of the rest of the kingdoms. Rhea immediately sent his last bird home and was rewarded by several more returning over the course of the next few days. It was a small boon that enabled the army to effectively communicate with the Council of Delegates in the capital.

"General, are there any missives you wish sent before we march?" he asked.

The hesitancy of being around such austere ranks was faded. Rhea had yet to lift his sword in battle, but he thought of himself as being seasoned in his own manner.

"No, lad. We've done all we need to do. Meisthelm cannot send us further aid. Let the boys do their jobs and we will be on our way home before long," Conn replied. His fatherly manner calmed Rhea's rising nerves.

The army deployed in a single column to minimize the area with which the enemy could strike them. Conn was confident in his commanders' ability to redeploy with haste in the event of battle. Unfortunately, those soldiers deeper in the column were going to choke on the dust kicked up by those in the front for the duration. The true life of a soldier was far from the glory and glamor inspired in bards' tales.

Dlorn stiffened as his eyes settled on two riders racing back from the forward position. "Continue the march," he ordered his commanders. "I will meet this. Come, Master Ailwin, let us see what news awaits."

Moments later he met the riders. Their worried looks left little doubt as to what their report was. Dlorn felt his nerves tremble his stomach. Decades of experience in the field and on campaign should have steeled his composure in the face of battle, yet being confronted with an army of unknown size and composition and trapped in a kingdom with only one entry point, left him on edge.

"General, they are coming," the ranking scout reported. His voice was thick with concern.

"Numbers?" Conn asked.

The scout shook his head. "More than we could count. Possibly tens of thousands."

Conn gripped the reins until his fingers bled white. *So many? How are we supposed to win against such odds?* "How far away are they?"

"A full day's ride, sir, and heading this way quickly." The scout paused, as if hesitant to continue. "Sir, there is more."

"Go on. You might as well kill me with the information now rather than later," Conn grumbled.

"Sir, Lord Kryte and his force splintered from the rest of us and headed east yesterday morning," he reported.

Conn winced, though he'd expected as much. The Golden Warrior commander had an odd air about him. Perhaps it was the war, for everyone was systematically being changed on fundamental levels. Unable to rely on that strength, Conn decided to make his stand.

"Return to the vanguard and order them to hold in place and establish defensive formations. We make our stand on this miserable plain. The main army will march as fast as possible. My orders are to hold unless threatened with defeat. Hurry, time is now our foe."

The scouts saluted Conn and fled back to their posts. Conn turned to Rhea and said, "It appears our fates will soon be decided."

Rhea did his best to show a brave face, while his innards threatened betrayal.

Andolus scowled as the warm breeze tousled his hair. His anger had continued to rise since rejoining the army. Sadith Oom was rumored to be the end of all things among his people. A legend he often looked down upon. At least until he was confronted with enduring the harsh environment firsthand. Somewhere on the Plains of Darkpool were the last of his kin. The elves of Dol'ir had gone forward with Aron Kryte to destroy the Staff of Life. His heart ached from not being able to join them.

The elf lord wondered if Long Shadow had gone forward or had he headed for the nearest port to return to his homeland across the sea? Sacrifice was a common theme among those invested in the war. How much more could he give before the pressure finally broke him? Andolus rode apart from Conn and the others, not out of an air of supremacy but from the need to resort his thoughts.

He thought of speaking with Genessen but the elf was already preparing his regiment for battle. So much had changed since fleeing the Mountains of the Fang. Andolus thought he had adjusted, only to have his conceptions thrown out after he'd narrowly survived the bridge explosion. Would he survive the coming battle? Would there be the rebirth of his people in faraway Dreamhaven? Questions, while valid, he had no answers to.

It took the better part of the day for the forward units of the army to reach the vanguard emplacement. Andolus desperately searched the men already digging in and preparing for battle for signs of his people. There were none. The elves were gone. He wished Jerns Palic luck in battle and decided to offer his services to Conn. Nothing more could be done for his people and the quest to destroy the Staff.

"General, where do you wish me during the coming battle?" he asked, finding Conn already pouring over hastily drawn maps of Sadith Oom, while his commanders formulated a viable battle plan.

Conn barely looked up. "I believe you would be best suited with Commander Genessen, unless you wish to be mired in the misery of the command staff?"

"Genessen's command will be sufficient," he replied. "Thank you."

Conn dismissed him with a nod. Too much needed doing to waste time on pleasantries. Andolus slipped through the mass of men and weapons to where his blood kin busied deploying his forces on the eastern flank. The vanguard had already established a clear line of defense across a third of a league. Scouts and pickets ranged just beyond vision range.

He found Genessen directing a unit of pikemen into place. The elves met by clasping forearms. "Andolus, what brings you to this lovely spot?"

"I needed something to do and Conn and I both agreed I would be better suited at your side," Andolus said.

"Comfort in familiarity," Genessen finished.

"I presume. Where can you use me?"

"On the flank, if you don't mind," Genessen said. "I will command from the center."

Andolus looked to the end of the line. If he chose to accept, he would be responsible for the far end of the army. Should he fail and the flank collapse, the enemy would sweep around and crush the only viable military force capable of stopping Arlyn from reasserting her control over the Free Lands.

"Very well," he replied. "Luck in battle, my friend."

"And to you, my lord."

The elves parted ways, each with his thoughts focused on different areas.

The hundred pickets and scouts deployed forward, raced back to the front lines shortly after dawn. An army of darklings, Rovers, and goblins stalked behind at steady pace. Final preparations brought the army of the Hierarchy to life. Armor was donned, weapons drawn, and shields interlocked. Thousands of soldiers made their peace and waited.

Siege engines were brought on line. Battalions of cavalry mounted and readied to ride forth. Conn wanted them to remain in reserve, needed only when the perfect opportunity presented itself. He watched with pride as his men, now hardened veterans, slid into position with remarkable ease. There was a time when he would have had doubts. Grim Mountain changed that. His biggest question now was how many of these men were not going to be leaving Sadith Oom alive.

Unlike Grim Mountain, where he needed his nimblest troops for the uphill assault, Conn placed his heaviest grunts in the center. Led by the pair of dwarves, Haf and now Jalos, who refused to continue traveling with Aron to Mordrun Hath, the middle of the line was the strongest position on the plains. Strong enough to make an enemy army break on their steel.

His gaze tracked across the mass of men, stopping only when he spied the dwarves. Their battlefield prowess was legendary across the kingdoms. Conn wished he had a battalion rather than a mere two. Without any other choice, he placed the survival of his army in the hands of two volatile individuals from the Wilderlands. Not bad odds, all things considered.

Jalos Carb watched as the distant, blurred mass neared and became individual beings. Thousands upon thousands of warriors coming to kill him. His grin spread from ear to ear, though was barely noticeable under his beard and moustache. The dwarf thumbed the edge of his axe as he reflected on the events leading him to this point.

As with a great many of his people, Jalos found life in the Drear Hills precisely that and left in search of a better life with more fulfillment. He found that in Hyrast, where he served as a senior military advisor for a time. His life changed, for the better, when the Golden Warriors arrived and liberated the city from the influences of the dark wizard.

Jalos spent the remainder of his time in the north fighting alongside Aron and the others, eventually reclaiming Meisthelm and heading south. He never expected to find one of his kin. Rumor had it they had enough troubles in the Goblin Lands and couldn't be spared for the war in the west. He didn't mind. War was an intimate affair. One he felt more comfortable entering on his personal terms and without the watchful eye of his superiors.

"That is a lot of bad guys," Haf commented.

Jalos spat and nodded. "Enough for both of us."

"Aye, though I wouldn't mind have a few more axes at our side," Haf replied. "I guess it is about time. Luck in battle, Jalos."

"Fight hard and die well."

The dwarves went to their respective commands to wait. They didn't wait long. The front ranks of the approaching horde, for there was no organization or discipline involved in their march, broke into an all-out run. Jalos watched them come, noticing how only darklings and a handful of goblins advanced. The Rovers and other men lingered behind, clearly not eager to join with such a heavily armed force. So be it. Their time would come soon enough. Jalos was about to bark orders when the thrum and whistle of catapult rounds slashing overhead filled the sky.

Watching the boulders slam into darklings filled him with joy, yet still they charged. Two hundred meters. A second salvo dropped into the advancing force, killing hundreds. Men cheered and brandished their weapons in the air. Jalos ignored them. One hundred meters. The enemy was closing faster than Conn's artillery could adjust their fire. The third salvo landed in the space between the attackers and the rest of their force. Fifty meters.

Jalos hefted his axe and bellowed, "Brace!"

Sergeants echoed the command. Jalos tested the weight of his axe with a casual swing as he looked left and right. Nervous men stared back. At Grim Mountain, they had been the ones assaulting, while Baron Mron's forces waited. It was their turn to stand the line now.

"Shields!"

A row of iron rose, protecting the front ranks from the hacking and slashing of the darklings. Jalos briefly wondered if the line would hold. The darklings crashed into him a moment later. Bellowing an ancient dwarven war cry, Jalos raised his axe and cleaved the nearest darkling from neck to groin as the enemy struck.

Blood splattered over his jerkin. He kicked the body aside and swung again, taking the next darkling at the knees. Mortally wounded, the darkling slashed across Jalos' armor. Sparks showered down. The dwarf was in his element. An inescapable tide collided with the soldiers on his flanks. Every darkling too close to his axe paid with his life. Jalos vented years of frustrations and pent up aggression.

The full weight of the darklings' crush pushed the shield wall back a step before the defenders settled and braced. Sergeants and captains shouted encouragement and the men responded. Pikes slipped through shield bearers to skewer darklings and goblins. Jalos watched the sloppy precision.

"Step!" he roared.

Pikes stabbed again and the shield wall regained their lost ground. Distracted, Jalos was swarmed to the ground by a handful of darklings. He punched and kicked, rewarded with grunts from those struck. His axe skittered away. Weaponless, the dwarf snatched the nearest darkling by the throat and squeezed. Small fists hammered into his armor. With his free hand Jalos drew the crude dagger at his belt and began stabbing wildly.

Darklings were hauled off him and killed, those few still living, giving Jalos the opportunity to regain his feet and slip back inside friendly lines. Exhausted and battered, the dwarf grinned savagely. These were the moments he was made for. A soldier handed him his axe with an astonished look on his face.

Jalos took the weapon and shouted, "What are you waiting for, you bastards? No one lives forever!"

The shield wall took another step forward. The slaughter was horrendous.

Night was dying. Hurst wasn't sure why but he always felt melancholy at this time of day. The former mercenary felt night provided the best opportunity to accomplish his purpose. He was a man who made his living avoiding true danger, surprising for a man selling his martial services to the highest bidder.

Somewhere ahead marched the army of the Hierarchy. Ten thousand bitter men seeking to kill him and those with him. Hurst lacked faith in his new army.

Most were already traitors of one cause. The rest were remnants of a much larger force battered and beaten down through an exceedingly violent campaign ranging most of the Free Lands. He needed Mron, loath as he was to admit it, if there was to be any hope of victory.

Arlyn insisted the future lay with him and his ability to wield the army. Hurst, ever the practical man, knew better. The motley collection of creatures at his disposal left him lamenting. An idea struck him, there on the lonely plain half shrouded in watered darkness. Terror was a weapon unexplored for him, but one he felt he needed to exploit. Hurst summoned Duoth N'nclogbar, the darkling leader. The time had finally come for the darklings to prove their worth in the new world order.

The darkling slinked up to him, cold red eyes glaring up at the horse-borne man. Hurst felt the animosity radiating from the smaller beast. *Good, little animal. Harness that anger and wield it against our foe. It may be the only thing saving us in the end.*

"Bring up the scrathes. We are within range," Hurst ordered.

Duoth hissed. His crooked fingers jabbed at Hurst. "Kill many men. We want our due."

"You shall have it. Send forth as many darklings as possible. Use every scrathe. We cannot meet that army head on." *Stupid creature! Oh, how I wish I had men to treat with rather than a beast with a limited mind. Arlyn Gert, what have you saddled me with*?

One hundred of the dragon-like creatures flew south from Suroc Tol. Each was capable of ferrying twenty darklings. Hurst reevaluated his plans. Two thousand darklings were about to drop behind enemy lines to give Conn what he hoped to be a very bad day.

"What are you waiting for? Go!" Hurst almost shouted after noticing the darkling hadn't moved.

If only he recognized the threat in Duoth's eyes. The darkling decided then that he would kill Hurst. No man deserved the darkling's loyalty, especially not a foul wretch like Hurst. Duoth once bent his knee to the Black Imelin, only to have those plans ripped out from under him. Any perceived weakness threatened to undermine his control over his people. Usurpers and murderers, darklings continually struggled to overthrow the current leader. Duoth needed to find a way to defeat the men of the north, if he had any chance of retaining his throne, and the power therein.

The darkling hobbled away, plans within plans forming.

THIRTY-THREE

The Battle of Sadith Oom

The sun was rising, shedding light on the massive sprawl of slaughter stretching across leagues. Bloodied yet brave, the army of the Hierarchy remained in control of the Plains. The initial darkling assault was repulsed with minimal casualties. Conn took this as a good sign. His men needed as much morale as he could muster.

Captured goblins, rather than submit to torture, bargained for their lives with intelligence. Conn remained dubious of their authenticity but copied their words in the hopes of being true. He first learned of a great citadel being constructed far to the south in what the goblins called Morthus. Conn also knew that the city had been emptied of all combat forces. He knew Arlyn Gert to be a shrewd woman from personal experience. For her to throw the entire weight of her forces at him, told the old general enough. She was as desperate to end the war as he.

With the enemy vanguard defeated, Conn knew it was but a matter of time before the rest of the army threw its full weight at him. He ordered catapult batteries to resupply. Archers were handed the last of the arrows and reinforcements filled holes in the shield wall. Surgeons' tents were already overflowing at the rear of his formation. They had defeated the darklings but at cost.

Cries of alarm rang out, first in one location and then spreading across the width of the army. Grabbing his sword belt, Conn hurried outside and looked to where a soldier pointed in the sky. Squinting through the intensity of the sun, he barely made out dark spots moving through the sky. Scores. The scrathes Aron once warned him of. Conn grimaced. He'd met this foe once before and was found wanting.

"Lord Andolus, I believe it is time to prove your worth," he said. His voice was soft yet commanding. "Have you readied your archers?"

The elf found the term confusing, given that crossbowmen were far from natural archers. Accurate to a point, they were all the elf had now that his people were off in the east. He wished them good fortune and pushed thoughts of them aside. More so, he longed to be back on the line with Genessen, but Conn's summons the night prior removed him from the front.

"The crossbowmen have been dispersed among the army in squads. We should reap a terrible price on those winged beasts," he snarled. Flashbacks of the fall of Dol'ir drove him on.

"Kill them all," Conn said. The general clasped Andolus' shoulder and went back into his tent to finish arming.

Andolus had barely gotten into position, when the first scrathes soared over the army. Waiting was the hardest part, for his every instinct screamed for revenge. He hadn't realized until now, how much fury his wiry frame contained. The elf lord drew his first arrow, his being the only long bow among the rear elements, the few companies of archers already being used on the front.

The first scrathe was almost overhead. He pulled back. Crossbows angled up, their armor piercing tips sufficient to rip through the toughened underbellies. Eyes shifted between the flying monsters and the elf. He complimented them for not giving in to fear and firing prematurely. Andolus pursed his lips. His muscles strained. *Just a moment longer*.

The bowstring thrummed. His arrow sped true, striking the scrathe in the exposed throat. Hundreds of crossbow bolts followed. Unnatural screams filled the sky. Darklings were pitched off, some falling to their deaths, while others were slaughtered by sword and spear. Andolus nocked and fired again.

Several scrathes fell, dead before they hit the ground. Yet for each one downed, ten more managed to drop their loads of darklings. Many of those darklings didn't live to touch the ground. Conn watched the aerial battle play out, helpless to do anything other than watch as life and death were doled out indiscriminately. He'd seldom known such frustration.

"General Conn! The enemy is advancing in full force!" a runner reported.

Conn turned from the fighting to follow the runner back to the front. Thousands of darklings and goblins were already engaged with his front lines, and those lines were being mauled. Already several sections were on the verge of collapsing. Secondary units waited to fill the gaps, but hundreds of darklings could pour through the lines in the meantime.

He snatched the runner by the collar and jerked him close. "My orders to the firing batteries, being firing at once. I want all rounds expended. Move, son!"

Hurry, before it is too late.

Zin Doluth watched as the enemy again clashed with the dwarf held center. The fighting was brutal and fast. He didn't envy the men dying. Doluth gave that and much more on Grim Mountain, yet after being returned to his adjutant position, he all but begged to be returned to his former command. Conn acquiesced, reluctantly, and gave Doluth back his command.

"Not a bad way to begin the day, hey, Lieutenant?"

He looked up as Sergeant Volm arrived. The veteran had his sword over one shoulder, seemingly nonchalant about their predicament.

"Sergeant."

Volm's eyes narrowed, taking in the massive force confronting them. "This looks to be much worse than the mountain. Have we gotten new orders?"

"Nothing yet. Keep the men ready. I don't expect our enemy to be gracious enough to only attack in one place," Doluth said.

Both men ignored the earlier scrathe attack. It was easy to avoid thinking about certain actions when they had nothing to do with them. The men in the rear were forced to deal with the airborne assault, leaving Doluth and his staff focused on the army to their front.

"Sir, didn't these bastards have men with them? Where are the Baron's men? Or the Rovers?" Volm asked.

Good question. Where have they disappeared to? He was about to answer when dust clouds filled the western sky. Doluth felt his stomach clench. There were no friendly units beyond his position on the flank. He feared the answers to Volm's questions were about to be presented.

"Ready the men, Sergeant. I believe our day is about to get busier."

The full Rover contingent and remnants of Hurst's mercenaries attacked Doluth's position with unprecedented ferocity. Volm got his fight and wished he hadn't. Most of the Rovers had endured decades of life on the run and fighting, making them harder than all but the senior most leaders in the army of the Hierarchy. The entire flank threatened to fold after an hour of heavy fighting.

Volm ripped his sword from a Rover's exposed chest and bent to help a wounded man up. Burning pain lanced his side, spreading up through his chest, toward his heart. Volm blinked, wincing as he failed to understand what happened. The agony exploded as his attacker drove the sword deeper and twisted.

Vision blurred, Volm turned to look upon his killer. He felt cold. Volm reached for the Rover with his empty hand but lacked strength. The arm dropped. Eyes rolled back into his head. Sergeant Volm, veteran and hero of Grim Mountain, died an inglorious death at the hands of a man he'd never met.

The battle raged on.

"General, we are losing the western flank!"

Conn punched a fist into his palm. "Deploy one third of the reserves and send the cavalry straight up their center. Break the Rovers or we all die!"

The captain saluted and sped away.

Andolus stepped forward. "Let me take the crossbowmen. Their bolts will pierce Rover armor. We must hold that flank."

"What if you are needed elsewhere?" Conn asked.

The center was holding. The dwarves knew their business. The east remained relatively quiet. All the enemy's gambit was focused on breaking the west and rolling the army up one company at a time. Andolus gave a look suggesting such and snatched an extra quiver from the small stockpile position before the battle began.

"Runner! Order Commander Tayhiro to attack the enemy center immediately." Conn brushed off the salute, his mind already focused on what damage his limited cavalry was capable of producing. Too small to win the day, Tayhiro would at least give those traitors pause before resuming their assault.

The easterner was a hard man, seasoned and smarter than many cavalry officers Conn ran across over the course of his career. He was also the only option the army had. Time became reflexive. The center held, appearing to have gained ground. Genessen, to the east, was taking advantage of the inaction on his flank and began to countermove what the Rovers were doing in the west. The pace was agonizingly slow, unlike where Doluth and his requested command fought for their lives.

"Hold a while longer, son. Hold," Conn whispered.

"Sir! We need to fall back! First Company is being overrun. Captain Salis is dead," the corporal shouted in panic.

Doluth didn't need the extra pressure. First Company was on their own, for he had nothing left to throw into the fight. Every able body was engaged. He cursed his luck for having to face the Rovers and mercenaries. His sword already dulled, it was all Doluth could do to ball his fists in silent rage.

Hundreds of men rushed past him from behind. Bitter looking men in Hierarchy colors. What was happening? Doluth stared confused, as fresh ranks slipped in between those already trying to hold with shields. Spying an elf, Doluth waded through the throng of soldiers.

"Lieutenant. I thought we could be of assistance," Andolus greeted.

Doluth almost wept, so certain that he was about to die. "We can use anything you bring us, my lord."

Nodding, the elf stood behind the second rank of spears and ordered, "Ready!"

His crossbowmen responded by raising their weapons. Drawing his first arrow, Andolus looked up and down the line. The Rovers hadn't noticed his addition. A mistake he would make them pay for. Enough enemy soldiers packed in against the defensive line, there was no need to aim.

"Fire!"

Hundreds of heavy bolts punched the front few ranks of Rovers off their feet. The thrum reverberated across the line, temporarily drowning out the cries of the wounded. Stunned, the Rovers paused long enough for a second volley. Andolus grimaced as he drew and fired, rewarded by taking a Rover officer in the throat.

Panic ensued. Doluth, stunned, watched as a sergeant ordered the shields forward. The defenders found new strength. A third volley cleared ten meters between the armies. Those Rovers in the back still had no idea what was happening and continued to push forward while those in the slaughter field tried to flee. A fourth volley broke all discipline.

"Now! Forward!" Andolus shouted.

The army responded. Swords hacked and slashed. Spears stabbed. Shields knocked dazed bodies aside as the army of the Hierarchy regained their lost ground, punishing their foes with each step. A horn sounded and the Rovers broke. Andolus admired how the Hierarchy soldiers ignored the urge to break into an all-out assault. Their attack was methodical and there were no prisoners taken.

The retreating Rovers struggled to escape the steel maw of the killing machine at their backs and were besieged by a renewed catapult barrage for their efforts. Hundreds were killed or maimed. Yet as effective as the barrage proved, it limited the infantry advance. Andolus took advantage of the pause and ordered his men to the frontline where they expended all ammunition. What remained of the Rover force, a skeletal shadow of what had once been, broke and ran for safety. Their will to fight was gone.

Satisfied he'd done what needed doing, Andolus collected his crossbowmen, men who blindly followed him after the multiple successes against the scrathes and now the Rovers, and readied to reinforce the center. Only he discovered an unanticipated sight awaiting where the dwarves busied holding the field.

Tayhiro lowered his visor and nudged his steed into a gallop. Hundreds more followed in tight wedges behind and off to the sides. They were Conn's armored fist. Infantry parted ranks just in time as the triple wedges met the combined darkling and goblin contingent. Though several horses and riders were dragged down by claws and daggers, no army in the Free Lands could withstand a cavalry charge. Tayhiro made them pay.

Sensing momentum turning, Haf Forager order his forces to attack. Their weight, combined with Tayhiro's assault to his front and Genessen's tactical movements to his right, forced the enemy into a fighting retreat. His orders were to hold, not advance, but Haf had a better view of the situation. He and Jalos Carb led the charge.

Unlike Doluth's command, the dwarves let their discipline fracture. Soldiers, eager to end this fight and seeing victory loom, raced in the wake of the cavalry. Haf stepped down to crush a wounded darkling's head with his boot before following the others. This was the type of war his kind excelled at. He only hoped Conn would recognize the moment and respond accordingly.

"General, the army is advancing and the enemy appears to be in rout!"

Conn raised the looking glass and was surprised and horrified to see his orders being disregarded across the entire line. It was never his intent to drive into the enemy. He wanted them to break on his steel. Still, battles were fluid and needed to be adjusted as they developed. Over a third of the enemy army was dead or wounded. There was no better time to attack.

He hadn't felt giddy since first commissioning, but the spirit of the battle swept over him. "All units advance. I want commanders to halt upon capturing the enemy command post," he ordered.

Defeat was still a possibility, and one he wasn't willing to embrace, but the prospect of snatching victory from a superior force proved too enticing to pass up. Conn had the reserves, what little remained of them, brought to the original defensive position and had them dig in and establish a fallback line in the event his gambit failed or the enemy had more surprises waiting to be sprung.

He raised the looking glass once more and did what many high-ranking commanders were forced to, watch as his soldiers battled for not only their lives, but for the continued existence of the Free Lands.

Duoth N'nclogbar left his dagger in a soldier's chest and turned to flee. His people were being systematically slaughtered on all sides. The promises of wizards burned to ash. What might remained of the darklings lacked cohesion. Their initial successes were gone. Naught but dying dreams of dominating the lands of men and elves. Duoth saw no escape, but there was the chance of revenge. A new plan formed. His people may be lost, his reign ended, but there was one option he had remaining.

The darkling ruler tripped a wounded goblin and leapt on him. Dust kicked up as the pair struggled. Duoth, having the element of surprise, circled his clawed hands around the goblin's throat and plunged his nails into the soft flesh. Blood flowed over his fingers as Duoth crushed the life from his former ally. The darkling snarled and looked around. If any noticed the betrayal, they failed to stop it. Duoth grabbed the goblin's short sword and continued running.

One final murder needed doing.

Chaos reigned across the Plains of Darkpool. Hurst watched, mouth agape, as his carefully laid plans were cast to ruin. His army, pathetic as it was to his mind's eye, was in total rout. Darklings and goblins were being slaughtered as fast as the enemy got within sword reach. His mercenaries, while being wise enough to fallback, weren't faring much better. The Rovers, from what little he was able to determine from distance, were taking the brunt of the casualties.

The battle, Hurst was forced to admit, was a disaster. He had nothing left to give. No reserves to draw upon. The mercenary snatched an extra sword belt and went to his horse. Escape back to Morthus was the only viable option. Facing Arlyn's wrath was on par with standing against the army of the Hierarchy, but he felt he could at least reason with her. His personal guard was already mounted, having anticipated his next move.

"This is pointless. We ride," Hurst told them.

He placed a boot in the stirrups and was jerked back when a great weight landed on his back. A horse snickered. Swords were drawn as men shouted in alarm. Hurst hit the ground and rolled away, drawing his weapon in the process. Vile red eyes glared back at him through the kicked-up dust.

"Traitor," Hurst hissed.

Duoth, goblin sword in hand, growled and attacked.

The darkling's natural speed and agility proved too much for the mercenary. His swing went wild as Duoth ducked low and slashed across the top of Hurst's left knee. Burning pain erupted as his leg gave out. Hurst swung again, eyes blinded by tears. Duoth hissed again and plunged the goblin sword into the mercenary's neck. Eyes bulging, Hurst collapsed in the dirt. His last sights were of Duoth being murdered by one of his guard.

Justice, but at great cost. His dying breath rattled out, unheard as the remnants of his army fell to the enemy. He'd done all he could but was no match for the discipline and tactics of the Hierarchy. They'd proved a worthy opponent, one he was inept to fight. Hurst hoped Arlyn met with better results and would seek revenge for the slaughter on the Plains of Darkpool.

Either way, his war was ended. Hurst died at the side of his men.

THIRTY-FOUR

Final Confrontation

Elxander stiffened. His eyes narrowed as he tipped his head back, as if sniffing the air. Moving faster than a man of his age should be able to, the wizard crossed the massive hall to find Aron. One hundred meters wide, the hall was once filled with wooden tables and roaring fires. It was a place where men and women congregated to celebrate the successes of the day and enjoy bonds of fellowship. Now the columns supporting the ceiling were dark, covered with cobwebs and the dust of generations. It, like the majority of Mordrun Hath, had become an empty place, void of life and mirth.

Old memories unexpectedly painful, Elxander swept over the sand covered floor. A scorpion crawled out of the way, tail poised to strike. The wizard ignored Horus and the group of radicals posing as rebels. He'd dealt with their kind before and found little purpose in their efforts. Rebels, along with protesters, were among the most useless of society.

Aron watched the old man come and braced for the approaching tirade. Since joining forces and entering the forge, the old man had turned abrasive, almost arrogant. Aron wanted nothing to do with him. He shifted, careful not to disturb the sleeping Karin as she leaned against him.

"Wizard, you look perplexed," Aron said.

Elxander's glare spoke volumes. "Matters have changed."

"In what way?"

He pursed his lips, as if debating the need to tell another. "I have felt powerful magic, close. We are discovered."

Aron gestured to the small army of trolls, men, goblins, and elves around him. "We were discovered a while ago, Elxander."

"No, this is different. A powerful wizard has arrived and is within these halls."

Aron stiffened. If what Elxander said was true, that could only mean one person. Arlyn Gert had arrived. "Are you certain it is her?"

"Her?"

"Arlyn," Aron said. He reached for the Staff.

Elxander shrugged. "I do not know who, only that danger stalks us. The time has come to destroy the Staff of Life."

At last. I can finally be rid of this totem and the world will know freedom. Aron had been anticipating this moment since first learning of his history. Only now that the time had arrived, he felt ill, as if his nerves threatened to rebel. He wasn't sure if he was strong enough or had the ability to perform what needed doing. Pressure threatened to break him, here at the bottom of the world where all things ended.

"Aron, what is it?" Karin asked, her voice hoarse and sleep laden.

"The Staff," he mumbled.

She pushed off him. Concern in her eyes, Karin squeezed his hand.

"We must hurry. Time is against us," Elxander insisted.

Sylin and Camden, having overheard part of the conversation, joined them. "What is it?"

Aron explained as more of their group circled around him. They listened with mixed emotions. Many saw the end to a long war. Others feared what happened next. Regardless of personal opinion, Aron needed to destroy the Staff.

Halvor entered the circle. "Lord Kryte, I have sworn to stand by your side until the end."

"I've made it this far, might as well stick around to see what happens next," Harrin added.

Others pledged their support, most surprising was Horus. The giant stopped beside Elxander in silent warning. Aron began to feel confidence in heading into the unknown but was still besieged with many issues. Mard's trolls were patrolling Mordrun Hath, so how had Arlyn managed to get inside unseen? Had she come alone? Where was her army?

"Quickly, time is against us," Elxander urged.

Aron rose. "What of the enemy army? I cannot believe she came by herself."

"No. There are others, but no military force in the vicinity. I fear she will prove more than a match for all of us," Elxander said. "The chamber is small, thus reducing the number who may accompany you. Sylin Marth, you are required, as is the elf priest. Choose but a few more."

Without pause, he addressed Poros. "There is a task you must attend. One I feel you were born for."

Poros spread his arms and cocked his head. "Go on."

His face dropped as Elxander described his task. Mard slapped him on the shoulder, his meaty palm nearly covering half of Poros' back as the troll barked a laugh.

"Good! It is about time we trolls found a real fight!" Mard said.

Poros, back aching, scowled and shook his head. Everyone was going crazy and he was locked in the spiral. Dying wasn't part of his plan and reluctant as he was to admit it, the leader of the Free Rebellion recognized his one true purpose. There was no denying Elxander's persuasion, nor was there much choice.

"Morthus is days from here. We would never arrive in time," he managed. *How many more friends must I lose before this nightmare ends*?

He saw them all staring back. Dom Scimitar, the stalwart dwarf who'd been at his side from almost the beginning. Matis, former goblin guard sworn to the pursuit of freedom as tyranny ranged unchecked. So many others who'd endured one hardship after the next. The ghosts of those already fallen flanked him, urging him to continue from their graves. Poros took comfort from that, knowing he would soon be among them once more.

Elxander said, "Leave that to me. There is still much power lurking in the depths. Combined with young Master Marth, I should be able to transport your entire force south. A journey of days will take but a few breaths."

"That does not sound comforting," Poros replied, his sentiments echoed on the faces of the others.

"Beasts have to traverse the entire continent to get here," Jou Amn snorted. The Golden Warrior stood with arms folded.

"I would gladly trade places with you," Poros offered.

Jou broke into a toothy grin. "Not for all the gold in the world. Enjoy your journey."

"Enough time has been wasted. The magic user is already heading deep underground to chambers only masters once used. She cannot be allowed to arrive first. Come, bring your army and I will create your path."

Poros still lacked confidence in the crotchety old man, but the time for deliberation was done. He led and his army followed.

Darkness choked the corridors. Aron lost track of how far they'd traveled, knowing only that they were deep underground in areas unexplored by the trolls during their occupation. Elxander assured him no other living soul had been this deep beneath Mordrun Hath since he was forced to flee one thousand years ago. When pressed, he said no more. Some pains were too personal to share.

Karin edged closer. She'd never cared for enclosed places. Walking beside Aron helped alleviate some of the pressure she felt though. His strength flowed through her. She was about to tell him when a vision exploded through her eyes. Brilliant flashes temporarily blinded her and the force of the vision dropped her to her knees.

"Karin!" Aron shouted.

"I'm fine," she lied.

"She had a vision. You did not tell me she was gifted with sight," Elxander scolded.

"What did you see?" Aron ignored the wizard.

"I saw pain. Suffering. The world burned as we rotted," she said with trembling voice. "Aron, I saw us losing this war."

Surprisingly, it was Horus who offered comfort. "Lady, I have not endured centuries of slumber merely to awaken to defeat. I shall not allow your vision to turn true. You have my word."

He leaned down to help her up. Karin placed her face close to his ear and whispered, "Do not trust the wizard. He will betray you before this ends."

Horus remained silent. His earlier apprehension was confirmed. Wizards hunted his people to extinction. He would not allow Elxander to finish what was once started. Horus held no illusions about the future. Death was stalking him, and he was ready for the cold embrace of nothingness. He missed his family. His people. Horus wanted to rejoin them in the next life. Yet no matter how deep his desires, Horus vowed to claim vengeance first.

"Are there other details you can tell us?" Sylin asked. He cast worried looks between Horus and Elxander. Their undisguised tension was spreading through the others. The spark had ignited and it was only a matter of time before the detonation.

Karin winced as pain spread across her head. She drank from Aron's canteen before answering. "I saw a woman in grey holding the Staff."

"Arlyn," Aron snarled. "Wizard, we must hurry."

Sylin's mind raced with possibilities. He addressed Garin, "My friend, we have endured many challenges. I ask you once more for your axe. Take your dwarves and ward the entrances. Danger stalks us."

The dwarf surprised him by breaking into a wide grin. He hefted his axe and said, "I've been waiting for you to say that since we entered this accursed land."

Elxander resumed his pace as the dwarves and handful of Golden Warriors remaining hurried off. The bowels of Mordrun Hath were near.

Door sealed for almost a millennium hissed open under a blast of sand and stale oxygen that forced them to duck and cover their faces. Aron choked on the dust. An ancient stench filled his nostrils, turning his stomach. The longer he spent in the forge, the more he began to understand how forgotten places needed to remain so. He didn't get a feeling of evil from the forge, but there was an almost malevolent presence lurking just out of reach.

Blinking away the residue, Aron straightened and drew his sword. Elxander warned there was no need for weapons but the Golden Warrior wasn't going to take unnecessary chances, nor was he willing to risk using the

Staff prematurely. Wary, he slipped past the wizard and froze. The chamber was larger than he'd imagined, stretching far into the distance. So far, that darkness occluded their vision.

Aron felt his breath catch. Cast iron forges ran the length of the chamber in two rows, spaced ten meters apart. Each was the size of a catapult and eerily quiet. Empty work benches and shelves decorated the walls. Tools covered in cobwebs and centuries of dust lay where they'd last been used. He half expected to find skeletons bent over their workstations or desiccated remains collapsed on the floor.

A complex system of mirrors and reflective panels funneled enough light into the closest part of the forge for them to see almost everything, including rack upon rack of gleaming weapons and suits of armor fit for royalty. Sylin came to stand beside Aron and could only stare. If the Hierarchy had been given access to such machinery, they might have been able to survive Arlyn's betrayal.

"There is nothing comparable in any of the kingdoms," he whispered.

Aron agreed. "There is only one problem. Those forges haven't been used in a long time. How are we going to ignite them to the point we can destroy the Staff?"

"Sylin and I shall handle that," Elxander told them. "Come, young Marth. We have work to do. The rest of you guard the doors. Arlyn must not be allowed entrance while we are in the middle of casting this spell."

No one moved, instead they looked to Aron for guidance. Aron gave a clipped nod. He wished more had stayed behind, but the wizard insisted the focus of evil in Sadith Oom was centered in the southern city of Morthus and it would take their combined strength to defeat it.

How much greater could the evil in the south be than the fury of what threatened the others here in the forge?

"I have it," Camden offered and drew his sword. He hoped this was his last action before slipping away to that forgotten corner of the world.

Sylin waited until they were backing out before admitting, "Elxander, I have the barest control of magic. What you ask is beyond me."

Elxander gave him a stern glare, like a teacher disciplining his pupil. "Close your eyes and clear your mind. Total concentration is required. Here."

Sylin hesitated before taking the slender finishing hammer Elxander extended.

"This will allow you to channel the energies surrounding us. It will give you focus."

Doubtful, Sylin decided the best course of action was to submit. He took the hammer and followed instructions. He felt nothing at first, and was about to give up, when a tingling began at the very tips of his fingers. They grew warm. The sensation was not unpleasant and soon spread throughout his body. Sylin wanted to smile. Never had he felt such raw power. It soothed him, caressed his fragile soul. It was euphoric.

The flame circled his inner being, lashing onto bone and sinew. Sylin pointed the hammer. The flame poured from his body. He trembled as conflicting sensations of full and empty threatened to tear him apart. Sylin scowled and collapsed as the flame abandoned him. He looked up with tear filled eyes, surprised to find Elxander as calm as the day they'd met. A flicker from the corner of his eye drew his attention. Sylin looked right and was amazed to see the first forge already blazing with blue-red flames.

"How?" he asked.

Elxander clasped his hands. "That… is true power."

The small explosion brought down part of the ceiling around them.

Arlyn Gert waited until nightfall before entering the Forge of Wizards, regretting that she hadn't thought to do so until the enemy invaded her new kingdom. Clearing out the nest of trolls would have proven problematic but was accomplishable. Any losses sustained would have proven traumatic to the rest of her army's warfighting ability however. Conn's unexpected quickness in crossing the Croom left her with little choice but to reinforce the roads south, leaving her alone to deal with those refugees now hiding in the forge.

Anger burned in her eyes as she pulled open the long-forgotten service door leading down into the lower levels. She'd used her magic to ensure there were no lurking traps of trip falls waiting. Whatever power the forge once held, it was long dried up. Arlyn found the reality of being in Mordrun Hath less than her expectations. Not all legends were what they were advertised.

She hurried through empty corridors and access tunnels between levels, eager to remain off the main thoroughfares. Arlyn had sensed when magic was used and sensed that the majority of those within were now elsewhere. Where wasn't her problem. All her focus was on reaching the forges where she could prevent the Staff of Life from being unmade.

Decades of planning, of want and greed, were finally coming to fruition. She, Arlyn Gert of a no-name village in the middle of obscurity, was about to claim her due. Giddy, she picked up the pace. Her heart clenched as she heard the voices before seeing those who remained behind. Those who'd beaten her to the forges.

Arlyn, with no time to formulate a plan, lashed out as she rounded the final corner. Men and women guarding the doorway collapsed as darkness robbed their consciousness. She took no hope from this, however, for none had been magic users. Arlyn slowed and poked her head into the forge. Her surprise at seeing Sylin Marth with a handful of others, including the upstart Kryte who possessed the Staff of Life, already lighting one of the forges. Frantic at the thought of being too late, Arlyn unleashed her magic on the ceiling. Killing them outright was her one chance.

Chonol Distan stared down at the charred remains, those which hadn't blown away with the breeze, of the crazed Bendix. He still wasn't certain why the old fool had been necessary or why the Guilds contracted him to find and deliver the man to Sadith Oom. Chonol was certain that his career as an assassin was all but finished after failing to keep his contract secure. Failure was akin to a death sentence.

Still, there might be a way to salvage his neck before the Guild Masters sent other Gen Haroud after him. Killing the one responsible for his failure might buy him a few more years to redeem his career. Or at the very least, an honorable death. Chonol kicked sand over the ash and stalked down the dune.

Trolls and goblins, that part surprised him, guarded the main entrance and despite his years of training and skillsets, Chonol had no desire to lock blades with a squad of the hulking brutes. Knowing there must be other, smaller entry points trolls would overlook, the assassin began searching. He didn't know why, but felt that time was running out. At night, when he was alone,

Chonol swore he heard sounds of battle coming from the plains to the west. If that was correct, war had finally come to this miserable kingdom.

And not a moment too soon. There is no redemption for any living soul down here. Best the knife through the heart and be done with it all. Musing, Chonol failed to see the lithe figure dressed in sand colored clothing rise from the ground to trail him. His focus was on gaining entry to the ruins without being discovered. The figure stalked him without sound. All but the dark hue of eyes concealed from the sun.

Chonol crested a long dune running parallel to the main entrance and spied a small door cast open. His nerves tingled, for this was not here earlier when he made his initial scout with Bendix. Another had come through, perhaps one of Poros' surviving rebels. He snorted. *What a wretched lot they had been. Death serves them better than Poros ever could.*

The assassin, satisfied the entry point was clear of traps, congratulated his good fortune and stepped into Mordrun Hath. The dank stench crinkled his nose. Disturbed with having to go underground where his senses would be dulled and his reactions hampered by constriction, Chonol forced himself deeper. He needed to return with a head to show for his efforts, or it would be his head on a pole in Meisthelm. The Gen Haroud were unforgiving.

His tail stopped at the edge of the doorway in the event she'd been discovered and the assassin was waiting for her. Using her magic, she scanned the steep stairwell for signs of life. There were none. Satisfied, she followed the assassin underground, curious to see where he was headed and who his intended target was.

THIRTY-FIVE

All Things End

Poros stabbed the goblin in the abdomen and punched with his mailed fist into the wounded creature's face. The goblin reeled, giving Poros enough space to rip his sword free and slice the goblin's throat. The combined army had entered Morthus within the outer walls, courtesy of Elxander's spell, and caught the defenders unaware. Poros was responsible for securing the perimeter, while Mard and his trolls stormed into the citadel, killing any fool enough to stand before them.

Fires sprang up from different quarters. Elves remained cohesive and gained high ground to cover the attackers. Their arrows reaped a wicked toll as the goblins struggled with being attacked simultaneously on so many fronts. Aron's Galdeans, comprising the armored fist of the assault, struck parallel to the trolls, each column plunging into the heart of Morthus. The attack, hastily conceived, was pacing ahead of Poros' expectations.

So why do I feel cold? What am I missing? They were in the heart of the enemy empire and had met with little resistance thus far. He'd never encountered Arlyn, yet only a fool would leave their seat of power undefended. Poros began to worry as echoes of the rebellion's slaughter resurfaced.

"Poros! Come quickly, the trolls are in danger."

His gaze swept over pockets of fighters in search of the speaker, eventually finding Jerns Palic looking up at him. The elf waved, almost frantic to Poros' untrained eye. Nervousness clutched his gut and he hurried down the stairs connecting the ramparts with the lower level barracks attached to the outer wall.

"What is it?" he asked, slightly out of breath.

Jerns was pale. His eyes wide. "A nightmare of old times. We can defeat it, but only through combined effort."

Confused, Poros pressed, "What are you saying? What nightmare?"

"I cannot explain. Follow me, quickly, else our cause is lost," Jerns insisted.

Reluctant to place his trust in a man he'd just met, Poros hefted his sword and ran beside the elf. A hundred others followed in their wake. They wound through the curving streets of Morthus, engaging the enemy only when there was no way around and avoiding skirmishes when possible. The elf remained reticent, giving Poros further cause to worry.

The first sign of true trouble was clear a moment later as Poros looked down upon the ruined figure of a troll warrior. His body was broken and twisted in awkward angles. Blood leaked from mouth and nostrils. Great wounds, reminding Poros of claws, ran diagonally down his chest. Agony contorted the troll's face. He had died in extreme pain.

"What could do this to a troll?" he asked, without realizing.

The elves shifted nervously but refused to say more. Poros swallowed his rising fear and continued to follow Jerns, who had slowed his pace to that of a stalker. Sounds of battle reached them and Poros again felt his heartbeat quicken. More trolls lined the streets. Many were dead, murdered similarly to the first. Others were severely wounded and being escorted away from the conflict.

Against his better judgment, Poros rounded the final corner and skid to a halt. Mard stood in the middle of the street, engaged in a titanic struggle with a creature that shouldn't exist. Unsure what he was looking at, Poros would only be able to describe the creature as evil when asked years later. He vomited on his boots. Several elves did the same. Others picked their moment to fire silver tipped arrows into the nightmare creature.

"Ware! Tis a grohl!" an elf cried.

The grohl jerked back in agony as the arrowheads bore deep into muscle. Emboldened by the sudden support, Mard hammered the grohl about the head and face. Dark ichor flew with each strike. The grohl reeled under the assault. Arrows continued to pepper his great hide. Mard seized the advantage and cracked his war bar across the grohl's throat. The bone shattering crunch echoed down the streets and alleys.

"Now! Kill the beast!" Jerns shouted.

His elves rushed forward and expended their arrows into what turned into a steaming carcass. Poros watched until he saw Mard collapse. The troll tried to roll to his side and rise but fell back under his great weight. Poros rushed to his side. Through dimmed eyes, Mard saw Poros and broke into a toothy grin.

"This… was a good… fight," the troll coughed. Blood spit with each syllable.

Poros finally saw the extent of Mard's wounds and knew there was naught to be done. The leader of the Dagger Trolls was already dead.

Placing his hand on Mard's shoulder, Poros choked. "Yes, my friend. A grand battle. I shall have a statue raised in your honor. All shall know the honor and valor with which you fought."

Mard gurgled once and stopped breathing.

Chonol knew there were many people within the ruins of Mordrun Hath. Finding them however, was proving elusive. He had no idea that the complex stretched as far and as deep as it did, leaving him at an extreme disadvantage. Knowing there was no way to return to his guild without a head to make up for his failure, Chonol grit his teeth and plunged deeper into the darkness.

He paused every few meters, certain he'd heard the scuff of slippered feet. Each time he turned, he was greeted only by emptiness. The acoustics of the underground levels played havoc with his senses, leaving him disoriented. Chonol needed to find his target and get away before madness consumed him.

Creeping upon a right angle, Chonol pressed against the cobweb covered wall and listened. There it was again. The subtlest whisper of footfalls skipping down the hall. He drew his second dagger, convinced he was being hunted. The assassin appreciated the irony. He'd made a life of hunting others, that he should find himself on the reverse end of that now, here, was oddly comforting.

Sensing the game was begun, Chonol slipped around the corner and searched out the perfect spot to lay in wait and ambush his hunter. Alcoves and locked doors filled the wide corridor. The first several he encountered refused to budge. Chonol slipped along the wall, feeling his way through the darkness. His gloves soon grew covered with ages old dust. He kicked against a skeleton. The bones shattered, collapsing into dust.

A faint glow lined the distance. Chonol assumed he'd found the others at last. It was nearly enough to make him forget his game of cat and mouse. His right boot scuffed the worn pavestones. Frowning at his incompetency, Chonol discovered open air on his right and entered the alcove. An ancient statue filled the center, likely one of the founding wizards. Their current descendants struck him as vain to the point of being unapproachable. Why should the originators be any different?

Settled in, Chonol began going through his mental exercises. Whoever was stalking him wasn't far behind, or ahead, leaving him with little time. He slowed his breathing, clearing his mind of diversions. Fingers clenched reflexively. His mind's eye envisioned a series of strikes, parries, and counterstrikes. Muscles loosened. Chonol closed his eyes and lashed into the hall with his right hand while swinging the left up in a move aimed at disemboweling his victim. His strikes met only air.

A slip of wind kissed his face. His neck felt wet, cold suddenly, as he tried to figure out where he went wrong. Chonol tried, failed, to raise his left arm. Burning sensations spread up his arm. The appendage fell limp, useless.

"Who?" he asked. Gargled blood poured down his chest.

The figure in tan emerged from the shadows. Chonol blinked rapidly as unholy darkness encroached his vision. His surprise upon seeing a woman, lithe and rather diminutive, standing before him with a bloodied needle tip dagger, stretched across his face.

"How?" he asked.

The woman, his killer, reached up and pulled the mask from her face. Red like blood. Kelanvex cocked her head. "I'd expected one of the Gen Haroud to put up more of a challenge. A shame. I never got to test my skills."

Chonol opened his mouth but the words didn't come. His knees buckled and the assassin fell dead at Kelanvex's feet. She skipped back to avoid getting blood on her slippers. Satisfied the immediate threat to the quest was removed, she replaced her face mask and hurried down to where Aron Kryte was about to destroy the Staff of Life. And if he didn't, if the pull of power grew too strong for his morals to withstand, she had a cure for him as well.

Dalstrom was right in sending her south. The assassin guilds operated with too much free reign. She and the other priests of the Red Brotherhood needed to counteract that to secure the peaceful transition from the Hierarchy to the Council of Delegates. Meters blurred past as the fledgling wizard and priest hurried to complete her task.

Aron's head pounded. His ears rang. Debris rained from the ceiling after the large chunks of stone had stopped falling. Unconsciousness threatened to claim him. The Golden Warrior shook off the cold fingers clutching him and looked about what remained of the forge. Instincts made him look for Karin. Her unconscious figure lay seemingly unharmed beside a massive chunk of ceiling. Squinting, he relaxed upon seeing the rise and fall of her chest.

"Sylin Marth, you surprise me," a woman's voice echoed. "I had long thought you hidden from the world. Finding you here is… troubling."

"Traitor," Sylin replied. He was calm, refusing to rise to her taunts.

Arlyn stepped into the forge. Her long robes flowed over debris and unconscious bodies. Disdain twisted her already pinched face. "Zye Terrio and the rest of the Council betrayed the Free Lands long before I made my decision. A pity you were not in Meisthelm when Imelin returned. No matter. Your time in this world ends today."

"How? You are hopelessly outnumbered," Aron coughed.

Arlyn turned her wicked glare on the last scion of Ils Kincannon. "I think not. That pathetic rabble you left to guard against me is being dealt with as we speak."

A bolt of dark, almost purple, power blasted Arlyn in the side, throwing her into the far wall. Elxander strode through the chaos. Electricity crackled around him. His long hair danced about his shoulders while madness lurked in his deep eyes. He unleashed a second, weaker blast, further pinning Arlyn to the wall.

"This insanity ends now," Elxander snapped. Spittle flew with each syllable. "Aron, destroy the Staff! Cast it into the forge-fire!"

Hands dragged the Golden Warrior to his feet. Aron thanked Camden with a nod and the pair, once Aron secured the Staff, stumbled toward the forge. Wild bolts of magic began to crisscross the forge as Arlyn counterattacked. One of the Golden Warriors chosen to remain was skewered by a blast, his flesh melting within his armor. Aron failed to see how any of them were going to survive.

"What was that?" Jou Amn raised his sword and turned back toward the forge. His displeasure with having been sent behind to ward the rear approach, evident.

Garin tugged on his beard. He too felt discarded, despite the confidence in which he'd accepted this position. "They have two wizards among them. More than enough to combat whatever enters."

"What of us?"

The dwarf was cut off as the ground shook. Confused, dwarves and men looked for the source of the commotion. Talrn was first to react. Axe in hand, he gestured to the ground where spouts of rock and dirt shot up all around. The floor shifted, heaving unsteadily. A dwarf slipped and fell. Ethereal hands, dozens of sickly green appendages dripping flesh and oozing from open lesions, burst from the floor to clasp the fallen dwarf. No amount of struggling helped. Clothing and flesh burst into flame wherever the hands touched him. They pulled the screaming dwarf down through the floor. Blood and gore were all that remained as his body was pulverized in the very stone.

Camden reacted first. "Ware the ground!"

"Back! Get back now!" Garin bellowed.

Man and dwarf fell back beyond the range of the trap. Scores of hands stretched up from their eternal prison, each questing.

"How can we fight that?" Jou said between ragged breaths.

Garin planted his axe blade on the ground and leaned on the handle. "We need a wizard."

Aron and Halvor ran as fast as they could while utilizing the wizard battle to their advantage. Flames in green and blue burned across the forge. Smoke issued from each of the three wizards. Aron failed to see how any would survive the nightmare. None of that mattered. He cared little for wizards and the damage they'd done to the Free Lands. Destroying the Staff promised a new dawn to a world free from the depredations of people like Arlyn and the Black Imelin. He just needed to reach the forge.

"Hurry, Aron. Time is short," Halvor urged.

The scarred elf priest dragged Aron closer. The end loomed. Heat from the forge flames nearly forced the pair into collapse, as it burned away tiny hairs on their face and hands. The Staff began to vibrate.

"I think it knows I am going to destroy it," Aron choked on noxious fumes.

Halvor nodded. The Red Brotherhood long suspected the totem of being sentient to influence the wielder. "Not much further. The forge is ahead. Take strength!"

Steeling his nerves, Aron forced each step forward. The Staff seemed heavier, as if attempting to pull him down. Each step was an effort. Aron began sweating. The forge was but a few steps away. He knew that it was time. Aron began unwrapping the Staff. His fingers curled around the freed material and the force of visions drove him to his knees.

Faces of men long dead flashed before his eyes. Men he'd killed over the course of his career. Aron blinked, hoping to clear his vision. The slaughter at the Unchar Pass, where he'd used the Staff to destroy thousands of darklings, taunted him. His arm grew heavy and began to drop.

"No! You must destroy the Staff!" Halvor shouted.

The forge trembled. Magic fire raced across the floor toward them. The elf raced to Aron's side and shoved him out of the way a breath before the flames arrived. Halvor wasn't as fortunate. The elf priest threw back his head and screamed as dark fires burned him from the inside out. His charred corpse fell.

Aron watched in horror as Halvor, who'd already suffered an attack of wizard fire in the long-forgotten ruins of Gelum Drol, died before his eyes. Anger welled in him. Too many friends who'd begun this quest no longer stood by his side. Halvor. Amean. They fell like sheathes of wheat on an autumn day. He wanted to cry. Aron rose on unsteady legs and threw the Staff with all his might.

Arlyn punched her right fist at Elxander and was rewarded with seeing the ancient wizard jerk back. His hands went to his throat. Snarling, Arlyn pulled her fist back and clenched. Elxander slammed into the floor, choking as tendrils of power squeezed his neck. All she needed to do was squeeze a little tighter and the last of the old wizards would die.

Movement out of the corner of her eye caught her attention. Arlyn snapped her head around and gasped as two men hurried to reach the forge. Glaring, she released her grip on Elxander and lashed out at Aron and the elf priest. Purple fire traced from her fingertips and ran a track across the floor.

"Not now, you little bastard," she whispered. "The Staff is mine."

The impact stung the side of her face. Confused, Arlyn reeled away. Her magic faded but not until one of the two was killed. Her fingers came away with blood as she gingerly touched the side of her head. No magic did this. Then what? A second impact drove her back another step. This time, she watched the fist-sized rock fall away. She was almost surprised to find Sylin standing a few meters away with another rock in hand.

Sylin leaned against a dust covered workbench for support. He was certain more than one rib was cracked. Each breath was painful. The former Councilman readied to cast his third rock when Arlyn turned on him. Time was up. His magic was spent. The limited wells of his power dried up. There was no way to stop Arlyn now, unless he got close enough to run his sword through her. The vehemence in her eyes, so bright they seemed to shine in the quasi-darkness, told him that wasn't going to happen. Sylin drew back to throw what would be his last rock when the explosion threw them all to the ground.

Arlyn screamed when she understood that Aron had successfully cast the Staff of Life back into the forge. Centuries of restrained magic was suddenly loosed upon the world. Cracks spread through the floor. A forge collapsed on itself and fell into the ground. Arlyn ran toward Aron, hoping to salvage the Staff. She never made it. A chunk of ceiling the size of a catapult caught her in midstride, pulverizing her entirely.

Horus watched the exchange of magic and was reviled. The old wounds of his people being slaughtered reopened, for they had died much the same way. Magic was corruption. His heart clutched when Elxander was slammed to the ground. The giant whispered a prayer to the old gods that his former persecutor was finally dead. Disappointment stirred when he saw Elxander still moving.

The explosion took him by surprise, but it also threw him closer to the wizards. Providence in his favor, Horus pushed off the floor. He hadn't known why he was awakened. Joining the war against the darkness seemed appropriate but ultimately unfulfilling. He knew there was more. One final piece necessary before attaining his destiny. This, Horus now understood, was why he'd returned. He, the final survivor of his people, was meant to be the instrument of vengeance. Retribution sat within the strength of his arm and the weight of iron he carried.

Horus stalked toward Elxander. He ignored the falling chunks of ceiling. Ignored the cut off scream of the witch woman responsible for this insanity. The giant loomed over the fallen wizard and drew back to strike.

Elxander, sensing a new threat, rolled over and lashed out with what little magic he had left. The weakened bolt of power caught Horus in the chest but not before the giant managed to follow through with his swing. Iron crunched into Elxander's skull, breaking bone and smashing brain. The wizard suffered an inglorious demise.

Horus collapsed atop his hated foe. Blood frothed around the corners of his mouth. His head felt heavy. Each breath produced unimaginable pain, yet he was satisfied. Soft hands touched him, caressing his tired cheek. He turned and saw Karin kneeling beside him. The seer he had vowed to save.

"Do not grieve for me, little one," Horus said. "My people have been avenged. I go now to meet them, for at last I shall be welcomed as an equal."

"Horus," Karin cried.

The giant managed a last smile before passing on to the next life where his wife and children waited. Karin laid her head down on his body and wept. So much destruction and waste of life and for what? She failed to understand. The forge collapsed around her. Convinced she was the only one still alive, Karin was resigned to join the others in death. There seemed little point in escape.

Aron picked himself up and surveyed what remained of the forge. Halvor was dead, as was Elxander and the giant, Horus. He found no trace of Arlyn. Despair began to settle, only to evaporate as he caught the gentle weeping of Karin. Moving as fast as his battered form allowed, the Golden Warrior hurried to her side.

"Come Karin, we must be away before this entire place collapses," he urged.

Stunned, Karin blinked away her tears. "Aron? I thought… I thought you were dead."

"Not yet, but there is not much time," he said.

She hugged him fiercely.

"Get her out of here!" Sylin shouted.

The Councilman limped across the forge. Cuts and bruises littered his body.

"Not until I find Arlyn. She must answer for this," Aron replied.

Shaking his head, Sylin replied, "Arlyn is dead, crushed by that rock. Go. I will keep the roof from collapsing until we are free."

Aron didn't hesitate. He pulled Karin to her feet and the pair headed for the doors. Only when they were clear did he stop to look back for Sylin. The Councilman smiled sadly before what remained of the ceiling dropped.

EPILOGUE

The blanket of night smothered the border city of Jerincon. What had once been a city on the verge of siege, was now returned to the normal quiet of obscurity. News of the war in Sadith Oom spread quickly and the goblin commanders immediately ordered their forces back to their lands rather than risk the wrath of the army of the Hierarchy. Not a drop of blood had been spilled.

A sliver of moon cut through the cloud clover, bathing only the smallest portions of the sprawling city. Most of the population had already turned in, retiring for the day. Most, but not all. Two squat figures, cloaked and unarmored, shuffled through the mix of shadow and light. They moved with precision, their destination known.

Once heavily guarded, the main command headquarters was a skeleton of its former glory. The citizen army of Jerincon disbanded back to their villages and in the case of the dwarves, back to the Drear Hills in the north. Only a handful remained. The two figures, dwarves themselves, entered the headquarters through the obscure side door and hurried, as quietly as dwarves could, up the single flight of stairs.

A quick check of the hall revealed their path clear, so they continued on. A soft glow of lamp light came from under the door at the end of the hall. One of the dwarves tried to run but was held back by the flat of an axe blade across his chest. Disappointed, he settled back into his normal gait. They reached the door and pushed.

"I figured you would come," Dremmin Giles snorted.

The dwarf commander of Jerincon's defense force stood with his meaty hands out to the side. He was unarmed.

Garin Stonebreaker lowered his hood, his brother Talrn did the same. It was Talrn who spoke. "This is for Gul Killingstone. A better dwarf than you or I shall ever be."

Garin closed the door behind them as his brother raised his axe.

Bells chimed throughout the golden city. Meisthelm was alive with music and joy. Six months had passed since the destruction of the Staff of Life. Six months in which the Free Lands began to rebuild. Kingdom rulers agreed that the Hierarchy was outdated and a new order necessary, if their people were to enter a new age of prosperity and more importantly, peace. The Council of Delegates was formed, with each kingdom sufficiently represented.

Elsyn cared nothing for that. She stood atop the steps of the former Hierarchy sanctum, hand in hand with her newly betrothed, Warrien. The two leaders, already strong members of the new Council, were married before a healthy crowd of men, elves, dwarves, trolls, and goblins.

Never had Meisthelm been host to such races. A mistake the new Council refused to make again. Members of all races sat on the Council. Elsyn looked over the crowd and missed her father. It seemed so long ago since he had been taken from her and the world plunged into chaos. Tear-filled eyes fell on Aron. The Golden Warrior was resplendent in his polished armor. At his side was Karin Kryte. All seemed right with the world.

Their escape from Mordrun Hath was well documented. Those missing pieces provided by Sylin

Marth. The former councilman had lost his right arm in the collapse but managed to escape using the same magic Elxander had shown him when they created the portal used to send Poros Pendyier and the others to Morthus.

He stood beside Poros and secretly missed Camden Hern. The two had grown close during their travels but Camden proved true to his word. The Journeyman made his peace and said good-bye at the Pillars of Creation. Sylin wished him well. Poros was asked, and accepted, to join the new Council. His efforts in Sadith Oom served as inspiration for many peoples. He hoped to live up to their expectations.

Warrien coughed under his breath, jerking Elsyn from her daydreaming. The queen of Galdea took a step forward to address the crowd. "People of Meisthelm, of the Free Lands, and my friends."

She scanned the crowd. Dlorn was in the front. He'd resigned his position as Field Marshal, only after suggesting a very capable Daril Perryman replace him, and accepted the position of General of the Army for the Free Lands. Conn retired upon leaving Sadith Oom. His heart and mind were no longer fit enough for duty. The once Rover Ute Hai, now a lieutenant in the Golden Warriors, stood in full armor among a company of his peers, veterans of the campaign all. Others she'd met during their travels filled the front few rows. The familiarity comforted her.

"The hours of warfare have faded. We now enter a time of peace and prosperity. Our kingdoms will rebuild. Our bonds strengthen as we renew relations that have long fallen into disrepair."

Her gaze fell on the elves. Andolus stood beside Long Shadow. The elf lord refused the offer to return to a better fortified Dol'ir, as did most of his elves. They were already reestablishing their colony at Dreamhaven.

A handful would rotate through the new fortress, adding their strength to the coalition of soldiers garrisoned in the Mountains of the Fang.

"Together we will remake the Free Lands, not into what it once was, but to the promise of what it may become."

People cheered and the clear call of trumpets pierced the morning air.

Long Shadow turned to Andolus and slapped his friend, whom he once thought dead in the Croom River, on the shoulder. "That, my dear friend, is one of the best speeches I have heard in a long time. Come, let us drink to the newlyweds!"

Those who knew Long Shadow, Andolus and Aron Kryte included, could only stare in mute awe as the once silent man from across the seas strode away chuckling. It was a new day indeed.

END

Enjoyed this series? Check out the acclaimed Northern Crusade series for more sword and sorcery action!

Hammers in the Wind: The Northern Crusade
Book I

ONE
A Foul Night

High-pitched screams pierced the wood and stone halls of Chadra Keep. Badron, the liege lord of Delranan, sprang from his ancient throne at the sound, his band of favored captains and counselors doing the same. His pale blue eyes boiled from shock to feral rage as he quickly registered what was happening. Screams could only mean one thing: his very family was under attack in what was supposed to be the most secure place in his kingdom. More screams and blood-choked cries mixed with the sound of clashing steel. Badron snarled grimly. The house guard, his guard, was locked in brutal struggle somewhere deep within the wooden halls of the Keep.

Badron drew his trusted sword and stormed off in search of the battle. The senior most lords and captains of Delranan followed him. Eight in all, they comprised a most lethal band of warriors. Their deeds had forged the kingdom from a pack of warring tribes and clans into a singular monarchy that quickly became the strongest of the northern kingdoms. They wordlessly chased at the wolf skin cloak of their king as he headed towards the royal sleeping chambers.

Fear drove Badron. Long red hair, now streaked through with gray, flowed angrily down broad shoulders. His normally pale blue eyes seethed red with rage. Wrath commanded him, wrath so strong it could threaten the foundations of his hard-fought kingdom and make the old gods of Malweir tremble in fear. Muscles bunched under his jerkin. His bulk filled the doorway. Badron felt the old energies flow into him. His was a warrior's life and this night but an extension of it. The sound of glass breaking drew his attention. Badron bellowed and charged, heedless of any lurking dangers.

Fleeting visions of battle appeared through the flickering torchlight. The flash of a sword. A spray of blood. The ruins of a body lay in the middle of the hall, a crumpled mass of flesh. Badron knelt beside the corpse. The smell of blood kissed the stagnant air. Deep cuts and gashes immolated the young house guard. Badron tried to close the eyes, if for no other reason than to avoid staring down into the pure agony. A feathered spear, broken at the hilt, was embedded in the lad's throat.

"Pell Darga," growled Jarrik. He rubbed his bald head and spat.

The king brought his gaze up to his friend and captain. "Rouse whatever watch remains, Jarrik. I want these monsters run down and skinned alive. The rest of you with me."

Badron led them further into the Keep. The inner doors to the royal chambers were smashed to ruins. One lay in splinters across the hall while what was left of the second hung in shreds by a single hinge. Smoke curled up from the chamber, running down the ceiling. Fresh blood stained the floor and walls in ragged patterns. More bodies. Badron grimaced. From the looks of it all of his private guard had been caught unaware and slain. Their furs and spiked helmets lay stained in growing pools of blood. Badron splashed his way past.

At last they came unto the king's chambers. The doors were similarly smashed, leaving a gaping maw, dark and uninviting. Shadows leaked into the hall. Unknown fears danced around the men and threatened their resolve. Preparing his mind for the worst, Badron bunched his shoulders and surged forward. Nothing in this world meant so much to him as the memory of his late wife Rialla and the children he'd sired.

Rough hands snatched at his collar and jerked him back. "No my lord, we cannot afford to lose you," Argis whispered. Harsh tones ground from his throat.

He gestured with his head and two of the largest guards crept forward to flank the doors. Satisfied the king wasn't going to do anything rash, Argis released him and tossed his torch to the nearest man. Inion snatched it and gave his battle brother an awkward look. A hint of smile, no more than the slight curve of his lips, caressed his face. It had been too long since they'd last gone to war. Inion hefted his tulwar and threw the torch into the bedchamber. He charged in after, Argis immediately following with a litany of battle cries. Berserker strength churned inside them.

Badron impatiently waited. Sounds came back to him, making the hairs on his neck stand. The breaking of furniture. A crash in the dark. He forced himself to stand by and wait while others rushed to defend his honor. The idea pained him, but he must be king before warrior. That was the price for the gift he'd usurped from his brother long ago. Inion reappeared a heartbeat later. Disbelief stained his naturally dark eyes. He mouthed words that were incoherent babble.

Badron pushed forward, forgetting all restraint. "Speak man, what of my family?'

The stunned captain could only point back at the broken door.

"Is she?" he whispered.

Inion could not bear to look his king and friend in the eye. "I don't know, sire. There are traces of blood but no bodies. It is clear that there was a struggle."

Emotions collided in a mass of confusion. Badron was beyond enraged and on the verge of breaking down. He'd never truthfully cared much for his daughter. In fact he constantly blamed her for the death of his precious

Rialla during childbirth. But Maleela was still his flesh and blood. He punched a massive fist into the nearest wall.

"Find my daughter or I'll have your heads on pikes by dawn. No one sleeps until the Pell Darga are found and killed. And bring me my son."

One by one they bowed and deployed throughout Chadra Keep. Only Harnin One Eye stood fast. Oldest and most loyal of the eight, Harnin watched his king with concern through his remaining eye.

"My lord, your daughter…" he whispered.

Badron shot him a cross look. "Do not remind me of what I know all too well. We shall deal with this when the time comes."

The bloodied halls of Chadra Keep felt surprisingly empty despite the flurry of activity. What remained of the decimated house guard began a room-by-room search for the royal family. Bodies were taken away and prepared for burial while servants scrubbed the blood from the walls and floor as best as they could. Many believed this night of terror was already finished. Badron knew it was only the beginning. Whatever evil the Pell had in mind would spark his final designs and begin a long anticipated war. Badron stormed through his Keep barking orders.

It was then that he came upon the body of his only son.

The young prince's head sharply drooped to the side. Pell Darga spears riddled his body. Blood wept from dozens of wounds. His sword was sheathed in blood. Badron's heart lurched. Clearly his boy had put up a good fight. Then he spied it. The gentle rise and fall of the chest. His son was not yet dead. Badron quickly dropped down and cradled his son to him.

"My son," he choked.

"They…came in….through the…windo…." Blood spit through his broken lips as he talked. Soon he would journey to the halls of his ancestors, no longer a pawn to the vagaries of life. "Took… Maleela…"

A last gasp made his body shake gently. The heir to the throne of Delranan was dead, at peace. Badron shook uncontrollably. Humbled and belittled, Badron could only stop and stare. He wanted to drop down and cradle the lad one last time, to let his tears flow free. But he was king, and kings do not do such things.

"He died honorably, sire," Harnin soothed. "We should all hope for such."

Badron spun on his friend. "Honorably? He died at the hands of cowards and assassins! Do not speak to me of honor!"

"Lord Badron!"

Jarrik strode purposefully down the hallway. "Lookouts spied men on horseback riding east. They claim to have caught the wisp of a woman's gown among the riders."

Anger's edge diminished, if only slightly. The desire for revenge grew.

"How many?" he asked.

"Between thirty and forty near as they could tell."

A cold gleam twisted Badron's eyes. "Reform the council. I want blood."

Badron reentered the throne room, his unfocused eyes streaked with red. The throne seemed less. The hearth fire was cold. It was only late summer and already winter's reach struggled to find purchase. The brightest of the summer sun had already faded. It wouldn't be much longer before the snow blew in from the cruel Northern Ocean. None of that mattered of course. Badron could see only despair in the near future. The threat of winter held no danger for him. His dreams, his very life, had come crashing down this night. All of the hard work he and his kind had done in building a mighty kingdom might well have died with his son. Delranan had no heir. None that is, except his unwanted daughter Maleela. Badron snarled.

His captains entered in somber procession. Each was armed and geared for campaign. Whatever they were now, they had all been among the very best warriors in the north countries. Now was the time for sharpened steel. Words and posturing didn't belong in the future Badron envisioned for his kingdom.

"The house of the king is ruined," Badron drawled. "The Pell Darga have shamed us all this night. My son is murdered and my *daughter* taken. How can this have happened under our noses? Chadra Keep is supposed to be the most secure building in Delranan."

His words dripped venom. All at once a chorus of rage echoed across the chamber. The call for war lifted their spirits. Frightened talk fell in hushed tones at the mention of the Pell though. Ancient hatred and superstitions cloaked the mountain dwellers. Some claimed they were nothing more than myth; one told to children to keep them in line during the long winter nights when mischief was prone to spark. No one living had ever seen one. Legend said they came from the Murdes Mountains far to the east, the Mountains of Death. No sane man volunteered to travel those dark paths.

"The Pell Darga do not exist. Surely we are missing some vital clue in all of this," Jarrik cautioned. For all of his great strengths, strategy was not one.

Harnin rose and cast down a blood-stained short spear. "Truly? Then explain this! Taken from the body of the king's own son as he lay dying. Mind your tongue, Jarrik. The Pell exist and it is time we confronted them."

The old man glowered at his rival, but said nothing else.

"How is it they managed to sneak past our guard and slay half of the house with us unaware?" Skaning, a burly man with coal black hair man, asked.

Badron grunted. "How do giants shape the mountains or the gods make war? You ask questions only a sorcerer might answer. This I tell you all. We have but two choices. Either we ignore this night's foul deeds." Chaotic roars swept through those assembled. Badron held his hands up for quiet, "Or we raise the Wolfsreik and march to war. To the very heart of the Murdes Mountains if need be."

"Sire, it will take a month or more to raise the full strength of the Wolfsreik," Harnin cautioned.

Ten thousand fully armed men complete with supplies and kit was no easy feat.

Badron had a familiar twinkle in his eyes. "Six weeks and we can march."

"On who exactly? The Pell Darga are not a nation. By rights we would be invading Rogscroft," Argis said.

Skaning stood. "Such an action would surely jeopardize your family more. If our goal is to retrieve the princess alive we need speed and secrecy, not the strength of arms."

"What would suggest then?" Badron asked sharply.

Clearing his throat, Skaning continued. "Send men to scour the inns and taverns. Find a stalwart band of mercenaries and adventurers willing to become heroes for a small price."

Harnin spat. "Not even a drunken fool would risk facing the Pell on their own territory. We must raise the army."

"I agree with Skaning," Jarrik seconded. "These are troubled times. Money can be a powerful motivator and the types of man we will attract are expendable at best."

"Battle against Man is one thing, but these are demons from the Old Times. I for one will not waste my life so recklessly," Harnin fell silent.

"Not even at the behest of your king?" Badron asked. "We are all led to a place of dark thought. Evil must be used to combat evil if we are to succeed."

No one noticed the sudden guarded look in Harnin's eye. "My apologies sire. I have forgotten my place. But the question remains. What fool would dare enter such a realm and risk certain death?"

"Every man has a price," Argis chipped in. "All we need do is find the right ones."

Badron thoughtfully rubbed the gray stubble on his chin. "This might work. Stouds has more than enough men of lesser quality for what we need. One Eye, since you so willingly champion this idea I place you in charge. You have two days to collect the men you deem necessary. After that I sound the muster and the Wolfsreik marches."

Harnin's smile was sharp, wicked. "Yes, sire."

The king pushed away from the table. He had heard enough. He paused in the doorway to look back over his shoulder and reiterate, "You have two days."

Chadra Keep's familiar shadows offered no comfort to the lone warrior marching through. Soft winds kissed the torch in his hand. Fractured darkness covered the windows. The first hint of dawn seeped through the cold grey night. Funeral pyres were already being erected in the main courtyard. Soon the bodies would be sent to their ancestors. Servants scurried about in an almost vain attempt to return the Keep to its former glory.

He ignored it all. Gaining the top of the stair, he quickly headed down to the cellars. He eased past the dungeons and food stores. His destination was perhaps the biggest secret in the Keep. Unknown to most, there was a secret tunnel leading out into the surrounding forest, but he knew. After all, he was the one who had left the exit unsecure and allowed the attackers inside in the first place. And it was the only way he was going to be able to elude the guard without questions.

He slowly pushed the ancient door open. The sky continued to brighten. It was now a muted shade of grey; still dark but light enough for him to see where he was going. He knew that Delranan, and perhaps all Malweir, was now locked in a season of change. It was a time for myths. Trolls and Goblins, dragons and wizards. It was a season for treachery and betrayal.

He took his first step towards freedom and was met by the touch of cold steel at his throat.

OTHER BOOKS BY CHRISTIAN WARREN FREED

ARMIES
of the
SILVER MAGE
CHRISTIAN WARREN
FREED

Malweir was once governed by the order of Mages, bringers of peace and light. Centuries past and the lands prospered. But all was not well. Unknown to most, one mage desired power above all else. He turned his will to the banished Dark Gods and brought war to the free lands. Only a handful of mages survived the betrayal and the Silver Mage was left free to twist the darker races to his bidding. The only thing he needs to complete his plan and rule the world forever are the four shards of the crystal of Tol Shere.

Having spent most of their lives dreaming about leaving their sleepy village and travelling the world, Delin Kerny and Fennic Attleford never thought that one day they would be forced to flee their town to save their lives. Everything changes when they discover the fabled Star Silver sword and learn that there are some who want the weapon for themselves. Hunted by a ruthless mercenary, the boys run from Fel Darrins and are forced into the adventure they only dreamed about.

Ever ashamed of the horrors his kind let loose on the world the last mage, Dakeb, lives his life in shadows. The only thing keeping him alive is his quest to stop the Silver Mage from reassembling the crystal. His chance finally comes through the hearts and wills of Delin and Fennic. Dakeb bestows upon them the crystal shard, entrusting them with the one thing capable of restoring peace to Malweir.

the Dragon Hunters
CHRISTIAN WARREN FREED

The Mage Wars are a fading memory. The kingdoms of Malweir focus on rebuilding what was lost and moving beyond the vast amounts of death and devastation. For some it is easy, others far worse. Some men are made in battle. Grelic of Thrae is one. A seasoned veteran of numerous campaigns and raids, Grelic is a warrior without a war. He languishes under mugs of ale and poor choices that eventually find him locked in the dungeons of King Rentor. His only chance at redemption is an offer tantamount to suicide: travel north with a misfit band of adventurers and learn the truth of what happened in the village of Gend.

Grelic, suddenly tired of his life, reluctantly agrees and meets the only survivor of the horrible massacre: Fitch Iane. Broken, mentally and physically, Fitch babbles about demons stalking through the mists and a terrible monster prowling the skies, breathing fire and death.

What begins as a simple reconnaissance mission quickly turns into a quest to stop Sidian, the Silver Mage from accomplishing his goals in the Deadlands. The last of the dark mages seeks to recover the four shards of the crystal of Tol Shere and open the gateway to release the dark gods from their eternal prison.

Grelic and his team are sorely outnumbered and ill prepared to deal with the combined threats of a dark mage and one of the great dragons from the west. Not even the might of the Aeldruin, high elf mercenaries, and Dakeb, the last of the mages, promises to be enough to stop evil and restore peace to Thrae.

DREAMS
OF
WINTER
A FORGOTTEN GODS TALE
CHRISTIAN WARREN FREED

It is a troubled time, for the old gods are returning and they want the universe back…

Under the rigid guidance of the Conclave, the seven hundred known worlds carve out a new empire with the compassion and wisdom the gods once offered. But a terrible secret, known only to the most powerful, threatens to undo three millennia of progress. The gods are not dead at all. They merely sleep. And they are being hunted.

Senior Inquisitor Tolde Breed is sent to the planet Crimeat to investigate the escape of one of the deadliest beings in the history of the universe: Amongeratix, one of the fabled THREE, sons of the god-king. Tolde arrives on a world where heresy breeds insurrection and war is only a matter of time. Aided by Sister Abigail of the Order of Blood Witches, and a company of Prekhauten Guards, Tolde hurries to find Amongeratix and return him to Conclave custody before he can restart his reign of terror.

What he doesn't know is that the Three are already operating on Crimeat.

BIO

Christian W. Freed was born in Buffalo, N.Y. more years ago than he would like to remember. After spending more than 20 years in the active duty US Army he has turned his talents to writing. Since retiring, he has gone on to publish more than 20 science fiction and fantasy novels as well as his combat memoirs from his time in Iraq and Afghanistan. His first book, Hammers in the Wind, has been the #1 free book on Kindle 4 times and he holds a fancy certificate from the L Ron Hubbard Writers of the Future Contest.

Passionate about history, he combines his knowledge of the past with modern military tactics to create an engaging, quasi-realistic world for the readers. He graduated from Campbell University with a degree in history and a Masters of Arts degree in Digital Communications from the University of North Carolina at Chapel Hill. He currently lives outside of Raleigh, N.C. and devotes his time to writing, his family, and their two Bernese Mountain Dogs. If you drive by you might just find him on the porch with a cigar in one hand and a pen in the other. You can find out more about his work by following him on:

Facebook: @https://www.facebook.com/ChristianFreed
Twitter: @ChristianWFreed
Instagram: @ christianwarrenfreed

Like what you read? Let him know with an email or review.

warfighterbooks@gmail.com

Twitter: @ChristianWFreed
Instagram: @christianwarrenfreed

CPSIA information can be obtained
at www.ICGtesting.com
Printed in the USA
BVHW041031180123
656516BV00005B/110